Charlottesville

STEPHEN KRAMMES

Copyright © 2014 Stephen L Krammes
All rights reserved.

ISBN: 1500997919
ISBN 13: 9781500997915

To My Wife—Always and Forever

March 2, 1865

They had stopped at the remains of a farm; much less apprehensive now that the sun had set. The night air was close; hot and humid. Lieutenant Garner Scott rode down the road a ways, then stood up in his stirrups and looked down into the valley. The entire area was dotted with the campfires of Grant's army. Scott sighed as he collapsed back into his saddle. They had been on the move all day, going far out of their way to avoid Yankee cavalry patrols. He turned his horse and headed back to the wagon where the general was waiting.

"Sir, the entire valley is filled up with Yanks, we won't be able to use this road any further."

"Well, this place is as good as any, I reckon," the general grunted. "Get them slaves up and moving. Tell Winters to move the wagons off the road down toward that burnt-out farmhouse."

"Yes, sir."

The lieutenant dismounted and tied his horse to a small sapling. He walked over to where two wagons were standing. There were four men wrapped in blankets on the ground, catching as much sleep as they could. Scott knelt down next to one of them and shook his shoulder.

"Winters. Winters. Get up, we're moving the wagons."

The man woke with a start.

"What? Wagons? Where we moving the wagons?"

"Not far, just down by the farm. Get these other men up and get the coloreds moving."

"We heading out, Lieutenant?" Winters asked.

"No, wake up Moses first and tell him to get the others ready to work. The general says we're going to have to unload the boxes here. There are Yankees everywhere up ahead."

"Yes, sir, I'll get him now."

In a short time the wagons had been pulled off the road and stood next to a ramshackle shed, the only farm building left halfway standing. The general was talking to one of the drivers.

"We don't have much time. We won't be able to bury the boxes, besides, that would leave traces. Where are them slaves?"

"Don't know, General."

"In the meantime, take the other drivers and look around for the well, it has to be somewhere close by."

The driver went over and relayed the order to the other men. They fanned out in the darkness, looking for some sign of a well. At that moment the men heard the muffled footsteps and soft mutterings of the slaves as they came into the farmyard. The one named Moses came up to the general and Scott.

"Yassur, what you wantin' us to do?"

"Have them spread out and help find the well, then we're going to unload the wagons and lower the boxes down. There's been a lot of rain, we'll dig out some near the top if we have to."

"Over here!" One of the drivers had found the well.

Working quickly, the wagons were moved next to it and the slaves began offloading two heavy wooden crates.

No one except the general knew what was contained in them, but the slaves and the drivers all had an idea. The only thing worth hiding was money and, from the weight of the boxes, it wasn't worthless Confederate paper money, it must be gold or silver.

In a little over an hour the boxes were well hidden on two ledges a short way down the top of the well. The men formed for instructions from the general.

"All right. Winters, you're going to load the coloreds into the wagons and head back down the road. You four are civilians, so you won't have any trouble with the Yanks. We're going to try and rejoin with Lee. We may not make it tonight and, if not, we'll be holed up somewhere until tomorrow night."

Scott moved closer to the general and whispered to him.

"But, sir, how can we leave this place unguarded? Like you said, the drivers are civilians and what about the slaves? They'll know where we hid the crates."

"Don't worry about it, lieutenant, it's not a concern."

"But…"

"Not a concern. Get ready to move out, we'll try and cover as much ground as possible before daybreak."

Lieutenant Scott saluted and within fifteen minutes the farmyard was deserted again.

Winters' wagon and the other one had covered about a mile or so down the road before he reined in the horses. The three or four slaves in each wagon were either sleeping or dozing. He climbed down and went over to the other wagon and spoke briefly to the driver. When he returned to his wagon he climbed into the seat and turned to the back. At the same time, each of the four men pulled out pistols and fired into the sleeping slaves. None of them were able to escape. The men pushed the bodies out onto the ground.

"Come on," Winters urged, "we got to get back and get some of that gold before the sun comes up."

"What are we going to do with it? We can't have it in the wagon; the Yanks will stop us for sure."

"We'll just take the boxes and hide them ourselves before that prissy lieutenant and moron general come back to get it. They won't know where we put them."

"You be a smart one, Winters," the other driver cackled.

"Someone's got to be. Let's get moving. We don't need both them wagons. Unhitch those horses and tie them on here, throw the gear in the back. Hurry."

Before long they were back at the farmhouse.

"How we gonna get them boxes back up?" Winters' co-driver asked.

"We got a rope and we got the extra harness. Saunders weighs next to nothing, we'll lower him down with the harness and he can tie a rope around a box and we'll haul it up."

"In the dark?" Saunders asked.

"Yes, damn it, in the dark. We're not far off the road and as soon as it gets light, there'll be Yank patrols all over this place."

Saunders was reluctantly persuaded to be lowered down into the dark hole and, by using his hands, he managed to find and secure a crate, laboriously followed by the second. The crates were hoisted in the back of the wagon.

"Now we're just going to put them somewheres else," Winter explained. "Let's dig up a little right next to that farmhouse, ain't nobody going to be living there for a spell."

The men cleared a place by the one remaining wall of the farmhouse and dug out a shallow hole. Then they dropped the first crate inside.

Winters walked over to the second crate still in the wagon. "Wait," he said, "we might need some traveling money. Let's see what we got in here."

He found a large rock and smashed the top of the wooden crate. The wood splintered and he hurriedly pried the pieces away until he could see the contents.

"What the hell?" he muttered.

He wasn't looking at Confederate gold or silver. He was looking at rocks.

The men quickly smashed open the remaining crate and discovered nothing more valuable than Virginia river rocks.

"God damn it to hell!" Winters cursed. "Where's the damn gold? That general and lieutenant must have taken and hidden it somewheres."

Winters and the others had no way of knowing it, but the lieutenant was sitting upright under a tree about two miles away. Blood was still trickling down his face from the bullet hole in his forehead.

The general was nowhere to be seen.

PART ONE

1

CLAYTON AND TILDEN INVESTIGATIONS LLC STARTS UP

"Jack?"

"What, Yolanda?"

"Do you think we should start a, I don't know, a scrapbook or something for all this stuff?" Yolanda pointed to several magazines and newspaper clippings stacked around their office.

"I don't know if I would call it a scrapbook, kind of thing. Maybe we should start a filing cabinet or something," Jack replied. "Besides, why do we want all that stuff anyway?"

Yolanda walked over to a side chair and picked up a copy of the Indianapolis Star and began reading. *"Former Indianapolis police detective, Jack Clayton and his young partner, Yolanda Tilden were instrumental in solving one of the city's most well-known cold cases. After quitting the force following a major drug war incident on the south side of the city, Ms. Tilden joined forces with Mr. Clayton to reopen the case of three missing children from the early 1990's. Reviewing old clues set them on the trail that eventually led to the discovery of the children's remains in an abandoned fallout shelter on the outskirts of Greenfield. They also found the body of the kidnapper, a Greenfield resident and teacher, Lynn Salyer.* And there's more," she added. She picked up a national news magazine. "We want to keep these things, Jack, they're all about what we managed to accomplish. And I do want to keep this one." She showed Jack the cover. "I really like the picture of me in this one and I really love the one where you're bent over in the background. Not your best angle, Jack," she giggled.

"Shut up, Yolanda."

Yolanda walked around the desk and gave him a quick kiss on the cheek. "You'd better be nice to me, partner. This working arrangement does have benefits that improve with proper behavior." This was followed by another giggle.

"If you think those benefits are going to allow you to be a smartass, you've got another think coming, Ms. Smarty-boots."

"Jack, seriously, you are the only person in the world who ever says smarty-boots."

"Well, maybe I'm the only one in the world who has to deal with one."

Yolanda laughed. "Jack, there's one thing that's been nagging at me about Salyer."

"Yeah, what's that?" Jack grunted as he tried to wedge a collapsible folder in a bottom desk drawer.

"It's those post cards. I don't see why he ever bothered sending post cards. I mean we don't have proof that he even wrote them, but it seems likely, doesn't it? No one else would have done that, would they?"

"Well," Jack thought a moment, "that first one about Annie; I think he was kind of proud of himself for orchestrating that. He was pretty much a loser and reading about the searches and the law enforcement involvement might have fed his ego. He didn't dare give any clue about himself, but I think he wanted someone to know that it was a kidnapping, so to speak, and he pulled it off."

"But what about the other two? He killed Gregory Watson, Jack, he flat out killed him."

"Yes, and he probably planned on killing Samantha and eventually Annie. His relationship with Annie? It had gone south and he felt trapped. He had lost his job and he didn't know Rucker had a stroke, he didn't know where the rent money was going to come from and he was getting desperate."

"Do you think he planned on killing Gregory, Jack?"

"No, but you know, I'm not sure what his intentions were. I think he wanted to show Annie that she owed him something; that he had taken her away from people like him. What he didn't understand was that Annie realized that he had also taken her away from people who loved her. As much as she didn't get along with her mother, she eventually knew that Salyer was a huge mistake."

"But he wrote two more post cards," Yolanda said.

"I think it was sort of for the same reason as the first, but this time he wanted to prove to himself that he had done something that needed some sort of recognition, even if it was only one-sided."

"You know what's sad? Even though it had been twenty years, I sort of had kind of a hope that we would find her in Davenport, Iowa or someplace with three ratty-looking kids, just like their dad."

"I know, but the important thing is that we did find her. She died a sad, sad death, but we took care of her, that's what you have to focus on. If it hadn't been for us, she would still be down there with him. We did save her in a way, that's the best way to look at it."

Yolanda just gave him a sad smile and then walked over and hugged him.

■ ■ ■

Following the successful conclusion of the kidnapped children, Yolanda had spent the next few months sifting through various offers from police departments, local law enforcement agencies, and even private families. Yolanda eventually convinced Jack to accept an offer from the Museum of the Confederacy regarding the search for the lost Confederate gold at the end of the Civil War. It seriously took a lot of convincing, but she eventually wore him down, just like she normally did. The next month or so involved setting up an office in a strip mall on the east side of Indianapolis. Yolanda was actually handling most of the details. She seemed to have a knack for business that Jack definitely lacked. One of the first things that she did was hire a receptionist to answer the phone and keep track of appointments. She didn't tell Jack until after the fact, so he was quite surprised one morning to walk into the office and see Rosa sitting behind a desk. She smiled broadly at Jack and pointed at a desk plate in front of her that read: ROSA MARTINEZ on the top line with the word RECEPTIONIST below it.

"Good morning, Officer Jack," she greeted.

"Uh…, uh…, good morning, Rosa. Uh…, so you work here now?"

"Sí, I mean yes, Officer Jack. Officer Yolanda hired me. I'm going to answer your phone for you," she smiled expansively one more time.

"Oh, I see, uh…, say, have you seen Yolanda? Uh, I mean Officer Yolanda. She left the house early this morning."

"No, sir, Officer Jack, Guillermo dropped me off this morning at eight o'clock, just like Officer Yolanda told me. She gave me the keys yesterday when she stopped by the house."

"Huh, I wonder where she is." Jack mumbled. He gave Rosa a little wave as he walked into the office that he had been given. It was still pretty Spartan. Yolanda had told him that there wasn't much point in putting a lot of money into an office that they would rarely work out of.

There was a stack of clippings and printed out computer articles that discussed the supposed Confederate gold that was still somewhere to be found by fortunate and hard-working treasure hunters. Jack still had deep reservations about its existence, but had learned that discussing the matter negatively with Yolanda had unwelcome consequences on the home front. "Home front," he mumbled to himself, "What have I gotten myself into? Home front?"

He had just finished rereading an article about clues found in a Virginia graveyard when Yolanda walked in.

"Hey, Jack! Good morning!" she said brightly.

"Where have you been?" he started right in.

"Whoa! No good morning back? What's the matter, Jack, a little grumpy this morning?"

"No, I just wondered where you went this morning, that's all. I mean, I'm just asking."

"OK, sorry, I was just in a hurry and you were taking so long in the bathroom." She paused for a moment and then added, "I understand that people of your age sometimes need some extra time in there." She grinned.

"What do you mean, people of my age? I'll have you know that…"

"Hey, stop!" she laughed. "I'm just teasing you. Calm down."

Jack's expression revealed that he didn't care for early morning teasing.

"And when did you decide to hire Rosa? Don't you think that we should discuss who we're hiring?"

Yolanda sighed and sat down on the corner of Jack's desk.

"Look, Jack, we're not getting off on a good foot this morning. I'm sorry. But you know, we both did decide that I would take the lead for setting up the office. OK, first of all, this morning I had an early appointment with a Verizon rep about setting up a computer/phone system for the office. It will make things much easier to handle. They'll be in tomorrow to install everything. And you are getting a touch-screen computer," she smiled.

"What do you mean, touch-screen?" Jack asked suspiciously.

"It's new technology, Jack; you don't need a mouse anymore."

"But I know how to use a mouse."

"Yes, I've seen how well you do that, Jack," she said encouragingly. *Oh, Jack, you are so sweet, but so Neanderthal about technology.* "Look, you can still have a mouse if you want one, but it will be wireless."

"Well, how will it work if there isn't a wire?"

Ugh, lightning make big fire. "Don't worry about it, Jack, you'll see. OK, about Rosa. We needed someone who could simply answer the phone, read and respond to emails, and to keep track of an appointment book for you and for me. I thought she and Guillermo could use some extra money. Her English is pretty good and she's quite capable of doing this job. I guess I just thought that you would be OK with it."

"I guess I'm OK with it; I was just surprised to see her, that's all."

"I promise to touch base with you in the future about stuff like that, OK?" Another smile.

"OK, I'd appreciate that." Jack sat up a little straighter in his chair.

Oh, boy. "Jack, we need to head out to Richmond soon. We've taken the time to research the cases we've been offered and I still think this one sounds like the most fun. I was thinking maybe the day after tomorrow. What do you think?"

"I guess so. I mean I've read so much of this on-line treasure hunting stuff, I'm ready to do something else. It's mid-summer though, you can bet it's going to be hot in Virginia."

"After the winter we had, I won't mind. OK, then, I'll call and get us tickets to Richmond for Thursday."

"Tickets?"

"Yes, Jack, we need tickets to get on an airplane; it's kind of a new thing you might not be aware of."

"No, we don't need to fly, we'll just drive there."

"Are you serious? That would be like a what? Twelve hour drive? Jack, we can be there in three hours. And you can have a cocktail from one of those tiny bottles!" she added.

"Look, Yolanda, there's not going to be a direct flight from Indianapolis to Richmond. That means that we'll have to sit in a terminal waiting for a connecting flight. By the time you add in security and luggage checking and retrieving, it's a lot longer than three hours."

"But I don't want to sit in a car for twelve hours!" she protested.

"We can take breaks, even stop for lunch. Plus it will give us time to discuss what our game plan is going to be," Jack explained.

Yolanda didn't look happy.

"And besides," Jack continued, "we'll need a car and I don't like driving rentals. You never know where the buttons are."

Oh, for Christ's sake! Now it's about the buttons?

Yolanda decided to let him win on this one. Besides, she knew Jack well enough that he wasn't going to budge much on a matter like this. He liked to drive, so he could just do it.

"All right, Jack, you win. We'll take your car. I would like to point out, however, that the museum contract includes a rental car or a museum van."

"Well," Jack smiled brightly, "I guess the museum will be able to save a little money on this boondoggle." Seeing Yolanda's expression darken, he added, "I mean this case, I really am looking forward to doing some historical stuff."

Yolanda looked at him suspiciously, but then nodded her head in agreement. "And it's in Virginia, Jack. So much happened there during the Civil War, it's going to be fun."

Fun? Boondoggle – wild goose chase is more like it.

2

ROAD TRIP

It was 8:00 a.m. on Thursday and the adventure started. Jack had finally gotten all of Yolanda's luggage crammed into the back seat. There was absolutely no more room in the trunk. He, on the other hand, had one medium suitcase and a smaller one, but wisely didn't make an issue of the luggage disparity. This drive to Richmond was going to be the first time that Jack and Yolanda had ever spent time in a car that was actually going someplace for a long distance. It turned out not to be without a little friction, but nothing terribly extreme. The initial mini-crisis occurred just as they left the I-465 outer belt and headed east on I-70 toward Dayton. The first thing that Yolanda did was pop a CD into the player. Jack liked to think about things when he drove and most of the time enjoyed the silence, sometimes he listened to music, usually piano, sometimes he liked listening to hits of the 60's and 70's. No Beatles though, he had overdosed on them during the early 70's. Yolanda's first selection of the trip was a song called Collision Course with Jay-Z and Linkin Park, at least that was what he was told when he asked. It was loud. Jack tolerated it for a long time, almost two minutes, before he reached down and turned the volume down.

"What's the matter, Jack? Need something?" Yolanda asked.

"Uh, no, I just thought it was a little loud."

"Well, you're supposed to play it loud, Jack, that's the point."

"You do know that experts are worried about hearing loss due to listening to loud music, don't you?"

"Jack, are you serious?"

It turned out he was. This initial disagreement extended for a bit and was concluded by Yolanda angrily plugging a set of ear buds into her iPod and cranking up the volume. It was so loud that it was actually uncomfortable, but she was angry and she was not going to give him the satisfaction of watching her turn it back down. Jack could even hear the strong thumping of the bass. He sighed and she continued to sulk.

The use of the ear buds ended the conflict regarding the CD player and the radio, but not the usual bickering that takes place during most long trips, even between members of the happiest families. Most of the arguments followed this line:

"So, Jack. You do realize that we could have been there by now, don't you?"

"Yes. For the umpteenth time I will agree with you, yes, we could have been there by now."

"And yet here we are in some desolate stretch of West Virginia looking at… Looking at what, Jack? There's nothing here but some cows and a few beat-up house trailers."

Jack sighed. *Jesus, it's like taking a kid on a trip.* "Listen, Yolanda, we've been over this. This is a nine to ten hour trip, but look, we would have had to go to the airport, park the car, get a shuttle bus, go through that security crap, and then wait around for the flight. I'm thinking that's a two-hour time slot right there."

"OK, two hours, but…"

"Damn it! Let me finish! Then it's a three hour flight to Atlanta, with who knows how long of a layover, then a couple of hours or so to Richmond…"

"But, we could…"

"Just a minute! Then we would have to wait to get out of the damn plane, wait for our luggage, and then go and find a rental car. When you think of all that, it makes sense to drive. Besides, I like driving my own car."

"God, you are so anal about things, Jack," she snorted. "Fine, instead of flying and getting little bottles of booze served to us, we get to see a part of America where dental hygiene was passed up in favor of Black Lung Disease." Yolanda turned in a huff and scrooched down in her seat, looking out the window.

Jack sighed again. Maybe I should have put her on an airplane. At least I could have some peace and quiet.

Yolanda saw a few more cows as they zipped by. *I wish I had a couple of bottles of airplane booze right now. Jesus, that house trailer is going to fall into that ravine.*

3

WELCOME, Y'ALL

The problem with most GPS devices often becomes apparent at the end of a trip. Oh, it was always easy to find an interstate connection or an alternate route around a traffic jam, but somehow they always managed to get confused when finding an address smack in the middle of a downtown area. This was the case with Jack's GPS. In spite of the arguments that had popped up from time to time, he and Yolanda had mostly enjoyed each other's company. He had even let her drive on I-64 after they got off the turnpike at Beckley, West Virginia. There was no way he was going to let her drive on that stretch of turnpike from Charleston; it was like a racetrack for all vehicles, including semi-tractor trailers.

Finally they arrived in downtown Richmond.

"Where in the hell is the god-damned hotel?" Jack shouted for the third time.

"I don't know, Jack, the GPS says that we've arrived at our destination."

"Well, where in the hell is it then? God damn it, I've been around this god-damned block three god-damned times!"

"Easy, Jack, your vein is out of control; and leave the Lord's name out of this." She knew better than to laugh, although she always got amused when Jack went off on one of his tirades. She had learned one thing about him. He always took almost everything calmly, but driving made him a different person.

He didn't suffer from road rage, but he was always ready to yell at other drivers for annoying him, and getting frustrated with his GPS also got similar results. "Look, pull over where you can and I'll get out and check."

Jack glared over at her, but didn't say anything. He didn't like comments about his vein and he wasn't in the mood to divert any of his anger from his GPS.

He found a loading zone spot and pulled into it. Yolanda got out of the car and headed down the sidewalk. He could see her in the rearview mirror as she stopped a man in a gray business suit. Moments later she was buckling her seatbelt again.

"See that white sign up there, Jack? Turn down that side street, the hotel is down there."

"Well, how in the hell was I supposed to know that? Don't they have a god-damned real address? Why, in the..."

"Jack! Stop! I get it; you're angry, now just count to ten or something. Jesus, you're driving me crazy. Look, it's been a long drive and we're almost there, so just breathe slowly, it's OK."

"It's just that it's this god-damned GPS and...," his voice trailed off as he saw Yolanda's expression. It revealed someone who was just about to lose her patience. "Yeah, OK," he grumbled.

Yolanda reached over and patted his arm. "That's good, Jack, pretty soon you'll be enjoying one of those awful scotches that you like so much," she smiled.

Jack just grunted.

The hotel was an older one, tucked in the middle of downtown Richmond, it was very nice though. Yolanda liked it right away; it looked like a Southern kind of place, chockfull of Southern charm. Jack, on the other hand, was just glad to finally be out of the car.

After handing the car keys to the parking valet, a second eager employee started stacking Yolanda's considerable number of suitcases onto a luggage cart in spite of Jack's protest that he could take care of them. After a few moments of rearranging the bags into a fairly safe pile, he escorted them to reception. An older lady in a lavender dress was working the desk. She looked up at them and smiled, and then hit a couple of keys on the computer keyboard before turning her full attention to them.

"Welcome to the Magnolia," she greeted them. "My name is Grace, Grace Levings. How may I help you this fine day?"

Yolanda took the lead, "Hello, Grace, your hotel is lovely, it's just like it could be in a magazine or something." She turned and made a sweeping gesture with her arm.

The lady smiled, "Oh, well, you know, the Magnolia has been featured several times in magazines. Why once there was even a movie scene shot right here in the lobby."

Jesus Christ, Jack thought. *Why in the hell do we have to have a god-damned conversation with everyone? Why can't we just check in?*

"Really?" Yolanda said, "That's fascinating, what film..."

Jack interrupted her. "We would just like to check in. We have a reservation, it's either under Clayton or Tilden."

The woman looked at Jack, her expression showed a touch of displeasure at his rudeness. She turned back to the computer and typed. It only took a moment.

"It's under Tilden," she said, "Yolanda Tilden."

"That's me!" Yolanda exclaimed. This earned her a warm smile from the lady, followed by another disapproving glance at Jack.

"Yolanda. That's such a beautiful name," Grace added.

Yeah, well, my name's Jack, that's fucking beautiful too. Jack was drumming his fingers on the counter as this exchange took place.

Grace reached under the counter and retrieved four keycards and ran them through a reader.

"Uh, I think we only need two cards," Jack said.

The lady looked up at him. "It's hotel policy that we give each guest two cards for the room," she said coldly. "Here, miss," another warm smile. "You're in room 814. And you, sir," no smile, "are in room 820."

"Oh, please, Grace, you can just call me Yolanda."

Both ladies beamed at each other.

"What? Two rooms?" Jack started, but Yolanda stopped him with a warning expression.

"Thank you so much, Grace," Yolanda said.

"Oh, it's my pleasure," the lady replied. "I see that the arrangements have been made by the Museum of the Confederacy. Are you connected with them?"

"As a matter of fact, we've been employed by them to do a little investigative work," Yolanda explained.

Jesus H. Christ! Let's go! Jack was growing impatient.

"Why, how fascinating. You know, living here in Richmond, we are just surrounded by history. It's a wonderful place to live, so rich in culture and tradition," the lady was gushing by now.

How in the hell does she do it? Every god-damned time we have to make friends with every god-damned person we run into!

"Oh, I can just feel that," Yolanda replied. "I don't know how long we'll be here in the city, but I know that I'll love every single moment. I've been doing a lot of reading…"

"OK, look, we're going to have to hurry to make that appointment," Jack blurted out. "Come on, Yolanda, we have to get going."

That interruption earned him two expressions, one mildly perturbed. That one belonged to Yolanda. The other one belonged to Grace. It went way past perturbed.

4

UNHAPPY JACK LEARNS EQUINE ANATOMY

"What is wrong with you, Jack?" Yolanda inquired as they took the elevator to the eighth floor. "I am standing there having a nice conversation with Grace and you have to make up some story about some appointment?"

"Damn it, we've been in the car for 11 hours and all I want to do is check in and lie down. You, on the other hand, seem to think that it's important to jump on the local Welcome Wagon and be buddy-buddy with every desk clerk and hobo we find on the street!"

"Welcome Wagon? What's that?"

"Never mind and what's the deal with two rooms?"

"Jack, I'm sure that the museum doesn't realize that you and I have an arrangement. Of course they would book two rooms. Don't get excited."

"I'm not excited," he snapped. "I was just looking forward to, you know, maybe something later."

"Given my current state of mind regarding your behavior, Jack, you'll be lucky if I'm in the same room with you tonight, let alone 'something later,' as you put it."

Yolanda crossed her arms and stared at the flashing of the floor numbers.

Crap, Jack thought, *she's in one of her moods.*

They completed the rest of the short ride in silence. Yolanda found her room number and slipped the keycard in the reader.

"You mean you're actually going to stay in this room?" Jack asked.

"OK, Jack," Yolanda turned to him. "You're right. It was a long ride and maybe I would like to lie down too. Not to mention that you've managed to piss me off. I might stay in this room tonight or I might not. I might stay in your room with you and you might not get anything from me but a sweet wish for a good night's sleep. You'd just better hope that I forget about how much of a horse's ass you were to Grace."

"What? Grace! Jesus Christ, Yolanda, she's just a hotel clerk! Why is that getting me all this crap?"

"Just a clerk. Really, Jack? You are an ass. I should apologize to the equine world for equating you with them." She glanced at her watch. "It's a quarter to five. I will see you again at five-thirty. I need a break." She pulled her suitcase into the room and firmly closed the door, leaving Jack staring at the numbers 814.

Shit.

5

REST DOES A BODY GOOD

Jack had just finished unpacking his suitcase. One of his idiosyncrasies about staying in a hotel or motel was unpacking. He refused to live out of a suitcase and always put his socks and underwear in a dresser drawer before hanging up his shirts and pants in the closet. He also had to arrange the contents of his shaving kit neatly in the bathroom. He had just finished doing that to his satisfaction. Then he sat down on the bed and took off his shoes and socks. He decided to take his shirt and pants off too in order to be more comfortable for his highly-anticipated nap. He had just hung them both over the back of the desk chair when a knock came at the door.

Ha, he thought, *it only took fifteen minutes for Yolanda to realize that she was wrong. Again!*

He quickly crossed to the door and flung it open. It wasn't Yolanda. It was a tall, thin man carrying a briefcase in one hand and holding an umbrella in the other. The man coughed, a little taken aback at Jack's lack of appropriate attire. Jack looked down and realized that he was just wearing his boxer shorts.

"Just a minute," Jack said and closed the door. He grabbed his pants and shirt and quickly wrestled them on. Then went back to the door where the man had been patiently waiting.

"Sorry about that," Jack apologized a little red-faced. "I thought you were someone else."

"Really?" the man drolly replied. "Do you know someone else in town besides your partner, Ms. Tilden? I wasn't aware that a gentleman would receive one's business partner while wearing one's undertrousers, especially a lady business partner."

Undertrousers?

"Uh, I guess, I was tired and all and wasn't really thinking," Jack offered. *Damn it, why am I making excuses to this guy?*

"Yes, travel can be disconcerting. Allow me to introduce myself. I am Howard Sedgewick, one of the curators of the Museum of the Confederacy. May I come in?"

"What? Oh, come in? Uh, certainly, come in," Jack stammered. *What is wrong with me?*

Mr. Sedgewick walked into the room and set his briefcase down on the desk and propped his umbrella next to it.

"Does it look like rain?" Jack asked.

"Rain? No, oh, you mean the umbrella," Mr. Sedgewick replied, "I believe that a gentleman should always be prepared for any eventuality, thus the umbrella."

This guy's a dick, Jack decided.

"Absolutely," Jack said, nodding his head, "I agree wholeheartedly, why my umbrella is right there in the closet, just waiting to get some fresh air later."

Mr. Sedgewick gave a slight, disbelieving snort before proceeding. "I just wish to make you aware of tomorrow's planned activities. We will send a car for you and Ms. Tilden at eight o'clock if that's satisfactory. We've arranged a viewing of artifacts that relate to the matter regarding the Confederate gold. You might find them of value and interest."

"Eight o'clock will be fine," Jack agreed. "I'll be having dinner with Ms. Tilden this evening and we will make arrangements to be ready on time."

"I do hope these lodging arrangements are satisfactory. The Magnolia is one of the jewels of our local history. It was actually built before the war, but didn't receive a great deal of damage. It was extensively rebuilt and modernized in 1939; there was a great increase in tourism due to Margaret Mitchell's novel, of course. More recently there was another remodeling and modernization done in the late 1990's. The owners have managed to retain much of the charm and quaintness of the hotel. Let me tell you about the wallpaper."

"Fascinating," Jack noted. *I can only imagine how well he and Yolanda are going to hit it off.* "Excuse me, Mr. Sedgewick, but, as you probably noticed, I was getting ready to get some rest after the long drive. If you don't mind, could we perhaps save this for tomorrow? I do love a good wallpaper story though."

Another polite snort escaped Mr. Sedgewick. "Ah, yes, I see. Well, indeed, it can wait for tomorrow. I know how taxing a long trip can be. As I understand it, you chose to motor here from Indiana?"

Motor?

"Yes, I do like motoring so much more than flying," Jack explained.

Another snort. Mr. Sedgewick stood up and retrieved his briefcase and umbrella. "Very good, Mr. Clayton. Until tomorrow morning at the museum. Please enjoy your evening in our fair city."

"I certainly plan to, thanks for coming by. I'll try to be dressed next time you stop in," Jack laughed.

Mr. Sedgewick stopped by the door and turned back and studied Jack for a moment. "Yes, that would be admirable," he sniffed and slipped out the door.

He really is a dick!

Jack looked at the clock. He had twenty minutes to nap and shower. He set his watch on timer for ten minutes and stretched out on the bed, but thoughts of an angry partner and a snooty visitor filled up most of the ten minutes. Jack sat up with a sigh and headed to the bathroom for a shower.

It was a little after five-thirty when another knock came at the door. Jack had finished his shower. He had on a t-shirt, boxers, and socks. Not wanting a repeat of the earlier issue, he quickly pulled on a pair of pants before going to the door. He looked out the peephole. This time it was Yolanda. Jack opened the door and stopped for a second. She was wearing a short, black cocktail dress and sandals. She looked beautiful.

"Wow, Yolanda, that dress is amazing," he complimented.

"Thanks, Jack; I see that you're not quite ready to go downstairs yet. Look, I'm still so tired, but I'm also very hungry. Tell you what, I'm going downstairs and getting a cocktail. If I were you, I'd get a move on. When the men in the lounge get a look at this dress, I'm not going to be paying for the drink. If you want to protect your territory, I wouldn't be long," she laughed.

6

JACK PULLS OUT A PLUM

Yolanda had been one-hundred percent correct. When Jack walked into the cocktail lounge he saw her sitting at the bar on the end stool. He also saw that there were two gentlemen standing to her right. They were attempting to engage her in conversation and there were already two drinks sitting in front of her. He walked over and took the open stool to Yolanda's left. She didn't see him sit down and the men certainly weren't paying any attention to him.

One of the men started what probably would have been an undoubtedly hilarious anecdote, which Jack interrupted with a slight cough. Yolanda swiveled around to face him.

"Hey! You finally made it! That was pretty quick, Jack." She then swiveled back to the two gentlemen. "I'm sorry, guys, but my date showed up," she smiled.

The two men looked at Jack and then at each other with confused expressions. In order to clarify the situation, Yolanda leaned over and gave Jack a quick kiss on the lips. That seemed to settle the matter and, although puzzled, the two men left in search of fresh game.

Jack watched them approach two ladies sitting at a table.

"Does this kind of stuff happen all the time?" Jack asked.

"Yes, pretty much," she answered. "I mean, after all, I'm sitting by myself, so it's just natural that men are going to come up and start talking to me."

"Well, isn't that kind of annoying?"

"Sometimes, but if I'm not interested, I flat out tell them. I was just killing time today waiting for you and look, two cocktails at no cost to you!" she laughed.

Jack motioned to the bartender and ordered a Johnny Walker Black on the rocks. As soon as his drink arrived, he raised the glass to Yolanda. "Here's to a new case, Yo."

She liked it when he called her that. It was sort of a pet name. In fact, she really liked it.

She picked the Cosmo over the Pina Colada and clinked Jack's glass.

"I think I can only handle one drink before dinner, I really am hungry," she said.

"Me too, I didn't get much to eat today, thanks to you."

"Having a fast food salad is about the only healthy way to go, Jack. You can't shove cheeseburgers and fries in your gut and then sit in the car for hours. It's just goes right to fat."

"Yes, I get it," he said resignedly. "Still, it's kind of traditional road trip food, you know."

"That could be, but it's no longer going to be traditional with you. When's the last time you had your cholesterol checked anyway?"

"Yolanda, …"

Oops, no Yo, I must have pushed one too many buttons with that one, she thought.

"…the state of my cholesterol is none of your business. I do thank you, however, for your concern, but I just might be shoving a steak and fries in my gut in the next 15 minutes."

"OK, Jack, sorry, you're a big boy. You just go right ahead and clog your arteries. I hear they can do miracles with heart attack victims nowadays, but maybe we should go and finish our drinks at a table. You could hurt your head if you keel over while sitting on a bar stool."

Yolanda stood up, grabbed her Cosmo, and then walked over to an empty table. Jack followed her, although not without a couple of dark thoughts clouding his brain.

Later, at dinner, Jack did order a steak, a ribeye, but he just had a salad and the vegetable of the day for the side. *I can't believe I let her psych me out of having French fries. Damn it, she's probably right, but I've got to stand up to her on this crap.*

Yolanda, true to form, ordered chicken on a bed of rice pilaf with the same vegetable side. She also had a glass of wine. Jack didn't order any more alcohol, because he still had hopes of a bit prurient nature and wanted to have his best game ready if needed.

They were both kind of quiet during dinner and when they got up to their rooms, Yolanda stopped at her door and turned to Jack.

"OK," she sighed, "I know you're wound up and I know what you've been thinking about all day, Jack. I still have my toothbrush and stuff back in my room. Just give me five minutes and I'll be back, I promise."

The expression on Jack's face was very close to a toddler's face looking under the tree on Christmas morning.

Jesus, she thought, *I do have a child on my hands.*

She didn't break her promise.

7

THE BREAKFAST HOUR

Yolanda woke up the next morning with plenty of time to scurry back to her room for a shower and to get dressed. She joined Jack down at the restaurant for breakfast. Like most places, the hotel offered a pricey buffet breakfast or one could simply order from the menu. Since the museum was picking up the tab, Jack had decided to establish his independence and chose the buffet. In fact, he had already piled up a plate with scrambled eggs and bacon with a couple of biscuits drowning in thick sausage gravy.

She looked down at his plate and started to say something, but stopped. Instead she just put on a smile and said, "Nice breakfast, Jack. That will help get you started on our first official day."

That took Jack by surprise. He had already prepared a couple of smartass comebacks, so her comment kind of deflated him.

She ordered the buffet too, but restricted her choices to a bowl of oatmeal and an assortment of fresh fruit. She sat down across from him and polished her spoon on a napkin after giving it a cursory examination.

She smiled at him, "You were very sweet last night, Jack. I really enjoyed being with you."

He grinned, a little conceitedly, and shoved a hunk of biscuit in his mouth.

Boy, I can play him like a fine violin, she thought.

"Did the man say when the car will pick us up, Jack?"

"Eight o'clock. I guess we get a mini-tour of some related relics to get us started."

"That'll be fun. You said that you liked history, so you should enjoy it."

"And you won't?" Jack asked.

"Oh, I don't know, it's sort of OK I guess, but it never really was my thing, if you know what I mean. I was more of a math and science person."

"Wow, that's completely opposite for me. I hated math. And as for science, I just think it's all magical. I mean really, I'm composed of tiny atoms? I don't think so."

Yolanda laughed. "OK, Jack. We won't get into any Darwinian discussions in the near future."

"You know, speaking of Darwin, you've never really discussed religion with me. What's your take on that?" he asked.

"Well," Yolanda slowly started, "I was raised Catholic. I mean I went through the whole First Communion thing and all that, but once I hit middle school and did Confirmation, I didn't really buy into it much anymore. So, I guess I'm officially a non-practicing Catholic. How about you?"

"That little farm town I told you about; well, going to Sunday School was sort of expected, although my parents never went. I guess they were helping me get on my way to heaven. It's kind of funny; all my teachers were these older ladies. I have to admit, I was kind of, well, not a positive participant."

"What do you mean, Jack?"

"Uh," he hesitated before continuing, "I was really a good kid at school. I didn't get into trouble, I think I was afraid to, but Sunday School? It was a time to not be so serious. After all, those ladies weren't real teachers. There was one kid who always memorized Bible verses and knew the books of the Bible. We mocked him a lot. I just wasn't interested. Hey, do you want to hear something hilarious?"

"Sure, what?"

"Every summer I got stuck going to Vacation Bible School. I mean it went on for two weeks! And it was kind of the same stuff as Sunday School, except we got refreshments, usually Kool-Aid and cookies, sometimes just graham crackers."

"So funny, Jack," Yolanda said.

"Just listen, damn it, I'm not done. Anyway one year we were learning about the disciples. My friend Marvin, who didn't live in town, got dropped off to stay with his grandmother and he was in my class..."

Yolanda started to interrupt, but Jack put his index finger to her lips in warning.

"...so our assignment was to cut out figures of the disciples and paste them onto a Biblical scene. Anyway, Marvin raises his hand and tells the teacher that he can't find his Peter. Now he was actually serious, he couldn't find the cutout, but we all started laughing, even harder when the teacher said, 'Class, Marvin's lost his Peter. Everyone help Marvin find his Peter.' And then her assistant said, 'Look and see if you're sitting on Marvin's Peter. He really needs his Peter.' Oh, God, it was so frigging funny, it still makes me laugh."

"OK, that is hilarious, Jack," she agreed. "But seriously, where do you and God stand today?"

"I call him the Supreme Being of Choice, because I'm so politically correct."

"Bullshit, Jack, you're about as politically correct as I am modest and unassuming."

"Ooh, that bad, huh?" Jack laughed, earning himself a punch in the arm. "Ouch!"

"Seriously, Jack, tell me."

"OK, well, I sort of strayed. I mean I go to church every now and then, but I have these nagging thoughts that when all is said and done, we're all just sort of dead armadillos lying along a Texas highway. You know, when the light goes out, that's all she wrote."

"Nice analogy, Jack. Armadillos, really?"

"Look, it's just that everyone wants to live forever. Maybe religion just does that for people, lets them hope that there's something else. I don't know, Yolanda, we're all carbon-based beings. If dogs and cats don't go to heaven, why do we think we get to?"

"I see what you mean, Jack." She looked at her watch. "Hey, we'd better get upstairs. I want to brush my teeth before we leave. We should definitely continue this discussion. I don't think Mrs. Salyer would be pleased if she knew your thoughts on the subject of an afterlife."

"You mean Sister Rhoda?" Jack laughed. "No, probably not. OK, let's go."

8

MUSEUM OF THE CONFEDERACY

Promptly at eight o'clock, a museum van pulled into the valet parking area. Jack and Yolanda were waiting on a bench near the front door. An aide stepped out of the passenger seat and opened the door to the second row of seats. Jack was relieved that Mr. Sedgewick was not in attendance. He figured that a later meeting was inevitable, but at least he wouldn't have to be lectured on the way to the museum about wallpaper or some significant section of sidewalk.

"You all folks the treasure hunters?" The driver looked back using the rearview mirror.

"Uh, treasure hunters?" Yolanda replied. "I guess you could call us that."

"Well, people around here been looking for that gold for a long time. Somebody must put a heap of faith in you all to find it," he continued.

"I guess you could call it faith," Yolanda laughed. "How about you? You ever do any treasure hunting?"

"Nah, my cousin, he goes out on weekends with his metal detector and all that, but folks be mighty particular about people stomping around on their property nowadays. Besides, everybody always wants a hunk of anything that they might find."

His partner decided to enter the discussion. "You all know much about this gold? By the way, ma'am, I thought only the South had beautiful ladies, but you certainly put many of our fair damsels to shame." He concluded that cloying remark with a sizeable grin.

"Well, aren't you sweet to say that," Yolanda smiled.

Jack noticed that she had the decency to blush, but also decided that he was going to nip this budding relationship right in the bud, so to speak.

"Look, we really don't want to discuss this before meeting with the curators this morning, you understand, don't you?" Jack interjected.

"We was just trying to be friendly, sir," he answered.

"Let's just be friendly about the weather, OK?" Jack replied, earning him a curious look from Yolanda.

With that, the man turned back to the front and the driver just paid attention to the traffic. The rest of the short trip was spent in a silence that was just a bit uncomfortable, but thankfully they soon pulled into a parking area behind the museum. Standing at the rear entrance was Jack's recent acquaintance, Mr. Sedgewick. Right next to him was another gentleman, just a bit rotund in appearance. Each of them was clad in an identical white suit. *Jesus,* Jack thought, *this is just like <u>Gone with the Wind</u> kind of nonsense.* He did note that Mr. Sedgewick was currently without an umbrella.

The aide jumped out of the front and opened the sliding door. His eyes dropped down to Yolanda's hemline as she maneuvered her way out of the seat, earning him a nice and extensive view of her legs. This did not go without Jack's notice. *What the hell? Eyes up top, asshole.*

The man offered Yolanda his arm as he helped her step down. No such arm was offered to Jack as he clambered from the van.

"Bye, ma'am, it was a pleasure meeting you," the aide mugged.

It was a pleasure checking out your legs, Jack thought.

"Thank you, it was nice meeting you too," Yolanda smiled.

No such homilies were thrown Jack's way. The aide just climbed back into the van and it pulled away. Mr. Sedgewick and his companion had made no move to come towards Yolanda and Jack, so they walked up the sidewalk to the back entrance. As they drew closer, Mr. Sedgewick stepped forward and stopped in front of Yolanda.

"Ms. Tilden, I presume," he said smoothly.

Well, it sure as hell isn't Doctor Livingston. Jack really found it difficult to like Mr. Sedgewick.

Yolanda smiled and offered her hand. Instead of shaking it, Mr. Sedgewick bowed slightly and brought it to his lips, bestowing a delicate kiss, something else chock full of Southern charm. Jack didn't like that either.

Mr. Sedgewick glanced over at Jack and gave a slight cough. "A pleasure to see you again, Mr. Clayton. I see that you are giving more thought to your attire today."

Jack could only think of what he wanted to say to that before replying, "Likewise, I'm sure. I noticed that neither of us remembered to bring our umbrellas."

Sedgewick snorted, then turned and gestured to the second man. "Allow me to introduce Doctor Claude Armbruster. Doctor Armbruster, this is Ms. Tilden and her colleague Mr. Clayton."

Seriously? Jack thought. *This guy looks like a bald Colonel Sanders.*

"Pleased to meet both of you," Dr. Armbruster politely intoned, but seemed to be more interested in Yolanda than Jack, as he also took the opportunity, Jack noted, to gum Yolanda's hand. In fact, as they turned to go into the museum each of them took a position at one of Yolanda's sides and made off toward the entrance as a threesome, leaving Jack to bring up the rear.

Once inside, they led the way to a medium-sized conference room. There was a projector set up on a small table and another larger table was covered with various objects.

Dr. Armbruster led Yolanda over to a chair and motioned for Jack to take a seat next to her. Jack noticed that he chose to guide Yolanda with the palm of his hand firmly planted on the small of her back. *Jesus, nothing but gawkers and polite feel-ups so far!*

"First of all," Dr. Armbruster began, "I want to give you a warm welcome to our museum. We are certainly happy to have you visit us and help us possibly close out a chapter in our state's glorious history."

Then Mr. Sedgewick weighed in. "As you know, rumors of the 'lost Confederate gold' have been existent since the end of the War Between the States…"

"You mean the Civil War?" Jack interrupted. This earned him a baleful look from Mr. Sedgewick.

"Yes, Mr. Clayton, that is the same conflict to which I was referring." Slight cough. "We prefer to call it the War Between the States."

Jack stared blankly at him, and then shrugged his shoulders.

At this point Dr. Armbruster took another turn. "You may wonder why we contacted you and set up this rather unique expedition."

"Isn't it simply to investigate and find the treasure?" Jack asked. "Is there something else we're not aware of?" Yolanda leaned forward in curiosity.

"Ah, yes," Dr. Armbruster responded. "My colleagues here at this museum and at others of this nature, that is to say, institutions that wish to maintain the glory and the dignity of the Confederacy, have long regarded this gold legend with disdain. For decades, uncaring, unprofessional persons have destroyed historical sites and made off with important artifacts, all as a result of this treasure hunt."

"This is where you come in, Mr. Clayton. And, of course, you, Ms. Tilden," Mr. Sedgewick warmly added. "You've gained a certain notoriety with your work in Indiana and we, the board of directors, Dr. Armbruster, and myself, decided that people with temporary high-profile, public personas, so to speak, might prove invaluable in finally putting this nonsense; this wild goose chase to rest."

"What?" Yolanda exclaimed. "What?" she repeated. "You mean you didn't hire us to find a treasure, just to prove that one doesn't exist?"

"No, not precisely, Ms. Tilden," Dr. Armbruster continued. "You see, all these mysteries thrive on conjecture and legend. We feel that you and Mr. Clayton, with the current notoriety that Mr. Sedgewick mentioned in passing, could either discover some validity to its existence or squelch this so-called treasure hunt once and for all."

"And for this you've given us a six-month contract?" Jack asked in disbelief.

"Mr. Clayton," Mr. Sedgewick sighed, "yes, we want to take advantage of your new-found fame to make this a high priority item in the press. I would emphasize again that curators such as Dr. Armbruster and myself are interested in preserving history, not conducting treasure hunts that are basically unfounded."

"Here, Ms. Tilden, Mr. Clayton, take a look at these items, all recovered from rumored sites," Dr. Armbruster encouraged. He swept a sheet-like covering from the table, revealing a few small, wooden kegs, some gold and silver coins, and some rusted digging implements such as picks and shovels.

Mr. Sedgewick stepped closer to the table and then gestured at some enlargements of what appeared to be hieroglyphics on the wall.

"At several random sites, more importantly Danville, Virginia and a town in northern Georgia, small kegs like this were discovered, each containing a fair amount of gold and silver. These markings," he indicated the enlargements, "were discovered on trees at the Green Hill Cemetery in Danville. Over the years people have assumed that they are a significant clue to the existence or whereabouts of a large amount of gold."

Jack and Yolanda moved to the wall and studied the markings.

"Yes," Jack responded, "We've already seen these after researching the treasure on the Internet."

"Ah, preparation," Mr. Sedgewick remarked. "Very admirable, Ms. Tilden."

Wait a damn minute! Nobody said only Yolanda did it!

"So," Dr. Armbruster began, "we would prefer that you start your investigation at Danville, it being so much closer and in-state. Besides there have been significant amounts of artifacts found there that might relate to the disposal or storage of an amount of gold and silver."

"Uh, no," Yolanda interjected, "not Danville or Georgia."

The two curators briefly glanced at one another before turning their full attention to Yolanda.

"Well, Ms. Tilden," Mr. Sedgewick said, "just where were you and Mr. Clayton planning to start your search?"

"Lynchburg," Yolanda answered, "The McIntosh Farm."

"You can't be serious," Dr. Armbruster said, "Why Lynchburg?"

"Yes," Mr. Sedgewick chimed in. "The only connection with any treasure at Lynchburg is nothing but wildly unsubstantiated rumors about some unnamed Confederate general using slaves to hide gold. There's no other hard evidence that links that site with the treasure."

"Exactly," Jack answered. "These other places have been searched fairly diligently and this," he motioned at the table, "is pretty much the sum total of what's been discovered in almost 150 years. Something tells me that, if there is something to be found, it's not going to be at Danville or in northern Georgia."

"Well," Dr. Armbruster mused, "this is something that we certainly hadn't considered, did we, Mr. Sedgewick? Although you must know that the McIntosh Farm has also had its share of amateur treasure hunters. Hmm.., so when do you propose to get started on this quest?"

"I think we'll leave for Lynchburg tomorrow morning," Jack answered. "It was arranged earlier that a van would be available for us. If we can pick that up today, we'll go and buy some supplies and load it up."

"Yes," Dr. Armbruster agreed, "we do have a full-size van reserved for you. I've also assigned two of our staff to accompany you."

"That won't be necessary," Yolanda chimed in. "Mr. Clayton and I will handle the investigation on our own. We won't need any assistance."

"But what if there's any heavy work involved? Won't you need some help?" Mr. Sedgewick asked. "After all, Ms. Tilden, a lady like yourself might not want to be involved in some of the more physical aspects of this project."

Yolanda suppressed a sarcastic comeback and simply stated, "If any heavy work turns up, it will mean that we've found something and believe me, you will be contacted immediately."

Sedgewick and the good doctor turned to each other and each of them shrugged. Jack could already tell that they were relieved that the museum would have as little involvement as possible. He still had the opinion that the existence of any treasure was doubtful, but he also was a little miffed at the cavalier attitude with which the project had been treated. He had already received a couple of dressing-downs from Yolanda about having a negative attitude, but now he kind of wished to prove those two white-suited dandies wrong.

"I guess we've seen about everything we need to see," Jack said. "Could we pick up the van now?"

"Ah, yes," Dr. Armbruster answered, "I'll have a staff member take you out to the parking garage. Will you be needing any more of our assistance?"

"No," Yolanda answered, "we just need a museum credit card for expenses. That was laid out in the agreement."

"Of course, of course," Armbruster said. "Mr. Sedgewick, would you take care of that matter, please? Ms. Tilden, why don't you accompany him to the treasurer's office. They will issue you the credit card and I'll have someone take Mr. Clayton to the garage."

Armbruster went to the door and motioned to someone. A moment later a custodian stepped inside and was given instructions to take Jack to pick up the van. As Jack left the room he noticed that Dr. Armbruster was busily rubbing his hands together, it seemed like a Pontius Pilate thing to Jack. He also noticed that Mr. Sedgewick had placed his hand on the same part of Yolanda's body that Dr. Armbruster had visited earlier. *Southern gentlemen, ha.*

Ten minutes later Jack was sitting in the van in front of the museum. He had only waited a couple of minutes before he saw Yolanda come out of the front entrance. He honked the horn and she immediately headed his way.

A spirited discussion began as soon as she climbed in the van and got buckled in.

"Jack, they just wanted to get rid of us."

"Ah, you noticed that too," he replied as he eased onto the street in front of the museum. "I guess the treasure search is not supposed to be successful at all, we're just supposed to sort of put an official end to the nonsense."

"Well, that certainly wasn't the understanding I got when all this was started. I don't get it, Jack. Why would they give us six months with the sole hope that we debunk the existence of the gold?"

"I know what you mean. But besides the fact that I don't like Mr. Sedgewick and that Armbruster looks like a Hollywood extra for some B-movie, I don't actually mind this set-up. Look, they're definitely not interested in what we do or where we're going, so that's a plus. Like you said when you talked me into this, it's a win-win situation for us. We get paid whether we find anything or not. And, if we do find something, we get a nice bonus."

"Yeah, I get that part too, but it still makes me a little angry. After all, I could have picked almost any cold case that I wanted, but this one sounded like it would be fun. I had no idea we were just picked not to find the treasure. I don't know, Jack. This just puts me in a bad mood. What should we do?"

"Look, don't let them bother you. We will either find something or not. It won't make any difference how we plan to handle this search. Let's go back to the hotel and have some lunch. We can make some plans. Then we can either get going this afternoon or head west to Lynchburg tomorrow morning like we planned."

"OK, lunch sounds good. It's funny, I don't know why, but I have a craving for fried chicken and I hardly ever eat anything like that."

Jack laughed. "I think you were given a subliminal message back at the museum. You can't spend much time talking to Armbruster without making a mental connection to Colonel Harlan Sanders."

"Shit, you're right! That didn't even cross my mind. He did look like Colonel Sanders, except he was bald!"

"Good eyes, Yo! OK then, let's go for the fried chicken, it must be an omen!"

9

THE PLAN

The hotel restaurant wasn't crowded and, like they had planned, Jack and Yolanda both ordered the Southern-fried chicken.

"I can't believe I get to eat fried chicken without hearing a load of crap from you," Jack remarked as the waitress set their plates in front of them.

"You are allowed to do a few things without my input, Jack. And yes, this is terrible for your body and for mine, but it's funny that I got a craving for it, so you're allowed to indulge too," she laughed. "Now, here's an etiquette question. Do we pick the chicken up or use a knife and fork to eat it?"

"I'm no expert," Jack said as he turned and tried to see if anyone else happened to be eating chicken. "You know, the hell with it. In Indiana we just pick it up and eat it. Nobody here knows us, so who cares. Let's just eat."

That act did earn both of them a few disdainful looks, mostly from a table of three matronly ladies who were horrified by such behavior in a restaurant known for its culture and its adherence to Southern values. Jack just looked over at them and waved a chicken leg as an acknowledgement, thereby setting off a round of whispered indignations.

"OK, Jack," Yolanda said as she nibbled at a piece of cornbread, "are we going today or tomorrow?"

"I think maybe tomorrow. It's about 2 and a half hours to Lynchburg, if we leave early enough, we can be there by 11."

"What do you think we should do first?"

Jack sighed. "You get angry every time I bring this up, but this could very well be a legend, a hoax, you name it, but just listen for a minute. This supposedly happened more than a hundred and fifty years ago. We had a lot of luck in finding Annie and that trail was only twenty years cold. I don't know, I think we need to go to the farm and just get a feel for the terrain."

"I guess that's as good of a start as any. How about after that?"

"Slow down, Yo, let's see what strikes us at the first impression. Then we'll figure out what we want to do next."

Yo again. She smiled.

"What?" Jack asked.

"Oh, nothing, it's just going to be nice working on a new case with you. Something so completely different than last time. We make a good team, don't we, Jack?" She looked at him earnestly.

"Yes, I think we do," he nodded. "Say, since we're not leaving until tomorrow, uh, maybe we could spend some, I don't know, quality time this afternoon," he smiled.

Yolanda didn't catch the meaning of the smile. "Well, Grace did tell me that there were two very nice art museums within walking distance of the hotel. We could just leave the van in the parking garage."

Jack's face fell.

"Jesus Christ," Yolanda whispered. "You're talking about sex, aren't you? No, Jack, we are not spending a sunny afternoon in bed having sex. Sometimes I don't know about you."

"I just figured that maybe it would have been nice," Jack mumbled.

"Yes, Jack, sex with you is nice, but you don't get to have it whenever you happen to want it. I want to see some artwork. You can either come along with me and make me happy or go up to your room and take care of your business by yourself. I do have to tell you that coming along with me will make me happy, and a happy me is much more likely to be agreeable about certain things later."

With that comment, Jack's expression considerably brightened. "Sure, I don't mind going to a museum. Can we maybe walk back by the Confederacy museum too? I would like to see some of their other exhibits."

Oh, Jack, you are so easy. Men. Why hasn't there been a woman president by now?

"Deal. Two museums, one art, one historical, and then I want to try dinner at someplace less stuffy than here. I don't like older ladies sniffling at us." Yolanda looked over at the three ladies and stifled the impulse to stick her tongue out at them. They did return the glance and then busily began whispering to one another. Yolanda just smiled at them. "Jack, let's go upstairs, I want to change clothes and start throwing some stuff into my suitcase in case we get rushed for time later."

"Uh, maybe I could come by and help you with maybe your zipper or something," Jack offered.

Yolanda stood up. "Jack, no, not now. Don't get me angry or you will be taking care of your own business. I swear to you."

Jack sighed and followed her out of the restaurant. A familiar song went through his head as he walked behind her. *Skyrockets in flight, afternoon…oh, shit.*

10

SATURDAY MORNING

It was 10 o'clock; they had been on the road for almost an hour. Jack was humming contentedly behind the wheel of the van. Friday afternoon had been entertaining. He didn't really like the art museum much. It was mostly modern, impressionist-type paintings and he didn't care for that at all. His taste in art ran to people doing things like waving swords or galleons firing cannons at each other. He did enjoy the Civil War exhibits at the Museum of the Confederacy and rejoiced that they avoided bumping in to either of their two sponsors.

Dinner was nice also. Jack had some seafood and Yolanda ordered some vegetarian thing. The best part of the evening came when they got back to the hotel. Yolanda stopped him just as they got off the elevator at their floor and gave him three simple instructions. One: go to his room and shave, she didn't care for whisker marks on her face. Two: brush his teeth. Three: knock on her door in 10 minutes. He was there in seven and was taking care of business in twelve.

Jack was humming some song. Yolanda glanced over at him and rolled her eyes. She knew he was reliving yesterday evening. She liked the sex too. Jack was different than anyone else she had ever been with. She actually hadn't had very many partners, but Jack cared more about pleasing her than himself. That was new for her and she really liked it. But it was still comical how Jack could stretch out the euphoria of sex over the next several hours. This morning he was just like a fat tomcat lying on his back in a patch of warm sunshine on a gray-painted porch. She giggled to herself at that image. Then she thought for a moment.

"Jack, we need a signal," she suddenly stated.

"What? A signal? A signal for what?"

"I was just thinking, I mean no one really knows much about us and that we're sort of more than partners."

"I know. Two rooms and stuff like that, is that what you mean?" he said.

"Exactly. I know you don't like that, but it's going to be OK. Anyway, maybe we just need something simple to remind us when we're in a situation like at the museum or someplace in public. Sometimes I just want to tell you how I feel about you, but having someone like Sedgewick or Armbruster around makes it difficult."

"So, what's the signal?" Jack asked.

Yolanda leaned over and tapped on the back of his hand three times.

"Three taps?"

"Yes, Jack. Three taps…I…love…you. Three taps."

Jack smiled at her. "I kind of like that, Yolanda."

"So every now and then, we can tell each other that we love each other, even if you're talking to the President or even the Pope." She settled back in her seat with a big smile on her face.

Jack smiled too and immediately went back to thinking about Friday night for a couple of minutes.

"So, Jack, what's the first thing we're going to do?" she inquired, interrupting his reverie.

"Huh, what?" The happy moment in his mind dissipated. "The first thing? Well, I guess we go to the farm and ask permission to tromp around on their land."

"That shouldn't be a problem. The museum let the owners know that we were coming and they were OK with it. I think they share the same feeling about the treasure that our two friends have. They are probably tired of chasing people off their land and would like the whole chapter to come to a close."

"That attitude should help speed things up. We do need to ask them some questions about what's on the property as far as buildings, old structures or what might be left of stuff that dates back to the war," Jack observed.

"I know you think this whole thing is bullshit, Jack. Are you going to really work this or are you just going to go through the motions?"

"No, I'm going to give it a shot. Honest. Look, legends grow for lots of reasons, sometimes there's a grain of truth to them or a reasonable explanation for them. This could be the case here. Besides, I don't like Sedgewick and Armbruster's attitudes."

"A grain of truth? For example?" she asked.

"OK, here's one. It's like the Sirens of Greek mythology. Maybe so many ships wrecked there because of the rocks or tides and the legend grew that there were beautiful temptresses luring ships to their doom. There's a similar story in Germany about a spirit called the Lorelei. Same sort of thing, it's a dangerous stretch of Rhine river with rocks and rapids. There was no surprise that ships crashed there. Then people started saying that a maiden leaped to her death after seeing her lover perish at the base of the cliff. Soon after, she reappeared as a spirit and lured more ships to disaster."

"OK," Yolanda laughed. "So now we have a legend about Confederate gold and we're going a little off-track, at least as far as the museum is concerned. What do you thing the grain of truth could be here?"

"Well," Jack collected his thoughts for a moment. "First of all, it wasn't Confederate paper money. If it existed, it had to be gold and silver. Four million dollars' worth equals a considerable weight, so more than three or four people would have had to be involved."

"So how does that lend a grain of truth to it?"

"All right, you have x number of people transporting the gold and silver. Let's say between 6 and 10 personnel hauling crates on wagons. There's absolutely no record of Union forces coming across that shipment, because finding that much gold and silver wouldn't have gone unreported. It also makes sense that if there were a maximum of 10 people, some of them would have most likely survived the war and, if the treasure had been hidden somewhere, they would also most likely have an inkling of where it disappeared."

"I see," Yolanda nodded, "but as far as an inkling goes, as you called it, doesn't it seem unlikely than no one ever came up with it?"

"Maybe, but let me remind you. You are the person who signed on for this project," Jack pointed out. "Hey, look at that house! How much money do you suppose that place is worth?"

Yolanda glanced at the large, brick mansion they were passing. "Who cares, Jack? It's just a big house. OK, one more question, why does the legend mention a well?"

Jack laughed. "How am I supposed to know? Would it make sense to hide gold in a well? I don't know. Seriously, Yolanda, this is what makes this case so vague. We have to try and find a 150-year old clue that no one else has ever found. It's a good thing that we're getting paid regardless."

"Yes, getting paid is great, especially for six months," Yolanda answered. "OK, here's what I think happened. I think that it was the end of the war and Union soldiers were all over Virginia. What do you suppose? Two, three, four wagons? It wouldn't have been easy to avoid being stopped and questioned, even if they were civilians. And, if they were Confederate soldiers, no way."

"So what are you saying?"

"That they might have hidden the money when it looked like there was no way they were going to be undetected," she explained.

"OK, here's another grain of truth," Jack offered, passing a rented RV that said "Visit Alaska" on the side. Virginia was a good piece from there. "I checked the meteorological reports from that time. The war ends at Appomattox in April. It had been a very wet spring with lots of rainfall, so any hand-dug well would have had a pretty good level of water in it."

"Yes, but water is still water. What's your point?" Yolanda asked.

"Yes, but…, as you so often like to say," Jack smirked, "what if they dug out an area above the waterline on the side of the well? Anybody looking for the money would assume it was at the bottom of the well. What if it wasn't?"

"OK, OK," she laughed. "I guess that almost any plausible explanation could be true. Heck, maybe aliens from outer space teleported the wagons into their mother ship."

That earned her a sterner glance from Jack. "Plausible, Yolanda, plausible."

11

LYNCHBURG

They arrived at Lynchburg and checked into their hotel. Once again Jack was a little annoyed that two rooms had been booked for their arrival. The clerk was all business, however, and Jack was pleased that Yolanda's typical bonding experience didn't take place. After they put their bags in their respective rooms, they met in the lobby in order to find someplace to have lunch. The clerk did offer a couple of suggestions, so they left the hotel and wandered down to the closest restaurant. It turned out to be Italian cuisine.

"Hmm…pasta for lunch, Jack. That's right up your alley," she grinned.

"Shut up, Yolanda. I'm in better shape now than I have been for a while. Besides, it's just lunch."

"OK, I was just joking. Come on, I want to eat and get out to that farm as soon as we can. I want to see this place."

After they were seated and ordered their meals, Jack coughed and caught Yolanda's attention.

"Something wrong, Jack?"

He coughed again. "Well, we don't know how long we're going to be here until we either find something or give up."

"Yes, Jack, I'm well aware of that. What is your point?"

Another cough. "It's just that…it's just that, how come you put your suitcase in the second room?"

Yolanda sighed and looked out the window at the ubiquitous Civil War statue in the square. "Jack, this is temporary. We are working for a museum. They don't know we are sort of a couple, they just think that we are business partners."

"Yes, but we're not just business partners."

"I know, Jack. Listen, let's make a compromise. I want our operation to look as professional as possible. This is not going to be our last case, Jack. I have several inquiries regarding cold cases that are anxious to provide funding for our investigation. Continued success in this regard requires publicity. One thing we don't need is our professional relationship tainted by people concerned about our sexual relationship."

"Tainted? It's none of their business what our sexual relationship is."

"Yes, Jack, I'm aware of that, but I also know that we are Clayton and Tilden Investigations, LLC. That is how I want the world to see us, not as two detectives who are overly chummy."

"Overly chummy? Is that how you view it?"

"No, Jack, damn it, just do it my way for now. It's not that important that we spend every night together. When we get back to Indianapolis, it will be different."

"Uh, a little while ago you mentioned something about a compromise or something."

Yolanda sighed. "Yes, I did and I was quite aware that it wouldn't have skipped your attention, Jack. Look, during this case, I promise that I will either visit you or let you visit me at regular intervals to keep you happy."

"What's a regular interval?"

"Jesus, I don't know!" This outburst attracted the attention of some nearby diners.

"Shh," Jack whispered. "It was just a simple question."

Yolanda briefly touched her first and middle finger to her forehead before answering.

"You do know that when you piss me off, you don't get special treatment from me, right?"

"Ha, do I ever."

"OK, I promise that I will be less critical and I will not use or withhold sex as a punishment, even if you irritate the hell out of me."

"I irritate you?"

"Jack, you're doing it right now, you're pissing me off."

"Oh, does that mean that you want to do it right now?" he winked at her.

"Are you fucking serious?" she glared at him.

Jack laughed, "No, I was just testing the waters."

The waiter arrived with their food.

"Just shut up and eat, Jack." But she smiled when she said it.

12

THE MCINTOSH FARM

The GPS led them right to the mailbox of the farm. Jack turned the van onto the greenish-looking gravel driveway and drove the short distance back to the farmhouse. They had no sooner gotten out of the van when the front door opened and two men stepped out and headed toward them.

"You're the detectives, I wager," said the taller man. He was dressed in casual work clothes and sported a neatly trimmed beard. The second man was similarly attired, no beard though. He had a dark complexion and had eyebrows that were wildly out of control. He just stood by without saying a word.

"Yes, I'm Jack Clayton and this is my partner, Yolanda Tilden," Jack said, offering his hand. They briefly shook hands. Jack was glad that the man wasn't one of the he-man types who try to bone-crush on a handshake.

"Josiah Potter. This is my foreman, Gene Segler. Mr. Sedgewick said that you would be stopping by this afternoon. Do you want to head out to the old farm site now?" the man asked.

"Yes," Jack replied, "we want to take a quick look around, just to get a feel for the place."

Jack noticed that the second man was not following the conversation at all; he seemed to have become fascinated in checking out Yolanda. *Seriously, do we have to go through this with every man we meet?*

Mr. Potter climbed into the passenger side of the van while Mr. Segler slid the side door open and motioned for Yolanda to get in. Jack was glad that she was wearing jeans; that prevented him from having a front row seat at another leg show like the one back at the museum. He was, however, paying way too much attention to her backside as she maneuvered into the second seat.

"Go on back down the drive," the man directed. "The original farmhouse was close to a side road about a half a mile down the road to the right."

Yolanda leaned forward. "Have you had lots of trouble with trespassers? You know, treasure hunters and the like?"

"Oh, it depends. We catch a lot of people nosing around the property. The worst times are after some history channel show runs an episode about the gold and we get mentioned. For the next couple of weeks we have to keep an eye out."

"In case they find something valuable?" Jack asked.

"No," the man laughed. "These people show up with all kinds of digging equipment. We basically try to chase them off before they end up hurting themselves."

Segler finally decided to speak. "One year some guy was digging a huge hole and ended up falling in and breaking his leg. He was down there for a good half day or so before we heard him yelling. It was a good thing we were out there; otherwise he could have stayed down there for days."

"See that post up there?" Mr. Potter pointed. "There's a turn-in right past it. That's the original access to the old farm."

Jack slowed down and squeezed the van between a fence post and a half-dead pine tree. He drove down the rutted lane for about thirty yards until the man told him to stop the van. After everyone climbed out he directed them toward a couple of scraggly cedar trees. Of course Yolanda had been helped out of the backseat by her overly polite companion.

"OK, there's really not much left here of the original buildings," Potter explained as he led them over to a flat area. There were several large rocks that were laid out in a rough L pattern. "You see, back then, they didn't have foundations like nowadays. They would simply find large stones and use them to support the corners and the midpoints before putting the floor joists down. You can see the original outline of the farmhouse. These stones were the original foundation. That's about all that's left; the place was burned down during the war and was never rebuilt."

Yolanda walked over and circled the foundation, staying clear of taller clumps of weeds. She had done her research and was a little concerned about the existence of the Eastern Diamondback Rattlesnake. Jack was more concerned about the location of the hand-dug well.

"Can you show us the location of the well?" he asked.

"Sure," Segler replied. "It's over here a bit. It's almost all filled in, but you can still see where it was."

Jack waved for Yolanda to come and join them.

Potter abandoned his explanation of early building techniques and started in on a history lesson.

"This whole situation revolves around a tale that was spun right at the end of the Civil War. I know you people know that already. But somehow it was rumored that the gold and silver were concealed in this well. That may have been the case, but I can personally state that this old well has been dug in and around repeatedly since the end of the Civil War and there's not been a single piece of silver or gold found here."

Jack nodded in agreement. "That appears to be in agreement with all the other supposed sites involving this so-called treasure," he said. "Still, rumors and legends usually have some basis in fact, even if it was small and insignificant, something must have happened around here to give rise to that."

Mr. Potter merely shrugged his shoulders. "You could be right; all I know is what I told you earlier. Nothing's ever been found here, I don't think anything ever will be."

Yolanda had a very disappointed look on her face. She had hoped that there would be something that stood out or would give her some inspiration, but old rocks and a slightly round depression among some dried weeds just didn't provide any insight.

"Look," Jack said. "Now that we know where this place is, why don't we drop you and Mr. Segler back at the house? Ms. Tilden and I will come back here and just look around a bit. I agree with you about the likelihood that there's nothing here, but still, we just want to get a historical feel for the place. We'll only be an hour or so before heading back to town."

"Sure, suit yourself," Potter replied.

"Just don't go digging any holes you might end up in," Segler wittily added.

"OK." Jack ignored the attempt at humor. "Yolanda, do you want to stay here? I'll be back in a few minutes."

"No, absolutely not, there could be snakes here."

"She's got a thing against snakes," Jack explained to the two men.

"Original sin," Segler pointed out, smiling at Yolanda.

That only earned him a baleful glance from both Yolanda and Jack.

13

THE RUINS

It took a little bit longer than 5 minutes. Mr. Potter signaled them to wait a moment and went into the house. He came back out with a small bag and two bottles of water and handed them off to Yolanda. Mr. Segler disappeared into an outbuilding and Mr. Potter had already gone back inside by the time Jack had put the van into gear.

"What's in the bag?" Jack asked.

Yolanda unfolded it and peered inside. "Ooh, a couple of apples and, oh, you'll like this, Jack, a couple of Hostess fruit pies."

"Really? That was nice of him. What flavor?"

"Uh, peach and apple. Yuck, you're not planning on eating this garbage are you, Jack?

"Well, it is fruit sort of, isn't it?"

"Jack, it's processed sugar and dough; we'll stick with the apples if we get hungry."

"It just seems that it would be a waste,…"

"Jack, empty calories, just listen to me."

By this time they were back at the ruined farmhouse.

The fruit pie issue bothered Jack. He shut off the engine and turned to face her. "You know that you're not my mother."

"Jack, don't pull that line on me, it's pointless. I am definitely not your mother, if you could possibly recall what happened last night; there was a non-mother and son event that took place. I get tired of you always fussing about this. We are partners, I worry about you. You lived your bachelor life for years, eating God knows what kind of junk every day. This sugary goop is not good for you. I need you around for a few more years, so cut the crap."

Jack knew the tone and he had heard the argument enough times to just let it go. He silently congratulated himself on his blend of wisdom and maturity. Besides, he would simply keep track of where she put the bag and help himself later.

They both got out of the van and walked over toward the site of the farmhouse. Jack went to one of the foundation rocks and sat down on it.

"So, Jack, what do you think?"

"I have no doubt that something happened here. But I know that the gold and silver isn't here. Some evidence of it would have been found by now."

"So what might have happened?"

Jack laughed. "This is what I told you about way back in Indy. One hundred and fifty year old events tend to lack a smoking gun. All I can offer you is conjecture at this point. Let's say that there was that much money. Whoever was in charge had the same problem that a pirate captain had. Somebody had to carry the treasure; somebody had to bury the treasure. The number of helpers equals the number of people who knew where it was. All it would take was one person to revisit the site and help themselves to the treasure. That's why so many pirates never made it back to the ship. Dead men tell no tales."

"So, our confederate pirate captain kind of guy killed all the helpers?"

Jack thought for a moment. "No, I don't think so. OK, it could have played out that way, but realistically I think that there wasn't any reason for him or whoever was in charge to kill anyone. Look, Yolanda, I'm betting that if there was a treasure, it never made it this far. I'm also betting that something was hidden here, maybe just to conclude whatever scam was going on, but I also believe that the treasure was somehow swapped out before it got here. I also think that this guy encouraged the rumors about the treasure to mask what really happened to it."

"Wow, Jack, that's a leap," she observed.

"Yeah, Yolanda, well, the whole thing's a leap. I just need to think about it some more."

She motioned for him to squeeze to his right; then she sat down on the same foundation stone. She looked out towards the well.

"I wish there was some kind of time machine viewer thingy," she said. "We could hook it up and go back to 1865 and actually see what happened here."

Jack laughed. "You know, that would make crime solving so simple. Actually I had a friend who was writing a science fiction kind of novel about just that idea."

"Really? Did he finish it?"

"I don't think so. It had a good premise, but maybe it was just a little too far-fetched," Jack replied.

"I don't think science fiction can be stretched too far. After all, we have aliens, atomic zapper guns, and teleportation. It seems to me that the sky's the limit," Yolanda observed.

"Maybe so," Jack said.

"Well, go on. What was so far-fetched about it?"

"Well, OK, here's a brief version. His novel theorized that all the dust motes and assorted junk floating in the air can only be displaced by a solid object. He called his novel *Traces*. So the protagonist invents this sort of atmospheric reader that could find this void kind of thing."

"OK, I'm beginning to sense the far-fetchedness. Is that a word?"

"I don't think so, but it's cute." He patted her knee. "Anyway, he developed a paint-fill program that would turn the void into a solid shape, sort of like those strange people in the Blue Man Group. Anyway, the main character went to Montana and recreated the final moments of Custer. At some point he went to the Atlantic in 1912 and saw the sinking of the Titanic."

"Hmm…, I don't know if that book would play out or not. Maybe that's why he never finished it."

"Yes, but it would be nice if we could focus it right on that well and go back to the Civil War. But you know; it would be a hell of a lot better if we could go to where the treasure was swapped out."

"OK, back to that," Yolanda said, "so you don't think the treasure was ever here?"

"No, I don't. Here's what I think. Remember when we were talking about it on the ride over here from Richmond? There had to be an x-number of people involved. Those crates or boxes were heavy and they must have been transported by horse and wagon."

"And…?"

"Patience, please. My point is that from the time those wagons left Richmond until they got here, they were never left unattended or unguarded."

"So that means you think the gold and silver were never in the wagons to begin with!" Yolanda said excitedly.

"Exactly," Jack said. "I think that whoever arranged this had replaced the gold and silver with something like rocks or junk metal before those crates were ever loaded onto the wagons. I don't see how anyone could have moved crates on and off during the trip without being noticed."

"You think pretty well when you're sitting down, Jack." She returned the pat on the knee. "So, where does that leave us?"

"It leaves us going back to Richmond, that's where all of this started. I've read all the stuff online about this, but government officials being government officials, even ones with a limited amount of time left, like the CSA, usually were consumed with documentation."

"So, we're going to spend more quality time with our friends at the Museum of the Confederacy?"

"More like in their archives, or at whichever museum or historical society paperwork of that type ended up. You know it's going to be boring as all get out."

"I know," she sighed. "I didn't consider archive searching when I got excited about this job. I saw us exploring caves and looking for hidden passages in old plantation mansions."

"Well, that might eventually happen, but more than likely we'll be exploring stacks of documents with no secret passages to be found."

With that remark, Yolanda nodded and stood up. She took Jack's hand as they walked back to the van.

The museum wouldn't be open on a Sunday, so they decided to stay around and do some mild sight-seeing around Lynchburg before driving over to Richmond on Sunday afternoon.

When Yolanda went to her room to shower, Jack had a Hostess peach pie.

14

GRACE VERSUS JACK

The Sunday drive back to Richmond went smoothly, it was only a two-hour trip and no points of contention were raised. Jack was looking forward to capping the day with a romantic evening, but, upon announcing his intent, Yolanda informed him that she was sort of benched from the starting line-up for the next several days. Jack was depressed.

The next morning Yolanda had to wake him up. She had stayed the night with him, it turned out that she felt pretty miserable during that particular time and liked to have her stomach held. Jack was happy to oblige.

They went down for breakfast and then back upstairs before leaving for the museum. Just as they passed the reception desk, Yolanda was hailed by a familiar voice.

"Yolanda! Yolanda! Yoo-hoo!" It was Grace, the desk clerk.

"Grace! Good morning," Yolanda responded.

Shit, Jack silently contributed.

"My, you look so lovely this morning," Grace cooed.

"And you, you are obviously what they mean when they speak of a Southern belle."

Holy shit. Jack involved religion in the thought process.

Grace actually tittered. "Did you enjoy the museums last week? Didn't you find them so lovely?"

"Yes, you were absolutely so dear to recommend them. Mr. Clayton enjoyed them too, didn't you, Jack?"

Jack grunted a reply, earning a look from Grace that was normally reserved for crossing a meadow filled with grazing cows and encountering something unpleasant on one's shoe.

"Say, Grace," Yolanda continued. "We're interested in doing some research on the Confederate government's actions at the end of the war. You know, like in archives. Do you have any suggestions for us? After all, your last ones were so enjoyable."

Grace absolutely beamed.

"Oh, Yolanda, you are so precious!" Grace leaned over the counter and touched Yolanda's arm. "I do think that your best place to look is at the museum, but there is another new museum that you could look at, it's called the American Civil War Center. I haven't been there yet, but it's built on the site of an ironworks factory that made cannons and the like for the Confederate Army."

"You really are such a great help," Yolanda said, "it's too bad that you can't come along with us."

Yeah, that would be great, Jack thought. *I would have to listen to this girl-to-girl prattle all day long.*

"What are you researching, dear?" Grace asked.

"Well," Yolanda leaned forward in a conspiring way, "it all has to do with missing Confederate gold."

"Oh, my, as I live and breathe," Grace gushed. "Treasure hunting! That sounds so exciting!"

"Maybe at the end, if we find any clues. Right now it's going to be pretty boring, looking through old papers and all."

"Perhaps Mr. Clayton will be of some help to you," Grace remarked, not even throwing a glance in Jack's direction.

Yes, maybe I'll be of some help, precious Yolanda. Jack's vein began throbbing.

"We're going to start at the museum; it's going to be a challenge, sort of a needle in a haystack kind of thing," Yolanda continued.

"Well, I can just tell by looking at you that you are up to that challenge, dearie." Grace leaned over again and this time patted Yolanda's hand.

"OK," Jack butted in. "Those archives aren't going to search themselves and I do promise to try and help a little."

Both Yolanda and Grace sighed a bit as they turned to face Jack.

"Yes, Jack, I'm aware of that. I was just chatting a bit with Grace. We'll be on our way in a minute, don't be in such a hurry."

Grace just gave Jack a cold stare before she made a slight harrumphing noise and looked back at Yolanda.

"Like I said, Yolanda, I'm sure that you'll do just fine. You certainly have my curiosity aroused about this treasure-hunting expedition. Please, please, keep me informed of your progress."

"Oh, you can bet on it, Grace. Wish us luck."

"I certainly do wish you…," she turned and gave Jack a cursory glance, "…wish both of you luck."

"Thanks, Grace," Jack said and grabbed Yolanda's forearm as he hustled her away from the desk.

"It's Ms. Levings to you, asshole," Grace softly directed this comment to Jack's back. *Oh, dear, and I'm a Southern lady. There's just something about that man that irritates me.*

15

THE ARCHIVES

Yolanda was quiet as they walked to the van, but, just as soon as Jack started the engine, she turned to him with a quizzical expression.

"Jack, why do you get so impatient when I'm talking to someone?"

Jack shrugged his shoulders and pretended to be way more interested in traffic patterns than usual.

"Was that shrug an answer, Jack? If so, its meaning escaped me. I mean that's twice now that I've talked to Grace and you get all pissy about it. I kind of got it the first time, you had driven all day and we had trouble finding the hotel. OK. But now? We're only going a few blocks to the museum, what was the big deal?"

"It's just..., it's just that..."

"What, Jack, just say it!"

"It's like everyone you meet suddenly becomes your best friend and starts these long conversations with you. It's like that bee-hive haired woman at that middle school. I mean within three minutes you've become life-long buddies."

"I'm just being friendly, Jack. I don't get why it bothers you."

Jack was at a loss at this point. He honestly didn't know why it bothered him so much.

"Jack? Do you have an explanation?"

Jack waited another moment before answering. "I don't know, Yolanda. I mean I just stand there and watch you trading pleasantries with complete strangers, when I don't see the need to get involved with them."

Yolanda frowned. "Well, Jack, I think the problem is with your pronouns. You don't see the need, but maybe I do. I like people, Jack. I like to talk to them. Look, in the future, just go find a chair and sit down on it. I got you a smart phone; you can Google things while I'm wasting my time getting to know people you don't care about."

"I didn't say you were wasting your time," he defended himself.

"No, you didn't say it, you implied it. Means the same thing, Jack."

"Look, maybe it's just that I don't get friendly with people like that. You can start up a conversation with anybody. I'm not like that."

"OK, that's a valid point. But Jack, I'm not going to stop being friendly to people just because it makes you impatient when I chat with them. Seriously, you will just have to go, sit, and find something to occupy your mind. You can be you, and I'll continue to be me."

"Fine, I'll try and remember that. Uh, you're not angry with me are you?"

"No, I just didn't get it. Now I have an idea what's going on in that head of yours. Don't worry, Jack, we'll be OK." She leaned over and tapped his right knee three times. "We're partners, Jack."

"I know, Yolanda, I like being partners, I really do." And he returned the taps on her left forearm.

Three minutes later they were already heading down the sidewalk toward the rear entrance of the museum. There was a security guard in a little kiosk by the door. He was a scrawny, elderly man. They showed him their temporary ID badges and he blinked a couple of times as he studied them. His lips moved as he read the names and then he decided to get talkative.

"Y'all them folk from the North, ain't you?"

"Uh, yes," Jack replied.

"You ain't from Ah-hi-yah, are you?"

"What? From where?" Jack was trying to figure out what that place was, when Yolanda stepped forward.

"No, we're from Indiana. Is there something about Ohio that interests you?"

Ah-hi-yah is the same thing as O-hi-o? Jack thought.

My great grand-pappy got shot by some Ah-hi-yah boys back in the War Between the States. Never been too overly fond of folk from there ever since."

"You or your Grand-Pappy?" Jack asked.

"That's a shame," Yolanda quickly interjected. "Well, we're all friends now, aren't we?" And she flashed him a winning smile.

The man grinned back at her, displaying some tobacco-stained teeth as he toyed with the collar of his too-large uniform shirt.

"Yeah, I reckon you're right about that. Don't have no problem with no Indiana folk anyways."

"But, Yolanda, you're from...," Jack started.

"Indiana! Indiana, Jack! Moonlight on the Wabash and all that!" she interrupted before turning back to the guard. "I do love being here in the South, especially around gentlemen like yourself."

This time Jack did pay more attention and realized that Yolanda just had a way of twisting people around her little finger. She was very good at it. Then he started wondering if he was a victim too.

"Can you tell us where the archived documents are stored," Yolanda asked sweetly.

The guard actually blushed. "Sure, ma'am, just go to your left when you get inside and there are doors to a stairwell on the right hand side. Go down one level and you'll find the document room down there."

"Thank you so very much," Yolanda looked down at his name badge, "uh, Officer Tingley," she smiled again.

"More than welcome, ma'am," and Tingley even threw her a salute. Jack just nodded his thanks as they went inside.

"OK, very impressive," Jack said as they walked down the stairs.

"What's impressive, Jack?" she asked.

"How you talk to people. I paid attention this time. You seem to know the right thing to say that gets people talking."

"Is that a compliment, Jack?"

Jack paused for a moment before answering. "Yes, it is. Honest. I was impressed."

Yolanda stopped and gave him a quick kiss on the cheek. "Thanks, partner."

"I'm going to give it a try in the archives. You just watch," he laughed.

They found the door to the archives. Jack held the right-side double door open for her and followed her inside. It wasn't quite the dreary place that they had imagined. It was brightly lit along with being brightly painted. Two clerks were sitting on tall stools behind a chest-high counter. One of them, who appeared to be a college-aged intern, looked up from his computer screen. "Just a minute," he said, returning to the screen display, "I just have to collate these docs."

The other clerk, a woman in her late 20's, swiveled around and faced them. "I'm sorry," she smiled, "Lionel gets wrapped up in his work and often forgets that we are public servants. Although to tell you the truth, we don't get a lot of customers down here. Most of the people like to go upstairs and look at the exhibits."

"That's fine," Jack replied, holding up his temporary badge. "We are on contract with the museum and need to go through the archives on a document search." He looked at her nameplate before adding, "Mary Louise." He smiled.

Mary Louise smiled back. It was time for Yolanda to observe Jack in action.

"Mary Louise is such a pretty name. Were you named after someone?" he asked.

"No," she giggled, "my Mom just liked the combination. My Dad wanted to name me Suzanne."

"Well, that definitely wouldn't have fit someone as pretty as you," Jack schmoozed, earning him another round of giggles.

Yolanda was beginning to see Jack's point of view. At least she talked to men and women; he seemed to reserve his charm for the ladies, she recalled the middle-school librarian.

"Well, kind sir, what area are you intending to research?"

"Quartermaster documents, especially those dating to the end of the hostilities, let's say from January to April of 1865," Jack explained.

"Hmm…," Mary Louise thought for a moment. "Lionel, have you organized and scanned quartermaster documents yet? I know I haven't." She looked back at Jack, "Just like everyone else, we're slowly digitizing all the archives, but Dr. Armbruster set priorities."

Lionel begrudgingly looked up from his screen. "No, not yet, we started with casualty records, then pay records, followed by recruiting documents. No one's touched the quartermaster docs."

"So, can you direct us to where we might find them?" Yolanda asked.

"Oh, of course, just let me do a quick search here." Mary Louise turned her stool around and punched some letters into the computer before hitting the enter button. In a moment a series of numbers appeared on the screen. She scrolled down and stopped, then she jotted down some numbers on a Post-it note.

"Lionel, you mind the shop, I'm going to take these people back to Annex N."

Lionel just grunted.

"Follow me, please," Mary Louise addressed both of them, but reserved a special look for Jack.

She led them through another set of double doors, then down a long corridor lined with doors marked with letters of the alphabet, right to the one marked N. She unlocked the door and turned to face them.

"The documents that we haven't scanned are stored in binders. They're pretty much sorted by dates, but they aren't organized in any particular way other than that."

"That's fine," Jack answered. "We're really just on a fishing expedition."

"Oh, you two are the treasure hunters, aren't you? It just dawned on me," Mary Louise said.

"That's us," Jack smiled. "And this is part of the hunt."

"You've been the talk of the museum staff for weeks. I'm glad that I could help you."

"Well, we have a lot of things to sort through. This is not the glamorous part of treasure hunting, but it is nice to meet someone who is glamorous," Jack raised an eyebrow. That comment earned him a wide grin from Mary Louise and a pained expression from Yolanda.

Mary Louise opened the door and flipped the light switch on. The room was small, about 12' by 12.' There were two tables on each side of the door with reading lamps on each. The walls were lined with cardboard boxes, each with labels showing the approximate dates of the documents.

"These are basically what have been cursorily identified as quartermaster documents. To tell you the truth, there may be other documents tossed in here. Like Lionel said, these haven't been a priority; they are mostly transit records of supplies and requisitions, nothing that most people have an interest in."

"Thanks, Mary Louise," Yolanda said, finally getting a chance to enter the conversation that had been exclusively between Mary Louise and Jack. "We have several hours of searching ahead of us. When do you lock up for the day?"

"At 4:30. Doctor Armbruster likes everything shut down and secured by five o'clock sharp."

"OK, that's no problem," Yolanda said. "We'll make sure and be out of here before then."

"And we'll be taking a lunch break, will you have to let us back in?" Jack asked.

"No, one of us will be at the desk all day, so you can leave this door unlocked as you come and go. We'll lock it up at the end of the day," Mary Louise explained.

"Great, well, we'd better get at it. Thanks again," Jack said, "you've been a real sweetheart."

Mary Louise just smiled and waved as she closed the door.

"See," Jack said, turning to Yolanda, "I can be just as charming and friendly as you."

"Really, Jack? 'You've been a real sweetheart?' I about threw up with that one. OK, Jack, you do fine with the ladies, let's see you charm Mr. Sedgewick next."

"OK," Jack laughed. "You have a point there, but I'm glad you at least admit that I do have a way with the ladies."

"I am not admitting anything, Jack. Let it rest. Seriously." She turned and surveyed the room. "OK, look at all these boxes. Where do we start?"

"OK, let's think about it. By January of 1865, the South was pretty much finished. The Union naval blockade had cut off food and military supplies and the desertion rate from the army was pretty high. Richmond was abandoned in April, so I think we can center our search on January through April."

"I hope we can find a clear piece of evidence in all this," Yolanda said.

"I know, this is really a shot in the dark, but we have to start someplace. Have a seat and I'll get us each a box."

There were fourteen boxes covering the dates in question, four covering January, five marked February, three in March and two in April. Jack set a January box in front of Yolanda and placed another one on the second table.

"So, let's see what we've got. If we're lucky, we'll find something about the wagons that ended up at the farm, but what we're really looking for is something of a similar nature, maybe the same number of wagons. I don't know, Yolanda, this really is a blind search."

"I agree, but at least it's a starting place. What concerns me is the fact that this is not the only museum where stuff like this ended up."

"That's so true, but let's dig in, we can only deal with the stuff that's here and hope. Good luck, partner."

"You too, partner," Yolanda laughed.

About four hours later, Yolanda stood up and stretched. "God, Jack, this is killing me. Let's go get something to eat; I don't think I can look at another document right now. This is about the most boring thing I've ever done and my hands smell like an old basement."

"Treasure hunting sure sounds exciting until you get mired down in something like this. I now know more about horse, mules, wagons, and hardtack than I ever thought I would."

"Yeah, let's go. A little fresh air and some food will clear my head," she said.

They went out onto the main street and found a mom and pop restaurant named Granny Bee's. They were seated at an end booth along a wall decorated with photos of past notable diners.

"Jack, who was Art Linkletter? Why was he famous?"

Jack glanced over at the photo. "He was a TV personality back in the 50's; I think he had a talk show or something. The woman next to him was a TV actress on some western, I don't remember which one."

"Gee, maybe we'll end up on the wall if we find the treasure," Yolanda laughed.

"Yes, I'll have to perfect a pose in case that happens."

"We could just use that one of you showing your backside," she laughed.

"Shut up, Yolanda."

After studying the menu, Jack opted for meatloaf and Yolanda ordered a salad and the soup of the day, tomato bisque.

"So, Jack, this archive searching, it's mind-numbing."

"If only Lionel had different priorities," Jack sighed. "It's just something we have to do, Yolanda, I don't see any way around it."

"I know," she sighed too. "But I'm going to be royally pissed if we go through all those boxes and don't find anything. I mean, I don't know how much Civil War era dust I'm inhaling."

"It's like searching for a shipwreck, there's a lot of ocean out there, but at least we only have twelve more boxes."

"Twelve? Holy shit, Jack!"

"OK, eleven and a half, make you feel better?"

"Makes me feel wonderful. Here come the salad and soup along with your mystery meat concoction."

"I love meatloaf, Yolanda. I've been hooked on it ever since my first elementary school lunch."

"I'm not giving you grief about it, Jack. I just wouldn't ever eat anything like that."

"I admit that it's an acquired taste. Thanks for the non-criticism."

They passed the rest of the meal commenting on other photos. Yolanda went back to the museum with an increased knowledge of B actors and actresses of the 1950's and 60's, learning that Duncan Renaldo was the Cisco Kid and he rode a horse named Diablo.

The afternoon passed with nothing to be found.

16

AN OLD FRIEND

Mary Louise had popped her head into the annex promptly at 4:30, earning a relieved smile from Yolanda who was more than ready to vacate the building. Jack was so tired that he didn't continue his verbal courtship. They returned to the hotel and passed the desk where Grace was not on duty. They agreed to meet in the cocktail lounge at 6:30. They both took showers in their respective rooms and Jack took a little nap. Looking at faded documents all day long had made his eyes tired.

He walked into the lounge right on time and he saw Yolanda in an animated conversation with a dark-haired man sitting on the bar stool to her left. He must have said something funny, because Yolanda was laughing. Jack walked up and stood between the two.

"Jack, you're here," she said.

Jack looked at the other man.

"Oh," she continued. "Jack, I want you to meet Galen Foster."

Galen Foster stood up and extended his right hand to Jack.

"Glad to meet you, Mr. Clayton, Yolanda has been telling me about you."

"Galen and I were at the academy together, we were in the same class," Yolanda explained.

"I see," Jack said. "This is a coincidence, isn't it?"

"It's a very pleasant coincidence," Galen pointed out. "I haven't seen her since she left the academy."

"Are you here on vacation?" Jack asked as he took the bar stool to Yolanda's right. He asked the bartender for a double Johnny Walker Black.

"No," Yolanda answered for him. "Galen is here working a case, it has something to do with domestic terrorism."

"Here in Richmond?" Jack asked.

Galen took a sip of his drink. Jack noted that it had fruit in it. His estimation of Galen Foster dropped a notch.

"Yeah, we're checking up on some leads. NSA picked up a lot of cell phone traffic between Virginia and Yemen last month. It's slowed down considerably, but we're looking into Yemeni nationals who are here legally and who might be abetting some fellow countrymen who entered the country on the sly."

"Galen is working here for a couple of weeks," Yolanda added.

"Then it's on up to Fredericksburg. Seems that the activity is up and down I-95," Galen explained, "and there's some indication that it might be along the I-64 corridor too. Staunton through Charlottesville to Richmond."

"Hey," Yolanda interjected. "We're going to have some dinner. Galen, do you want to join us?"

"Tempting offer, Yolanda, but we have a debriefing scheduled in...," Galen looked at his watch, "...in twenty minutes. Maybe we can set something up later. Maybe we can go out and continue catching up."

"Yes, that would be nice, Galen. We'll be in touch."

Galen stood up and then leaned over and gave Yolanda a quick kiss on the cheek.

"Bye, Yolanda, we'll definitely be in touch."

Jack didn't like the kiss and Jack, being Jack, went into auto-pout mode.

"That was so nice. It's hard to believe that it's been three years since I've seen him," Yolanda said, watching Galen leave the lounge.

"Yeah, nice, very nice," Jack grunted, then took a long pull on his scotch.

Yolanda didn't pick up on that remark, but the next one was solidly telegraphed.

"He was one of the better-looking guys in my class at the academy and I have to admit, he's still pretty hot."

"Yeah? Well, maybe you can ogle him at your upcoming dinner date. And what the hell was that kissing all about?"

"What? Kissing? Jack, he just kissed me on the cheek, don't make such a big deal out of it. You would have probably kissed Mary Louise if you had thought of it."

"Humph."

"Oh, Jesus, you're in one of your pouty moods, aren't you? Jack, Galen and I are just friends. Knock it off, I mean it. You make me so angry when you get like this."

"I'm fine, nothing's the matter, and I'm not pouting."

"If you say so," she sighed. "Good, come on, let's go get some dinner. If you really promise not to pout, I'll buy you a martini."

"The museum is buying the martini, Yolanda."

"Well, the museum won't be in bed with you tonight, how about that?"

Jack's mood brightened.

17

PAPERS, PAPERS, AND MORE PAPERS

Jack walked over and unceremoniously dumped a pile of folders in front of Yolanda.

"Jesus Christ, I'm getting tired of this," he moaned, rubbing his eyes. "This stuff is so disorganized. I don't have a feel for anything; this is seriously like a needle in a haystack. I thought it would be easier."

"Believe me, Jack, you're not the Lone Ranger here. Other than the fact that everything is filed under the month, it's just all one big mess."

They had been working all morning, took a quick lunch break and it was now mid-afternoon of the third day of searching. So far it had netted absolutely nothing, no clue about any other shipment leaving Richmond.

"I'm going to the restroom, Yolanda, I'll be right back."

Yolanda waved as he left the room. Then she opened up the first folder. It seemed to contain shipping manifests. According to Jack, that would be unique due to the Union blockade of Southern ports. He really did know a lot about the Civil War, and he hadn't really been lecturing her, he just gave her details when certain pieces of information were uncovered.

She was so tired that she almost missed the clue. It was in the second file. She had been rifling through the papers and, to her credit, she had been going at it for hours. It caught her attention because it was a different color paper. It was dark yellow. She read it carefully, set it on the table, and waited for Jack to return. It was only a couple of minutes before he opened the door.

"Jack! Come here! Take a look at this! It's a shipping order!" she said excitedly.

Jack hurried over to the table and picked it up.

"Let's see. Transit Order #7207, two wagons, four drivers, two crates of rifles and ammunition."

"The numbers match up with the Lynchburg stories, Jack, and look at the date."

"February 26, 1865."

"The war is over in about four or five weeks, Jack."

"OK, OK, hold on a second, Yolanda. This paper's been torn, the destination is missing. We don't know where it was headed. Let's look through the rest of the folders in this box, maybe it's in there someplace."

They each grabbed a folder and thumbed through the assorted documents. Jack was working on the third folder when it caught his eye. He had just flipped over a consignment order for four hundred pounds of salt pork, when he saw a dark yellow piece of paper stuck to the reverse side of the order. He carefully peeled it off the back and held it up to the first piece. It matched.

"Holy shit, Yo, here's the destination."

"Where, Jack? Where did it go?"

Jack looked at her. "Lynchburg, Yolanda, Lynchburg," he repeated.

"Do you think that might be the gold, Jack?"

"No. Well, I don't know. Look, all we have here is a shipping manifest. For all we know it's exactly what it says it is."

"So it's worthless?"

"No, not at all. But we have to keep looking. We need to find out if there were two shipments on the 26th. That would give us a viable lead, because otherwise we don't know where this one ended up."

"But it says Lynchburg."

"Yes, but Virginia was blanketed with Union troops during the last month of the war. There were cavalry patrols covering the roads. Two heavily loaded wagons would have been difficult to hide if they were seen. They may have been forced to take numerous detours. Long story short, if they were prevented from getting to their original destination, they had to end up someplace."

"So?"

"So, grab some more folders. Here's an idea to speed things up. Let's zip through the folders and see if there are more manifests with the same color. It can't hurt," Jack added.

Yolanda was already ahead of him, a quick search of the remaining folders turned up seven more pieces of dark yellow papers, each one of them completely intact.

Jack gave a cursory glance at each one.

"Ammunition, canteens and mess kits, hardtack." Then he stopped. "Yolanda, listen, two wagons, four drivers, two crates of rifles and ammunition."

"Where to, Jack?"

Jack looked up from the paper with a puzzled expression. "Charlottesville, Yolanda."

"Where exactly is Charlottesville, Jack?"

"It's about an hour and a half west of here. Your FBI friend mentioned it yesterday. We actually drove past it on the way here, but you were taking a nap."

Yolanda took the paper from him. "February 26, 1865! Jack, it's the same date!"

"OK, let's consider this for a bit. There are two shipping orders, both originating from Richmond, each containing the same cargo, one is going to Lynchburg and the second one is going to Charlottesville."

"We already know that nothing's ever turned up in Lynchburg, Jack. What do you know about Charlottesville?"

"There's a lot I know about Charlottesville. Monticello is just south of there. It's the home of the University of Virginia, and it's horse and wine country."

"And the Civil War?"

"Open up your laptop and run a search on Charlottesville and the Civil War. I'm drawing a blank."

Yolanda went over to the other table and opened up the Google search page. Within seconds she had the information.

"Jack, look at this. It doesn't seem like much happened there. There's only one entry, it seems like General Custer attacked some artillery units around someplace called Rio Hill."

"General Custer? Really? That's it?"

"That's all that it says here," she affirmed.

Jack sat down on the table and was quiet for a minute.

"What are you thinking about, Jack? Do you have some idea about this?"

Jack hesitated a moment before answering. "OK, here's a theory. Let's say that some important figure in the Confederacy wanted to conceal a sizeable amount of gold and silver. He somehow arranges to have duplicate transportation orders written. According to the orders, each shipment contains weapons and ammo, but each of them has a different destination."

"So, one of them had gold?"

"Hold on a minute, there's something bothering me about this."

"What, Jack?"

"Just wait! I have to think this through."

Yolanda rolled her eyes, but she went back over to her laptop and began searching again.

After a few minutes, Jack stood up and started pacing.

"We have two sets of wagons," he started. "If they were really carrying munitions, or if they were supposed to be, would there really have been a point to it? The war is practically over, why would they ship stuff to Charlottesville? On the other hand, Lynchburg would make sense, there was much more action around there."

"So you think that the gold went to Charlottesville and the rifles to Lynchburg? That makes sense to me, Jack. I mean I've double-checked some other search engines and I'm not getting anything else different from what Google listed."

"Here's the thing that's nagging me. Each order specifically mentions a driver."

"Why not? Wouldn't they need people to drive the wagons?"

"Yes, but why not use military personnel? If we're on the right track, there was a lot of gold in that shipment and they were moving through territory with a lot of enemy soldiers."

"Maybe they thought it would look less conspicuous if they were civilians," Yolanda observed. "Maybe they thought it would be easier to pass through without being stopped."

"No, sorry, I don't buy that. Two wagons? They would have been stopped by any patrol that would come in contact with them and you can be sure that somebody would have been checking the contents of those crates."

"Well, Jack, what's your take then?"

Jack glanced at his watch. "Holy shit, it's after 4:30!"

As if by signal, Mary Louise popped her head in the door.

"Hey, treasure hunters!" she cried. "It's time to close up shop! I had almost forgotten you were down here, it's a good thing I remembered, because once those alarms go on, you would have been guests all night here!"

"Well, we wouldn't want that to happen," Jack laughed, "unless we had enough change for the vending machines."

"Yes," she laughed too, "but seriously, Doctor Armbruster would freak out. I'd better put a Post-it note on my computer screen to remind me from now on."

With that, she ushered them out of the room, locking it as soon as they were in the hallway.

18

MAY AULD ACQUAINTANCE...

Jack was sort of getting fond of the daily ritual. They would go back to the hotel, get a little nap in, shower, and then head down for a cocktail before dinner. His fondness died a quick death as he once again saw Yolanda deep in conversation with Agent Foster.

Shit.

"Hey, Jack!" She looked over at Galen. "You'll appreciate that I don't yell 'Hi, Jack!' in front of an FBI agent," she laughed.

Agent Foster laughed too. A bit too loudly and forced in Jack's opinion.

"So, you're here again," Jack observed.

"You can't blame someone for stopping by here when you know you can have a drink with an attractive young lady." Galen beamed at Yolanda who smiled back.

"Thanks," she said.

If Jack had been wearing a mood ring, it would have been quite dark by now.

"So, Yolanda, have you given any thought to our reunion dinner?" Galen asked.

"No, actually I haven't, but I think it would be fun. When do you have in mind?"

"How about tomorrow night? I have a light schedule on Thursday, so we can stay out as late as you want to."

Jack's mood ring would have exploded at that suggestion.

"Jack, that's OK with you, isn't it? Galen and I just want to get caught up on people and things that wouldn't interest you."

"What?" Jack replied with studied disinterest. "Oh, sure, perfectly fine with me. It will give me a chance to take care of some things."

"Great!" Galen exclaimed. "It will be fun to discuss all the things that have happened since the academy. I really want to know what you've been up to."

I bet. Jack thought.

"Oh, you'll be bored," Yolanda laughed. "Should we meet down here at when? Six?

"Sure," Galen replied, "that will give us time to get to the restaurant. I'll make reservations; I know this nice place near Short Pump. It's on the northwest side."

"I'll be looking forward to it," Yolanda said. "So, Jack, do you want to eat here or go down the street and explore for a new restaurant?"

"I don't care," Jack shrugged, "I'll leave that decision up to you."

"OK, then, let's go and see what we can find. Bye, Galen, see you tomorrow evening."

This exchange was followed by Galen once again bestowing a hug and a quick kiss on Yolanda's cheek.

Jack went through a silent litany as they left the cocktail lounge. *It's no big deal, it's no big deal, they are just friends, they are just friends. It's no big deal.*

"You're quiet, Jack, what are you thinking about?"

"Huh? Thinking? Oh, just running over some ideas about the case."

"Good, partner, I like it when you start developing ideas." Yolanda put her arm in his and leaned her head on his shoulder as they walked down the sidewalk.

It's no big deal.

They found a Greek restaurant within two blocks of the Magnolia. After ordering they sat in silence for a few minutes. Yolanda looked at Jack.

"Jack, is that thing with Galen bothering you? I just want you to know that it's just dinner between two old acquaintances. You've been awfully quiet since we left the hotel."

"No, no, it's OK. I understand. Heck, one of these days I'll stumble across someone I knew back in the day and the same thing might happen. Relax, Yolanda, I get it."

"OK, then," she smiled. "I'm sorry, Jack, I just know how you can get sometimes. I'm glad that you're OK with it."

Jack gave her what he considered to be a warm smile, but it wouldn't have passed close inspection.

"Have you given any more thought to the two sets of wagons?" she asked.

"Honestly, no, I've had some other things on my mind since we left the museum. Give me a minute." Jack toyed with the knife from his bread plate.

"Well," Yolanda said, "I think there's definitely a connection with those two manifests. I mean how common would it be to have duplicate transits on the same day with the same cargo?"

"Maybe not when the war was in full swing, but yes, you're right. Anyway, here's a thought about it." Jack paused as the waitress brought Yolanda a Greek salad and his bowl of lemon-grass chicken soup.

"What's the thought, Jack?"

"This really is a long-shot, but this couldn't have been a one-person job." Jack stopped for a moment and tasted his soup. "The thing about the civilian drivers puzzles me. What if maybe one of the pair of wagons was a set-up, sort of a decoy and the other wagons that held the gold were manned by insiders working for the man in charge. That would have gotten rid of random military personnel who might not have been cooperative."

"But the other wagons had civilians with them too."

"Yes, but what if it was a scam. What if the guy in charge sort of leaked the information that it was really gold instead of weapons? That would have kept the drivers occupied with a plan of how to get the gold in their possession."

Yolanda's fork paused in mid-air. "You think that one group was in cahoots all the way and they had the real gold. The other group suspected or were led on that they were carrying gold."

"Exactly."

"So, how would that all have turned out?" she asked.

Jack laughed. "Something happened over one hundred and fifty years ago and I'm only offering a shot-in-the-dark speculation about what went down, keep that in mind."

"Well, it sounds good, Jack."

He laughed again. "You know, almost anything could probably sound good."

"OK, tell me how you think it went down," she directed.

"As soon as I finish this soup, it's getting cold."

Within minutes the plates had been cleared. As they waited on their entrees, Jack launched into his theory.

"I'm tired of saying 'the man in charge,' I'm going to call him Mr. Big. Mr. Big is placed in charge of transporting the gold and silver. He must be a high-ranking military man or a high-ranking government official. I'm betting military. He arranges a dummy shipment filled with scrap metal, rocks, or anything that would be heavy enough to seem like gold. He puts his cronies in charge of the wagons with the gold. Mr. Big has duplicate orders cut and then he somehow makes a comment to someone, probably one of the drivers, about the nature of the cargo. Of course they most likely start scheming about how to get their hands on it."

"Do you think the gold went to Charlottesville?"

"Hold on, just wait a minute."

The waiting coincided with the arrival of the food. After the waiter made the appropriate comments and asked the standard questions, they were once again left alone.

"So, Jack, Charlottesville – gold; Lynchburg – rocks or scrap metal. What are you thinking?"

Jack put a forkful of his grilled fish into his mouth. "I like Charlottesville," he said. "Here's why. Most of the action was taking place in Georgia and along the Atlantic Coast in Virginia."

"So a shipment heading west out of Richmond wouldn't have been as likely to be spotted by the Union patrols," Yolanda tossed in. "But, Jack, here's maybe a dumb question. Why did a place in central Virginia, I mean sort of a major city, not attract any attention from the Union Army?"

"It's where it's located. Directly west of Charlottesville are the Blue Ridge Mountains. Armies don't like to traverse mountains, Yolanda. A formidable terrain feature like that would have acted as a funnel diverting troop movements away from it."

"This opens up a whole new area for us to consider, Jack. Look at it this way; if the only skirmish of note took place at this Rio Hill place, we don't really have a single clue where we should start looking."

"Yes, but three days ago we were just as lost. Now we just need to do some detective work and see if any viable leads pop up. Hey, like you've said lots of times, we're getting paid regardless. Let's go to Charlottesville tomorrow and see what we can scare up."

"Maybe the day after tomorrow? I'm meeting Galen tomorrow night," she reminded him.

"What? Oh, yeah, I forgot about that. OK, we'll stay another day."

Yolanda marked Jack's silence during the remainder of his meal to his fondness of Greek food. That wasn't it. That wasn't it by a long shot.

19

JACK GETS, WELL, TO BE HONEST, UPSET

They spent the next day looking for any supporting evidence regarding the shipments, but they didn't find anything. After saying good-bye to Mary Louise, they drove back to the hotel. Yolanda went to her room to shower. Jack tried to take a nap, but the Foster thing prevented that. He didn't bother going down for dinner. He didn't really want to eat by himself and he was in no mood to see Yolanda leave on a "dinner date" with Agent Foster. He looked over the room service menu and then decided to just have a pizza. He hadn't had a pizza in a long time, mainly because of the health food lectures Yolanda would deliver at the mere mention of a pizza.

So, he decided to indulge and order a pepperoni and green olive pizza from a place listed in the guest handbook.

Yolanda did take a short nap after her shower and then put on her black cocktail dress. She walked into the lounge right at six and found Agent Foster waiting for her at the bar. He was drinking something pink and foamy.

He held up his glass in a mock salute. "Wow, you look amazing in that dress. Would you like a drink before we go?" he asked.

"Um…, no, I don't think I need one just yet. I can wait until we get to the restaurant," Yolanda replied.

"Sure thing," Galen said. "Let's go, the valet has my car out front already." He set his glass down on the bar and walked with her through the lobby.

His car turned out to be a standard-issue government sedan, black of course.

He went to the passenger side and opened the door for Yolanda and, just like the museum staff had done, he treated himself to as much of her legs as he could discretely get away with as she sat down on the front seat.

Within moments he was navigating the downtown traffic heading for the interstate that would put them on the northwest side of Richmond. Only twenty minutes or so passed before he turned into the parking lot of the restaurant.

It was one of those brick and ivy-covered Italian places, not a chain, just a local place that had been around for years. Yolanda really liked the charm of the place.

They were seated immediately. Galen had asked for an outside table. The dining area was covered with wrought-iron fencing lush with greenery and flowers. He ordered a mai-tai and Yolanda considered her choices for a moment before requesting a sea breeze.

"A sea breeze?" Galen noted. "I don't think I've ever had one of those. What's in one?"

"Oh, rum, lime, and grapefruit juice. I don't know why it's called a sea breeze, but I really like them. This restaurant is lovely, Galen, how often have you come here?"

"Oh, a couple of times a year, it's really good; it's the kind of place that you know you're always going to revisit when you're back in a certain area. I mean there are all the standard chain places and little corner restaurants, but this one is very special to me."

"So, have you entertained several young ladies here?" Yolanda laughed.

Galen smiled, "Well, maybe yes, maybe no, but I choose not to discuss other young ladies in the presence of such a beauty." He glanced at the top of Yolanda's dress that was just cut low enough to give a hint of what might be covered up.

"Ooh, a compliment," she laughed. "Don't get any ideas, Galen, this is strictly a reunion dinner!"

Galen put up his hands in mock surrender. "The thought hadn't crossed my mind. I'm completely innocent." Actually his thought processes were in complete opposition to his words. The image of her legs as she got into the car remained topmost in his mind along with the little amount of cleavage that her cocktail dress offered.

The waiter brought their cocktails and delivered the dinner menus. They chatted as they looked at the entrees. Yolanda decided on the shrimp alfredo and Galen ordered lasagna.

"Hmm...," he commented, "our dinner choices leave us with little compromise room for wine selection. Let's just order by the glass. OK with you?"

"Sure, let me see, do they have a Riesling? I know that a pinot grigio or sauvignon blanc might be more customary, but I love German wines."

"Wow, you know about wines," Galen remarked. "Yes, here's a Riesling. I'm going to have a merlot; I love merlots with Italian food." *Maybe a little alcohol will pay dividends later.*

The rest of the cocktail time and the dinner were filled with various reports regarding former classmates, favorite instructors, disliked instructors, and ended with Yolanda telling Galen about the Greenfield case and how it landed her and Jack in Virginia.

"I read about that case," Galen said. "I'm sorry, I was wrapped up in something else at the time. I didn't pay much attention to it, but I overheard a lot of people talking about it. So that was you? That's simply amazing. You took on a twenty-year old cold case and managed to solve it."

"It wasn't just me, Galen. My partner, Jack, gets most of the credit. He was remarkable. He put so many clues together to solve that case."

Galen sort of nodded in agreement, but his body language didn't agree with Yolanda's assessment of Jack. He wasn't quite sure about her relationship with Jack. The guy was a lot older then her, but there seemed to be some kind of connection that was hard to nail down.

Yolanda turned down dessert and after Galen settled the bill, they walked back to the parking lot. Her cocktail and the two glasses of wine had made her a little careless and this time Galen's determined vigilance was rewarded with a bit more than her legs. He actually was treated to a lot of leg and even a brief glimpse of black panties as she entered the car. This led his thoughts regarding his former classmate to be more and more open for review.

The evening traffic was light as they drove back downtown to the hotel. After he turned the keys over to the valet, he escorted Yolanda into the lounge area.

"Hey, Yolanda, we might be moving out in a day or so and this might be our last chance to talk for, who knows how long? How about one more drink before we call it a night?" Galen was hoping that the "one" more drink would make it a night to remember.

Yolanda glanced at her watch. It wasn't even nine o'clock yet, and although she was tired from the archives and the dinner drinks, she decided that it would be okay.

"Fine, Galen, but just one. I'm feeling the wine from dinner," she smiled.

"Great, come on over here, there's a cocktail table open."

Galen held her elbow as she climbed up onto the high stool and managed to slide his hand down to her hip in the process.

"Thank you, sir," she said, really not noticing what Galen's hands were up to.

"Anytime," he grinned.

The waitress quickly took their drink orders, another mai-tai for Galen and this time Yolanda went for her favorite, a cosmo. *All I have to do is make it to the elevator and find the right floor,* she rationalized.

"You kind of implied that you're dating around, Galen, is that the way it really is?"

"Yeah, this job. It's kind of hard to be in a permanent relationship when you have to spend so much time on the road working cases. How about you?" He kept thinking about the black panties he had recently seen and was imagining about how nice it would be to slip them down her legs.

Yolanda paused for a moment.

"Well, you know, this might seem a little out there, but actually Jack and I are sort of…, gee I don't know how to describe it. We're just sort of together."

"Really? Jack? You mean in a relationship? Huh, who would have thought? I mean, isn't he kind of a lot older than you?"

"Yes, yes, he is. But, you know, we connect, Jack and I do. I just don't pay a whole lot of attention to the age issue."

The drinks arrived. The news about Jack had severely derailed Galen's plans for an accompanied elevator ride to Yolanda's room and what might have ensued from a serious good night's kiss. It appeared that seeing her panties was going to be the highlight of the evening.

Shit.

With the prospect of a happy ending seeming most likely remote, Galen's feigned fascination with Yolanda's Indianapolis police exploits waned quite a bit, but Yolanda failed to pick up on his drop in interest. Still Galen hadn't given up all hope. Unseen by Yolanda he signaled the bartender for two more drinks. Yolanda looked up in surprise when another cosmo was set in front of her.

"Oh, Galen, I've really had enough to drink," she objected.

"Come on, Yolanda, look, it's not even nine-thirty yet. Besides, we haven't seen each other for such a long time," he pleaded. *And liquor's quicker,* he thought.

Yolanda laughed. "OK, I guess I can drink at least some of it."

"So, tell me more about that drug thing," Galen said. "I know about the missing children, but you didn't say much about the drugs." Galen took advantage of his renewed interest to scoot his stool closer to Yolanda.

"It was crazy," she started. "And it even involved firecrackers. Oops, I'm getting a little ahead of myself," she giggled. *Whoa, girl, what's with the giggling?*

"Take your time," Galen encouraged and offered his glass in a toast, getting Yolanda to take the first sip of her new cocktail.

"OK, the Mexicans who got me in trouble…"

Galen could really care less. He was taking advantage of his new, closer position to look down the front of Yolanda's dress as she leaned forward. He had already discovered that she was wearing a black bra that matched her panties and, at times, he was getting tantalizingly close to seeing more of her breasts than Yolanda would have guessed possible.

In spite of Galen's hopes, the evening would have probably ended without incident, but, unfortunately, something occurred that would have far-reaching effects.

Jack had consumed two beers with his pizza, but he felt like one more would taste pretty good. Besides he was kind of tired of sitting in his room. He figured that he could check out the baseball scores on the bar TV. So he headed downstairs and ordered an IPA. He had just settled down on what was turning out to be his favorite end barstool, when he noticed Yolanda and Foster sitting over on the far side of the lounge.

Huh, I guess dinner included drinks afterward.

He decided to focus on the TV. He knew Yolanda too well. If she saw him at the bar she would accuse him of coming down just to spy on her. He decided to quickly finish his beer and avoid an inevitable confrontation. A recap of the Yankees/Red Sox game had just ended as he finished the last of the beer.

He had just set his empty bottle back down on the bar and pulled out his wallet to settle up. He glanced over at Yolanda's table just as Galen took advantage of a pause in Yolanda's discourse. He slipped his arm around her and suddenly leaned in and kissed her. It was not just a full on the lips kiss, he took advantage of her surprise to use his tongue. Yolanda made a surprised sound, but, as a result of the alcohol, actually put her arm around Galen's neck and returned his kiss for a moment. Galen pulled away for a moment and slid off his stool. He took Yolanda by the arm and pulled her off her stool into his arms and kissed her again, this time sliding his hand down and cupping her bottom.

Feeling his hand on her bottom brought Yolanda back to reality. "Whoa there!" she laughed, pushing him away from her. "Hold on, Galen! That's a bit too friendly!"

"Sorry," he grinned. "You're just so beautiful and all. I guess I couldn't help myself." He leaned forward to kiss her again.

"No, Galen! Stop it! Look, I'm sorry, we drank too much. It's OK, I understand." She shook her head to clear it. "Wow, I guess that's what happens after too much wine and cocktails. Seriously, Galen, I'm with Jack now, you have to understand that. I'm sorry if I led you on to think that what you did was OK. Let's just forget that it happened."

"I'm sorry, Yolanda." *Not.* "I'm really sorry, it's just that you're so beautiful and all, I couldn't help myself," he smiled sheepishly. *I would have liked to help myself to a lot more.*

"OK, I accept your apology," she laughed. "That last drink was pretty strong. We'd better call it a night and I'd better head upstairs before you get frisky again. I did have fun tonight, Galen. Maybe I'll see you tomorrow."

"Yeah, maybe, I guess I'll go over and check out some of the scores before calling it a night. It was great talking to you, Yolanda. Seriously, I'm so sorry."

"Forget it, Galen, it's OK," and she gave him a quick hug, but with no accompanying peck on the cheek before heading to the elevators.

Agent Foster walked over to the bar and sat down. There weren't any other customers at the bar, just an empty beer bottle and a ten-dollar bill.

20

IT'S A LONG, LONG WAY TO CHARLOTTESVILLE

The alarm woke Yolanda up. She sat up in bed, just a little disoriented. She was alone in her hotel room. She quickly went over the events of the previous evening. She realized that she had been a little tipsy when she came up the elevator. Then she remembered knocking on Jack's door, but there was no answer. That's why she was back in her room. Then she also remembered Galen kissing her. *What the hell was he thinking?* She also recalled kissing him back. It made her feel a little guilty. *OK, too much alcohol makes Yolanda a bit careless.*

She got up and noticed that she had gone to bed wearing only her panties. She usually wore a tank top. *I guess I really did have too much to drink.*

Still, she didn't have any glimmering of a hangover. She went into the bathroom and turned on the shower.

After getting dressed and putting her clothes into the two suitcases she had brought on the trip, she went down the hallway and knocked on Jack's door. Still no answer. *Maybe he's in the bathroom, he gets so mad when I tease him about being in the bathroom so long.*

She listened carefully at the door, but didn't hear anything, so she decided to go on down to the dining room. When she walked in the door, she was surprised to see Jack sitting at a table. A near empty plate had been pushed to one side and he was drinking a cup of coffee.

"Jack?"

He looked up at her.

"How come you didn't wait for me, Jack? I thought we would have breakfast together."

"I got up early and figured that you might still be asleep. After all you were out late last night carousing."

"Carousing?" She laughed. "I would hardly call it carousing, Jack. We went out and had dinner. It was fun, there were so many things that we talked about. There were people and stuff that I hadn't thought about for years."

"Glad you had a good time," Jack said.

There was something in Jack's tone that made Yolanda a little suspicious, but she couldn't quite put her finger on it.

"Let me go get some fruit. Do you want a refill on that coffee?" she asked.

"No, thanks." Jack stood up.

"What? Jack? Aren't you going to keep me company?"

"No, I have to get my stuff packed up before check-out time. We want to get out of here as soon as possible. It will give us some extra time in Charlottesville to get a feeling for the place."

"Oh," she said, a little disappointed. "OK, I guess either you come to my room or I'll stop by your room, whoever's ready first."

"Sounds good. Enjoy your fruit."

Yolanda didn't exactly enjoy her fruit, because she felt there was something going on with Jack. She still didn't have the slightest idea what might be wrong other than the dinner date with Galen. That had to be it. *Oh, Jack, you just have to roll with it sometimes.*

She finished her fruit and even treated herself to a peach yogurt. She liked peaches. Since she had packed before breakfast, it didn't take her long to brush her teeth and put her travel cosmetics bag next to her suitcases. Then, taking one last look around to check for stray items, she pushed her bags out into the hallway and took a second trip down to Jack's door. Once again, there was no answer. *What the hell?*

She pulled her luggage onto the elevator and impatiently tapped her foot as the numbers went by. The doors opened onto the lobby, but there was no Jack in sight. She went over to the front desk and saw that Grace was looking through a couple of blue file folders.

"Good morning, Grace!" she said brightly.

"Oh, Yolanda! It's so nice to see you. I'm glad I could catch you before you left."

"How did you know I was leaving?"

Grace gave what could be considered a cold shudder. "Your…uh, partner already cleared your account. He said that you were going to Charlottesville for a bit." Grace leaned closer and said in a soft voice, "Dearie, I just don't know about that man. Don't you think you could find a better partner who is at least a little polite?"

Yolanda patted Grace's arm. "Jack is a little rough around the edges, Grace, but you just have to get to know him. He's really quite nice."

"Humph" was Grace's take on that idea. Then Yolanda spied Jack standing out in front of the hotel talking to the parking valet. The white museum van was already there and a bell hop was putting Jack's luggage in the back.

"Bye, Grace, I'm sure that we'll be back in a few days. I'll look forward to talking to you soon."

"Bye, Sweetie. Be sure and visit Monticello if you get a chance." And once again Grace leaned forward. "And don't you believe all that nonsense about Thomas Jefferson and that Sally Hemings hussy. I know that a noble Virginian like Mr. Jefferson would not have done the things some folks claim that he did."

"Uh, I'm sure you're right, Grace. I have to run. Mr. Clayton is already outside."

With a quick wave, Yolanda headed out the automatic doors and turned left towards the van. The same bellhop took her bags and loaded them. Jack was already in the driver's seat when she hopped in next to him.

"Hey, Yolanda," Jack said.

"Jack, what is going on with you?"

"Huh? What do you mean 'going on?' There's nothing going on."

"Well, here's what's going on. You ditched me for breakfast, then you were supposed to come to my room to get me and instead you come down here by yourself."

"Well, I figured it would take some time for the valet to get the van, so I thought I wouldn't have to make you stand around and wait for it too. Besides, I know women sometimes need some extra time in the mornings to get ready. It's not always men who need more time in the bathroom," he stated.

OK, that did sort of sound logical to Yolanda, but she could read Jack pretty well. She also knew that if there really was something going on, he wouldn't be able to keep it to himself very long. He was just not built that way.

The drive to the bypass and to I-64 West was made in silence. Jack appeared to be seriously studying the traffic and Yolanda contented herself with listening to her iPod.

After about 20 minutes into the drive, she popped her ear buds out and tried to start a conversation.

"Looks like what, another hour or so, Jack?"

He grunted something that sounded like an assent.

"What, Jack? I didn't quite catch that."

"Yeah, something like an hour, I guess."

"Grace said something to me before I left the hotel," Yolanda started, "something about Thomas Jefferson and a Sally something, Cummings, maybe?"

"Hemings," Jack answered, "Sally Hemings. I guess life at Monticello was lonely and it seems that Tom had a fling with one of his slaves."

"Seriously? Wow, I didn't think our Founding Fathers would have been up to something like that."

"It seems that lots of people who aren't supposed to be up to something do it anyway," Jack commented.

Yolanda didn't quite understand the meaning to that remark.

"Jack, I hate to ask this question, but is there something wrong? There just seems to be, I don't know, something a little out of whack."

"Out of whack? That's kind of a funny saying isn't it? Out of whack."

"Yes, Jack, it's quite amusing, but you didn't answer my question."

"No, there's nothing wrong, Yolanda, don't worry about it."

A few more minutes passed in silence.

"Uh, so, why don't you tell me how your dinner date went?"

"It was dinner, Jack, not a date. You know that."

"OK, sure, so how did the dinner go?"

"It was a lot of fun. Like I told you this morning, that chapter in my life seems so long ago. I really thought that was going to be who I was, you know, an FBI field agent. Talking with Galen brought back a lot of memories. But I'm so happy with what we're doing now, you and me, Partner," she smiled warmly at Jack.

"And were you happy with what you and Foster were doing last night?" Jack stared straight ahead at the road.

"I just said that it was a lot of fun, what's the matter, Jack? Something is bothering you."

Jack gripped the steering wheel tightly before answering. "I saw you, Yolanda. I saw you in the lounge. He had his tongue down your throat and his hand on your ass and you were kissing him back. You were fucking kissing him back!" Jack punctuated that with six hard slaps on the steering wheel to match each of the last six syllables. He still didn't trust himself to look at her.

Oh, holy shit, she thought, *oh, holy fucking shit. Where do I start?*

"Jack, I'm so sorry you saw that, I had no idea you were there."

"You're sorry I saw it? That's it? You're fucking sorry I saw it?"

"No, I mean yes. Stop, Jack just listen to me!"

"When you said it was fun, I had no idea how much fucking fun you meant."

"Jack, please, let me talk," she pleaded. "Look at me."

"I'm fucking driving, I can't look at you," he snapped.

Yolanda began to cry. "I didn't know he was going to do that, Jack. I had too much to drink and then he just lunged in on me. I didn't mean to have that happen."

"You can knock off the crying, Yolanda. So you go out on a harmless dinner date and end up getting felt up in a cocktail lounge and I wasn't ever supposed to know. Was that all or was there a Chapter Two?"

"No, Jack, damn it," she started crying again. "Would you just listen? I was sitting there and he just leaned over and kissed me. He took me by surprise and then he pulled me off the bar stool. I wasn't even aware he was touching me, Jack, honest."

"Well, he did touch you. During the second, that's right, the second tongue thrust, he put his hand right on your ass."

"Jack, he tried to kiss me again, but I pushed him away. I told him to stop, didn't you see that?"

"No, no I didn't." This time Jack glanced over at her. "After I had heard nothing from you but stories about how it wasn't a date, it was just an innocent reunion, a reunion that ended with him feeling you up, I threw some money on the bar and left. I didn't want to see what was going to happen next."

"Jack," she sobbed, "nothing happened next. Honest. I told him that he had gone too far and that I was with you."

Jack just stared ahead and didn't say anything.

"Jack, say something, please. I'm so sorry, I wouldn't hurt you for the world, you know that."

"Do I know that? That's funny. You stick your tongue down some guy's throat, let him grab your ass, all because you wouldn't hurt me for the world. That's so fucking comforting."

Yolanda just sobbed.

Eventually she stopped and just stared out the side window. The rest of the drive to Charlottesville was spent in silence.

21

THE HOME OF JEFFERSON

The trip took longer than planned, since a minor accident had closed one lane of the highway. They didn't arrive in Charlottesville until after twelve o'clock. Once they exited I-64, Yolanda sat up straight and decided to break the silence and deal with the elephant.

"Do you have a place to stay in mind, Jack, or are we just going to find someplace."

Jack shrugged. "I'm not sure. I looked at some motels, but the ones in town are off of Route 29 and that road is a mess."

"Jack?"

"What?"

"About Galen. Are we going to be OK? I honestly didn't mean to have that happen."

"Just leave it for now, Yolanda. I don't want to talk about it."

"But, Jack, we need …"

"Drop it," Jack insisted. "I don't feel like talking about it right now. I'm too angry and I don't want to get into a pointless argument about what you did or didn't intend to have happen. You said that nothing else happened, OK, I'll accept that. So that's it, but the next time you want to go out on 'just a dinner date,' remember this, guys just want to get in your pants, that's what he had planned all along. I knew it and you kept reassuring me that it wouldn't happen. Well, it did happen. I saw it. We can drop it now, I believe you, it caught you by surprise, but just remember what happened and don't be so quick to blow me off."

Yolanda sniffled, reached for a tissue and blew her nose. "I won't, Jack. I'll be more careful. I promise that something like that won't happen again." She blew her nose again.

"Listen, Yolanda, it's behind me. Let's get back to what we're supposed to do here. I'm seriously clueless about where to start. Northside? Southside? At the university? Monticello?"

"OK, we'll leave it for now, but I mean everything I said, Jack. I'm so sorry. You know that I love you."

"Sure, I mean it too, but I don't want to talk about it anymore. Understand?"

"Yes, I get it," she sighed. "OK, let's change the subject. Let's go up and find the Custer skirmish thing. Might as well take a look at it. It's up on the north side near a Kroger," Yolanda offered.

"I guess it's a start."

Jack turned off the 250 bypass and landed smack in the middle of bumper-to-bumper traffic on Route 29.

"See what I mean about this highway," he said.

"Didn't doubt you for a minute, Partner. Jack?" she asked encouragingly.

"What?"

"Since we're sort of on our own, we don't have to get two rooms," she smiled. "I bet you'd like that."

"Yeah, we'll see. The museum might notice if we only have one room and, like you pointed out, we're supposed to be professionals. Besides, maybe I need some time to myself."

"Yeah, you're probably right." *You're still mad. Damn it, why did you have to be in the bar. How am I going to fix this?*

After navigating several more traffic lights and unanticipated lane changes by various local motorists, Jack spied the Kroger store on the left hand side of the road. After making the turn, they drove around the parking lot.

"I don't see a marker or anything, Jack. Should we just get out and take a look?"

"I suppose so. I wasn't expecting Gettysburg, but I don't see anything either."

They got out of the car and spent a few minutes wandering around. The Kroger store was in a small strip mall with a few restaurants and assorted shops. Yolanda reached down for Jack's hand and was relieved that he at least seemed agreeable to hold hers. Jack eventually stopped a passerby and asked about the monument. He and Yolanda were directed down a sidewalk past the front entrance of the grocery store. There, emblazoned on a wall, was the story of Custer and the skirmish at Rio Hill.

"This is it?" Jack commented.

Yolanda laughed. "Well, a minor skirmish deserves a minor monument. I was expecting more than a sign on a supermarket wall though."

"OK, this is not an 'aha' moment."

"Do you want to get some lunch. Look, there's a restaurant over there, we can get something," Yolanda said.

"You mean that Thai place?"

"God no, Jack, you know I hate Asian food. No, the other place two doors down. We can talk about our next step."

It was an American cuisine restaurant. They ate a hurried lunch, and then started discussing what to do next and where to go next.

"So, as far as we know, wagons were dispatched from Richmond to here on the same day that an identical shipment was sent to Lynchburg," Yolanda started.

"And somehow we need to pick up a trail that's about one hundred and fifty years old," Jack sort of complained.

"Yes, Jack, that's been a part of your song and dance number since we started this. Look what we've accomplished so far. You can't deny that we've found some solid clues."

"Solid? Only if you put the best possible spin on those shipping manifests. For all we know there were two legitimate shipments of weapons. We have no idea if there was gold on this one or not."

"Granted," Yolanda conceded, "But still, we're treasure hunters, Jack. This is going to be fun."

"OK, OK, fun it is," Jack replied. "Here's what I think we should do next. Let's go to a library or the local newspaper and take a look at what was going on in town immediately following the war. That might give us a clue. If somebody was sitting on a pile of money, it might have started being spent."

"Right," Yolanda agreed, "because those Confederate dollars were worthless and the Southern economy was in shambles."

"Yes, sounds like you've been doing some research."

Yolanda beamed.

Following lunch, Jack's mood seemed to be better. That renewed Yolanda's hope that maybe he'd be able to get over the Galen fiasco.

They decided to visit the local newspaper, the Daily Progress. Much to Jack's surprise and a little relief, Yolanda failed to bond with the rather disinterested receptionist who kept texting someone during their inquiry. At the appropriate time, she sighed heavily and, after reluctantly laying her smart phone on the counter, directed them to a bank of computers in a neighboring room. They provided a searchable archive of local newspapers predating the Civil War.

Before they left the counter, Yolanda did come up with a question. "Excuse me, but this paper. Was it in publication during the Civil War?"

"Good question, Yo," Jack stated, much to her happiness.

"No, the Progress dates back to the 1890's. There were two papers during the War Between the States published here, the Daily Chronicle and the Jeffersonian Republican. Our archives actually include them also," droned the clerk glancing wistfully at the phone. It was buzzing.

"Thanks," Jack said, "we'll let you get back to more pressing matters." As soon as they turned, the phone was snatched up like a lollipop in a kindergarten class.

There were six computer terminals and a painfully thin Asian gentleman was sitting at the far end, selectively typing in search words using his index fingers. Jack smugly observed this technique, since he felt he was a bit gifted in keyboarding, although Yolanda knew that he had learned it on manual typewriters in the olden days.

They sat down at the two computers on the far left and began discussing their plan.

"Let's do this a little like we did the archives in Richmond. I'll search from, let's say February to April and you take the months right after the war ended, May to, I don't know, July maybe?" Jack offered.

"Sure," Yolanda replied. "So I should look for maybe business start-ups?"

"Yes, and check land acquisitions. Real estate would have been in turmoil following the war, so lots of property might have been up for sale."

If they had thought leafing through musty documents had been tedious, it seemed nothing compared to trying to read scanned copies of yellowed newsprint. Jack actually had it somewhat easier, since news of the war was front page material, while Yolanda had to search more carefully. Before they knew it, it was already four o'clock and nothing had come up.

"Jack, we still haven't found a place to stay. Let's call it a day and pick it up tomorrow."

Jack leaned back in his chair and rubbed his eyes, "Yeah, you're right. You know, there was a lot of propaganda cranked out at the end. These reporters were taking any minor success and building it up as a major victory. It was sort of the same in Germany and Japan at the end of World War II."

"So, nothing yet, huh?"

"Nope, I didn't hear any 'aha' from you, so I'm assuming you had similar results."

"Yeah, this was pretty dry reading. You were right, things were a mess. I mean I did read about carpetbaggers and stuff in high school history class and it turns out that Mr. Harris was pretty accurate, but I just didn't care that much about it back then," she laughed.

"See. Now you're smack in the middle of American history. Just goes to show."

"I know, life's lessons and all that. Let's go. I'm tired."

"Right with you," he answered.

They left the office and drove north on 29. Jack had seen that there was a Doubletree Suites on the north side of town. He wanted to avoid the congested area closer to the university.

When they checked in, he did ask for two rooms. While the clerk was punching in the required information on the computer, Yolanda turned to face him.

"Jack, are you serious? You don't have to do this."

"No, you gave me a talk in Richmond about this – our professional relationship. Besides, maybe I need to have some quiet time to think about you and Foster. I do believe you, Yolanda, just give me some time. Besides, I can focus on that gold shipment. You never know, I might get a sudden burst of insight. It's happened before."

"I'm sorry you feel this way, Jack, and I'm so sorry about what happened. But, OK, if that's what you want to do, I understand," she sadly stated.

"The clerk said that there are lots of places to eat downtown and there's a shopping complex just north of here with a supermarket, a Target store and some Italian and sandwich restaurants. What do you say we meet down here at six and head up that way? Six o'clock downtown is not the place to try and be," Jack said.

They reached the bank of elevators. After the doors opened, Jack pushed the three button and then he turned to her. "I knew about the kissing, Yolanda, and all the time you were pretending that nothing happened between you two. That's what upset me. You can't blame me for that."

"I know. I know," she answered. "I promise I'll make it up to you and I want you to forgive me. What I told you is the absolute truth, Jack. I didn't tell you about what he did, because I knew it would make you angry. Maybe I should have, I would have told you right away that it was his doing and not mine. I didn't have any idea you saw it, that's why I kept it to myself."

Jack just nodded.

Their rooms were on the third floor and the rest of the ride in the elevator was accomplished in complete silence.

22

JACK FINDS A CLUE

Dinner the previous evening had been a bit awkward. Jack found a little Italian place and then discovered a liquor store a few doors down. He went in and Yolanda tagged along behind him.

"Laying in some booze, Jack?"

"I don't know, I guess I don't like hanging around in hotel bars as much. I thought I would maybe buy some scotch or something."

"I really don't know how you can drink that disgusting stuff. It smells so bad, like dirt."

"Ah, you see, to the discerning taste, that's the peatiness you're noticing."

"Well, whatever it is, it's god awful."

"I happen to like it. Unlike some people, I don't have to festoon my cocktails with fruit and umbrellas."

"Festoon? What the heck does that mean? Oh, I get it. It's about Galen, isn't it? Jack, please, let it go, damn it."

"Why do you think I mean him?" he answered innocently. "And are you defending him? Why would that be, as if I didn't know."

"Damn it, Jack! I've confessed that it happened. I know you saw it! You need to forgive me and move on. I said I was sorry. You know I'm not defending him."

By this time the clerk at the liquor store had taken a vested interest in the exchange in Aisle 3.

"Look, I just never dreamed that I would witness that. It was like a kick in my groin, you know that?" Jack lowered his voice during his last exchange since he did notice the clerk hanging over the counter listening.

"All right, Jack, now I'm getting angry. I had too much to drink and a guy took advantage of that. He kissed me, Jack, then he grabbed me. I told him he was way out of line and that was that. I had no idea you were there and I wanted to sweep it under the rug. Now you can either get over it or believe me or you're going to piss me off big time. I can only say I'm sorry so many times."

Jack didn't reply. He walked up to the counter and set the bottle down a bit too firmly.

"Little trouble with the lady?" the clerk asked.

Jack just glared at him and asked, "How much?"

The clerk shrugged and pointed at the register display. Jack counted out the amount, grabbed the bottle and headed for the door.

"Hey," the clerk shouted, "what about the receipt and your change?"

"Keep it, you nosey bastard. Just keep it." Yolanda had to hurry to catch up with him.

Needless to say, that was why the dinner had been pretty much eaten in silence.

After getting dressed the next morning, Yolanda promised to be positive and happy. She was not going to keep the grudge or snit, or whatever else he might call it, going with Jack.

The thing with Jack was this. He really wanted to yell at Yolanda, but he was afraid to. She had a way with twisting things around. He had played it over and over in his head and he knew that it was going to come down to the fact that he had supposedly been spying on her, then she would be self-righteously angry. She always tossed the original bone of contention out the window and managed to fabricate something that landed right on top of him. The kiss would be forgotten and lost in the verbal shuffle. She was damn good at it and he hadn't figured out how to beat her at that game just yet. She was one of the most stubborn people he had ever known.

So, Jack decided to let it go. Maybe he had read more into that kiss than was actually there. She sure looked like she enjoyed it though. Then he remembered the hand on the ass. It took him a minute to process that thought. *The guy probably was just on the make. She keeps saying it was just dinner. Hell, I don't know, just forget it.* He congratulated himself on his new level of maturity regarding Yolanda and that incident.

They met downstairs. As much as Jack liked eating breakfast out, it was really getting kind of tiring. Most of the hotel food was the same. Sure, eggs are eggs, but it was losing its charm. The one thing that amused Yolanda was the fact that he always ordered V-8 or tomato juice. He never drank it at home, only when he was at a restaurant. She had asked him about it once, but he really didn't know why he did. It was a mystery to him too.

The first few minutes of breakfast featured über-cordial sparring. The level of politeness harked back to their first few days after that morning when they finally buried the hatchet in Jack's living room. Still, all in all, neither of them noticed what the other one was up to, so they each took credit for the sterling display of friendship and trust.

After a short trip upstairs for tooth brushing and Jack's required solo flight in the bathroom, they headed back to the newspaper office.

They had been there for a little over two hours when Jack suddenly sat up straight in his chair, then leaned forward to more closely read the article on the screen.

"Yolanda! Slide over here and take a look!"

Yolanda pushed her chair over to Jack's computer.

"Where, Jack?"

"This article here. It says that Union forces were moving toward Charlottesville in March of 1865. It was Custer again and some of Sheridan's cavalry. Hold on a second; let me check on the Internet. Jack ran another search and found another incident besides the Rio Hill skirmish.

"Here's something," he said excitedly. Yolanda pushed closer to see. It says that there was some big attack planned for Richmond and Custer was assigned to head toward Charlottesville as a diversionary force. It was supposed to draw Confederate troops away from Richmond."

"Does it give a date, Jack?"

"Let's see. Uh, yeah, look! It was March the third."

"Jack, that's just a week from the date those wagons left Richmond."

"I know. OK, that had to be a surprise to whoever was in charge of those wagons. If we are right in assuming they picked Charlottesville because it would be out of the action, it would have been a shock to run into, let me see…the Union 3rd Cavalry Division."

"Does it say what they did?"

"Just a minute. OK, besides the military hospital there was a factory that produced uniforms and shoes for the Confederates. It says here that they burned a bridge over the James River and then they burned down the factory. Some local big shot talked to Custer and convinced him to leave the university alone. I guess he dropped the Jefferson name and Custer bought into it. That was the only damage done to the city."

"So what does that mean, Jack, do you have any ideas?"

"Well, other than some country roads, there were only two main roads, actually pretty much like today, one running from Richmond over the mountains to Staunton and north/south to Culpeper and Lynchburg."

"So we think that they would have used the Richmond highway?"

"Yes, and side roads when necessary. But the first thing that Custer would have done was post sentries on every road in and out of the city. If the wagons didn't make it before the 3rd, there's no way they could have entered the city undetected."

"Jack, something that might help would be if we knew what day of the week the 26th and the 3rd were on."

"You're right, that might put this in context."

"Just type in the February date and see what comes up, then we can check the 3rd."

In a moment several options were listed, one of them actually said Sunday, February 2, 1865. He had to open another site and found that the 3rd of March was a Friday.

"Couldn't you have just figured that out, Jack?"

"I just wanted to be sure, Ms. Math Teacher."

"OK, sorry. Jack, that means that those wagons had four days to get here."

"Well, five days if they left first thing Sunday morning."

"I don't know. Is that about the right time for traveling from Richmond to here?"

Jack thought for a moment. "I'm guessing that they might have had to hide from Union patrols. There were Northern soldiers all over Virginia around that time. It's possible that they even traveled by night. Their progress might have been agonizingly slow."

"So this unexpected move by the Union Army may have derailed the plans for Charlottesville," Yolanda remarked.

"They had to be careful; they probably had a couple of people in civilian clothes riding as scouts."

"How would that have worked, Jack?" she asked.

"They would have two outriders. The second one would ride behind the first one, but still remain in sight of the wagons. That way if the first rider was stopped, the second one could signal the wagons to stop also."

"So if the first guy was stopped by a sentry, they would change their route somehow?"

"Yes, to avoid that particular place and try and find another way around it."

"You know a lot about this kind of stuff, don't you, Jack?"

Jack laughed. "No, you have to remember that I'm making most of this stuff up as we go. One hundred and fifty years have passed since what we think went down. This could all be a pipe dream. All I know is what I might do in a similar situation. Whether or not it actually took place is anyone's guess."

"So now we don't know if the shipment made it here or not. What's next?"

"Now we have two things to look at. Either the wagons got here on the Thursday or the Union troops had occupied the city before they arrived."

"Other than that factory, was there anything else the cavalry would have been looking for?" she asked.

"There was a military hospital; it was located somewhere near the university. I guess there's a cemetery there where they buried the casualties. I don't think it was a major concern. Even though there was a lot of hatred, it didn't really extend to the abuse of wounded men, regardless of whether they wore gray or blue. Besides, with the war winding down, I don't know if retribution was much of a factor. It probably would have been different if it was Sherman, he would have burned down everything."

"So what now?"

Jack sighed. "We keep looking."

23

NO LIGHT AT THE END OF THE TUNNEL

They spend the rest of that afternoon and most of the next day looking at the newspapers. Yolanda even went past their initial dates into the next two months and wasn't able to come up with anything. It was just after three o'clock when Jack decided that he had read enough.

"Come on, Yolanda, let's get out of here."

"Where are we going, Jack? Did you find something?"

"No, but I get the feeling that there's nothing here. I've read countless articles and I haven't picked up anything helpful and you haven't either."

"So what are we going to do?"

"Let's go get a drink," Jack offered.

Yolanda looked at her watch. "It's not even four o'clock."

"I don't care. Besides, we deserve a break and maybe something will come to us if we just back away from it for a while."

"That's fine with me. I think I know way too much about Charlottesville in 1865 than most people," she laughed.

They drove back to the Target store area and found a restaurant that had outdoor seating. Jack ordered his traditional Johnny Walker Black on the rocks and Yolanda decided on a gin and tonic. She remembered what happened after a couple of cocktails with Galen and decided to stay away from cosmos for a bit.

After they got their drinks, they sat in silence for a few minutes. Then Jack looked at her with a thoughtful expression.

"Jack, are you thinking about the case or about me?" she teased.

"Well, I spend a lot of time thinking about you, but this time it's the case. Maybe we need to rethink something."

"Like what?"

"Let's get back to that Lynchburg thing. We think those wagons were a decoy and the real shipment, the gold, was supposed to come here."

"It's what you said earlier, Jack, and I agree. We're creating a story about something that happened a long time ago and we don't have any real evidence to back up what we think took place."

"I know, it's silly, isn't it?" he laughed. "I mean I come up with all these theories and I can actually see what I think went on, at that point I stop and realize that it's all just conjecture."

"Yes," Yolanda agreed, "but even though we can't prove anything yet, we have developed something plausible. That's a lot more than anyone else has ever done."

"True," Jack laughed again. "I guess even a half-assed guess and theory are better than none."

"Jack, you said we need to look at Lynchburg again. I was thinking, even if that was a decoy, we decided that somebody in charge of that shipment knew it was a fake."

"Yeah, that was what we thought."

"Well, we talked about a pirate captain killing people so they wouldn't know where the treasure was and you pointed out that he wouldn't have had to do that, since it wasn't a real treasure."

"Yes, you remember well, so what's your point?" Jack asked, taking another big sip of scotch.

"That guy would have either taken some of his pirates into his confidence or maybe he didn't tell anyone. So after they unloaded the crates and hid them, he knew where the real treasure was headed and he would have made a beeline for Charlottesville," Yolanda offered.

"We don't know what day they may have arrived at Lynchburg, it's closer than Charlottesville." Jack made a defeated gesture with his hands. "Yo, this is so…, so…, intangible. Each time we get an idea, I realize how impossible this whole thing probably is."

"Yes, Jack, I agree, but we've been over this. In the long run it's not going to make any difference, we've got six months. You have to get past the long-shot notion. Now I have another idea."

"What?"

"I think we need to look at a list of Southern generals. We know someone pretty high up had to be in charge of all that money and most likely it was a military man. Let's find out who was around in late 1865 and maybe what they did after the war. That might give us a place and time to backtrack."

Jack took another drink of scotch and studied the remaining amount in his glass. He signaled the bartender for a refill before answering.

"You know why I love you, Yo?"

Yo! "Probably, but I'd like to hear it."

"You have such good ideas," Jack smiled.

"Huh, I thought you were going to go for body parts," she laughed.

"Well, now that you mention it."

"No, stop it; I want to know what you think of that idea before you get in one of your moods," she ordered.

"OK, OK, you win." Jack put up his hands in surrender. "I think that the general thing is a great idea. Tell you what, let's go ahead and order dinner here, then we'll go back to the hotel and go to bed early. We can kick off that search tomorrow at the library."

"Yay! You liked my idea!" she exclaimed. *And you called me Yo!*

24

WHO'S WHO IN THE CSA

There was no one using the computer terminals at the library the next morning. It was relatively easy to find Confederate generals - lists abounded on the Internet. Jack and Yolanda divided one such list and each ended up with about eight possibilities to research.

"Jack, it's possible that we need two people, right? Maybe both generals?" she asked.

"Well, that's just another assumption we're making, that it could involve a general. It could also be a high-ranking government official, but I'm going to lean in the direction of the military. Especially for the actual gold shipment, that would be more important to whoever was running this scheme," Jack explained.

"OK, well, here we go," Yolanda laughed.

It took less than a half hour for them to eliminate the generals who were casualties before March of 1865. The next step was dropping the ones from the Western theater from the list. This left them with a few that needed a little more research: James Longstreet, George Pickett, Braxton Bragg, and A.P. Hill.

Jack took Longstreet and Pickett. Yolanda got Bragg and Hill.

"Look and see what they were doing at the end of the war," Jack said. "One or more of these guys might be plausibly linked to what we think was going down."

"Gotcha," Yolanda agreed.

This search took a little longer, since they cross-referenced sources to see if they could uncover some connection to either the Lynchburg or the Charlottesville shipment. After an hour had passed, Jack stood up and stretched.

"Hey, Yolanda, I printed some stuff off. Grab anything you have and let's go take a coffee break and compare notes."

"Sure thing, Jack. You know, I think I might have found something we need to take a closer look at," she told him.

"Really? That's great, because I didn't come up with anything."

They left the library and found a small coffee house down the street. They ordered and then went outside to sit.

Jack started first. "Since you might have found something, let me tell you right off the bat that Longstreet and Pickett don't seem to be viable candidates. Longstreet was wounded in late spring of 1864 and had a long period of recuperation. He did end up being in charge of the defenses around Richmond, but I couldn't find anything about Lynchburg or how he could have been involved."

"And Pickett? Was he the one at Gettysburg?" Yolanda asked.

"Following Gettysburg, it seems he was pretty much a screw-up. Same deal as with Longstreet, but what did you come up with?"

"Do you remember that we said it might not be two generals? Look, I think I found something suspicious and I also found a reference to a general that we didn't consider."

"Go on," Jack urged, "what's the suspicious thing?"

"OK, just like most of the fighting at the end, this A.P. Hill guy was around Richmond, but it turns out that he gets really sick in March. March, Jack."

"So?"

"So, he's not fighting anymore and he's in Richmond to recuperate."

"And that's suspicious?" Jack asked.

"Just wait. Jack, A.P. Hill doesn't survive the end of the war. He was shot and killed near Petersburg on April 2, that's a week before Lee surrenders."

"I still don't see anything suspicious, Yolanda."

"Here's the thing, Jack. He was a general and when he was killed, he was with one staff officer. One staff officer, Jack. You know how generals are, they like underlings hanging around."

"All right, I agree, that's a little out of the ordinary. What else did you find?"

"I think we can cross Braxton Bragg off the list. He was having trouble like Pickett, it seems. Besides, he was basically operating in the Carolinas at the end, so he wouldn't have been around Richmond."

"Go ahead, what was the connection? You're killing me here."

"OK, get this, Jack. One of Bragg's assignments was to improve the army's supply system. It turns out that he had conflicts with so many people, especially a man named John C. Breckinridge. Breckinridge was a major general, but in February of 1865, he gets named Secretary of War. He ended up being in charge of all the military and government records of the Confederacy."

Jack whistled. "Way to go, Yolanda!"

"Jack, what if Breckinridge masterminded this? He would have definitely known that the Confederacy was doomed."

"Go on and build a theory, I'm listening," Jack said.

"So he's the Secretary of War. He's in charge. He creates a dual transport manifest and sends A.P. Hill with the contingent to Charlottesville in late February, right before Hill is incapacitated. In the meantime, let's say that he takes the responsibility for the decoy shipment to Lynchburg."

"OK, for complete conjecture, I like the way you're piecing it together. Can I toss something in here?"

"Sure, Jack, that's about all I have right now. What do you think?"

"That Sheridan thing keeps coming to mind. OK, let's accept your theory as reality. Breckinridge guides the dummy shipment to Lynchburg. He has the crates unloaded and maybe hidden. Then he leaves and heads for Charlottesville. If I were him, I wouldn't have anyone in that group knowing it was a fake. After he left, he wouldn't have cared what happened to the crates, he wouldn't have worried about them. It only makes sense that whoever helped unload them would most likely double back and try to see what was in them. It would have been a big surprise to find scrap metal or something instead of gold."

"What do you mean about the Sheridan thing? You kind of lost me there, Jack."

"Huh? Oh, sorry, I rambled off track. OK, here's what I mean. If A.P. Hill was heading to Charlottesville, he wasn't expecting to find it occupied by Federal troops, especially Sheridan's cavalry. Like I said earlier, Custer would have sealed off every route into and out of the city. I don't have a clue what the final destination of that shipment was, but there was no way it was going to make it past the checkpoints. He would have had to go someplace else."

"And in a hurry," Yolanda added, "because there were more and more Union troops showing up every day. It would have been hard to escape being spotted by random cavalry patrols."

"OK, I tell you what. Let's drop this for now. Tomorrow let's look around and see what other possibilities might have been there for Hill to move the wagons."

"All right. You know, Jack, I think we might be onto the right track with this. I really do."

Jack just smiled as he finished his cup of coffee.

25

CAN I PHONE A FRIEND?

Jack surprised Yolanda the next morning. Instead of his usual massive breakfast, he sat down with a plate piled with pineapple, peaches, and a banana perched on one side.

"Jack, the fruit? What gives?"

"Well, we've been doing a lot of sitting lately and this morning I sort of noticed that my pants were a little, uh, snug, so I figured I should cut down a little on the calories. Don't make a big deal out of it."

"No, I won't, you're right. I've missed working out, but we really haven't had any time. Speaking of that, what are we doing today? I don't know what else to do or where else to look for clues, do you?"

Jack sighed. "Well, I'm not going to like doing this, but to save time, I'm going to call the museum and get in touch with either Sedgewick or Armbruster."

"Do you think they might know something about Breckinridge and Hill?" Yolanda asked.

"I don't know, but I want to keep them as much in the dark as we can. I bet they know all the Civil War buffs in the area. We just need the names of a couple so we can interview them. We don't want to waste our time doing aimless research when we should be able to get the information we need from them."

"Oh, that's a great idea, Jack. You are such a genius."

"Really? That's kind of high praise coming from you."

"No, I mean it. I was dreading spending another day either looking at a computer screen or sifting through musty documents."

"OK, I'll take it then," he laughed. "By the way, do you really like oatmeal or do you just eat it because it's healthy?"

"My Mom always made me oatmeal before school when I was growing up. I guess when I see it all prepared and everything, I just like to have it."

"I tried it for a long time. The doctor said it would help my cholesterol, but I kind of overdosed on it. It wasn't a happy mealtime for me."

"I've noticed that you've strayed a bit from the healthier aspect of breakfast, Jack."

"And yet you don't nag me as much as you used to."

Yolanda smiled. "Yes, because I've noticed you do a lot better with your other meals. Maybe I'm having more of a positive impact on your life than you thought."

"I just like to think I am making more mature choices. All on my own, I might add."

"Sure, Jack, you just keep thinking like that. So, when are you going to call?"

Jack looked at his watch. "It's 8:15. The museum opens at nine, so after breakfast I'll take a cup of coffee upstairs, watch some ESPN, and call then."

"Maybe I'll take some time and go to the fitness room. Your comments about nutrition kind of got me thinking especially now with your bulging waistline and all."

"I didn't say bulging!" Jack raised his voice a little, attracting some attention from fellow diners.

"Calm down, Jack, I was just messing with you. I haven't had time to practice my annoyance skills lately," she laughed.

That reminded Jack that he was supposed to be angry with her about the kissing thing. Then he also remembered that he was taking the high road on that issue, but the delay in responding was noticed by Yolanda.

"Jack, are you OK? You had a weird look on your face. Isn't the pineapple any good?"

"No, it was nothing. I guess I was dreading talking to either of those Bozos at the museum." *Nice recovery,* he congratulated himself.

"I see your point. OK, I'm going to go change. After I finish working out and shower, you can tell me what they said. Hey, why don't you call from my room? That way you can fill me in when I'm done. I won't work out too long."

Yolanda stood up, handed Jack a key card, and then leaned over and gave him a quick kiss on his cheek. "Good luck with that phone call, Jack. And try to be polite if it's Sedgewick."

"I'll ask him if he needs any tips on where to put his umbrella if his hands are full."

Yolanda laughed and then left to go upstairs.

Jack sat there for a moment, then his mind wandered back to that kissing thing. *I mean maybe it didn't mean anything. It sure wasn't a friendly kiss and he did have his hand way lower than it should have been. No, it was definitely on her ass. But she's right, it was all on him.* He sighed and then got up and walked over to get a coffee to go. *I can let it go, I will let it go.*

Yolanda was already gone by the time Jack settled down on the sofa with his coffee and turned on ESPN. Jack liked the New York Yankees. There was no particular reason, other than the fact that his father had been a Yankee fan, also for no particular reason. Jack often surmised that his father simply liked backing an almost perennial winner. Jack also had a very peculiar personality quirk regarding sports. If he was somehow emotionally involved with a team, he was too nervous to watch a game on live television. It used to bother Yolanda at first, but now she was sort of used to it. For example, Jack also liked the Steelers and the Packers. Yolanda loved football, mostly college, but she would watch NFL games with Jack on Sundays. However, when either Green Bay or Pittsburgh was on, Jack would pace up and down and find all kinds of mini-tasks to do around the house. Only when it was clear that victory was imminent would he sit down and enjoy the ending. This was why he watched ESPN, he could catch the highlights after the issue was no longer in doubt. The Yankees won last night, so Jack was quietly content. Then he saw that it was 9:05. Time to call.

"Good morning, the Museum of the Confederacy, Janet speaking, to whom may I direct your call?"

"Hi, uh, Janet, this is Jack Clayton. I was wondering if either Mr. Sedgewick or Dr. Armbruster were around this morning."

"Sure, let me put you on hold and I'll try both of their offices. It will be just a moment."

"Thanks." As soon as he was put on hold, some kind of martial music came on, probably something from the Civil War he reasoned.

Janet came back on the line. "Mr. Clayton?"

"Yes."

"Doctor Armbruster is out at a dig today. Mr. Sedgewick has a brief matter to attend to, but he said he can call you back in ten minutes or so. Would that be all right?"

"Sure, tell him to use my cell number, he should have it."

"Of course. "Is there anything else I can help you with this morning?"

"No, thanks, Janet, I'll just wait for him to call. Bye."

"Have a nice day, Mr. Clayton."

Jack put his cell phone down just as Yolanda opened the door to the room. She was soaking wet.

"Jesus, what kind of a workout got you that sweaty in twenty-five minutes?"

"I just got on a treadmill and cranked it up to seven miles per hour. I was really moving."

"Yeah, I can see that."

Yolanda pulled off her tank top and tugged her shorts off. Jack's jaw dropped. She had been wearing the running shorts with the built-in panties. When she turned around, just wearing a sports bra, she saw him staring at her.

"For Christ's sake, Jack, you've seen me naked lots of times. What's wrong with you?"

"Do you think for a moment that I would ever get tired of looking?"

Yolanda smiled, "Well, a look is all you're going to get when I'm sweaty like this and as a rule; I'm not much for morning sex. Here's a treat for you." She grabbed the bottom of her bra and pulled it up over her head. "Here, Jack, the complete package for you to enjoy!" And then she walked to the bathroom and closed the door.

Wow!

The phone rang.

Jack grimaced. *I really hate having to talk with this dick.*

"Mr. Sedgewick?"

"Ah, yes, Mr. Clayton, I presume"

Again with the Stanley-Livingston routine?

"Yes, this is Jack Clayton."

"Very good, so, in what endeavor may I be of assistance this morning? Or are you calling with a progress report? Dr. Armbruster and I were just discussing the seeming lack of progress accounting for the paucity of communication."

Paucity? "As a matter of fact, we have developed a fairly sound theory; we just want to pursue it further before giving you a report. Rest assured, you will be informed as soon as we have something concrete."

"Might we get to the purpose of this interchange then? I do have some matters that demand my attention this morning."

Dick, dick, dick.

"Ms. Tilden and I need the names and contact information of anyone in the Charlottesville area who you would consider to be an expert on the Civil War."

"Ah, you mean 'whom' I would consider."

Seriously a mega-dick.

"Yes, whom," Jack said through gritted teeth.

"Just a moment, let me consult my tablet."

As Jack waited, the bathroom door opened and Yolanda emerged, just as amazingly naked as when she had gone in, but noticeably less sweaty and with a towel wrapped around her head. Jack followed her as she walked over to her suitcase. She stopped once, glanced at him, and then just shook her head before proceeding. She grabbed a pair of panties and a bra and went back into the bathroom.

"Mr. Clayton?"

"Yeah?"

A snort. "I have three contacts who would meet your criteria. Do you have a writing implement and paper on hand?"

"Yeah, let 'er rip, Mr. Sedgewick."

This time a cough. "Jackson McCormick, 434-970-6112, he's a professor at the university; Claude Rankin, 434-970-9834, he is the president of the Charlottesville Historical Society; and lastly Roger Douglas, 434-970-3957. He is actually an amateur historian, now retired from his job in sales. He's authored several well-received pamphlets regarding the War Between the States."

"I bet you call it that instead of the Civil War, because war is rarely civil. Would that be it?" Jack inquired.

He knew that was a bad joke, but he just wanted to annoy Mr. Sedgewick.

"No, Mr. Clayton, although your droll humor is admirable. As I explained when you were at the museum, we Southerners do not refer to the conflict with the same name as people from the Northern states. Will there be anything else? Anything I need to pass along to Dr. Armbruster?"

"No, like I said, we'll let you know as soon as we have something definite. You can tell him that we do have a lead we're pursuing."

"I believe you mean I may tell him, my ability to use the spoken language has not been in doubt."

Argggghhhhhh!

"Oh, thank you ever so much for that grammatical tip. Now I'm sure you're anxious to get to those tasks you mentioned earlier."

"Yes, indeed, good day, Mr. Clayton. My best to Ms. Tilden."

"Sure, see you."

Jack put his cell phone down. He didn't know how that pompous ass managed to get under his skin, but he was sure good at it. Yolanda made another appearance. She had put on her underwear, matching silver and black panties and bra. Jack really just couldn't take his eyes off of her. She walked over and sat down on his lap.

"Jack, I can tell you're excited, but we're not going to do anything about it right now."

"So, why are you in my lap?"

"Because this is the third time this morning that I've noticed you being a little, uh, interested in watching me."

"And?"

"And this is all you're going to get until maybe tonight."

She proceeded to give him a very passionate kiss, so passionate that his left hand automatically wrapped itself around her left breast. She allowed it to stay there until he tried to worm his finger inside the cup.

"OK, Mister, that's enough for now." She removed his hand from her bra, "I'm finishing getting dressed."

"But, it's not good for me, uh, it's not good for men to get excited like this and then just be left alone."

Yolanda smiled. "Suffer, Jack. I'm sorry, but that argument never works."

He could tell she wasn't sorry.

26

RULES ARE NOT SET IN STONE

Jack got over his discomfort and his disappointment. Yolanda was right in a way; he had seen her naked lots of times, although it was true that he never got tired of seeing her. For some reason watching her take off those shorts a bit earlier had flipped an automatic switch.

After she had gotten dressed, Jack filled her in on the phone call.

"That's funny," she said. "That Sedgewick guy just sets you off, doesn't he?"

"He's such a prig. He even corrected my grammar. Twice!"

Yolanda laughed. "And you're Mr. Double Negative Man!"

"Shut up, Yolanda."

"Ooh, a little touchy after that mean Mr. Sedgewick took you down again?"

"I mean it or else I won't tell you what we're doing today."

"OK, I can see that you need to take it out on me. Go ahead, no spanking though."

That remark actually gave Jack a couple of quick mental images. They gave him pause before continuing.

"He managed to snort out three names of people who might be able to help us. Give me a second and I'll call them. One's retired, one's a history professor, and the other one is the president of the local historical society."

"Well, the professor is most likely busy and the society guy sounds OK, but maybe the retired guy has some time on his hands."

"I agree. Let's start with him and see how it goes. Hey, I have an idea."

"What?"

"You know the way you have with people, especially old codgers. Why don't you call and ask."

"That's OK with me; I do seem to charm the older fellows. Don't I, Jack?" Yolanda fluttered her eyelashes at him.

"Oh, so now I'm lumped in with your older admirers, am I?"

"Just teasing, you big baby. Here, give me your phone."

Yolanda punched in the numbers and waited for the call to go through.

"Mr. Douglas? Mr. Roger Douglas?" she asked.

She nodded an affirmative at Jack.

"Mr. Douglas, my name is Yolanda Tilden. Let me tell you why I've called. My partner, Mr. Jack Clayton and I are currently under contract to the Museum of the Confederacy…, yes, that's right, Richmond. And we…, uh, no, no relation to Samuel Tilden, I don't think. Anyway, we were wondering…, yes, I'm not from around here. Please, Mr. Douglas, if you would just let me…, no, Mr. Douglas, I called you, you didn't call me. Uh, no…I didn't know Mr. Bell wanted people to answer the phone saying ahoy, that's interesting. Listen, please, can we come by and see you? Why?" Yolanda shot Jack an exasperated look. "We want to learn about the end of the Civil War in Charlottesville." She finished in a rush.

"Yes, you're right," she continued, "I should have just said so in the first place." Jack caught another confounded look from her. "Yes, yes, this afternoon would be fine…at one o'clock…your house. And what is the address? Yes, Mr. Douglas we have a car. No, it's not a convertible. You do? That's nice, Mr. Douglas, but it's not a convertible, and you won't need a cap. The address, please!"

Yolanda started pacing around the room wildly gesturing with her free hand.

"104 Ashton Street, got it, oh, you are so right, I should just get to the point. Yes, I don't like long conversations either. Fine, yes, one o'clock. No, Mr. Douglas, for the last time, it's a van, just a van. Right, right, no, the top doesn't go down. No, I don't hold a grudge against Rutherford B. Hayes. No, my parents don't either. The popular vote, yes, I get that. Yes, Mr. Douglas, good-bye to you too."

Yolanda put the phone down and plopped down on the sofa bed.

"Holy, Jesus Christ, Jack! Maybe we'd better try somebody else. This guy won't shut up. He might be just a tad senile to boot. Why would I hold a grudge against Rutherford B. Hayes?"

"Look, let's give him a chance. If it doesn't work out, we'll try someone else. As far as Hayes, it was the election of 1876. Samuel Tilden won the popular vote, but there was a lot of fraud and Hayes ended up president. It was pretty controversial at the time. I guess your last name got him excited. Look, it's ten o'clock and we don't have to be where exactly? Ashton Street? Until one?"

"Yup." Yolanda stood up, kicked off her shoes, and unbuckled the belt of her jeans.

"What are you doing, Yolanda? Changing again?"

"No, after that phone call I know exactly how I need to spend the next two hours."

She pushed her jeans down past her hips and stepped out of them.

"Two hours? Doing what?" Jack asked.

Yolanda tossed her jeans on the sofa and turned to face Jack. "I'm going to get naked and climb into that bed. If you know what's good for you, your naked ass will be in there right after mine hits those sheets. Good news, Jack, it's going to be morning sex time."

Jack knew what was good for him.

27

SIT DOWN, SONNY, AND I'LL TELL YOU A STORY

They did spend two hours lying in bed. The Confederate gold was not mentioned. It was the longest time that they had spent just talking and laughing since they had left Indianapolis. Jack realized how much he had missed just being close to her. She felt the same way.

At about twelve o'clock she propped herself up on her elbows and kissed him lightly on the lips. "I love you, Jack Clayton."

"I love you too, Yo."

Yo!

"I'm going to grab a quick shower, Jack. Are you going to take one after me?"

"No, I don't think so, we might be running short on time. If we don't get there right at one, the old guy might forget we're going to show up," he laughed.

"OK." She kissed him again. "I really loved this morning," she said.

"Me too, now scoot," And he treated himself to the view of her fanny as she walked to the bathroom. As soon as he heard the shower start, Jack got out of bed and started collecting his clothes that had been thrown all around the room in his earlier rush.

He was all dressed when Yolanda came out of the bathroom. She was naked again. He sighed happily and went in to use the bathroom before they left.

They had time to stop for a quick lunch before the GPS led them to Mr. Douglas' house. It was a small Dutch colonial in the older part of Charlottesville.

"Boy, I sure hope this conversation goes better than the one on the phone," Yolanda said as they walked up a narrow sidewalk to the front door.

"I promise, if it's all bats in the belfry, we'll try one of the other two guys."

"Bats in the belfry? Jack, no one talks like that anymore. Good grief."

"Don't be so critical about my vocabulary, you don't want me to start relating you to Sedgewick."

"OK, good point. Well, here we go," she said, ringing the doorbell.

They waited a minute, and then she rang the doorbell twice in a row.

The front door was suddenly flung open and Jack was struck with the business end of a kitchen broom.

"Damn you kids! Take that, you little bastard!" The short man in a red sweater vest raised the broom up again.

"Hey!" Jack yelled and grabbed the handle of the broom as the old man struggled to hit him again. Yolanda reached in and pushed the man's glasses from on top of his head down to where they belonged.

"Stop!" she cried out. "Look! We're not little kids! We're the people who are supposed to be here at one and its one o'clock right now!"

Mr. Douglas, because that's who it turned out to be, gave first Yolanda, then Jack a suspicious once-over.

"One o'clock?" he asked.

"Yes," Jack replied, brushing off some of the broom bristles from his jacket. "We want to talk to you about the Civil War. Ms. Tilden spoke with you about that on the phone this morning."

"Well, of course, I remember that. You're the folks with the convertible. I love convertibles. I have one of them hats folks wear when they ride in convertibles," he said proudly.

Yolanda looked at Jack with a "see what I mean" expression.

Jack reached out and patted Mr. Douglas on his shoulder. "You know," Jack said, "maybe we came at a bad time. Perhaps we'll set up a meeting when you're not so…, so stressed."

"Nonsense, Sonny, I'm not stressed. Why would you think I'm stressed? What you got there? A broom! Well, not your typical hostess gift, but I always say, never look a gift horse in the mouth."

Jack started to say something, then thought better of it and just meekly handed over the broom.

"Come on in, I've been waiting for you." Mr. Douglas turned and looked at Yolanda and then raised his right eyebrow three times.

Holy crap, Yolanda thought, *is he flirting with me?*

Mr. Douglas led them through a tidy, little kitchen into an amazingly cluttered and dirty living room.

"Wow, you have a lot of stuff in here," Yolanda said.

"What? Stuff? Yeah, I suppose," he answered. "Have a seat."

Both Jack and Yolanda looked around for an open place to sit, but there wasn't one. Jack ended up moving a stack of random magazines from one side of an overstuffed chair to the floor and motioned for Yolanda to sit down. Mr. Douglas had already settled down in a seedy looking lounge chair of indiscriminant age. Jack grabbed several books and added them to other existing stacks that covered most of a musty smelling sofa. He finally had enough space to sit down.

"I might as well tell you up front that I don't need any more life insurance," Mr. Douglas stated.

"Uh, Mr. Douglas," Jack started, "we're not selling life insurance. We're here to talk with you about the Civil War."

"Mr. Douglas, this is kind of personal, but can I ask you a question?" Yolanda inquired.

"Sure, sweetie, I'm always happy to assist a beautiful young lady."

That eyebrow thing again. Holy crap!

"Are you taking any prescribed medications?" she asked.

"Well, I'm supposed to, but I keep losing that damn little bottle," Mr. Douglas giggled.

"I tell you what," Yolanda continued, "why don't you sit and talk with Mr. Clayton and I'll go and see if I can help you find it."

Mr. Douglas nodded. "OK, Sweetie, that would be nice. They're green, you know."

"Green?" Yolanda asked.

"The pills," Mr. Douglas answered, "the pills are green, wait a minute, maybe they're pink." He turned to Jack. "Do you remember what color they were?"

"Uh, no, not exactly," Jack answered.

"Well, a hell of a lot of help you are!" Mr. Douglas shouted.

"Calm down, Mr. Douglas," Yolanda said in a soothing voice. "Why don't you tell Mr. Clayton about your life as a salesman while I go look in your bathroom."

"You know, in France they often have the bathtub in one room and the toilet in another," Mr. Douglas offered.

"Fascinating," Yolanda replied, "you can probably tell Mr. Clayton all about that too. I'll be back in a couple of minutes."

Mr. Douglas turned back to Jack. "Now in Russia, sometimes you have to buy the toilet paper when you go into a restroom."

"That's nice, Mr. Douglas, you've actually made two connected statements for the first time this afternoon," Jack said.

Mr. Douglas gave him another suspicious stare. "You making fun of me, Sonny?"

That was the last thing Yolanda heard as she left the room. *Mr. Douglas likes me, but I don't think he likes Jack!*

Yolanda went back into the kitchen and looked around. She didn't see any prescription bottles on any of the counters. She pulled open a couple of drawers. There were old ballpoint pens and pencils mixed in with the knives and forks. Another drawer held some t-shirts and several unmatched socks. She gave up on the kitchen and went down another hallway and found the stairs.

The bathroom was at the top of the stairs to the right. It was small, but thankfully clean; she had been worried about what condition it might be in. The obvious first place she looked was the medicine cabinet. It appeared to contain a rudimentary can-opener, several pieces of broken crayons, and a postcard from Utah. *Jesus, it's no wonder he can't find anything. I wonder how Jack's doing.*

Jack was doing sort of OK. He had been able to get Mr. Douglas to forget about his bathroom comment by inquiring about the issue with the neighborhood children. That was definitely a hot-button topic for Mr. Douglas. He carried on for several minutes listing the shortcomings of parents and the American educational system and even managed to include a brief mention of the weather patterns of the Santa Ana winds.

Yolanda gave up on the bathroom, just like she had in the kitchen. She opened the door to a barely furnished bedroom. It only contained a bed and a dresser with a mirror. She went to the only other door and pushed it open. OK, it was Mr. Douglas' bedroom and it had the similar appearance of the living room, only this time it included random piles of clothing mixed in with more books and pamphlets. The bed was piled high with clothes with only a narrow spot where Mr. Douglas must have carved out a place to sleep. There was also a strong smell of dirty laundry. Yolanda pulled the door back and forth several times to see if she could get some fresh air in the room.

OK, I couldn't find it in the kitchen or the bathroom. Really it could be anywhere and I don't want to dig through dirty laundry to find it.

She took a deep breath and stepped into the room, at the very same moment that Jack was being informed that Glen Campbell's song, The Wichita Lineman, was not about college football at all.

Yolanda gingerly stepped over what appeared to be the socks that matched the ones in the kitchen and paused at the foot of the bed. She made a slow turn, looking around the room hoping to spot the bottle. Sadly it wasn't in plain sight.

OK, where would it be, it wouldn't be in plain sight, because even he would eventually see it. It also doesn't appear that anything is where it's supposed to be in this house. He's not the kind of person who would put anything away logically then, so it must have been…

Suddenly Yolanda had an idea. If he had no clue where it was, it must have accidentally ended up someplace. She dropped to her knees beside the bed and looked underneath. There, lying next to an empty McDonald's Kid's Meal box and a dried up apple core, was a prescription bottle. She looked around to see if there was any likelihood of being bitten by a mouse or something, then she quickly grabbed the bottle and stood up. She popped the cap and looked at the pills.

Blue. Really?

Just as Jack was learning that the first cheerleaders were actually male, although Mr. Douglas had offered his theory that modern female cheerleaders were just the logical evolution from the female camp-followers of the Middle Ages, Yolanda walked in with a glass of water and two blue pills in her hand.

"Here, Mr. Douglas, take these," she directed.

"Is it Viagra, Sweetie?" he asked.

"Uh, no, Mr. Douglas, I think one of the last things you need at the moment is an erection," she replied.

Jesus, enough with the eyebrows!

"Say, Mr. Douglas, why don't we make you a little something for lunch? You can kick back in your recliner and get a little cat nap in while we're fixing it," Jack said.

"Well, Sonny, I am a bit fatigued. You've been talking my leg off."

"Uh, right, sorry about that," Jack said.

Mr. Douglas pushed his recliner back and put both of his hands behind his head. "Of course, I was about to mention that the French Foreign Legion was extremely pivotal in…"

He started snoring.

Yolanda gestured for Jack to follow her to the kitchen.

"Are we really making him lunch or are we just getting the hell out of here?" she asked.

"Let's wait and see what those pills do. I've already invested way too much time listening to him go on and on to give up on him now."

"OK," she sighed. "Let me see if there's actually anything edible in here." She opened the refrigerator door. "Nope, I don't think all these things are supposed to be green. By the way, Jack, did you notice that the pills were blue?"

"No, did you have trouble finding them?"

"Uh, yeah.., like I might have to take time to scald my hand because of some the things I had to touch. Maybe there's something in the cabinet."

Yolanda found a can of soup that had only expired two months earlier and what looked like a reasonably clean saucepan, bowl, and spoon.

"Chicken noodle, Jack, best thing in the world for Mr. Douglas," she remarked.

"Who in the hell are you and what in the hell are you doing in my kitchen," came a voice from the hallway door.

"Mr. Douglas!" they both shouted. He took a frightened step back.

"It's us, the people from the museum, don't you remember, you got tired and took a little nap. Ms. Tilden is making some soup for you," Jack explained.

"Well, I do think it's a bit forward of you to just let yourselves in my house and make yourselves at home, even if it was to make me lunch," Mr. Douglas remarked.

"We do apologize, Mr. Douglas, but here, sit down and have some soup."

"Any crackers?" he asked.

"Uh, yes, but they were so stale you couldn't even snap one in two. Just soup today," Yolanda said.

"You both might as well sit down too. Now tell me what you needed to see me about."

And the slurping of soup commenced.

28

HE'S BAAAAAAACK!

There was little point in starting a conversation while Mr. Douglas was finishing his soup. From all appearances, he had skipped a few meals, so it didn't take him long to polish it off, even tipping the bowl up in order to get the last of it.

He wiped his face with his shirt sleeve and then looked expectantly at both of them. "Well?" he said.

"Great," Jack said, "We were told that you were an expert on the Civil War, especially as it related to Virginia."

"I wouldn't say expert," Mr. Douglas said modestly, "but I have done a lot of research on it."

"We're interested in what happened in and around Charlottesville. We already know about Rio Hill," Jack added.

"Actually the Battle of Rio Hill was the first major incident of the war in Charlottesville and that didn't occur until the end of February in 1864."

"It was more like a skirmish, wasn't it?" Yolanda asked.

"Yes, that's pretty accurate. Probably the most interesting aspect about it was the fact that it was Brigadier General George Armstrong Custer who was in command of the Union forces. He stumbled across elements of the Stuart Horse Artillery Battalion and led a cavalry charge that actually cleared the Confederate camp," Mr. Douglas explained.

"And that was it?" Jack asked.

"Pretty much so, in all the confusion, Custer thought that the artillery was being reinforced, so the Union cavalry withdrew."

"What about later?" Yolanda asked. "What about the things that went on in late February and early March of 1865?"

"You see," Mr. Douglas continued, "Charlottesville was really on the fringe of the war most of the time. The best avenues of approach for the Northern armies were further to the east and, of course, the Blue Ridge Mountains made a formidable obstacle, so no army was likely going to traverse over them."

"But Custer paid a return visit, right?" Jack said.

"That entire incident is most intriguing," Mr. Douglas continued. "Charlottesville had a small foundry and a factory that produced uniforms for the South. The actual goal of the Union operation was Richmond. The South basically knew that their war effort was doomed, but they were massing their remaining forces for the defense of that city. The only reason Grant sent Sheridan's cavalry so far to the west was to be a diversionary force to draw Confederate troops away from there."

"We picked up on a lot of that from reading the newspaper archives," Jack said. "Was there anything else of note?"

"Like any Confederate generals in town?" Yolanda hurriedly added.

Mr. Douglas looked at her a bit strangely.

"No, I don't know anything about any Confederate generals being here for any significant amount of time," he said.

"Let's go back to that diversionary raid," Jack said. "When exactly was that?"

"Custer showed up on the 3rd of March. That was in 1865, the war was over in about a month. There was talk about what he and his soldiers might do as far as looting and burning, but nothing came of it. The mayor at the time, Christopher H. Fowler, and a couple of respected townsmen met with Custer and persuaded him to leave the university and the town undisturbed. Maybe it helped that it was Thomas Jefferson who founded the university. For whatever reason it worked."

"We were hoping that something else might turn up," Yolanda said disappointedly.

"Well, like I said, not much happened here," Mr. Douglas shrugged.

"So Charlottesville ended up being occupied until the end of the war?" Jack asked.

"Oh, no, not at all. After three days Custer and his men moved out to support the operations against the Richmond defenses," Mr. Douglas explained.

"Three days!" Jack raised his voice. "So, like on the 6th of March there weren't any more Union forces in town?"

"That's what I said, Mr. Clayton. Three days." he repeated.

Jack exchanged a look with Yolanda.

"Excuse me, Mr. Douglas, but I need to have a moment with my partner," Jack said.

"That's fine, use the living room. I'm going to see if there's anything else to eat. I'm still kind of hungry." Mr. Douglas started opening up cabinet doors as Jack pulled Yolanda into the living room.

"What's going on, Jack? What do you need to tell me?" she asked.

"I just want to bounce an idea off of you. Listen, we think that the wagons might not have made it here by the 3rd and if the Union soldiers left on the 6th, that would have made it Monday. Whoever was in charge of those wagons had to go someplace besides Charlottesville. He couldn't take the risk of being discovered in the open by some random patrol."

"Do you think Mr. Douglas might have some idea that would give us a clue?" Yolanda asked.

"It couldn't hurt, let's give it a shot. Come on." They went back into the kitchen and found Mr. Douglas had just opened a box of animal crackers.

"Look," he said, "I found these behind a jar of pickles in that cabinet. Wonder where I got them."

"Let me see," Yolanda said, taking the box from him. "Good grief, Mr. Douglas! This says best when used by April 10, 2002! These animal crackers are over ten years old! Who buys your groceries?"

"I can take care of myself, thank you very much. But I did think they tasted a little funny," he answered as he went back to the bank of cabinets.

"Mr. Douglas," Jack started. "Right around the 3rd of March, was there anything else going on? I don't mean in Charlottesville, but maybe in the general area."

Mr. Douglas paused for a moment as he replaced the spark plug he had just found by the same jar of pickles.

"Well, there used to be another hospital not too far from here, but it closed in 1863. That was in Scottsville. The Yankees came across the James River and did some damage. They tore up the canal locks so the river couldn't be used to ship anything. They also wanted to put that section of the Virginia Central Railroad out of commission."

"Scottsville," Jack repeated. "How far away is that? Oh, and do you recall when all that happened?"

"Of course, I can recall, I'm not senile, Mr. Clayton."

Jack and Yolanda exchanged yet another glance.

Mr. Douglas reluctantly abandoned his search for food and leaned against the sink. "That happened on March the 6th, the same day that the Union troops left here. There were two columns, all together around 10,000 soldiers. Custer was in charge of one, and the other was commanded by a lesser known general, a Major General Wesley Merritt. He moved into one of the plantation houses and used it for a temporary headquarters. They really did a number on Scottsville, they burned any building of value; it took years for the town to recover."

"And how far away is Scottsville?" Yolanda prompted.

"Oh, that's right, you wanted to know that. It's just about 20 miles south of here."

"One more question, Mr. Douglas, well, maybe two. This is kind of obscure, but do you know what the weather was like around that time?"

"According to Union accounts, a lot of rain and the spring thaw had made the roads pretty difficult to use; probably slowed them down a great deal. What's the other question?"

"It's about Scottsville, is there anything there now that would be pertinent to that particular time period?" Jack continued.

"Pertinent? I don't know that I could tell you anything like that. I mean some of the buildings are still standing; the hospital was actually located in several buildings. One of the buildings is a hotel and it's still there. Oh, it doesn't have anything to do with the Union attack on the city, but there is a small cemetery where they buried the casualties, the Confederate soldiers who died at the hospital. Maybe you should drive down there and take a look-see."

"That's a good idea, Mr. Douglas. Mr. Clayton likes to go places just to get a feel for what might have happened there. I guess we can head down there tomorrow," Yolanda added.

"Say, would you mind if I kind of tagged along? I haven't been down there for a spell and maybe I can think of some other tidbits about the area," Mr. Douglas offered.

"Sure," Jack nodded, "we'd be happy to have you along."

"About nine o'clock then? I don't get up as early as I used to," Mr. Douglas explained.

"Nine o'clock it is," Jack agreed.

"And Mr. Douglas," Yolanda chimed in, "you need to go grocery shopping today. Seriously."

Mr. Douglas just waved his hand at her as he ushered them to the door.

29

WE NEED A PLAN

They didn't do much after leaving Mr. Douglas' house. Jack had stopped at the Sam's Club next to the hotel and gassed up the van for the road trip. Yolanda wanted to shower before dinner, having been in much closer contact with Mr. Douglas' laundry than Jack had been.

He went down to the lounge while she was still getting ready and ordered a scotch. He was already on his second one when Yolanda found his table.

"Hey," she said.

"Hey, Yolanda."

"OK, let's talk about today. You know, I don't know exactly what those pills are, but they certainly made a change in our expert," she laughed.

"I know, he was all over the place when you were looking for the bottle."

"So, Jack, what's your take on everything that he told us?"

"I think one of the most interesting items was the weather. I checked out the distances and Charlottesville is about 30 miles closer to Richmond than Lynchburg is, but according to what I read, it wasn't as rainy down there."

"So that would account for the wagons taking so long, plus all the lost time hiding from Union soldiers," Yolanda noted.

"Exactly," Jack agreed. "And here's something else. If it was A.P. Hill and he discovers that Custer has occupied Charlottesville with 10,000 soldiers, he knows that he needs to make those wagons and crates disappear fast."

"Do you think he went to Scottsville?"

"That's impossible to say with any great certainty. I don't think he would have gone north or east and the mountains would have prevented him from going west. It seems like south would have been his safest bet."

"What about Monticello? Could he have gone there?" she asked.

Jack laughed. "Yolanda, I haven't got a clue. You know, even if Custer had stayed out of Charlottesville, we wouldn't have had the slightest idea where to look, but at least we were pretty sure that was the destination. When was Hill killed?"

"April 2nd."

"So where could he have gone between March the 3rd and April 2nd? Christ, I might as well just sit here and drink all night; it's about the only productive thing I can think of to do right now."

"Don't give up, Jack. I mean we're going to do something tomorrow, I know it might be hopeless, but we're still going to work it, aren't we?"

Jack snorted. "Yes, I agreed to this weeks ago. I'm sorry; I'm just a little discouraged right now."

Yolanda scooted closer to him and put her hand on his forearm.

"I know, I feel that way too, but I think maybe it's a good thing that it's not here, Scottsville isn't as big. You never know, we might find a clue," she said encouragingly.

"Don't forget that Hill was laid up most of the month of March, Jack. Come to think of it, what if it was due to exposure to all that rain and dampness? I mean he would have been on the road for at least seven or eight days."

"I did forget that. By the way, I hope Mr. Douglas doesn't lose his medicine by tomorrow morning. It'll be one thing to remind him to take it, because it didn't seem to take long to work, but it's completely another thing if you have to search the house for it again."

"Yuck, you're telling me. His bedroom could use a serious fumigating."

"You mentioned Monticello," Jack said, "that was probably too close to Charlottesville. The modern part of the city expanded to the north, so Monticello would have been a risk, plus it most likely would have been a place Union soldiers would have wanted to check out."

"I don't know why he would have decided to go all the way to Scottsville though, twenty miles on muddy roads was quite a journey," Yolanda offered.

"You know, if I completely accept the theory that he headed there, I can't come up with any solid reasons as to why either. They had to have had a plan to conceal the gold in Charlottesville, so Hill obviously wasn't afraid to be in a town. Do you suppose that he kept the same plan and just switched towns?" Jack asked.

"He and Breckinridge must have worked something out. They would have had to sit on the gold for a couple of years; I would think that their actions, especially Breckinridge's would have been heavily scrutinized, especially since he was in charge of shipments at the end of the war," Yolanda theorized.

"Maybe that's why he let Hill take the gold shipment and he took the fake one. He would have come under a lot of suspicion. So, we have to go there tomorrow and see if anything jumps out at us. Now let's go get something to eat. Two scotches and no food aren't helping the thinking process."

"OK, partner," she replied.

30

MORE LESSONS TO LEARN

Promptly at nine o'clock, Yolanda rang the doorbell of 104 Ashton Street. Just like the day before, no one seemed inclined to respond.

"Should I try two again, Jack? It worked yesterday."

"Sure, just let me stand back away from the door."

Yolanda stepped to the far side of the door and leaned way over to her left to reach the button. She gave it three quick jabs before straightening up.

The door opened.

"Damn it, you don't need to play that thing like it's a piano!" Mr. Douglas offered.

"Hi, Mr. Douglas, how are you this morning?" Yolanda asked.

"Well, hello, Doll," he replied.

Oh, crap, he hasn't taken his medicine yet, she thought. Jack shared that opinion.

Mr. Douglas' smile disappeared as he turned and saw Jack. "Who the hell are you?"

"Mr. Douglas, please try and remember. We were here yesterday. You talked to us about the Civil War and Scottsville. Ms. Tilden made you a bowl of soup."

Mr. Douglas screwed up his face with the effort of recalling those incidents. He looked back at Yolanda. "I do seem to recollect seeing you." This was followed by his trademark eyebrow move.

Oh, Jesus.

"That's right," she said, "and you had a wonderful time chatting with Mr. Clayton. Now, can we come in for a moment?"

"But what do you want?" he asked.

"I wanted to see what kind of groceries you bought yesterday. You wanted me to stop by and see them," Yolanda continued.

Mr. Douglas got a crooked grin. "I think you should stop by and leave the big fellow at home. I got a few things besides groceries I could show you." Eyebrow, eyebrow, eyebrow.

Good grief, what if he did get his hands on some Viagra. Not a woman in Charlottesville would be safe.

"I'm sure you do, Mr. Douglas, but that would be unprofessional of both of us," she pointed out. "Now, let's go take a look at something I don't mind seeing." She pushed past him and went into the kitchen. Jack and Mr. Douglas trailed in after her.

There were three shopping bags on the counter. She looked in the first one and found canned vegetables and soups. The second one had a loaf of bread, peanut butter, raspberry jam, and some powdered donuts. The third one had a package of chicken and one more containing pork chops. Yolanda picked up the chicken.

"Mr. Douglas, when did you buy these groceries?"

"Yesterday afternoon. I kind of remember you telling me to go and buy some."

Yolanda sighed. "Yes, but you forgot to put the meat in the refrigerator. It sat out all night. Now it just has to be thrown away."

"Are you sure? It looks OK."

"Trust me, Mr. Douglas. Now where do you suppose your bottle of blue pills went?"

"Those pills! It's like they have a mind of their own. You know, dug-in fortifications are called pillboxes."

I wish everyone involved in the present conversation had a mind, Jack thought.

Yolanda sighed again. "That's good to know. Look, you help Mr. Clayton put your groceries away and, if you haven't eaten this morning, try one of those doughnuts." She left the room.

"You know, Sonny, doughnuts were made with a hole like this so they get cooked in the middle."

"Fascinating," Jack replied. *Hurry up and find the pills, Yolanda!*

Yolanda was luckier this time; she found the pill bottle right away. It was protruding from between the seat and back of the recliner. She tugged it loose. *I wonder what else might be found down there. It won't be me doing the searching; no way in hell would I stick my hand down there.*

She triumphantly returned to the kitchen, just in time to hear that Mr. Douglas' one-time neighbor had possessed a rubber plant named Trojan.

"Here," she said. "It was in your recliner, it must have fallen out of your pocket. Tell you what, why don't I hold onto them for the time being. That way the pills will be around when you need them." She shook out two and got him a glass of water.

"These aren't Viagra, are they?"

Yet another sigh. "No, Mr. Douglas, we discussed that yesterday too, you don't need any Viagra, I don't believe you're presently in a relationship."

"You never know, doll, you never know." Eyebrow, eyebrow, eyebrow.

Yolanda didn't say anything, she just handed him the two pills and the glass of water.

"Let's get a move on, I want to get there as soon as possible," Jack said.

"Where we going?" Mr. Douglas inquired.

"To the town you told us about yesterday. Scottsville," Jack explained.

"Why in the hell are we going there? There's not much to do or see in Scottsville."

"We're just taking a little road trip, Mr. Douglas. You need a change of scenery," Yolanda said. "Uh, aren't those the same clothes you were wearing yesterday?"

"There wasn't any point to putting on new clothes, I didn't get these dirty," Mr. Douglas pointed out. "I like this sweater vest. Do you suppose they make them like this or do they remove the arms later?"

"Yes, you look nice in red, but…, OK, to be honest, they just don't smell, uh…, fresh," she said. "And no, they don't make them with arms first."

"This is why I never got married. If you don't like the way I smell, you should just quit smelling me."

"It's called breathing, Mr. Douglas, not smelling. Please, just for me, would you go upstairs and change clothes? And I mean change everything," she finished up that request with an engaging smile.

"Fine," he grumbled, then brightened up a bit. "Would you like to come along and maybe help me pick something out?" Eyebrow, eyebrow, eyebrow.

Oh, Jesus. Come on pills, kick in!

"No, I'll just stay down here and tidy up the kitchen a bit. Now run along, Mr. Douglas, Mr. Clayton is in a hurry."

Visibly disappointed, Mr. Douglas made his way up the stairs.

Jack laughed. "So, your skill of interacting with people sometimes puts you in awkward positions, doesn't it?"

"Seriously, he needs someone to check on him every day. He is kind of cute when he gets all frisky though."

"I wonder how long he's been without…uh, let's call it female companionship," Jack said.

"Maybe he needs to go to Reno like you used to do."

"I think professional escorts might be a bit too much for Mr. Douglas," Jack observed. "It's more likely that participating in events at the local senior center would pay greater dividends."

"That's a good idea, Jack. We'll have to mention that to him. I bet church activities might be a good place for him to meet lonely ladies too."

"Maybe we should take some of our money and buy some stock in Pfizer," Jack said.

"Pfizer?"

"They manufacture Viagra. If Mr. Douglas embraces his friskiness persona, there could be a big jump in sales," Jack laughed.

Before Yolanda could reply to Jack's financial plan, Mr. Douglas reappeared.

"You people seem to make a habit of barging in here and hanging around my kitchen," he observed.

"You know you invited us in, Mr. Douglas. You just have to think hard about it," Yolanda said. "Stop being so antisocial. Let's see what you put on."

He had changed into a pair of gray pants and had put on a blue shirt with a pale yellow sweater vest.

Yolanda did a tentative sniff test. Although he wasn't exactly fresh as a daisy, it was an improvement. *What he probably needs is a good bath, but I sure as hell am not going to suggest he get naked. I can only guess where his mind would go with that idea.*

It was obvious that the pills had their designed effect. Mr. Douglas had returned to his Civil War expert personality.

"Weren't you talking about going someplace earlier," he asked.

"Yes," Jack patiently replied. "We discussed going to Scottsville to take a look around today. You wanted to come along."

"I suppose lunch is included?"

"Yes," Yolanda said, "lunch is definitely included. Now, are you ready?"

"Sure, I'm not the one holding up this expedition," Mr. Douglas stated.

Jack and Yolanda just looked at each other. Jack shrugged his shoulders.

"Yes, I'll take the blame for that," Jack said. "Let's go."

31

SCOTTSVILLE

The trip to Scottsville took about 45 minutes. The first several minutes were spent navigating the heavy traffic through Charlottesville on Route 29. Jack made the exit to VA Route 20 and was relieved to find the traffic much lighter. Mr. Douglas promptly fell asleep, but did cost them a little more time when he woke up and needed to use the restroom. Jack found a gas station and the trip resumed.

It was about eleven o'clock. Route 20 turned into Valley Street. Jack found a parking spot downtown and they got out of the van.

"Now, if you look around," Mr. Douglas said, "you can spot some of the older buildings that survived the Union attack. Most of the historical buildings and residences predate the Civil War by twenty or thirty years."

He led them down to a walkway that paralleled the James River and a railroad line. They turned eastward and walked until they reached a warehouse.

"This building dates back to the early 1840's. It was typical of the warehouses built along the river. Most of them were burned down, but this one survived." He pointed out the old ferry landing, then took them on a loop back down Main Street to Valley Street. He pointed at a brick building on the northwest corner.

"That's the Carlton House; it was also built in the 1840's."

"So, it's a hotel?" Yolanda asked.

"Yes, but its interest to you lies in the fact that it served as a Confederate hospital from the beginning of the war until 1863. Then the Confederate government closed it down. Come on, there's two more places you might want to see."

"Wait just a minute, Mr. Douglas," Jack said. He then went to the corner and stood quietly for a moment.

"What's your partner doing?" Mr. Douglas asked Yolanda.

"Jack, I mean Mr. Clayton, has a knack for sensing things. He just likes to take a moment and get a feel for a place like this. I can't explain it, but it's part of the way he does things."

Jack turned back around and smiled. "OK, lead on, Mr. Douglas. Where to next?"

"Let's cross the street here, I want to show you Old Hall. It's just around the next corner."

A couple of minutes later they reached the house. It was an impressive, brick plantation home.

"When the Yankees got here in March of '65, General Merritt kicked the family out of their house and moved his headquarters into it."

"But they didn't stay here long did they? The Yankees, I mean," Yolanda asked.

"No, just for a few days. The Beal family lived here. They were in the mercantile business and their wealth was destroyed as a result of the raid. Now we need to get back to the van, we have to drive to the next place."

"Why don't we get lunch here? I'm kind of hungry," Jack said.

"Good idea, Mr. Clayton, there's a nice place called Horseshoe Bend. It's back on Valley Street pretty close to where you parked the car."

They walked to the restaurant and were seated right away.

"I like this place," Yolanda said, "especially the checkered floor."

"It's got a good reputation," Mr. Douglas said, "just to be sure, you did say lunch was on you, didn't you?"

"Yes, Mr. Douglas. Actually it's going to be on the Museum of the Confederacy, so order away," Jack laughed.

Mr. Douglas took him at his word. He ordered a bowl of chowder for an appetizer, a dinner-sized steak with steak fries and ended up with a huge slab of peach cobbler. Yolanda had soup and a salad and Jack had a crab sandwich.

The meal took much longer than Jack had anticipated because of two things. First of all the sheer quantity of the food that Mr. Douglas had ordered and secondly, he kept filling them in on local history, much of it unrelated to the Civil War.

At long last he pushed his empty cobbler plate to one side and sighed contentedly.

"So, we can get going now?" Jack asked.

"Just a minute, I need to use the restroom." With that Mr. Douglas slowly stood up and made his way towards the men's room.

"Wow! Can you believe how much he stuffed in himself?" Yolanda said.

"I noticed you didn't give him grief about steak and potatoes or even the cobbler," Jack replied.

"Well, I have a feeling that he doesn't eat much normally, I mean look at what his kitchen was like. It's a good thing I found that chicken. He could have died of salmonella if he had cooked it."

"Yeah, it's probably getting to a point where he does need to find a lady friend or at least go into an assisted care facility."

"That's sad, isn't it, Jack?"

"It's probably the number one thing that old people fear the most, losing their independence. But really, for Mr. Douglas? It probably would be a good thing. It's obvious that when he goes off his medication, he really can't take care of himself. I kind of like the crazy talk, I have to admit," Jack laughed.

"Oops, here he comes, let's get up before he decides to order something else."

They met Mr. Douglas by the hostess station and herded him out the door and towards the van. After they made sure he was securely buckled in, Jack asked him which way he should drive.

"Go back north towards Charlottesville, then look for the signs to the Confederate Cemetery. Don't turn right on Jefferson Street, but you kind of have to veer right onto Hardware Street, it's a weird intersection," Mr. Douglas directed.

Jack made the slight turn as told.

"The cemetery is just up ahead. Turn on Confederate Street and the cemetery is on the left-hand side. There's plenty of places to park."

Jack pulled the van into the parking area. The cemetery was very small.

"How many people are buried here?" Yolanda asked.

"There's forty headstones. Over there is a plaque with the names of the soldiers," Mr. Douglas pointed out.

Yolanda stepped closer to one of the stones. "There's not a name on this one," she called out.

"Oh, none of them have a name on them. They just say a Confederate soldier," he said.

"Who are the names on the plaque then?" Jack asked.

"Well, around the turn of the century, they researched the records and found the names of the men who died at the hospital. Or hospitals, I don't know if I told you, but the hospital was actually housed in four buildings in Scottsville. Oh, and there's actually forty-one names on that plaque, one of the bodies was shipped home for burial."

"That seems like a pretty low number of casualties. I mean from what I've read, a battlefield wound was likely to be fatal due to the conditions and the lack of proper medical treatment," Jack noted.

"Well, you are probably right. There has been some controversy about whether there are more bodies buried around here. There were skeletal remains discovered at a construction site, so it is quite possible that more bodies are around here in unmarked graves."

"Well, I think that about wraps up everything we need to see here, Mr. Douglas. Let's get you back home," Jack said.

"Did you sense anything? Your partner said you did that," he said.

"Maybe a little something," Jack replied. "I do have something to think about for a while before I make up my mind about it. Let's go. Come on, Yolanda."

32

JACK REVEALS HIS PLAN

Jack and Yolanda dropped Mr. Douglas off at his house around four in the afternoon. They had stopped at a local supermarket and Yolanda replaced the chicken and pork chops from yesterday and made sure they went into the refrigerator. She also purchased a small frozen casserole that she put in the oven and set the timer.

"Mr. Douglas," she pointed out, "when the timer goes off, take this out and let it cool down for ten minutes or so. It will be too hot for you to eat right away. Oh, and don't forget to turn the oven off. Got that?"

"Of course, what do you take me for? An idiot?" he replied.

"No, Mr. Douglas, I just wanted to make sure you understood. Also, I've taken two sets of your blue pills and put them into these plastic baggies. After you eat dinner tonight, take two of them and be sure to take the next two first thing in the morning. It looks like you're due for a refill, so I'll take the bottle with me. We'll be over in the morning to see how you're doing."

"Don't understand what all the fuss is about. I'll be fine, always am."

"Yeah, well, we'll still just check in tomorrow." Yolanda leaned over and patted his shoulder. "Don't forget the pills, I mean it."

"I don't need any nursemaid, now just vamoose. I think I need a little nap. That is unless you'd like to stay and keep me company, you know what I mean?" Eyebrow, eyebrow, eyebrow.

"No, I'm determined not to know what you mean, believe me," Yolanda laughed. "Come on, Jack, we need to stop at a pharmacy."

Once in the car, Yolanda checked the address on the pill bottle. "It's a Kroger pharmacy, Jack, the address is on the south side, so it's not up on Rio Hill."

"Do you think we might be overstepping our bounds with Mr. Douglas? I mean, why are we suddenly spending so much time worrying about him?"

"Seriously, Jack? Have you not seen the man in action? Someone needs to keep an eye out for him and it's going to be us, or at least me."

"OK, OK, I get it, Yolanda, it's fine."

"And I was thinking, Jack, I think Mr. Douglas needs some kind of goal in his life. How about letting him tag along with us for a few days? When he's taking his medicine, he's just fine and he certainly can be helpful about the war and all that."

Jack glanced over at her. "Are you seriously considering adopting the man, Yolanda? He's not a stray dog, you know."

"Damn it, Jack, I just like him. And I feel sorry for him. Look, he won't be in the way and it might make him feel good to be part of something useful."

"That's because he doesn't call you Sonny and yell at you. Plus there's all that eyebrow wagging and Viagra talk. You really want to put up with that for several more days?"

"Oh, Jack, he's harmless." She smiled. "You're not a little jealous of him, are you, Jack?"

"Why in the hell would I be...," Jack stopped when she started laughing.

"Oh, you are a little jealous. Jack, that is just hilarious. Honestly, how do you get yourself worked up over stuff like this? He's an old man!"

"Yeah, he's an old man who has implied several times that he wants to get it on with you. I don't think that's so hilarious."

By this time they had reached the Kroger parking lot and Jack parked in the fire lane next to the walk-up pharmacy window.

"Jack?" Yolanda asked.

"What?"

She put her hand behind his neck and pulled him towards her, delivering a very serious, very long kiss. When she broke it off, she stayed very close to his face.

"It doesn't make any difference who flirts with me, you are the person I want to be with, Jack. I love you, you know that. Please just stop being jealous. I like Mr. Douglas a lot and I want to help him."

"I know, it's just that after I saw you and…," Jack stopped; he had almost moved something from the back burner. "…nothing," he continued. "I just can't help it, I guess. I'll stop acting this way, I know you care for the old guy and sure, he can tag along with us, but only if he wants to."

Yolanda smiled, then gave him a quick kiss on the cheek. "Thanks, partner, you won't regret it. I'll be right back."

Jack just nodded, thinking to himself that there was probably going to be a lot to regret.

Yolanda returned five minutes later.

"They won't be able to refill it for an hour or two. We can just swing by in the morning and pick it up. What do you want to do now?"

"It's about five o'clock," he noticed. "It's too early for dinner and I'm not in the mood for a cocktail. Let's head down to the campus area. I want to take a look at something."

As they headed toward the university, Yolanda's cell phone rang. It was Rosa.

"Hello, Rosa, what's up?"

"Hello, Officer Yolanda. I just wanted to tell you that some kind of tax papers came in today's mail. I don't know what to do with them."

"Well, what do they say? Can you figure out what they are about?"

"It says something about underpayment and a fine. I asked Guillermo, but he didn't know what it meant either."

"Oh, great," Yolanda breathed.

"What is it?" Jack asked.

"Taxes," she whispered back.

"Listen, Rosa, it's pretty late today, but I will text you the fax number of the hotel. First thing tomorrow I want you to fax me those documents so I can see what the problem is, OK?"

"Sí.., I mean yes. I will do that first thing tomorrow, don't you worry."

"OK, how is everything else going back in Indianapolis?"

"Good. Guillermo loves his job with the forklift. And just about every day there are letters in the mail from some persons or police departments talking about unsolved cases. I did like you told me to do and put them in boxes with the same kinds of cases. I have three boxes so far."

"Good to hear that, Rosa. OK, Mr. Clayton and I are in the middle of something here. I'll check in the morning for the faxes. Have a good evening."

"You too, Officer Yolanda. Bye."

"Shit," Yolanda offered.

"What was that all about?" Jack asked. "Bad news?"

"I don't know, we got some kind of paperwork from the IRS. I won't know until tomorrow what they're about. From what Rosa said it had something to do with underpaying and some kind of fine."

"Taxes for what?" Jack asked.

"Income from those magazine articles and the advance from the museum. Damn it, I thought I sent enough money to cover us."

"We do have money, don't we?" Jack asked.

"Yes, we have plenty of money, but I had to guess what our tax liability might be. Looks like I might have to refigure it. That's one area that I'm not so good at, Jack. I'm sorry."

"Look, you know a hell of a lot more about this stuff than I do. I mean, you set up the LLC, you got us offices, phones, a computer network, and you hired Rosa. Let's face it, who really knows what the IRS is up to. Don't worry about it, Yolanda, you'll do all right."

She smiled at him. "Thanks, partner, I promise to keep us out of jail."

"Duly noted, partner."

Jack pulled into a parking garage near the university hospital and found an empty spot on the third level.

"So, what are we here to look at, Jack?"

"Come on, there's a park bench over there. Let's sit down and recap a bit."

He led her over to a brightly painted blue and orange bench, the colors of the university.

Jack looked at her for a moment after they sat down.

"What is it, Jack? Tell me."

Jack paused another moment. "OK, what you said about keeping us out of jail, I have a theory, Yolanda. And it might just land us in jail."

"Holy shit! What are you talking about?" she exclaimed.

"After being in Scottsville today, I sort of had to rethink everything."

"You mean you have an idea about what happened down there?"

"More like I have an idea about what didn't happen down there. I started with the premise that Hill couldn't get into Charlottesville because of the Union troops. Then I figured that the next place he would head to might be Scottsville, that's why I wanted to take a look down there."

"So now you don't think that's what happened?" she asked.

"We know he had been on the move for the week prior to that Friday. Let's say that he was already sick when he got here. There was no way that he would want to travel twenty or so miles with the roads in such bad condition."

"You think he just held up around the outskirts?"

"I bet he was a pretty smart man. I would bet that he would somehow get a spy into the city to see what was going on. Soldiers talk. Drunken soldiers talk even more. Let's just say that he discovered that the army wasn't setting up for a permanent occupation and he also learned that they were heading down to Scottsville on Sunday."

"So he would have been jumping from one big problem to another one," Yolanda observed.

"Right. So given the condition of the roads and the movement of the Union cavalry, it wouldn't have made any sense to head south. He wouldn't have gone up into the mountains and Sheridan's men were all over the eastern and northern approaches."

"So it only makes sense that he would hide the wagon someplace safe and wait until they left," Yolanda agreed.

"That's my new theory," Jack explained.

"Where does the part about us going to jail come in?" she asked.

Jack laughed. "OK, you wanted to know what I sensed about being in Scottsville. Here's the thing. Hill was going to have to hide the money in a safe place until after the war. Let's say that he does hide it. Then, before he recovers from his illness and finds Breckenridge, he's killed by that Yankee sentry. He's the only one who knew where he put it.

"What about his pirate helpers? Wouldn't they know too? The manifest said that there were civilian drivers," Yolanda noted.

"Yes, but they thought they were hauling munitions. It was probable that Breckenridge leaked the false story about the gold to the Lynchburg contingent. So what if Hill told the men that it was hopeless and they should just take off and make it back to Confederate lines. There was no point in delivering munitions to a city that had just surrendered to Custer. That would take care of his pirate helpers."

"But wouldn't the crates be too heavy for just two men to handle?" she asked.

"That's a good point. I guess they could have shoved the crates off the wagon. I guess it's more likely that they would have had to offload the gold by hand."

"OK, Jack, this is one of your leaps again, but I like it. But you still haven't told me about Scottsville. What was wrong with that place?"

"It was small. Plus there was something about that cemetery. There were only 40 some bodies buried there and the hospital closed down sometime in 1863. That's why we're here, Yo."

"Where's here exactly, Jack?"

"The Confederacy ran a major hospital here in Charlottesville, Yolanda. Right on the other side of this garage is a Confederate cemetery."

"So?" she asked.

"Before A.P. Hill told his people to clear out, they could have transferred the second crate and kept just one wagon. He wasn't planning on going very far. So, if he just kept one adjutant with him, they would have been able to shove the crates off the wagon and into a hiding place where no one would look."

"Really, Jack? Do you think they buried the treasure in this cemetery? Do you think this is where the gold has been the entire time?"

"OK, slow down. Here comes some more conjecture at you. We don't know what the original destination of the gold was supposed to be, maybe it was headed to a warehouse or some local leader's root cellar, but here's what I think. Once Hill found the city occupied, he decided to wait it out. In the meantime his physical condition was worsening and, by the time the Yanks moved out, he was in no condition to complete the original delivery."

"So he improvised," Yolanda added.

"Look at it this way; you have an active hospital with numerous casualties every day. They basically get unceremoniously buried, it's the end of the war and no one was going to notice if there were two extra graves that suddenly appeared. Hill and his adjutant move the wagon into the city from the southwest; the university was pretty much on the outer edge of the city then. They move at night and pull into the cemetery. The ground was wet, so it wouldn't have taken them long to dig a hole, they didn't have to go six feet down. Even with Hill being sick, they could have managed that. Then they tipped the crates out of the wagon and into the hole. They must have dug one to match the size of a traditional grave."

"And then Hill goes back to Richmond to recover and is killed before he can pass the location of the gold to Breckenridge," Yolanda excitedly summed up. "But what about the adjutant?"

Jack thought for a moment. "Well, Yolanda, I have a feeling that the adjutant might have ended up suffering the same fate that a member of the pirate crew would have had. I'd be pretty sure that he ended up with a bullet in his head and maybe there are two graves in this cemetery that are connected with this whole operation."

"You mean that dead men tell no tales?"

"Exactly, not pretty, but most likely; the same thing could have happened in Lynchburg."

"Jack, if they did bury the crates at night, I bet he wouldn't have killed his helper in the cemetery. I mean, it was still a town and a gunshot, even during war might draw attention. Besides he would have needed him to help get rid of the wagon and horses."

"That's a good point, Yo, and he wouldn't have to bury the body, he could just dump it in the woods."

Yolanda beamed.

Suddenly Jack laughed. "I don't know. I mean if it really did indeed happen that way? Who knows? We've come up with a good theory, it really is, but you know what we're going to have to do next?"

"That's the jail part, isn't it?"

"Yeah, we're going to have to do some old-fashioned grave robbing or at least search the cemetery. Unfortunately it's not what we call being in an isolated area."

"So, do you have a plan? Are we going to sneak out here at night and snoop around?"

"No, I don't think that's such a good idea, the campus police do regular patrols; I have thought of something, but I want to think about it a little more before I share it. Let's go for a walk."

They walked past the parking garage and found the cemetery.

"Jack, there are a lot of graves here," Yolanda said. "Where are we going to start?"

"Let's check out that statue first of all."

They stood in front of a statue of a young, Confederate soldier. He was holding a rifle in one hand. There were four plates at the base, naming the soldiers who were buried there.

"OK, I've seen enough," Jack said.

"What? What did you see, Jack?"

"Just let me think about it overnight, Yolanda. Let's go have dinner and call it a day. Besides, I want to bounce a couple of ideas off of Mr. Douglas, who I guess, happens to be our new partner."

Yolanda smiled and put her head on Jack's right shoulder.

33

WELCOME ABOARD, PARTNER!

Leaving the hotel the next morning took much longer than usual. Yolanda had retrieved the documents from the IRS that Rosa had faxed when they had returned the previous evening. As she had explained to Jack over dinner, it was simply a case of guessing how much tax money to prepay. Jack had a little issue with the concept.

"What do you mean? I pay my taxes every April 15th, what do they want money now for?"

"Look, Jack," Yolanda explained, "this is different. Since we don't really have any idea of how much money we're going to make, I have to make estimated payments every quarter. Otherwise we can get stuck with a big penalty."

"So how can you estimate something if you don't know how much it's going to be?"

Yolanda sighed. "Jack, don't worry about it, I can handle it. It just turned out that I underestimated, but I'm going to have Rosa send in an additional check. It won't be a problem."

"But…,"

"Seriously, Jack, I can do this. Remember, I'm the one in charge of the business stuff, you're the one who has the ideas on the cases. You've been doing great with this one."

Jack snorted. "It's funny, Yolanda. We left Indianapolis a couple of weeks ago. We've been discussing this case since last spring. When you say that I've been doing great, you do realize, don't you, that I've done basically nothing but create a scenario that could be 100% fairy tale mixed with some pixie dust?"

Yolanda just sighed. "I know, Jack. It's just that I want to believe. Those two shipments, there's something funny about them, I just know it. And we know where they were headed, we think that there's nothing in Lynchburg, so there's something here. I'm sure of it."

"Well, all I can say is that we've put together a reasonable chain of events. Whether it ever took place is something we're going to find out soon. If this doesn't pan out, I'm at a loss at where to go next."

"It will pan out," Yolanda reassured him. "It most definitely will pan out."

By the time Jack had finished breakfast Yolanda had called Rosa and told her how to fill out the required paperwork and to draw a check on the LLC account. It was after 9:30 before they left the hotel.

"Don't forget, Jack, we need to stop by the pharmacy and get Mr. Douglas' medication."

"Well, I would have forgotten that, thanks for reminding me, I guess."

"You know that he's going to be a lot more help on his medication. You know what he's like without those blue pills."

"Yes," Jack agreed, "but it seems that his libido is a little fired up whether he's on or off those pills."

Yolanda laughed. "Yes, that's why we need to get him involved in some senior citizen activities. He's just lonely, Jack."

"Lonely doesn't always mean horny, Yolanda. I mean he's already invited you up to his room a couple of times. And that was with me standing in the same room!"

"Mr. Douglas certainly isn't aware of our relationship, Jack. Don't worry, I've seen his room and there is no way that I would consider going into it again, even as a casual visitor. Now, just drop it and park right here. I'll be right back."

It only took a few minutes for Yolanda to pick up the prescription and get back to the car.

"OK, I'm not going to be very positive that he took the medicine I gave him last night, but maybe he did."

"At least we know to be careful when we're standing at his front door," Jack laughed. "It's funny when the pills kick in and he always wants to know what we're doing in his house."

"Well, a little funny, but sad too, Jack. I think taking him along with us will do him a lot of good."

Jack had already turned onto Ashton Street.

"Well, we don't have to worry about knocking on the door this morning," Jack said.

"Why not, Jack?"

"Look who's sitting on the front steps."

It was Mr. Douglas. He was wearing his signature red sweater vest and was holding a small paper bag in his right hand. As Jack maneuvered into a parking spot, Yolanda watched Mr. Douglas peer intently up and down the sidewalk.

"It looks like he's looking for someone or something," she said.

"Maybe he's expecting us, but I've basically parked in front of him and he's ignored us so far," Jack said.

They sat in the car for a few more minutes, just watching. Mr. Douglas continued his keen observations of non-existent sidewalk traffic, pausing on occasion to peer into the paper bag.

"OK," Jack sighed. "Time to get this over with."

"I know," Yolanda agreed. "Let's see what's going on."

They got out of the car and approached Mr. Douglas.

"Good morning, Mr. Douglas!" Yolanda happily greeted him.

This didn't earn her a direct response. Mr. Douglas merely waved a hand in her direction as he carefully studied the area under an adjacent shrub.

"Mr. Douglas!" she repeated.

Still no response.

This time Yolanda placed herself in his direct line of sight, seemingly aimed at the lower branches of a scraggly locust tree in his side yard.

"Mr. Douglas, what are you doing? Are you looking for something?"

Standing in front of him finally broke through his intense level of concentration.

"Looking for something? Hell, yes, I'm looking for something. What in the hell do you think I'm doing, mowing my lawn?"

"Gee, Mr. Douglas, I'm sorry, but you don't need to yell at me," she said. "What are you looking for? Maybe we can help you find it."

"It's Fluffy. He didn't come home last night."

"Fluffy?" Jack asked. "Is that a cat?"

Mr. Douglas slowly turned his head and looked at Jack. "Yes, it's a damn cat, you idiot, Fluffy is a cat's name, it's sure as hell not a dog!"

"Whoa there, Mr. Douglas," Yolanda chimed in. "Just calm down a little bit. Mr. Clayton was just asking. What does Fluffy look like?"

Mr. Douglas turned his attention to her, but he did soften up a bit.

"Well, it's hard to say. Sometimes he's gray and then on other days he's sort of white with orange splotches."

Jack and Yolanda looked at each other.

"So," Jack started, "Fluffy kind of changes colors from day to day?"

"Yes, it's the darndest thing," Mr. Douglas responded. "I noticed it right after I got him. I figure he's one of them chameleon cats you read about. Why once he showed up completely black."

Jack and Yolanda looked at each other again.

"That's fascinating, Mr. Douglas," Yolanda said. "By the way, what's in the bag?"

"Catnip. Fluffy loves catnip. He just rolls around on it like there's no tomorrow," he laughed.

"Mr. Douglas," Yolanda continued, "did you happen to take your blue pills like I told you to?"

"Well," he said thoughtfully, "I'm pretty sure I remembered last night, but you know, I don't think I saw them this morning. They weren't where I left them."

"Where did you leave them?" Jack asked.

"Where did I leave what?"

"The blue pills, Mr. Douglas, the blue pills in the plastic bag I gave you."

"You know, when they ask you if you want paper or plastic at the supermarket, they really want you to say plastic. It's cheaper."

"Fascinating," Jack commented.

"Well, Sonny, if you were more observant, you would know these things. You wouldn't have to be such a smartass either," Mr. Douglas scolded.

At that moment a scruffy-looking yellow tomcat came out from under the next door neighbor's porch.

"Fluffy!" Mr. Douglas exclaimed and shook some catnip out into the palm of his hand.

The cat meandered over and began enthusiastically rubbing on Mr. Douglas' ankles. "See, I told you he'd show up," he declared.

"I know," Yolanda agreed, "what a nice kitty cat."

"Yep," Mr. Douglas agreed. "I like dogs too, but they shit all over the place. Nowadays you have to clean it up or people get mad. Cats just take care of it themselves." He glanced at Jack. "That's what you need those plastic bags for, Sonny."

In the meantime the cat had discovered the catnip that had fallen onto the sidewalk and was happily wallowing in it on his back.

"It looks like Fluffy is having a good time, Mr. Douglas. Why don't we step inside and see if we can't find your plastic bag. Even if we can't, I picked up some of these for you."

Yolanda waved the pharmacy bag.

"That wouldn't happen to be Viagra in there, would it?" Eyebrow, eyebrow, eyebrow.

"Holy shit, Mr. Douglas, would you give that Viagra nonsense a rest? Ms. Tilden is not interested in having sex with you!" Jack yelled.

That outburst only got Jack a cold stare, followed by a much warmer glance at Yolanda as they went into his living room.

"You know, Missy," he said as he leaned against the door frame, "I might not need any of them peter pills, if you know what I mean." Eyebrow, eyebrow, eyebrow.

Yolanda shut her eyes and put her thumb and forefinger on the bridge of her nose before replying.

"Mr. Douglas. I think you're a sweet man, but I also think it's a bit forward for a gentleman of your standing to so blatantly propose having sexual relations. I'm happy that you're a healthy, vigorous man, but I think you need to find someone more in line with your age group. Here comes a great disappointment, I am simply not interested. Zero interest. Zilch, can you grasp that?"

Mr. Douglas chuckled. "Can't blame a person for trying. I mean look at that Hugh Hefner fellow. He doesn't have to go to Gray Panther meetings to meet the ladies."

"Yes, Mr. Douglas, but your lifestyle and Mr. Hefner's are quite far apart."

"Way far apart," Jack interjected. "Now, I want you to take two of those pills. I have to talk to you about something important."

Mr. Douglas bristled. "Look, Sonny, I might need a peter pill every now and then, but I'm sure as hell not impotent. You got a lot of nerve."

"Jesus Christ, Mr. Douglas! I said important, not impotent!" Jack yelled.

Mr. Douglas eyed Jack warily. "Nice recovery, Sonny," Mr. Douglas snorted. "OK, fine, give me those damn pills." He stomped into the kitchen, hopefully to get a glass of water.

For the umpteenth time that morning, or so it seemed, Jack and Yolanda just exchanged looks.

"OK, Jack," she said. "We know he'll be fine in a few minutes."

"But seriously, Yolanda, a chameleon cat named Fluffy? Those pills are really miracle workers."

"I know, he really is a sweet man, Jack. And you're right; those pills are like night and day with him. I wonder if he thinks he has a cat when he's more normal."

"Beats me, let's find out."

Mr. Douglas came back into the living room.

"Well, we've been to Scottsville," he said, "why do I have the honor of your presence today?"

"Ms. Tilden was curious whether you would like to come along with us for the next few days. She thought it would give you something to do and I guess I'm in agreement," Jack shrugged.

"What exactly are we going to be doing?" Mr. Douglas asked.

"Take a seat and we'll tell you," Jack instructed. "By the way, do you own a cat?"

"What? A cat? Hell, no, who wants a worthless cat! Why do you ask?"

"We were just curious," Yolanda said. "We thought maybe you would have a pet for companionship."

"Nope, don't need a cat to keep me company. So, tell me what's going on?"

34

MR. DOUGLAS JOINS THE CIRCLE

"All right, Mr. Douglas, here's the real reason that we're here in Charlottesville. It's true that we were hired by the Museum of the Confederacy, but not just to do research. The curators of the museum wanted us to either prove or disprove something."

"That something being the existence of a Confederate gold shipment that supposedly disappeared at the end of the Civil War," Yolanda interrupted, earning a disapproving glance from Jack.

Mr. Douglas laughed. "Seriously? Do you know how many numbskulls have been chasing after that? Do you know how much they've found? Nothing! A big nothing! And are you serious? Those idiots in Richmond are paying you good money to traipse around on a wild goose chase?"

This time it was Yolanda's turn to get a little angry. "Just a minute, Mr. Douglas, maybe you're just being a little too hasty in discarding our efforts. You don't have to act so snooty about this."

"OK, OK, I'm sorry," he laughed. "Still you have to understand that this is a legend, a fairy tale of sorts. OK, like I said, I'm sorry; go ahead, tell me more."

"I understand your skepticism, Mr. Douglas. As a matter of fact, the museum is more concerned with us debunking this legend, just to put it to rest forever," Jack went on.

"So, you've been looking. Did you find anything?" Mr. Douglas asked.

"Did we ever!" Yolanda exclaimed.

"Yolanda, just calm down a little," Jack said. "Let me handle this."

She shot him a very unhappy look.

Jack continued, "OK, Mr. Douglas, first of all we didn't go to the typical places, the ones that the curators directed us to. Ms. Tilden had a feeling that there was a connection between Lynchburg and the gold."

"The well thing?" Mr. Douglas remarked. "Yes, gold was supposedly hidden in a hand-dug well on a farm, McIntosh, if I remember correctly. Yes, people have spent a lot of time searching around there. So, what did you find out down there?"

"Mr. Clayton came up with a theory!" Yolanda couldn't help herself.

Jack just coughed before continuing. "We decided that nothing happens in a bureaucracy, even one that was on the point of collapse, without some sort of paperwork. We spent several days searching through shipping manifests back at the museum."

"And you found something?" Mr. Douglas asked.

"Yes!" Yolanda almost yelled it.

"Jesus, Yolanda, give it a rest!" Jack admonished.

"Listen, Jack Clayton, I'm just as much a part of this as you are!"

"Stop it, you two," Mr. Douglas scolded. "I don't care who did what, just get to the point."

"Here's the point, Mr. Douglas. We searched the manifests for the last few months of the war and Ms. Tilden found a shipment of munitions. It was headed here, to Charlottesville."

"So? It was wartime and armies need munitions," Mr. Douglas smugly noted.

"Yes, but we also found a second manifest dated the same day with the exact same cargo, but its destination was Lynchburg."

"Once again, what does that prove?"

"We have a theory, Mr. Douglas," Yolanda started. "We think that the dual shipments were authorized by John Breckenridge. We also think that he sent a dummy shipment to Lynchburg and leaked that it was gold. That's why so much attention was given to Lynchburg after the war even until today. We think that the real shipment of gold was sent here."

"Did I say earlier that the legend was sort of a fairy tale? If your last name was Grimm instead of Clayton, I could buy into this nonsense," Mr. Douglas noted.

"Yes, you have a point, Mr. Douglas," Jack sighed, "Ms. Tilden and I have discussed that same point repeatedly. It is blatant conjecture, but just listen for another minute or two."

Mr. Douglas rolled his eyes, but he waved his right hand in assent.

"We took a look at the important people who might have been involved. Ms. Tilden came up with Breckenridge. You know what he was doing at the end of the war, you're the expert. He was in charge of logistics. Here's the other high profile person, General A.P. Hill. We think Breckenridge accompanied the shipment to Lynchburg. We think it was crates filled with scrap iron. We think Hill brought the gold shipment to Charlottesville, but when he finally arrived here, he discovered that Custer's cavalry had occupied the town."

"And what's your theory regarding about where the gold ended up?"

Jack glanced over at Yolanda before beginning. She smiled encouragingly at him.

"You already told us how miserable the weather was during that stretch of time. I originally thought that perhaps he had headed to Scottsville as an alternative destination, but it turns out that Hill was deathly ill, most likely due to continued exposure for the week after leaving Richmond. We believe that he found out that the Union forces were heading to Scottsville on Sunday and decided to lay low until they left."

"So you think the treasure ended up here? Why didn't anyone claim it after the war? There's no record that it was ever found or that Breckenridge benefited from it. Hill was killed before Appomattox," Mr. Douglas noted.

Yolanda noticed that he was at least a little interested at this point.

Jack leaned forward. "Here's some more fairy tale for you. After visiting Scottsville, I just didn't get a feel for that. Plus, if he had gone there, he was dead center in the path of the next Union movement. I think he went west of Charlottesville, toward the mountains and hid the wagon. He only had a small window of opportunity, because there would be other forces moving into town."

"Yes, that would have been a Pennsylvania cavalry regiment from the Army of the James," Mr. Douglas confirmed.

"So, whatever plans they had to deliver or conceal the treasure were most likely scrapped and Hill had to do something quickly."

"And?" Mr. Douglas inquired.

"That Confederate cemetery down by the university – we think, Ms. Tilden and I, that there are two graves there that didn't come from the hospital. One of them might contain the original crates shipped from Richmond and the second one might be whoever was helping Hill with the shipment."

"Really? And does somebody live happily ever after at the conclusion of this story?" Mr. Douglas asked sarcastically.

"Yes, maybe somebody does," Yolanda snapped. "There's some plausibility to this."

"Plausibility?" he snorted.

"Look, Mr. Douglas," Jack said, "Ms. Tilden wants to know if you would like to help us investigate this theory."

"Wait a minute, you still haven't explained to me why you think those crates might be in that cemetery and why would I want to be a part of this nonsense?"

"It's because Hill was so sick," Jack continued. "He was recuperating for over a month.

With all the upheaval and uncertainty during March and the beginning of April, we don't think he was able to pass the word along to Breckenridge. He knew that the gold was safe, so it didn't make any difference; they would have had to keep it hidden for a couple of years following the war anyway. A military cemetery was a place that the South would always consider sacred grounds."

"That's about the truest point you've made yet. Say, I'm getting hungry. Do you think the museum will foot the bill for another lunch? There's a nice Italian restaurant off of Ivy Road, it's called Vivace's."

"Damn it, Mr. Douglas, let Jack explain!" Yolanda yelled.

The yelling took Mr. Douglas back a bit.

"OK," Jack continued, "just a couple of more minutes, Mr. Douglas, then we'll go get lunch, I promise. The legend of the gold exists, because supposedly it was real, but it's never been found or discovered. Here's our last theory. Hill is back in action. All he has to do is survive a couple of more weeks and the war is over. Instead it turns out that he exposes himself to enemy fire and a Union soldier shoots and kills him. The location of the gold dies with him. When Breckenridge heard of this he must have been beside himself. He really didn't have much of a clue what Hill did with the crates."

Mr. Douglas sat still for a few moments, and then he slowly nodded his head. "OK, you promised me lunch. Let me think about this, I'm going to have some more questions for you."

Yolanda smiled at both of them.

35

LUNCH

The ride to the restaurant was strangely quiet. Mr. Douglas sat in the middle seat and was humming some marching songs from the Civil War. At least that's what Jack and Yolanda thought anyway.

At the restaurant, Mr. Douglas stated a preference for outdoor seating and the host took them to a table on the far side of a nice patio.

The flowers and furniture were enough like the Italian restaurant in Short Pump to make Yolanda feel vaguely uncomfortable. It wasn't the dinner with Galen that nagged at her conscience; it was still the kiss in the hotel lounge that bothered her. She had always thought him to be attractive and her reaction to his kiss still surprised her.

Mr. Douglas was able to duplicate his rather extensive luncheon order from the Scottsville trip. This time, however, he did have several questions for Jack and Yolanda.

"This thing about graves," he began, "you said that the manifest was for two crates, and then you said there might be two graves. Tell me again why that would be."

"It's all about pirates, Mr. Douglas," Yolanda said.

"Pirates!" he exclaimed. "Where in the hell do pirates figure into this?"

"Just a minute, Mr. Douglas." She grabbed his arm, just as he was about to shovel a remarkably large forkful of lasagna into his mouth. "Look, we think only the two people in charge wanted to know where the gold ended up. Jack told me how pirate captains would often murder the crewmembers who helped them hide treasure. We think General Hill turned the drivers and helpers loose after they reached Charlottesville. He only kept one person with him to help drive the wagon, probably a member of his staff. After they put the gold into the grave, it's likely that Hill killed him. The same thing might have happened at Lynchburg, even though it was a decoy."

"And that would account for the second grave," Jack added. "They would all be marked as unknown; that narrows down the search. Plus, both of them should be close by."

"That is a stretch," Mr. Douglas noted. "However at the end of the war, there were a lot of MIA's, so someone disappearing like that wouldn't have raised much curiosity. But the whole deal about A.P. Hill going a month or longer without making contact with Breckenridge doesn't seem likely either."

"Two things contribute to that being possible," Jack stated. "Hill is seriously ill and Breckenridge has his hands full trying to defend Richmond from the Union armies. As soon as he discovered that Hill was back in Richmond, he would have known that the gold was taken care of. All he had to do was wait for the inevitable end of the war. Both men knew that the South would be in turmoil for decades and waiting two or three years for the dust to settle wasn't that much to ask."

"All right, I see your point, but you have to admit that it's a long shot."

"Mr. Douglas, Jack and I have done nothing but remind each other about exactly how much of a long shot this entire theory is," Yolanda said. "But you know, we're pretty much down to it right now. We're either going to find something or we'll have to admit that we don't have a clue about what to do next."

"So how are you planning on examining the cemetery?" Mr. Douglas asked. "Are you going to ask the university for permission to go poking around?"

"No," Jack answered. "At first I considered sneaking around and pretending to be university employees, but then I realized that the museum could clear us for an upfront examination of the gravesites. I think they can arrange to get us permission to search with metal detectors. I sort of lost track that we are actually official in that regard."

"So, have you contacted the museum yet?" Mr. Douglas asked.

Jack sighed. "No, I don't really like communicating with the curators, so I've kind of put it off as long as I can."

"Jack," Yolanda said, putting her hand on his shoulder. "Just be businesslike and don't let Mr. Sedgewick bother you. Most of the issues you have with him are in your head."

"What's your problem with Sedgewick?" Mr. Douglas inquired. "I seem to remember meeting him at some conference or the other. Kind of a skinny, officious type, right?"

"Officious hardly covers it," Jack said wryly. "OK, I'll make the phone call after lunch. I promise."

"Do you suppose I could have two desserts?" Mr. Douglas asked.

36

FULL SPEED AHEAD

They dropped Mr. Douglas back at his house. Yolanda made him take two of his pills and then put two more in another plastic bag for the next morning. She also directed him upstairs and had him collect a laundry basket of unwashed clothes from his bedroom. She carefully watched him as he loaded the washer and added the correct amount of detergent. It was anyone's guess whether the clothes would eventually make it to the dryer, but Jack and Yolanda had things to do and they didn't want to wait for the wash cycle to finish. To Yolanda's relief, this was all accomplished without any eyebrow-wagging. It seemed that Mr. Douglas' libido was in direct correlation to the taking or non-taking of his prescription drug.

Back at the hotel, Yolanda stretched out on her stomach across the bed while Jack reluctantly went to the desk to make his phone call to the museum.

"Remember, Jack, just stay calm and assured. You are simply making a request to help us on this case," she directed.

Jack wasn't in the mood for any stage directions from his partner. He just looked at her.

"OK, OK, I'm sorry," she said. She rolled over on her back and pulled a pillow down over her head. "I'll just lie here quietly until you're finished. But if he upsets you, I don't need to hear about it," she warned.

Jack sighed and dialed the number.

"Museum of the Confederacy, Raymond speaking. How may I assist you today?"

"This is Jack Clayton, we're on a field assignment for the museum and I need to speak with either Mr. Sedgewick or Doctor Armbruster."

"Of course, Mr. Clayton, we are all aware of your particular assignment on behalf of our museum. Please hold a moment."

"Thank you, Raymond." Jack waited patiently, while something or the other seemed to have affected Yolanda's funny bone.

"What the hell are you laughing about," Jack whispered.

She giggled before continuing. "Hello, Mr. Sedgewick, this is Jack Clayton speaking, well, of course, I'm speaking or else you couldn't hear me. Well, unless I wasn't talking loud enough, I mean Richmond is so far away from here. Oh my, hear and here sound alike, I hope I didn't confuse you. Oh, I have a new umbrella!" This was delivered in a deep voice, vaguely muffled by the pillow.

"So help me if I weren't on the phone right now…"

Yolanda sat up and grinned at Jack. "Really, what would you do, Mr. Clayton? I'm over here shaking in fear!"

Jack just glowered at her.

"Mr. Clayton? This is Raymond again. I'm having difficulty locating either of those gentlemen at this moment. May I please return your call as soon as I find out their whereabouts?"

"Of course, Raymond, here's the number, 904-561-2332, Room 314."

Yolanda was still giggling under the pillow and didn't know Jack had hung up the phone. He walked over and stood by the bed for a moment, then jumped right on top of her.

She screamed.

Jack yanked the pillow from her head. "All right, Ms. Smarty-Boots, now you're going to find out why you should have been shaking in fear."

Yolanda looked at him in mock terror, and then affected her best Southern accent. "Oh, kind sir, I do pray that your intent is not to ravage my virgin body!"

"Oh, you're going to get ravaged, all right, Scarlett! I promise!"

Jack grabbed her belt and quickly unbuckled it before unbuttoning and unzipping her jeans. Then he stripped them off of her, turning them inside out. Yolanda modestly clamped her legs together.

"No, no, you shall not take the flower of my virginity!" she cried.

Jack grabbed the bottom of her shirt and tugged it up over her head. She immediately crossed her arms over her chest.

"Please, please, no man's eyes have yet to gaze upon these modest beauties!"

Jack gave his best wild man snarl and pushed her bra up, uncovering those modest beauties and in an instant they were not only gazed upon, but were undergoing a serious interaction with the fair maiden's attacker.

Someone knocked on the door.

"Ignore it, Jack, I like what you're doing!" she whispered.

"Gotcha," Jack agreed.

Another knock, this time accompanied by the ringing of the telephone.

"God damn it!" Jack got up and scooped up the phone. "Yes, what do you want?" he snapped.

"Mr. Clayton? This is Raymond from the Museum of the Confederacy."

"Yes?"

"I just received a phone call from Mr. Sedgewick. The front desk of the Doubletree wouldn't release your room number, but I told him that you had just given it to me. I do believe that he and Dr. Armbruster on their way to your room."

Another knock, this time accompanied by a voice. "Mr. Clayton, are you there?"

Holy shit, that's Sedgewick! "What? Really? Uh, OK, Raymond, thanks for the information. Bye."

Jack gestured at Yolanda to grab her clothes and run into the bathroom. He went over to the bed and tried to smooth out the covers as neatly as he could. "Just a minute," he yelled.

He looked around the room, it looked sort of OK and any physical response he had earlier enjoyed had faded with the phone call.

Jack walked over to the door and opened it. There stood his nemesis and the Colonel Sanders clone. Mr. Sedgewick did indeed have his umbrella in tow.

"Good day, Mr. Clayton, might we ask to come in?" Mr. Sedgewick inquired. Dr. Armbruster smiled expectantly.

"What? Come in? Oh, sure, certainly." Jack made a sweeping gesture that he immediately regretted.

As soon as the duo made their entrance, the door to the bathroom opened and Yolanda stepped into the room. She made a small wave in their general direction, and then busied herself looking for her shoes.

"It's a pleasure to see you again, Ms. Tilden," Dr. Armbruster remarked.

And I'm standing here too, asshole, Jack thought.

Yolanda's hair was actually kind of disheveled looking, but that wasn't the worst part of the situation.

"Uh, Ms. Tilden," Mr. Sedgewick began, "might I be allowed to draw attention to the fact that you seem to have donned your attractive and tasteful top, uh, backwards or something. I do believe that is the tag I see at the front."

"What? Backwards?" Yolanda asked. Then she looked down at her shirt. "Shit. I mean crap. I mean…OK, hold on a minute." She scampered back into the bathroom.

Mr. Sedgewick gave Jack a cool stare. "I would believe that an alert gentleman would have noticed Ms. Tilden's fashion mishap and corrected it. It is early afternoon after all."

What a dick! "Well, Ms. Tilden and I have been working so hard that my customary watchfulness must have failed me."

Mr. Sedgewick gave one of his trademark snorts.

Yolanda reappeared, this time with the shirt correctly oriented and her hair a little more in place.

"We were getting a little curious regarding the progress of your investigation," Dr. Armbruster began. "I know we gave you great latitude in your actions, but Mr. Sedgewick and I felt we deserved an update. You implied on the phone that you had made some type of breakthrough regarding the matter."

"Look," Jack replied. "Instead of standing around this small room, let's meet downstairs in the restaurant. I can give you the details and, it's pretty good timing on your part, we're getting ready to put our theory to the test."

"Splendid," Sedgewick intoned, giving the impression that the meaning of the word was bathed in insincerity.

"Fine," Dr. Armbruster agreed. "We'll be waiting downstairs. I'm sure that Ms. Tilden will want to freshen up a bit before joining us."

"Uh, yes," she agreed. "I'll, uh, just go to my room for a minute or two."

"May we escort you on our way?" Sedgewick asked.

"Uh, no, I need to have a minute or two with Mr. Clayton also."

"Very well, but please hurry, we are most anxious to hear your theory," Dr. Armbruster said. Mr. Sedgewick just snorted.

37

IT'S GETTING TO BE SHOWTIME

"Shit!" This was the one-word catch phrase that Jack and Yolanda simultaneously shared.

"I can't believe that they just showed up here," Yolanda said.

"And not at a very good time," Jack added in a disappointed voice. "I was really getting into deflowering you."

Yolanda laughed. "Maybe we can work on that later, Jack. Maybe I should get one of those Southern belle gowns and we could recreate the cover of a romance novel."

Jack thought that one over for a minute. "Yeah, maybe I could be a Union soldier or something and we could…"

"Stop right there, Jack," Yolanda put her index finger to his lips, and then gave him a quick kiss. "We don't have time to work on sexual fantasies right now; we'd better get downstairs and get it over with."

Jack grinned. "OK, Scarlett, but I think you're going to be amazed at some Yankee ingenuity later."

Yolanda just shook her head. "Look, I'm going to fix my hair, it will just take a minute."

That was all the time it took. They found Mr. Sedgewick and Dr. Armbruster seated at a corner table in the restaurant. Both of them rushed to stand up when they saw Yolanda coming.

"My," Mr. Sedgewick began, "you certainly did wonders to your hair, Ms. Tilden."

"Very becoming," Dr. Armbruster added.

God damn it, was Jack's silent contribution to the greeting process.

As soon as they were seated, a waitress came by with menus, but with the exception of Yolanda, they all ordered coffee. She asked for hot tea.

"So," Dr. Armbruster said, leaning forward with his elbows firmly planted on the table, "we know that there are several months remaining on our contract, but all indications seem that you've made some kind of quick progress on this matter."

"Yes," Mr. Sedgewick chimed in, "we came to Charlottesville for a full briefing. We are indeed curious."

Indeed, my ass. Another silent contribution from Jack.

"That's fine," Yolanda agreed. "I guess I'll let Jack fill you in."

It took over a half hour for Jack to go through the steps that had brought them to Charlottesville and the Confederate cemetery.

"That's about it," he concluded. "We figure that all we need to do is go over the grave sites with a metal detector. If the gold is there, it should register very strongly."

Sedgewick and Armbruster briefly looked at one another.

"I have to admit, that is a fascinating theory," Dr. Armbruster said. "I can understand your interpretation of events and you've managed to somewhat tie them in to the events of the last few months of the war."

"Although it does appear to be quite a stretch," Mr. Sedgewick observed, "not only of the truth, but also the imagination."

Jack didn't let that one bother him. "Yes, I know. We know. You brought us on board to either prove or disprove a myth. Yes, we agree, we've found certain indications that led us here. Now we just have to see."

"When do you intend to inspect the cemetery?" Dr. Armbruster asked.

"Tomorrow morning seems as good a time as ever," Jack said. "We have the help of a local man, Mr. Roger Douglas. You gave me his name over the phone," Jack nodded at Mr. Sedgewick. "If you get permission from the university, all we have to do is get the two metal detectors from the back of the van and walk the gravesites."

"Capital!" Mr. Sedgewick exclaimed. "Then after this fails to find anything, we can just terminate the contract earlier than planned."

"But we would still have more time remaining," Yolanda protested.

"Yes, but let's be realistic. We do admire your efforts, but this seems to be your optimum solution. It would appear to be futile to start from the beginning again," Dr. Armbruster stated, "and it would indeed accomplish what we intended to do regarding putting this entire matter to rest."

"Fine," Jack shrugged, "let's just go there tomorrow and see what we can find out."

"Shall we make the arrangements at, let's say nine o'clock?" Dr. Armbruster offered.

"Sure, that's as good a time as any," Jack agreed. "Come on, Ms. Tilden, we have some things to get ready."

Once again the two Southern gentlemen stood up as Yolanda and Jack left.

Instead of going back upstairs, Jack stopped Yolanda by the front desk.

"Let's go for a ride, Yolanda," he said.

"Are we going to go get the metal detectors ready? Where are we going?" she asked.

"I want to go back down to the cemetery to look around a bit."

"OK with me, it will give our friends some time to clear out."

The drive downtown to the university was quiet. Jack appeared lost in his thoughts. Yolanda was just wondering what he was up to.

Jack parked at the garage next to the university hospital and they walked over to the statue of the Confederate soldier.

Jack pointed at a nearby bench. "Just go sit down there for a few minutes, OK? I just want to walk around a bit."

She watched him as he wandered down towards the area that held the graves from the final months of the war. He stopped for several minutes and slowly turned around and carefully studied the cemetery in all directions. Finally he began walking back toward the bench and sat down heavily next to her.

"Jack, what is it? Something's bothering you, isn't it?"

Jack sighed and then turned to face her. "Yolanda, I don't know, it's finally come down to this. I just don't know if it's here or not."

"But, Jack, this is our end game. This is where we figured out the gold is."

"I know and that's what Armbruster has concluded. He said this was going to be it, Yolanda, but what if we don't find it here?"

She looked out at the hundreds of grave markers and waited a moment before replying.

"Jack, like you said, it's finally going to be yes or no. I can't believe Sedgewick and Armbruster both said that it's over if this turns out to be nothing."

"I know, but this is a good shot. I mean we tracked likely possibilities and this seems the most probable. Maybe we won't find anything, but you know, I still think we're close to it, no matter what. You've converted me. There was gold and it's around here someplace."

Yolanda leaned over and gave him a kiss on his cheek. "Let's not worry about it, Jack. Maybe some dinner will help you feel better. I'll tell you what, even though they might pull the plug on our expense account, they still have to pay us for the six months, that's in the contract."

Jack smiled at her. "Maybe I'm wrong about my feeling, we'll just have to wait and see. You are right about something though, dinner is a good idea."

38

SHOWTIME

It was nine o'clock the next morning and the search party was all there. Even Mr. Douglas had already taken his pills by the time Jack and Yolanda stopped to pick him up. Dr. Armbruster and Mr. Sedgewick were dressed in matching outfits that appeared to be designed for a safari or a jungle expedition, the most striking feature were their pith helmets.

"How do you plan to do this?" Mr. Sedgewick asked. "We're eager to get started."

"We're going to start at the far end and run sweeps over two rows at the same time. Ms. Tilden will take one detector and I'll take the other. You can pick either one of us and walk along."

It was no surprise to Jack, but when they arrived at the starting point, all three men had chosen to stand next to Yolanda. At that point, much to Jack's displeasure, Dr. Armbruster pulled rank and ordered a bitter Sedgewick to accompany Jack, leaving only Mr. Douglas as a competitor for Yolanda's attention.

"OK," Jack directed, "let's take it slow and easy. If it's here, we're going to get a very strong reading."

"Yes," Dr. Armbruster observed, "but at that point we will have to get an exhumation order. You can't just start digging in a graveyard, you know."

"Yes, we're well aware of that," Yolanda said impatiently. "So, let's go."

They started a slow sweep of the adjacent rows, only getting minor blips that indicated nothing more than perhaps uniform buttons, random bits of metal, and most likely the ubiquitous pop tabs that blanketed America during the sixties through the nineties.

It took them over an hour and a half to cover the cemetery. The end result was what Jack had feared. There didn't appear to be any significant amount of metal that would equate to the amount of gold they expected to find. They met back at the van to put the detectors away and held a short debriefing.

"Well, well," Mr. Sedgewick began, "a noble effort, Ms. Tilden, but in spite of your conjectures and predictions, it seems that the supposed treasure remains a myth."

"You know, Mr. Sedgewick," Jack slowly said, "Ms. Tilden and I are partners. You don't always have to address her as being the sole person on this assignment. I'm getting tired of it."

"Tut, tut, Mr. Clayton," he replied, "so sorry to give you that impression." His tone suggested no such apologetic intent.

"Mr. Sedgewick and I will be leaving for Richmond immediately. We do intend to cancel the remainder of the contract," Dr. Armbruster stated. Yolanda started to say something and he quickly continued. "We will, of course, honor the remaining amount due to you both, but the expense account will be terminated. You can wrap things up here, but we would expect the van to be returned by, hmm..., let's say Thursday. That will give you two days to get back to Richmond."

Both of the curators displayed wide grins as they prepared to get into their car. Jack was sorely tempted to just punch Sedgewick, but took out his frustration by roughly tossing the metal detectors into the back of the van.

"Mr. Clayton! Please treat those a little more gently if you please, they are museum property!" Dr. Armbruster exclaimed.

Jack just grunted and slammed the rear doors closed.

"Ms. Tilden," Mr. Sedgewick purred, "it was such a pleasure meeting you, perhaps I could treat you to dinner when you return to Richmond."

"I don't think so, Mr. Sedgewick, to tell you the truth I don't feel like ever eating again right now."

Visibly disappointed, although Dr. Armbruster had enjoyed the exchange, Sedgewick made his way around to the driver's door and slid in, pointedly avoiding a farewell to Jack.

After their car had left the parking area, Jack folded his arms and leaned against the van.

"God damn it to hell," he said. "God friggin'damn it to hell. I hate those assholes."

"Jack, I'm so sorry, I thought we had this cold, I really did," Yolanda said, and then she started crying. "I fucking can't believe we didn't find that gold," she sobbed.

Mr. Douglas, who had remained strangely quiet during the entire search, seemed a little taken aback by Yolanda dropping the F-Bomb.

"I'm sorry, Ms. Tilden. And you too, Mr. Clayton. I tried to explain to you that this was highly unlikely, although I have to admit that I was caught up in the excitement. Now that it's all over, you'll have to admit this was all based on a very thin string of evidence. And I am a bit surprised by your reaction, Ms. Tilden."

"What reaction?" Yolanda asked.

"I was just trying to say that I didn't expect to hear such language from such a lovely young lady," he stammered.

Yolanda turned to face him and put both hands on her hips. "Well, fucking forgive me if my fucking language has upset your fucking delicate sense of manners!" Yolanda yelled. "Just get in the fucking van, because I want to get out of this fucking place!"

Mr. Douglas meekly scrambled into the middle seat faster than he had ever moved before. Yolanda climbed in the passenger side and slammed the door as hard as she could. Jack got in behind the wheel and turned to face her.

"I'm sorry, Yo. I knew that it was a long shot, but I agree with you, I thought it was going to happen." He handed her a tissue. "Here, blow your nose."

Yolanda had stopped crying right after her yelling fit at Mr. Douglas, but she accepted the tissue, because she did indeed need it.

"So what do we do now, Jack?" she asked.

"I guess we take Mr. Douglas home and go back to the hotel. Then we'll pack up and leave in the morning. You know, we have to come back this way after we return the van. Maybe something will come to us. Like I said earlier, I do believe that gold is around here someplace."

"Uh, can I say something?" Came a voice from the middle seat.

"What?" they both yelled simultaneously.

Mr. Douglas blinked several times. "Uh, when we get to my house, can you both come in for a few minutes? I have an idea."

Yolanda sighed and turned back and stared listlessly out the window.

Jack turned back to driving. "Sure," he answered, "I guess we can give you a few minutes."

The remaining minutes were spent in silence. Yolanda was nursing her disappointment. Jack was nursing his anger at Sedgewick. Mr. Douglas was actually nursing a craving for some Chinese carryout, but he knew better than to ask.

Jack pulled up in front of Mr. Douglas' house. The scraggly-looking yellow tomcat was sunning himself at the top of the stairs. As they got out of the van, Mr. Douglas clapped his hands and yelled, "Scat!" The cat quickly jumped up and disappeared under Mr. Douglas' front porch.

"Damn cat," he mumbled. "I don't know why he hangs around here." Yolanda and Jack just exchanged bemused glances.

They followed Mr. Douglas through the still tidy kitchen and into the still unkempt living room. Their previously cleared off seating options were still available. Mr. Douglas sat down in his lounger and squirmed a bit to make himself comfortable. Jack and Yolanda waited just a little impatiently for him to begin.

After a few minutes slipped by, Jack finally cleared his throat. "Mr. Douglas, what did you want to tell us?"

"Oh, right, sorry. I had a thought about your cemetery thing."

"What's that?" Yolanda asked.

"Hiding the gold in a grave would have been a perfect way to keep it undiscovered," Mr. Douglas explained.

"Well, yes, it would have been perfect," Jack replied, "but we just proved that it didn't happen."

"You just proved that he didn't bury the gold at that particular cemetery," Mr. Douglas said.

Yolanda leaned forward. "You think it's in another cemetery?" she asked. "Which one?"

"Hold on a second, let me explain. That cemetery near the university? It was hardly isolated at the end of the war. It was right next to the hospital and it was still packed with wounded soldiers and staff members. It's a safe bet that Custer would have deployed guards around it. It would have been difficult to go unnoticed, even in the middle of the night, because there was always someone up and about. Medicine wasn't as advanced as it is now and supplies were short."

He now had their rapt attention.

"You already have a theory that A.P. Hill was holed up on the west side of Charlottesville. Well, there's another cemetery near there, an old one. Well, it's not exactly a normal cemetery, I mean there aren't any headstones, but it dates back to the end of the American Revolution. There were some captured British soldiers kept here in town and several of them were buried there. There's a small monument there. Like I said, it's west of here up towards the mountains and there wouldn't have been any Yankees around."

"Great, Mr. Douglas!" Yolanda exclaimed. "That's an excellent idea."

"Well, your cemetery thing has merit. With all the construction around Charlottesville since then, it's quite likely that it could have been discovered by accident by now. Nobody is going to disturb an historic cemetery."

"Can you take us out there now?" Jack asked.

"Uh, yes," Mr. Douglas slowly replied. "Uh, do either of you have a little hankering for some Chinese food? I'm feeling a little hungry."

THE DAILY PROGRESS

Charlottesville, Virginia

Geraldo Rivera might feel vindicated and the vaults of Al Capone can slip a bit further into the distant past.

Private Investigators under the employment of the Museum of the Confederacy mounted a search for the infamous Lost Gold of the Confederacy in the cemetery near the UVA Hospital.

According to museum curator, Dr. Claude Armbruster, the museum contacted the private investigators due to their recent success in solving an Indiana cold case involving the kidnapping of several small children. Dr. Armbruster also stated that they were selected because of their deductive talent. He explained that their particular skills would be invaluable in either proving the existence of the gold or, more likely, debunking the myth and ending the myth of the gold once and for all.

The search began early yesterday morning and continued for two hours. In spite of careful screening of each gravesite with the use of metal detectors, no significant amounts of metal were discovered and the search was declared a failure.

Mr. Howard Sedgewick, also of the museum, noted that proving it's non-existence was the goal of the museum the entire time, since so many valuable sites and artifacts had been disturbed or stolen as a result of hundreds of random amateur searches of historical sites. He concluded his remarks with this quote, "It has long been the contention of not only our museum, but the hundreds of similar museums that keep the glory of our Southern heritage, needed this groundless legend to finally be put to rest. I applaud the energetic efforts and creative thinking of the investigators that led them to the highly plausible conclusion that the gold would be found in the Charlottesville cemetery, but I also take comfort that their mission has concluded and no other attempts to discover a non-existent treasure will hamper the preservation of our glorious past."

The investigators had teamed with a local expert in seeking out the location of the treasure, but all three of them declined to comment on the outcome of the search.

39

MR. DOUGLAS WILL BE HUNGRY IN TWO HOURS

Jack drove the van to a Chinese restaurant near the university. Mr. Douglas had wanted to go to a Chinese buffet, but Jack could only imagine how long that meal would have lasted.

After their entrees arrived, preceded by Mr. Douglas enjoying hot and sour soup and eggrolls, Yolanda finally got him to address the topic.

"So, Mr. Douglas," she began, "tell us more about this old cemetery."

"Like I said earlier, it dates back to the American Revolution; they buried some British soldiers there who died while they were interned here."

"I wonder if Hill would have thought of that." Jack said.

"Who knows?" Yolanda offered. "It does present another opportunity though."

"Uh," Mr. Douglas mumbled, "there might be a little problem with it."

"What's that?" Yolanda asked.

"Um..., well, it's kind of like on private property."

"You mean like a farm?" Jack responded.

"No, more like a private residence," came the answer.

Jack looked over at Yolanda.

"Well, that raises a big issue," he said. "I mean looking at the Confederate cemetery was one thing, but going into somebody's yard with metal detectors is a whole different matter."

"What are we going to do, Jack?" she asked.

Mr. Douglas was unsuccessfully trying to spear a piece of chicken with one chopstick.

"I guess you could just ask them," he said.

"Maybe," Yolanda said. "Here, Mr. Douglas, put the chopsticks between your index finger and thumb like this," she demonstrated.

Mr. Douglas made a brave attempt, but didn't produce a credible amount, but he did manage to flip one of the chopsticks onto Jack's plate.

Jack quickly lost patience. "Here, use a fork! We don't want to spend the entire afternoon here while you try to pick up a stray grain of rice."

"I was just trying to celebrate the Asian culture," Mr. Douglas defended himself.

"Well, celebrate the invention of the fork instead," Jack growled.

"Just enjoy your lunch, Mr. Douglas," Yolanda said, turning to Jack. "Any ideas, Jack?"

Jack thought a minute. "Yeah, I have an idea how we can probably get onto their property. What bothers me is how we deal with the gold if we find it. I mean, does it belong to the people who own the property? I don't know."

"Well, come on, what's your idea."

"We're going to drop Mr. Douglas off at his house, and then we'll go take care of it. I'll fill you in later."

Yolanda made an unhappy face, but she knew she wasn't going to get anything out of Jack. He was just stubborn that way. In the meantime, Mr. Douglas had used his fork with such expertise that he joined the Clean Plate Club.

40

PUBLIC WORKS

Mr. Douglas was dropped off with explicit instructions to take a nap. He was quite happy to oblige since he had consumed way more Chinese food than either Jack or Yolanda had ever seen anyone pack away.

"OK, Jack..." she started.

"Hold on, I told you I'd tell you. Just stay calm. Here's the deal, we're going to one of those banner stores and get some magnetic signs for the van. Then we're going to a uniform supply store and buy three sets of coveralls and hard hats. There's a quick turn around with the signs, so they should be ready by tomorrow. Then we'll go to the cemetery."

"Why coveralls? What's going to be on the signs?"

"We are going to be sewer and water line inspectors for the county," he said.

"Do you think the property owners will buy it?"

"I don't see why not. I'm just going to tell them that we're running a routine check of a water line that runs parallel to the road. I'll stress that they wouldn't be responsible for any damage or costs."

"But what if they want to see identification or a work order?"

Jack smiled. "We'll stop by an office supply store tomorrow morning and use our driver's licenses, a scanner, and a laminator and we'll be able to show them proper identification."

"Pretty ballsy, Jack," she said, "but I like it. I think it might work."

"You can count on it. Look, there's the sign store on that corner."

Within minutes, Jack and Yolanda were waiting at the counter. There was a man completing a purchase of signs similar in nature to the ones Jack wanted. He peeked over the man's shoulder and was able to make out the words "Green" and "Schools." After the man paid and collected his signs, it was their turn. Yolanda listened as Jack outlined what he wanted printed on them. They were told that the signs would be ready by ten o'clock the next morning.

After they left the sign store, Jack drove to a uniform supply store. He let Yolanda pick the color of the coveralls and she chose light green ones. They took a guess at Mr. Douglas' size and bought a pair for him. They were also able to purchase three yellow hardhats that Yolanda thought complemented their outfits. Jack was amused.

Neither of them was hungry for dinner, so Jack drove back to the restaurant near the Target that had outdoor seating. Jack ordered his typical scotch and Yolanda had her typical white wine, a Riesling.

"So, Jack, give me your plan in detail, please," she said.

Jack swirled the ice around in his glass and took a long drink before answering.

"OK, Yolanda, here's what I think. Mr. Douglas may or may not have a point about this. We thought the university cemetery was our best shot and it didn't pan out. Other than the fact that this is also a cemetery and it's on the west side of town, we don't have any basis for thinking the gold is there. We're going to put the magnetic signs on the side of the van. I'll go up and knock on the door and tell them we're checking the county drainage system and we'll be spending an hour or so inspecting and tracking the lines. Douglas said that it was a small cemetery, so it won't take long to cover the area. With our fake ID's and our uniforms, I don't think the owners will question us."

"Are we going to quit if we don't find it, Jack? Are we just going to drive back to Indianapolis?"

"No, I don't think so. We will have to take the van back and get my car. Look, I know that I didn't start out on this case with much optimism, but you've found lots of things that give some credence to it. You've been amazing at this, Yo."

Yolanda smiled.

Jack continued, "You know that sometimes I can get a feel for things. I don't know if that gold is in that cemetery or not, but for some crazy reason, I do think it's around here."

"Well," Yolanda said, "I would love to find it tomorrow, but it would make life a whole lot simpler if it weren't on private property. Like you said, to whom would the gold belong?"

Jack laughed, "I still don't know the answer to that, but I like the way you used the word 'whom'!"

Yolanda smiled again.

41

WE'RE JUST HERE TO HELP

Jack and Yolanda stopped and picked up the magnetic signs for the van. Jack put them on each side of the van which now proclaimed it to be an official vehicle of the Albemarle County Engineering Department.

"OK," Yolanda said, "I have to admit, it does look pretty good, Jack."

"As in saying you have to admit to something? You could just plain say it, you know."

"You know what I mean; it's just an expression, Jack."

"I know, I'm just giving you grief."

"You're such an ass sometimes!"

"Well, that was certainly disrespectful. I need to remind you that I am the site supervisor for the Albemarle County Engineering Department and you're just a crew member."

"What makes you think I can't be the site supervisor?" she asked.

"This," Jack reported and pulled a laminated card clearly labeled: Jack Clayton, Site Supervisor, Albemarle County Engineering Department. "Here's your ID," he continued, "note where it says Yolanda Tilden, Site Crew."

"You are an ass, Jack Clayton, you really are," she said and then delivered one of her patented punches to the upper arm.

"Ouch! Damn it! That was hard," he exclaimed.

"Serves you right, Mr. Supervisor. Now, I'm going to climb in the back of the van and put my coveralls on, it's your turn next. No peeking or I'll file a harassment complaint."

"Really? I thought I could help you slip it on. After, of course, I helped you slip out of your present outfit," Jack smiled encouragingly.

"Let me think about that for a second. No!" And she slammed the door shut.

Less than five minutes later, she reappeared in the light green coveralls. She had put her hair in a ponytail and had plopped the yellow hard hat on her head. Jack had to admit that she still looked darn good even in that outfit.

"Your turn, supervisor. Hurry up, we want to go get Mr. Douglas," she ordered.

"Yes, ma'am," he replied. Before closing the door, he turned and said, "I don't suppose you would mind helping me. I wouldn't file any complaints."

"I would be glad to help, but I have a problem with getting certain body parts caught in zippers and I don't think you would want that to happen. Now hurry up and get changed, I mean it."

Jack sighed and closed the door. It crossed his mind that they had plenty of room in the back of the van and they hadn't used it for any recreational activity yet. He made a mental note to address that issue in the near future.

After they arrived at Mr. Douglas' house, Yolanda carried the coveralls inside. She didn't want to encourage Mr. Douglas to change his clothes anywhere near her. After they made sure he had taken his pills, they loaded up in the van and headed west out of the city on Ivy Farm Road.

"What are we going to do when we get there?" Yolanda inquired.

"I guess I'll just go up and knock on the door and tell them we're here to check out some drainage lines," Jack replied.

"Sure sounds plausible enough," Yolanda commented. Jack just grunted.

"It's right up there on the left," Mr. Douglas chimed in.

Jack pulled the van off the road, just past the entrance to the drive. They could see the monument to the British soldiers; it was about 4' by 6' and was just about 3 feet high. Right behind it was an old brick farmhouse.

"Go ahead and get the metal detectors out of the back, I'll go up and knock on the door," Jack directed.

By the time Yolanda had dragged the metal detectors out of the back of the van and briefly instructed Mr. Douglas regarding its operation, Jack was back from the front porch.

"Looks like no one is at home. That's even better, so let's get started."

The graves weren't marked, so they just began sweeping in the general area. It only took about 20 minutes to cover all the suspected sites. Other than a couple of small beeps, nothing else registered, especially what would have been a sizeable amount of gold.

"What now, Jack?" Yolanda asked.

"OK, so this doesn't seem to be it, but it was worth checking out." Jack turned to Mr. Douglas. "Do you have maps at your house that show this area at the end of the Civil War?"

"Sure do, I have several maps. Why?"

"Do you have an idea about something, Jack? What is it?" Yolanda asked.

"I think that Hill had to have concealed the gold somewhere around here and it had to be someplace where no one would stumble on it by accident. If we look at a map, we might get a clue about where to look. I seriously do think the cemeteries make the ideal place to look."

"Sounds like the best alternative to me," Yolanda said. "Let's go."

Jack tossed his hard hat in the back of the van and climbed in the driver's side. Yolanda helped Mr. Douglas climb in the second row and closed the sliding door.

"I guess we didn't need to spend the money on the coveralls and the signs," Jack said.

"You don't know that. They might still come in handy, Jack. Maybe we'll still need them."

"Maybe," Jack replied.

The rest of the drive back to Mr. Douglas' house was made in silence.

42

A CLUE

Mr. Douglas came into the kitchen and set a folder of maps in front of Jack and Yolanda.

"Here's all I have of the area, leastways for that period of time," he commented.

Jack quickly shuffled through the maps and then pulled one out and carefully studied it.

"What is it, Jack? Do you see something?" Yolanda anxiously inquired.

"Yeah, maybe. Hey, Mr. Douglas, take a look at this."

Mr. Douglas stepped over to the table and peered over Jack's shoulder.

"So," Jack began, "this shows the southwest quadrant of Charlottesville. If we're right in assuming that Hill stayed clear of the city and went west to avoid Union patrols, that would have put him in the vicinity of this little town, Ivy. What can you tell us about it?"

"Well, it was just a little farm village. It's not much bigger now, but they do have a traffic light."

"What about cemeteries?" Jack asked.

"There was a church cemetery. The church is still there today, but the original building isn't standing anymore. It's St. Paul's Episcopal Church. The cemetery was originally a family plot, but the church took it over in the early 1860's. It was the Lewis family, I believe."

"Yolanda, do you remember what I told you at the Confederate cemetery next to the university?"

"Uh, not exactly, Jack. What did you tell me?"

"I said that we might have to do some old-fashioned grave robbery. I think we need to drive out to Ivy and take a look around tonight."

"When you say grave-robbing, what exactly do you mean?" Mr. Douglas asked.

"I mean that we're not going to have the museum to run interference for us, so we might as well do this at night without alerting anyone at the church or any local law enforcement," Jack explained. "It's just like before, if we don't find anything, it's no big deal. If we do, then we'll have to figure out what to do next."

"It's two-thirty now. What should we do the rest of the day?" Yolanda asked.

"We don't need to be at the cemetery until after midnight, probably between one and two would be the best time. I think we need to go back to the hotel and get some sleep. Mr. Douglas, you need to go upstairs and lie down too. We'll be back here around midnight. You are still in on this, aren't you?"

"You bet, Sonny, you got me curious."

"OK, it's settled then," Yolanda said. "We'll make sure you take your pills before we head out. Have a nice nap, Mr. Douglas."

Mr. Douglas' eyebrows signaled that he could delay the onset of the nap, but Yolanda pointedly ignored him.

He wasn't the only one motivated to postpone the nap. When Yolanda came out of the bathroom in panties and a tank top, she discovered that Jack had already climbed into bed without benefit of clothing.

"You planning something, Jack?" she smiled.

"It's just kind of early and I'm not exactly sleepy yet, I just kind of figured…" His voice trailed off, but his face still held a hopeful expression.

She slipped under the sheet and blanket and used her left hand to do a quick examination of Jack's state of readiness. He certainly appeared ready.

She wasn't really tired, so she snuggled against him with a kiss. Somehow Jack managed to set a land speed record in removing the two articles of clothing she had planned on sleeping in. The panties had barely settled to the floor before Jack was fully engaged in that afternoon delight thing that he was so fond of.

43

BIMBOS AND MARTINIS

Jack had set the alarm for 10 p.m. He got up and quickly showered while Yolanda remained sleeping. He went ahead and put on the coveralls again. He figured that they might provide a scant alibi in case someone might spot them in the graveyard. He knelt down by Yolanda's side of the bed.

"Hey, Yo, wake up. It's time to get cleaned up and dressed."

Yolanda sat up in bed and the sheets fell down to her waist. Jack's breath caught as he saw that her nipples had hardened in the cooled air of the room. He reached out with his left hand and captured her right nipple in his fingers. He moved in to kiss her.

"Whoa, Jack," she said, as she pushed his hand off of her breast. "We don't have time to start anything like that right now. Besides, you already had some fun today."

"Well, there's always time for some more fun," he pleaded.

"No, Jack, I need to shower," she laughed. "Maybe tomorrow we can have a bout of celebratory love-making, right now I feel like there are parts of me that demand some scrubbing."

"I could even help with that," Jack noted.

Yolanda sighed. "Jack, Jack. I'll let you watch me go into the bathroom, but that's the extent of it for now. Just relax."

She threw back the covers and walked to the bathroom door and then she disappeared, firmly closing the door behind her.

Jack wished he had set the alarm for nine-thirty.

Yolanda was ready in record time. To Jack's disappointment she must have had some underwear in the bathroom already, because she came out wearing a bra and panties. She read the expression on his face and just shook her head as she slipped into her coveralls.

By eleven o'clock they were in the van.

"We told him we'd be there around midnight. What are we going to do for an hour?" she asked.

"Let's stop and get something to eat. I'm sure Mr. Douglas doesn't have anything at his house, so if we show up a little early, we can eat in his kitchen before driving to Ivy."

"I'm excited, Jack," Yolanda said. "This sounds so logical."

Jack laughed. "Yolanda, this is really no more based in reality than anything we've done so far."

"I know, but even you have changed your attitude about the whole thing. I'm so proud of you!"

Jack laughed again. "I don't know if I've done anything to make you proud. I don't know, if this doesn't pan out, we can't cover every single cemetery in Virginia, I guess we have to call it quits."

"I know," Yolanda added sadly. "But no matter what, Jack, I do love working with you. I'm so glad that I quit the force. And don't worry, even if we do give up on this, there are several more offers waiting to see if we'll accept any of them. We'll be gainfully employed for a long time to come," she brightly concluded.

"Maybe something fresher than one hundred and fifty years?"

That earned him a Yolanda arm punch.

They decided on stopping at a Subway. They got Mr. Douglas a ham, turkey, and cheese sub. Yolanda got the same, and Jack opted for an Italian sub. Jack didn't say anything, but it always amused him when Yolanda ordered from Subway, which didn't happen very often. She was definitely not a fast-food person. Her approach was to simply ignore the bread and just eat the contents of the sandwich. He asked her once why she simply didn't order a sub with no bread, but that was just met with a look of disbelief.

Mr. Douglas answered the door wearing a t-shirt and a baggy pair of pajama bottoms brightly decorated with scantily clad women wrapped around large martini glasses.

"Nice pajamas," Jack remarked.

"Women and martinis, Sonny, now there's a combination for you." At this point his eyebrows performed their traditional Yolanda greeting.

"No martinis, Mr. Douglas," she sighed, "but let's get some pills into you, then go upstairs and put on the coveralls. After you get dressed, we're going to eat some sandwiches."

Yolanda led him into the kitchen. Once she had discovered that the pill bottle almost always ended up missing, she had stockpiled several doses in various places in the kitchen. She retrieved a baggie from the very top of the silverware drawer and found a reasonably clean glass. After that was accomplished, Mr. Douglas was sent upstairs. She also noted that a shower would not have been out of the question, but the time involved, plus the fact that a naked Mr. Douglas in the house was not a good idea, led her to abandon that idea. Besides, he always sits in the middle seat of the van, safely isolated.

Within fifteen minutes they were seated at the kitchen table. Mr. Douglas was warily watching Yolanda dismantle her sandwich. He started to say something, but Jack caught his attention and silently passed on the recommendation not to say anything. Freshly loaded with pills, Mr. Douglas was more in tune with his surroundings than usual.

As they finished up, Jack started his council of war.

"I went online and found a map of the church and the cemetery. We only have to search the oldest part of the grounds and since it opened in the early 1860's, we don't have to cover that much territory. We'll park the van in the church parking lot; a passerby will just think it's a church van. We'll get the detectors out and start sweeping the gravesites. There's enough moonlight for us to see what we're doing, but hopefully the coveralls are dark enough so we're not conspicuous."

"What if you find something, Sonny?"

"If we get a sizeable hit, we're going to open the grave," Jack said.

Mr. Douglas whistled. "That really could get us in trouble."

"Yes," Yolanda added, "but if it's only gold and no body, it won't end up being an issue."

Jack stood up. Mr. Douglas stood up too. Jack leaned over and brushed a quite large accumulation of bread crumbs and lettuce bits from Mr. Douglas's pants. Once again, Yolanda noted that was an activity that she wouldn't even contemplate performing.

Within minutes, the house was locked. The yellow tomcat was chased into the neighbor's yard, and they were headed to the village of Ivy.

44

WHERE IS IGOR WHEN YOU NEED HIM?

It was a little past one-thirty when Jack pulled into the church parking lot. He drove as close as he could to the oldest part of the cemetery before shutting the motor off. They got out of the van and quickly pulled the metal detectors from the back of the van.

"What about the shovels?" Yolanda asked.

"Just leave them here. Just in case somebody notices us, we can still say were investigating a possible sewer leak," Jack explained.

"At two in the morning?" Mr. Douglas offered.

"Sewers aren't on a time clock, Mr. Douglas," Jack grunted. "This way we don't have to explain away the shovels too, although they would make sense. It just helps if we would have to get out of here fast."

Jack took one detector and handed the other to Yolanda and Mr. Douglas. He led the way to the part of the cemetery that would have been used in the mid 1860's. There was sufficient moonlight, but there were still a couple of stumbles and inappropriate language when they tripped over unseen markers.

Finally Jack stopped. "OK," he whispered, "let's do like we did in Charlottesville. We can go down two rows at once. A lot of these are laid out haphazardly, so go slow."

They set off. Jack was the first one to take a fall. He stepped into a sunken hole with a fragmented head stone that put him right on his face. Mr. Douglas was oblivious to the muffled cursing, but Yolanda rushed over to help him back up.

"You OK, Jack?"

"Ow! Yes, damn it! That hurt!" he whispered.

"I'm sorry, Jack."

"It's OK, can't help it now. Let's keep going."

It was twenty minutes later. They had progressed through 12 lines of gravesites when Jack heard Yolanda and Mr. Douglas start whispering excitedly.

"Jack! Get over here!" Yolanda called out.

"Hey! I think something happened. This machine made a lot of racket!" Mr. Douglas added.

Jack hurried over to where Mr. Douglas and Yolanda were standing. Jack turned on his detector and went to where Mr. Douglas indicated. Suddenly his detector emitted a loud series of beeps. Jack ran the detector over the area and roughed out a size a little smaller than one would expect a casket to be.

"Look, we're almost at the end of this part of the cemetery. Mr. Douglas, you stay here with this detector. Yolanda and I will take this one back to the van and get the shovels." Jack looked at his watch, "it's still not three o'clock, so we have enough time to take a look before it gets light. Come on, Yolanda."

Jack and Yolanda walked back to the van as quickly as the darkness and the threat of random headstones allowed. Jack put his metal detector in the back of the van.

"Jack, we found something!" she said excitedly. "Do you think it's the gold?"

"You're right, it's something. It could be gold or it could be a metal casket. I mean as a rule, people were buried in pine boxes, but don't get your hopes up, OK?"

"Oh, my hopes are up, way up. Jack, hurry and give me a shovel!"

Within moments they were headed back to where they had left Mr. Douglas. They were only interrupted once when a car stopped at the 4-way stop and turned, throwing its headlight beam across the cemetery. Jack grabbed Yolanda's shoulder and pulled her down low to avoid being seen.

"Was that a police car?" she whispered.

"I don't know," Jack answered, "but they've gone on. Come on."

Mr. Douglas was resting against a tree. He stood up when they reached the grave. "You're really going to do this?" he asked.

"We didn't come out here to do nothing," Jack replied. "Don't worry; we'll leave you out of it if it all goes south. Now, that's a funny expression at this point in time," he laughed.

"I wonder what the penalty is for grave-robbing." Yolanda wondered.

"Hopefully we won't find out," Jack replied. "Well, here we go."

He quickly shone the flashlight on the weather-worn headstone. It simply said "CSA, UNK."

The ground was hard and rocky. It took a lot of effort to get through the layer of grass and it didn't get any easier. He and Yolanda were digging at opposite ends of the rectangle. At intervals he would tell her to climb out of the way and he would attack the middle before digging at the ends again. Jack looked at his watch; it was getting close to four o'clock.

"This isn't good," he observed. "It's taking a lot longer than I thought. This damn ground is so hard."

"Do you want me to try a spell?" Mr. Douglas offered.

"No," Yolanda answered, "Jack's right, you better stay out of this."

Jack had her step out of the hole again while he began to level the middle. Then his shovel caught on something. He tossed it to the side and dropped to his knees.

"What is it, Jack? Is it the gold?" Yolanda asked.

"I don't know, it isn't metal." Jack felt around in the hard dirt. His hands felt something like cloth. He tugged on it and a piece tore off. "Kneel down here and use your flashlight, Yolanda."

Suddenly they were illuminated by the high-beam headlights of a car that turned into the church parking lot.

"Shit, it's a sheriff's car," Jack whispered.

"What are we going to do, Jack? What are we going to do?" Yolanda whispered back.

Mr. Douglas was edging back toward the cover of a couple of scraggly trees.

"Mr. Douglas! Get back here, it's too late, they've already seen you." Jack turned to Yolanda, "Just follow my lead."

The car had pulled up to the edge of the cemetery and a large, out-of-shape deputy clambered out of it. He put the beam of a large flashlight directly on Jack, then moved it slowly to the other two. Placing his hand on his service revolver, he walked to within about ten feet of them.

"What are you all people doing here in the middle of the night?" he asked. "Hey, you, old-timer, get over here, you ain't going nowhere." Mr. Douglas stopped and meekly took up a position behind Yolanda.

"Well, it's not for fun," Jack laughed. "We got a report that there was some sewer or water line issue here at the church."

"At four in the morning? You don't even have any lights or generators going," the deputy observed.

"They just sent us out here to check it out, we haven't found anything so far. We're using this to see how far the lines extend." Jack pointed at the metal detector Mr. Douglas was still holding.

"It seems there wouldn't be any water lines in the cemetery itself. That would be stupid," the deputy observed.

"Oh, yeah, we're not looking here. We were taking a short cut through to the other side of the sanctuary," Jack explained.

"Huh," came the answer. "You got some ID?"

"Of course," Jack replied. He had put his laminated ID tag on a lanyard and tugged it up and over his head, and then handed it to the deputy. He looked it over carefully and then walked over to Yolanda and Mr. Douglas, who dutifully pulled their cards for him to peruse.

"Huh," he grunted again. "You folks wait here a second." He walked back to his car, still carrying Jack's ID.

"Oh, shit," Yolanda whispered, "what's he going to do?"

"No idea," Jack whispered back, "I guess he's checking with either the Sheriff's Department or Albemarle County Water Department."

They waited for a few more minutes in uncomfortable silence.

"Here he comes," Yolanda whispered, "you know, he really can't arrest us, we weren't doing anything wrong."

"Well, we are in the middle of a church graveyard with metal detectors and shovels. I think even the dumbest person in the world would be a bit suspicious."

"I called headquarters," the deputy began, "turns out they can't get ahold of nobody at the water and sewage department, it being so early and all. The dispatcher done told me that I should just stay here and keep an eye on you until you finish your business."

Shit. Three minds shared that thought; two immediately, one a second or two later.

"Come on then," Jack directed. "We just have that area over by the far parking lot to check out."

All four of them headed to the indicated destination. Jack wasted no time in setting up a metal detector and quickly covered the area. About fifteen minutes later, he shut it down. The deputy had taken a seat on a low fence rail that separated the church from the graveyard. Jack walked over to him.

"Darndest thing," he said. "The guy at the church said there was standing water. We didn't find anything and it's taken hours. How much longer have you got on your shift?"

"That's too bad," the deputy agreed. "I came on at midnight, I was just doing my second round when I caught sight of you guys working. Let me see," he checked his watch. "Yup, about five, I only have until eight and I still got a donut stop to look forward to."

"Sounds good," Jack nodded. "We're going to load up and get out of here. I need some solid shut-eye."

"Say," the deputy whispered. "What about that girl? She going out with anybody? I thought maybe I'd see if she wanted to maybe go out or something. Chicks like uniforms and she looks good, even in them coveralls."

"Ah," Jack remarked. "Uh, listen, I'm sorry, but she's one of them who don't exactly go for the men, if you catch my drift."

"Are you kidding me?" The deputy spit a good-sized hocker in a respectable arc over his right shoulder. "Just between you and me, I think a lot of them women have just never been with a real man, know what I mean?"

"Oh, yeah, exactly, but what are you going to do?" Jack shrugged, then he turned to where Yolanda and Mr. Douglas were pretending to search for water-related issues. "Hey, you guys! Grab your gear and let's get to the van, there's nothing here, some idiot wasted our time and a good night's sleep." Then he turned back to the deputy. "Well, at least it broke up the boredom of your shift. It was good talking to you."

"Yeah, no problem. Believe me, I get called out to take a look at stuff all the time that turns out to be nothing."

"Well, at least we get paid for it, don't we," Jack laughed.

"Not nearly enough," also accompanied by a laugh.

Within minutes, both vehicles were pulling out of the church lot; the deputy toward Ivy and the van back towards Charlottesville.

"God damn it!" Yolanda exclaimed. "What the hell kind of luck was that?"

"I know," Jack agreed, "all we needed was another half hour or so."

"So what do we do now, Jack? Are we going to turn around?"

"No, it's too close to sunrise. We have to wait until tonight."

"But what if we get caught again? If it's the same deputy on duty, he'll be sure to check the graveyard, just to see."

"I know, but we're keeping the same game plan, we're just changing how we're going about it this time."

"What do you mean?" Yolanda asked.

"We're going to stop somewhere and have breakfast. I'll explain over some eggs or something."

"Please not that Waffle House again," Yolanda pleaded.

"I saw something a little better just a little north of there, it looked like a place with Old World charm," Jack added.

Yolanda thought that sounded intriguing, but that feeling only lasted as long as it took her to realize that Jack had just turned into an IHOP.

"Old World charm? What were you talking about? This is an IHOP!"

"Yummy," came a voice from the back seat.

"It's international, Yolanda. Lighten up," Jack laughed.

"It's a good thing that I'm tired, Jack Clayton. It's a good thing."

They had to scramble to catch up with Mr. Douglas who had launched himself from the van as soon as it stopped. Even Yolanda was mildly mollified when she discovered that she could order a waffle with fresh strawberries. Mr. Douglas went for a double stack that he proceeded to drench with syrup. Jack ordered a breakfast sandwich with home fries.

They quickly finished eating, then Jack told them his plan over a last cup of coffee.

"OK, we know there's something suspicious out there, but we can't risk getting caught two nights in a row. Here's what we're going to do; we're ditching the van tonight and we'll get a rental car, something big enough to hold the tools, but small enough to be inconspicuous from the road. We're also getting rid of the coveralls and hard hats. We're wearing black shirts and pants. We're also going to blacken our faces."

"So, we're going commando?" Mr. Douglas asked.

Yolanda about spit her tea across the table.

"Uh, yeah, you might put it like that," Jack laughed, catching Yolanda's eye.

"Are we going about the same time?" Yolanda asked.

"No, we'll try earlier. Mr. Douglas, we'll be at your house around ten thirty."

"But there might be more traffic that early in the night, Jack," Yolanda said.

"Yes, I know, but there won't be much, and it should be fairly quiet around midnight. Besides, we're going at this differently. Mr. Douglas is going to be our lookout." Jack turned to him, "The first time you see the hint of a headlight, we're hitting the ground until the car or truck passes. We'll be almost invisible as long as someone doesn't get suspicious and stops for a closer look."

"Gotcha, Sonny," came the reply.

"OK, then, let's drop you off. I'm beat and I'm sure everyone else is too. Get some sleep. We'll bring some sandwiches to eat at your place before we leave. We'll try to get to the church around eleven thirty."

They left Mr. Douglas at his house after Yolanda set three baggies of medicine on his kitchen table with firm instructions to take the last dose right at ten p.m.

Jack and Yolanda went back to the Doubletree, took turns showering, stuck the Do Not Disturb sign on the door handle, and were fast asleep within a few minutes.

Jack woke up around two. Yolanda was still asleep. He got dressed and went down to the lobby for a newspaper and another cup of coffee. He went back up and sat at the desk while he read. By the time he finished, it was almost 2:30. He walked over and knelt by the side of the bed. "Yo," he whispered. "Yo, we need to go get the rental car, so you'll need to come along with me to either drive it or the van back."

She slowly opened her eyes, "Nooooo, I just want to lie here. Come back to bed, Jack, we can snuggle."

"I would love to, Yolanda, but we have to get this done," he leaned over and tried to kiss her.

"Yuck, no, Jack, I haven't brushed my teeth yet."

"I just had some coffee. Does that change your mind?"

"Yes, I love coffee kisses," she laughed and pulled Jack close to her for a long kiss.

"See, that wasn't so bad, was it?" Jack laughed. "Now, get up and get dressed, we want to get this done."

It only took a few minutes for Yolanda to get ready, since she knew she would be putting blacking all over her face in the evening, it didn't make any sense to deal with make-up.

The desk clerk directed them to an Enterprise rental office off of Route 29. Jack picked out a maroon, full-size sedan. Since he signed it out in his name, he drove it back to the hotel and Yolanda followed in the van. He transferred the spades and the shovels to the trunk of the rental.

"What about the metal detectors, Jack? Are we going to take them?"

"No, they would take up too much room and besides, we know where we're going to dig."

They decided to grab an early dinner and then try to relax before driving over to Mr. Douglas' house. They went back to their favorite shopping area by Target and found a little Italian pizza place a few doors down from a hamburger joint. Afterwards they stopped at the liquor store and picked up a chilled bottle of Riesling to take back to the room.

Jack sat on the desk chair and gave Yolanda the armchair. They used the bathroom glasses for the wine.

"We haven't talked about what might happen tonight, Jack," Yolanda said, "There was definitely a solid hit at that grave."

"I know, it could be a pile of rusted metal that just got shoved there and gradually sank down and got covered up over the years or it could be some rifles that got tossed there…"

"Or it might be gold and silver bars!" Yolanda added excitedly.

"Yes, it might be," Jack smiled. "We're going to find out in," he checked his watch, "about five hours." He took the last sip of wine. "I'm going to go brush my teeth, then try to catch some sleep. How about you?"

"Can we lie in bed and talk a little?"

Jack smiled. "Sure, Yo, maybe I'll even scratch your back."

She smiled back, "Jack, are you going commando too?"

He laughed.

45

PAY DIRT

They stopped and got deli sandwiches and coffee. Yolanda ran up to Mr. Douglas' house while Jack waited in the car. She checked to see if he had taken his medications. He had. They spent a quiet time in Mr. Douglas' kitchen eating. Then it was time to leave.

Once again it was a quiet ride to Ivy. It was already dark and each of them seemed to have things to think about.

Jack came to the four-way stop and looked long in both directions.

"OK, I'm going to park on the far side of the church away from the road. All we have to do is carry the spades and shovels over to the graveyard. No one will see the car from the road."

They got out of the car. Jack had purchased black baseball caps for each of them. Then he reached in a small plastic bag and pulled out a container of blacking.

"Here, put this on your faces and hands, we can't get caught tonight because we will be leaving evidence of digging," he directed.

It didn't take long to reach the gravesite. Since it was in the oldest part of the cemetery, Jack had been confident that the marks left from their previous digging wouldn't have been noticed. He went to the area that he had dug in before the deputy showed up. He dropped to his knees and dug around in the dirt with his hands. He found the same flap of material that he had discovered the night before.

"Yolanda, come over here with the flashlight."

Yolanda covered the lens of the flashlight and placed the beam on Jack's hand. It was a ragged piece of cloth. It was impossible to tell what color it was; it was completely covered with dirt. Jack scraped some more dirt to one side and tugged on the material again, uncovering more of it. This time when they inspected it, they saw that there were two, dirt-covered buttons. Jack rubbed one of them on the leg of his pants until the dirt was gone. The button had a raised "CSA" on it. Jack knelt down at the far end of the gravesite and used the side of his shovel to gently scrape the dirt away. Within moments he had uncovered a skull. He pried it out of the ground. There was a bullet hole in the forehead.

"Yo," he whispered, "I think we've just found our pirate crew member."

"Holy shit," she whispered back.

"OK, now we have a problem. We've just opened a grave with a body in it," he said.

"What are we going to do, Jack? Cover him back up?" she asked.

"Damn it, no. The gold is underneath him. Hill wouldn't have dug a six-foot grave, we don't have far to go." He checked his watch again. "We have a long time until it gets light. Dig down along the sides. When we hit whatever is down there, maybe we can bring it up and not disturb too much of the remains."

Ten minutes later, Yolanda's shovel hit something. "It feels like a rock, Jack."

Jack took out his flashlight and shone it where the tip of her shovel was resting. He reached down and saw a bright gold scrape on what appeared to be a long rock. He used his shovel to pry it loose.

"What is it?" Mr. Douglas anxiously asked.

Jack used the leg of his pants again and rubbed the dirt off of one side of it, a dull gold color in contrast to the bright streak where Yolanda's shovel had scraped it.

"It's a gold bar," he exclaimed. "Yolanda! Mr. Douglas! It's a fucking gold bar! We fucking found the gold!"

Yolanda literally jumped for joy. Then she turned and gave Mr. Douglas a big hug. "We found it! We found it! We couldn't have done it without your help, Mr. Douglas!"

Mr. Douglas beamed and also took advantage of the happiness of the moment to place his right hand firmly on Yolanda's left bottom. She grabbed his hand and pushed it away. "Mr. Douglas, please do not forget you're a Southern gentleman!" Then she skipped over to Jack and gave him a similar hug. Jack didn't have to grab her bottom, he had a feeling that there was going to be a celebration that was going to include a lot more than copping a random feel.

"What do we do now, Jack?"

"Now we call the police or in this case, the county sheriff," he answered.

"But what about the body we dug up in the grave, Jack? Won't that get us in trouble?"

"Maybe a little, at first, but when we contact the museum and explain the historical significance of the body, let alone the gold, I think it will be overlooked," he explained.

"I'll be damned," Mr. Douglas chipped in. "I can't believe this fairy tale came true."

This time Yolanda high-fived him, carefully maintaining space between him and her bottom.

46

SCREW YOU, SEDGEWICK

Within twenty minutes there were six sheriff cars surrounding the rental car. In spite of the fast approaching dawn, deputies had set up a light frame using a small generator to illuminate the grave. In the bright light, it was possible to ascertain that the skeletal remains were still covered in the tattered fragments of a gray, wool uniform. It took another thirty minutes for the county coroner to arrive and begin removing the bones.

Jack had been right to a certain extent. Within minutes of the sheriff and deputies arriving, all three of them had been read their rights and placed in individual cars and questioned.

Jack explained their assignment and attempted to call Sedgewick's cell phone, and then Armbruster's, not getting an answer from either one.

"So, let's go over this again," the sheriff said. "You and this Tilden woman were hired by the Museum of the Confederacy to track down missing gold. You end up illegally digging in a church graveyard and you find a considerable amount of gold and silver ingots. Just how in the hell did you do that?"

Jack shrugged, "You know, I have to tell you. It was luck and guess work. We went after several false leads, but then logic kind of put us in the right place."

In one car over, Yolanda was basically telling the same story to an equally disbelieving deputy sheriff. "So if you did figure you would find the gold here, why didn't you simply ask permission?" he asked her.

"I guess it's because we were in a hurry. The museum was cancelling our assignment; in fact we were supposed to be returning the van to Richmond today. My partner is amazing. He figured this out; it was like he was thinking just like the Confederate general who hid the gold there."

In the third car, a deputy was being given a lecture about the arrival of starlings from Europe because of a Shakespearean play, quickly followed by a discourse on the importance of the ablative case in Latin as far as prepositions were concerned, along with a brief tie-in to Alexander Hamilton and the Hamilton Tiger-Cats of the Canadian Football League. Yolanda had forgotten to bring more pills along.

Promptly at nine o'clock, the sheriff called the museum. Raymond answered the phone and quickly located Mr. Sedgewick. He verified that Jack and Yolanda were indeed under a contract to the museum, although he did point out to the sheriff that they were due back that very day and were supposed to return a borrowed museum van. The sheriff handed Jack the phone.

"Mr. Sedgewick, how the hell are you?"

"Ah, Mr. Clayton, always the casual one. Let me inform you that I have no idea how you have run afoul of the local constabulary, but the termination of your contract provides no legal assistance for you or your partner, although I can hardly imagine Ms. Tilden being involved in any nefarious activities." He managed to end that sentence with one of his patented snorts.

"Well, Sedgie. Ms. Tilden and I have some news for you. You might want to clear your social calendar, find Armbruster, and get your butts to Ivy. It's a small town a few miles west of Charlottesville."

"Really, Mr. Clayton, I don't feel our relationship is of such a personal nature for nicknames to be tossed about."

"You know, I don't really give a crap. Here's what I do know, however, you'd better bring a truck and as many legal documents as you might need to claim a pretty big pile of gold and silver bars. We found it, Sedgie! We found the Confederate gold!"

There was a long silence on the other end.

"You still there, Sedgie?" Jack asked.

"You are serious?" Sedgewick finally found his voice. "This is not a joke?"

"No joke. Get here quickly, the press is on the way and you might want to get that ugly mug of yours on TV." Jack pushed the off button and handed the phone back to the sheriff.

"That didn't sound like a lot of positive interaction," the sheriff observed.

"Wait until you meet this guy," Jack replied.

By this time a sizeable number of news trucks had arrived along with the local minister and several members of the congregation. They expressed consternation when the coroner and his assistant wheeled a gurney out to a hearse with a body bag on it. They were more used to seeing bodies go into the cemetery, not out of it. The assistant pastor did allow all three of them to use the church restrooms in order to scrub most of the blacking off their faces and hands. Jack had to send Mr. Douglas back in order to remove a noticeable Adolf Hitler smudge that he had missed. After the rudimentary clean-up they met up outside the church for the long wait.

Mr. Douglas stretched out on the grass along the fence of the cemetery and fell asleep. Yolanda was relieved, because she didn't want to send him back to his house alone and she certainly didn't want to miss the arrival of Mr. Sedgewick and Dr. Armbruster. She walked over to Jack and the sheriff.

"The reporters are getting antsy," she said.

"Yes, but our contract says any discovery and the resulting press conference has to include both parties, so we have to wait," Jack explained.

"Damn it," Yolanda exclaimed, "I forgot about that. I wish we could just go do it. After all, we found it."

"It'll be OK, Yolanda. They'll be here by noon easily. I am hungry though." He turned to the sheriff. "Would it be OK if we go get something to eat? Besides our associate here," Jack pointed to Mr. Douglas, "needs to take some medicine. It's nine-thirty right now; we'll be back by eleven thirty at the latest."

"Sure, I guess, I mean you maybe really aren't technically under arrest anymore," the sheriff said. "No one's moving that gold until the museum people get here. Plus, I've had some calls from the church about claiming it. I think someone's going to have some legal battles to fight."

"Great, we'll be back." Jack walked over and wakened Mr. Douglas. "Come on, Mr. Douglas, you can nap in the van. We're going to your house to get some medicine, then I'm going to order you the biggest breakfast in Charlottesville."

"Did you drive a convertible?" Mr. Douglas asked.

"No," Jack sighed, "not today."

47

MONEY, MONEY, MONEY

After stopping and getting some pills in Mr. Douglas, Jack fulfilled his promise and took Mr. Douglas to the Waffle House on Route 29. This was definitely not one of Yolanda's types of restaurants. She busied herself with cleaning up globs of syrup that the bus person had overlooked while cleaning up after the previous diners. She had never eaten at a Waffle House before and was a little confused when both Jack and Mr. Douglas started babbling about the relative merits of smothering, covering, chunking, and capping. Needless to say, she opted for an English muffin and a cup of tea.

After the waitress took their orders, Yolanda just looked at Jack for a moment.

"I can't believe we just did what we did, Jack. It hasn't hit home yet," she said.

"I know what you mean. I don't know if it's because I'm so tired, but I'm not even sleepy. Maybe this breakfast will kick in and get me back to normal."

"How much do you guess that gold is worth?" Mr. Douglas interjected.

"I have no idea," Jack replied. "Two whole crates? How much gold and how much silver? I guess we'll leave that to the museum to figure out."

"Jack," Yolanda began, "do you realize how much money we're going to get from this? We don't have to be detectives anymore. We can buy a vacation home in Florida or a country home in Maine or a mansion in California!"

"Slow down, Yolanda. That money could be tied up for years before we see any of it. We already know that the church is claiming it, who knows how many other people are going to want some of it."

"John Breckenridge never had a clue," Mr. Douglas observed. "He must have come here after the war and looked around. It would never have occurred to him that A.P. Hill took those crates all the way to Ivy. How did you figure that out, Sonny?"

"Mr. Douglas, honestly, from the very beginning we just took wild guesses at this. Yolanda made the big break when she found the duplicate shipping manifests. We had already arrived at the conclusion that Lynchburg was a dead end, so we decided that Charlottesville was the destination."

"And we figured that the safest place to hide the gold would be in a fake grave," Yolanda chimed in.

The waitress brought Jack's breakfast and Yolanda's muffin. She returned a few seconds later with the three plates that comprised Mr. Douglas' meal.

After Mr. Douglas polished off the last of his omelet, the three got back in the car and drove back to Ivy. When they got near the church, the road turned into a long, narrow parking lot. There were camera trucks, police cars, and assorted automobiles from curious gawkers as far as one could see.

"I didn't anticipate this," Jack said. "Shit."

"I wonder how long it will take," Yolanda commented.

"Considering that they're all going to the same place, I think we're pretty much locked in here. Yolanda, open your door and stand up. Can you see what's around this stupid truck?"

Yolanda unbuckled her seat belt, opened the door and leaned out as far as she could.

"It's just a grassy berm," she said.

"OK, buckle back up," Jack directed. As soon as she was, Jack turned the car to the right and started slowly driving up the side of the road. They made decent progress, disregarding the honking of horns as they narrowly missed side view mirrors. They made it to within a quarter mile of the church before the appearance of a culvert stopped their progress.

"Looks like we'll have to walk from here," Yolanda observed.

"Yeah," Jack answered. "You up for a little stroll, Mr. Douglas?"

"Don't worry about me, Sonny. I want to hear what those men from the museum are going to say at the press conference."

It took about ten minutes to cover the distance to the church. Jack was heartened when they got close enough that he could see Doctor Armbruster and Mr. Sedgewick, again sporting the pith helmets they had worn in Charlottesville.

As soon as they caught sight of Jack and Yolanda coming across the cemetery, Dr. Armbruster started waving frantically. Mr. Sedgewick remained stoic.

"Ms. Tilden! Mr. Clayton! How did you do this? We thought the cemetery in Charlottesville was your last guess," Armbruster said excitedly.

"We came to a new conclusion, Dr. Armbruster. We went back to Mr. Douglas' and brainstormed it. Ivy seemed like a natural solution to Hill's problem with the Union cavalry."

"But you were also correct regarding the body. How do you suppose Hill could have justified murdering his adjutant?"

"Two large crates of gold and silver, Dr. Armbruster, two large crates of gold and silver. You can imagine how Breckenridge felt after he heard of Hill's death. All the risk and the planning to get the gold out of Richmond and he didn't have the slightest clue where it ended up," Jack explained.

"Well, it's remarkable, no, it's unbelievable that you traced it here. No one else has even come close to this," Armbruster gushed.

At this point Yolanda decided to join the conversation. "Dr. Armbruster, we've been up for a long time and it's been physically and emotionally exhausting. Do you mind if we speed this up a bit and get the press conference over?"

"Oh, I am so sorry, Ms. Tilden. Of course, how thoughtless of me. Mr. Sedgewick! Let's have the deputies put those reporters in some sort of order so we can begin the presentation."

In less than ten minutes, the five of them stood in front of several microphones and cameras. Dr. Armbruster began the press conference.

"Welcome, ladies and gentlemen. I am Dr. Claude Armbruster of the Museum of the Confederacy in Richmond. Allow me to introduce my esteemed colleague, Mr. Howard Sedgewick." Sedgewick gave a gallant wave while displaying a cheesy smile. "Several months ago we learned of the exploits of two former Indianapolis detectives, who managed to resolve a twenty-year old cold case. We decided that they had the deductive skills to do the same with the one hundred and fifty-year old legend of lost Confederate gold. Mr. Sedgewick and I had the utmost confidence that they had the skills and intelligence to uncover the clues that had eluded countless professional and amateur treasure seekers and be able to trace the movement of a long lost shipment of gold and silver..."

Bullshit. Jack and Yolanda shared the same thought at the same moment.

"...and with the help of a renowned local Civil War expert, Mr. Roger Douglas, we can proudly stand before you today and tell all of you that the search ended here early this morning. Successfully ended might I add. Now let me have Mr. Jack Clayton say a few words regarding this endeavor."

The press section burst into a babble of shouted questions as cameras focused on Jack. He simply held up his hands until it got quiet again.

"This was a long shot," he began. "I've got to tell you that I doubted this from the very beginning. It was only through the perseverance and foresight of my partner, Ms. Yolanda Tilden, that we ended up here this morning. And you know, when more of the story is told, lots of you will say it was luck. It really wasn't. We worked so hard at putting together a logical sequence of events that it all fell into place. We had our share of failures and false leads, but the underlying interpretation was right on the money. That's about it for now. I'll let Dr. Armbruster and Mr. Sedgewick finish up. Ms. Tilden, Mr. Douglas, and I are a little tired and we need some time to unwind."

With that, Mr. Sedgewick stepped forward and began answering questions. Jack took Yolanda's arm and led her to the side of the reporters and back down to where they had left the car. Mr. Douglas brought up the rear. It took quite a bit of maneuvering to get the car pointed away from the ongoing press conference, but Yolanda helped by standing outside and letting Jack know when he was about to scrape a news truck. Eventually they were bumping back along the berm until Jack could move over into the east-bound lane towards Charlottesville. They dropped Mr. Douglas off at his house. Yolanda checked and made sure that there were sufficient baggies set out for him. They promised that they would pick him up for dinner that night around six-thirty before heading back to the Doubletree.

48

THE GOLDEN GLOW

As soon as they entered their room, Yolanda went to the bed and plopped face down on it. Jack sat down on the desk chair and began taking his shoes off. Yolanda turned on her side to face him.

"I am so tired," she said. "And I am so excited, but I'm too tired to deal with it right now. Does that make sense?"

"I know what you mean," Jack answered. "It hasn't all hit me just yet."

"OK, I'm going to go shower now and then I just want to close my eyes. They feel so gritty."

"Go ahead, and then I'll take my turn, unless you…"

"No. I know what you're going to say, Jack. I'm tired. My turn, then your turn," she firmly stated.

Jack knew that was probably going to be the answer, but he couldn't let a possible opportunity pass by.

Within fifteen minutes Yolanda was asleep on her stomach with her head under the pillows. Jack was asleep next to her with his hand resting on the small of her back.

■ ■ ■

Jack woke up first. He looked over at the clock radio. It was almost four-thirty. He climbed out of bed and stretched. Then he walked over to Yolanda's side of the bed and knelt down. He gently lifted up the pillow and uncovered her head. He leaned forward and kissed her cheek, then he whispered, "Yolanda."

It took a couple more kisses before she squirmed a bit and then opened her eyes. She was still half-asleep. "Hmm...what is it, Jack? Why did you wake me up?"

"We're going to get Mr. Douglas in a little over an hour and I want to talk to you about what happened this morning before we pick him up."

"Umm...OK, let me go wash my face and get dressed. I also need to put on make-up before we go out."

"That's fine, we can talk while you do that."

Jack followed her into the bathroom and sat down on the floor with his back to the closed door. Yolanda washed her face and then opened up her cosmetic bag.

"Jack, how much money do you think our share will be?"

"We wouldn't know until all of it is recovered and valued. But it's like I said earlier, Yolanda. There will be so many claims laid on that gold and silver, that it might be years before we get to see any of it, or maybe none at all."

"But that wouldn't be fair, Jack, that was part of our deal with the museum."

Jack watched her doing something to her eye with some kind of clamp-like instrument that looked dangerous to him.

"Yes, but remember, the museum thought it was nonsense and we were just supposed to prove it didn't exist. Their claim to the gold really doesn't have much substance. Supposedly the church wants a cut of it, but I have a sneaking suspicion about who's going to walk off with it."

"Who, Jack?"

"The Federal Government, that's who. They're going to claim that any goods or valuables that once belonged to the Confederate States of America are going to pass to the United States Treasury as a result of the Treaty of Appomattox. That's my take on it."

"But we had a contract."

"Yes, but governments go crazy about stuff like this. Some group of investors helped fund the recovery of a ship wreck a few years ago. Somehow they found it and recovered something like forty million dollars' worth. Unfortunately the investors never saw a cent of it."

"So this was all for nothing?" she asked sadly.

"No, not the way you sometimes look at things. You were so proud of all the cases we were offered after we found Annie, just think of how many more we're going to get now. We might not get that mansion in Florida or California you were talking about just yet, but we're going to have lots of cases to consider."

"Yeah, I see your point."

"And besides, we don't want to sit around doing nothing. We're Clayton and Tilden Investigations. Oh, I forgot the LLC," he laughed.

"I guess you're right, Jack. I just didn't see that stuff about the money being tied up coming."

"OK, I'll let you finish up, then let's go get Roger." Jack left the bathroom and got dressed for dinner.

THE DAILY PROGRESS

Charlottesville, Virginia

Sorry, Geraldo, you and Al Capone are back in the running.

An amazing event occurred yesterday morning in a church cemetery in Ivy. The same investigators, who unsuccessfully searched the Confederate cemetery in Charlottesville a few days ago, discovered the final resting place of the Confederate gold that had only been an unsubstantiated rumor since the spring of 1865.

Museum of the Confederacy officials made a hasty return visit to the Charlottesville area when notified of the discovery. County sheriffs were also on the scene earlier, when the investigators notified them not only of the discovery of the gold, but also unearthing the remains of a Confederate soldier.

Although initially detained for trespassing and disturbing a gravesite, the historical significance of the find led to the charges against the three persons involved.

Mr. Jack Clayton stated that the discovery of the location did not involve as much guesswork as it did the careful application of logic. He and his partner, Ms. Yolanda Tilden, had recreated the probable chain of events from period documents, weather conditions, actions of the Union forces, and finally the desperation of the personnel in charge of the gold shipment at the end of the war.

Mr. Clayton credited his partner with the initial discovery of the documents that led them to Charlottesville and also the Civil War expert who assisted them during the search for the site, Mr. Roger Douglas of Charlottesville.

Museum officials, who earlier had expressed relief at the debunking of the gold legend, seemed overjoyed that the discovery had finally been made. The private investigators pleaded exhaustion and left the remainder of the interviews and explanations to the museum curators.

The final disposition of the gold and silver bars remains in contention from several parties including the museum, the church where the gravesite was found, and several federal and state government agencies. As Doctor Claude Armbruster pointed out, the ownership rights of the treasure might not be decided for months.

49

A NIGHT OUT WITH ROGER

Much to their surprise, Roger was waiting for them in front of his house when they pulled up. Jack still had the rental car from the previous day and thought it would be more comfortable than the museum van. An even bigger surprise came when Roger climbed into the back seat.

"Roger," Yolanda said slowly, "you smell nice this evening."

"Well, since we're maybe going to be a little famous for a bit, I thought I'd better gussy myself up a bit. Never know if you might run into a lovely lady or two," he smiled.

"You'd better stick to just one at a time," Jack advised. "So, Roger, where to for dinner? Italian? Chinese?"

"Please not Chinese," Yolanda begged.

"Well, it's a bit further out, but how about German?" Roger asked.

"German?" Jack and Yolanda both said.

"I love German food," Jack added.

"I don't know," Yolanda said, "isn't it just sausage and something called a schnitzel? What is a schnitzel anyway?"

"There's a place way up in northern Greene County called the Bavarian Chef. It's got really good food," Roger replied. "Oh, and a schnitzel? It's usually either breaded veal or pork."

Jack made the necessary turns and went north on Route 29. A few miles out of town, Roger pointed out a large, modern building on the right.

"That's an Army place," he explained. "It's actually the Army's intelligence center. No place for tourists though, hush-hush secret stuff."

"Really?" Yolanda said, "In Charlottesville? Isn't this kind of backwater for something like that? Is it sort of CIA-related?"

"I guess," Roger replied, "I've known some folks who work there. I think they basically take CIA documents, change a few words and phrases, and then claim them as their own. Not too well respected in the intelligence community."

"Huh," Jack added, "I was in the Army Security Agency back in the day, I guess that's ancient history now."

"Can I have a beer when we get there?" Roger asked.

"You can have all the beer you want," Yolanda turned and patted his arm, "You deserve it, Roger."

Roger probably had the biggest smile since they had met him.

Jack found the restaurant on the left side of the highway. They parked the car and went inside. Luckily they didn't have to wait for a table; a young lady in a dirndl led them upstairs to a quaint German dining table.

Yolanda was a little hesitant about ordering, but went for a sausage appetizer and a bowl of tomato bisque soup with crab meat. Both Jack and Roger ordered pork chops that were soon served on an enormous plate.

"You think both of you can eat all that?" Yolanda asked.

"Just watch us," Jack laughed.

During the meal they made plans for their next step.

"Mr. Douglas, how would you like to come with us back to Richmond, say the day after tomorrow? We have to return the van and there will probably be at least one or two more press conferences," Jack added.

"Sure, I kind of like all this attention," he answered.

"I'll turn the rental car in tomorrow and we'll head out pretty early. I do want to get rid of the museum van and say a fond farewell to Armbruster and Sedgewick." Jack's expression revealed how fond that farewell would be.

"I can't believe you guys ate those humongous pork chops." That was Yolanda's final contribution to the victory dinner.

50

BACK IN RICHMOND

Wednesday passed uneventfully. Jack did get the rental car returned and that was the major accomplishment of the day. After breakfast at the hotel, they picked up Mr. Douglas by 8:30. His luggage consisted of a rather beat-up looking suitcase and a blue gym bag. Before leaving, Yolanda made sure that there was an ample supply of blue pills in her purse.

Jack didn't need his GPS to find the hotel this time, but he groaned a bit when he saw that Grace was at the main desk.

"Yolanda!" Grace happily greeted them.

There's more than one person standing here. Jack decided to stay calm and let the gabfest run its course.

"Grace! Have you heard the news? We found the gold! We really did!" Yolanda excitedly announced.

"Oh, my gracious, yes! Why it's been the talk of the town! It's been all over the newspapers and the TV news! I am so proud of you, dear."

Humph, is that "you" singular or plural, Jack thought.

"It took a lot of thinking and guesswork to get that done, Grace, we were so fortunate. Oh, and it wasn't just Jack and me." She turned and pulled Mr. Douglas up to the desk. "Let me introduce you to our friend and Civil War expert, Grace. Roger Douglas, this is Grace Levings, we met her when we first came to Richmond. Grace, Roger was invaluable in helping us discover the whereabouts of the gold."

"Pleased to meet you, Mr. Douglas. My, a Civil War expert, you must have so many interesting stories to tell," Grace smiled.

"Well, maybe a few," Roger replied, accompanied by his trademark eyebrow waggle.

Holy crap, Yolanda thought, *Roger is putting on his game face!*

"Uh, Grace," Yolanda interrupted, "we're going out to dinner this evening, around seven or so, would you like to join us? We can tell you about the treasure hunt and maybe Mr. Douglas can share some of those stories he mentioned."

"Oh, that would be wonderful," Grace replied, gazing at Mr. Douglas with new-found interest.

Are you kidding me? Jack asked himself. *Now I have to spend an evening with her?*

"When does your shift end, Grace?" Yolanda asked.

"I'm done at four this afternoon. That will give me time to go home and freshen up," Grace said.

"I'm sure that task would be nothing more than gilding a lily," Mr. Douglas noted.

Grace actually blushed, then reached out and patted his arm, "You are such a gentleman," she gushed.

Eyebrow, eyebrow, eyebrow.

Holy crap! A thought shared by two other people standing at the front desk.

Grace gave Yolanda her address and then distributed three room keycards. They escorted Mr. Douglas to his room and gave him instructions to take a nap, then shower and pick out something appropriate to wear to dinner. Yolanda also made sure that he took two of his pills.

"So, two rooms again?" Jack noted.

"Yes, but we're only using one, don't worry, Jack." She kissed him on the cheek. "I think we can dispense with the formality during the rest of this trip."

That cheered Jack up immensely. "Oh, and did you notice how nice I was to Grace today?" he asked.

"Yes, Jack, you have come such a long way in your dealings with others," she noted, with just a touch of sarcasm.

"Just saying."

"Yes, Jack, I get it. We are unpacking and getting a nap in too. A nap, Jack, don't get any ideas, I'm not in the mood today."

Well, I guess that was a wasted "nice."

■ ■ ■

At six o'clock they collected Mr. Douglas. Yolanda inspected his attire and approved it, but she did send him back into the bathroom to seriously re-comb his hair. It appeared that he had reversed the nap-shower sequence to shower-nap. His hair-do looked like he had stuck a paper clip into an electrical outlet.

Jack reclaimed his Buick and punched Grace's address into the GPS. She didn't live very far from downtown and in less than fifteen minutes, Jack pulled up in front of a small, Craftsman-style bungalow.

"I'll go and ring the doorbell," Mr. Douglas said as he quickly unbuckled his seatbelt and opened the car door.

"Fine," Jack said as he watched him hustle up the sidewalk. "You know," he turned to look at Yolanda. "I think Mr. Douglas is kind of motivated about something. What do you think?"

"We both saw the eyebrow waggles. At least I'm no longer the intended target. I wonder if that should make me feel sad?" she laughed.

"I wonder if he made another trip to the pharmacy for some of his 'peter pills.' Oops, here they come."

Mr. Douglas gallantly opened the door for Grace, then walked around behind the car and got in next to her.

"We forgot one important thing, Grace," Yolanda said, "we never decided where we should go. Do you have a suggestion?"

"Oh, you all would love Bookbinder's! It is so good and it's near the river. Steaks and seafood! So scrumptious," she exclaimed.

"That sounds good to me," Mr. Douglas agreed. Eyebrow, eyebrow, eyebrow.

"All I need is an address to put in the GPS," Jack said.

"Jack, let me take care of it," Yolanda said, picking up her cell phone. She punched in the name and, in a few moments, got Jack headed in the right direction.

"I didn't know your cell phone had a GPS on it. Does mine?" he asked.

"Uh no, Jack, I got you one that, well, is a little simpler to deal with."

Jack frowned and was about to say something when Yolanda whispered, "Just let it go, Jack, we don't need things on our phones that we wouldn't use much. Besides, I really like your GPS."

Jack smiled at that. *Seriously*, she thought, *I should write a book on relationships.*

Grace's suggestion was a good one; they thoroughly enjoyed their entrees and Mr. Douglas entertained them with funny stories about his sales career and left the Civil War pretty much out of it.

51

MR. DOUGLAS HITS THE JACKPOT

For the second time that evening, Jack stopped in front of Grace's house.

"Would you all like to come in for some coffee?" she invited.

"No thanks, not tonight, Grace," Yolanda said. "I'm stuffed and I think I just want to go back to the hotel and put on some pajamas and relax."

"Oh, that's too bad, maybe the next time," Grace said. Then she turned to Mr. Douglas, "I do have some interesting historical books dating back to the antebellum South, if you would like to come in for a bit. I'll be glad to drop you back off at your hotel later this evening."

Mr. Douglas took that bait like a starving rainbow trout in a mountain lake.

Yolanda and Jack watched as he offered his arm and proceeded to lead her up the sidewalk to her porch before heading back to the hotel.

"Uh, Jack, do you think Grace has plans for Mr. Douglas?" she asked.

"I have a feeling that a couple of the historical items he's going to be checking out are quite likely a bit personal in nature," Jack laughed. "Good for him."

"I can't believe Grace is a first date kind of lady, Jack. She seems so prim and proper."

"Well, I imagine that she's not been, uh, with anyone for about as long as our friend, Roger. Good for her too, I guess. Uh, maybe there's a 'good for me' coming up soon," Jack looked over at Yolanda and waggled his eyebrow.

"That's funny, Jack, but please don't do that again. And no, there's no good time coming your way for at least five to six days."

"You mean…"

"Yes, I mean that exactly. Now get us back, I really do need to go to bed, I ache all over."

I never would have thought that Mr. Douglas was going to get more action than me tonight. Sigh.

52

JACK HEARS A STORY

A lot happened the next day. First off Jack and Yolanda were treated to the sight of Mr. Douglas sneaking into the lobby while they were finishing breakfast. It appeared that he had misplaced his tie and his hair was sticking up all over the place again. He didn't see them in the hotel dining room, but the expression on his face was one of complete self-satisfaction.

After breakfast they knocked on his door and actually got him out of bed. His excuse? He had difficulty falling asleep last night after Ms. Levings had dropped him off. That was met with great sympathy. The next stop was the museum, where Jack dropped off the van at its service garage. Yolanda had followed him in his Buick. Dr. Armbruster had arranged another press conference. Most of the questions had to do with the whereabouts or the dispersal of the gold and silver. Obviously the museum was no longer in possession of it, so Jack figured it was a hundred miles or so north in another well-known city.

That afternoon they went to a local TV station where they were interviewed for a feature on the six o'clock and eleven o'clock news. Everything was wrapped up by late afternoon. Yolanda wanted to stop and have a light, early dinner. After they got back to the hotel she decided that maybe a visit to the hotel fitness room would make her feel better or at least take her mind off her aches and pains.

Jack decided that he would just go down to the bar and have a drink. He certainly wasn't interested in working out.

The bartender had just put Jack's scotch in front of him when two men wearing dark suits came in and sat a couple of stools down from him. They looked to be in their mid to late twenties. With 90% certainty, Jack pegged them as FBI. Their cocktails arrived and he also noticed that they had fruit in them. *What's the world coming to?*

After a few minutes had gone by, one of them leaned forward and looked over at Jack.

"Hey, I saw you on the news just now. Aren't you the guy who discovered all that Confederate gold?" he asked.

Jack nodded, "Yeah, that was me, with a lot of help."

The two men stood up, picked up their drinks, and moved to the stools on Jack's right.

"I thought that was you," the closer one remarked. Jack identified him as Blue Tie. "You've been all over the TV news and even the local papers."

"That was so cool," the second one added. *Green Tie.* "I mean to go after something that far-fetched and to actually find it is amazing."

"There was a lot of luck involved," Jack shrugged and took a sip of his scotch. "Let me guess something. Both of you are FBI, right? Or Homeland Security?"

"FBI," Green Tie affirmed. "How could you tell?"

Jack didn't explain that dark suits, conservative ties, and ubiquitous sunglasses hanging from a suit pocket didn't leave much room for doubt, he just shrugged.

"What was the big break? I mean what made you decide to look in that cemetery?" Blue Tie asked.

"Well," Jack studied the level of scotch remaining in his glass, "the break came when we found duplicate manifests for the same cargo, one listing Lynchburg as the destination and the second one was sent to Charlottesville. That's what led us there. I can't take the credit for that one, my partner found them. Once we got there, it was just some lucky deductive reasoning," Jack explained.

"What was the deductive reasoning?" Green Tie wanted to know.

Jack sighed and motioned for a refill.

"A.P. Hill had two crates of gold and silver and found himself in the middle of Sheridan's cavalry. He needed to hide it someplace that wouldn't be accidently found. We figured that a graveyard would fulfill that need."

"But what led you to that graveyard in Ivy?" Blue Tie chipped in.

Jack's second scotch had arrived. "It was the logical direction from Charlottesville, but believe me, it wasn't the first cemetery we searched. We knew that Custer had patrols on the southern and eastern sides of the city, so we borrowed an old map from a local historian, tried to figure out a logical course of action, and took a shot at Ivy. Turned out to be the right one."

"Amazing," Green Tie remarked.

"So, you guys doing the Yemeni domestic terrorist thing?" Jack asked.

"How do you know about that?" Green Tie asked.

"I met one of the other agents here a couple of weeks ago. Galen Foster. He told me that the FBI was working the I-95 and I-64 corridors for Yemen sympathizers."

Blue Tie and Green Tie exchanged wide grins.

"What's so funny?" Jack asked.

"Uh, it's just that Foster filled us in on a couple of things," Blue Tie explained.

"What kind of things? You lost me there," Jack said.

Blue Tie leaned closer to Jack. "It's your partner, that hot babe you work with."

"What about her?"

Another exchange of grins. "You know how it goes with guys," Green Tie said, "Foster just shared some good intelligence about her. They went out on a date the last time he was in Richmond."

"It wasn't exactly a date," Jack said. "They went out to dinner to get caught up on things since the academy."

"Well, it may not have been a date, but according to Foster, she threw him one of the wildest fucks he's ever had," Green Tie giggled.

Jack sat up straight and turned to face Green Tie.

"What are you talking about?"

"I guess they had some drinks at the restaurant and on the way back, she reaches over, pulls his dick out, and gives him a case of road head right on the outerbelt!" Green Tie exclaimed.

"And then they had a couple of drinks at the hotel bar, when she stands up and sticks her tongue further down his throat than anyone ever had," Blue Tie added.

"And then she took him up to her room and did him every which way but loose. I mean she straddled him, did him straight, and then got on her hands and knees and he pounded her from behind. Foster was really disappointed that you guys left the next day, because he really wanted a go at Round Two," Green Tie laughed.

"Hell, we would have all liked to get some of that," Blue Tie added. "I mean, you're a lot older than her, so you might not know what she does in her free time, but she sounds pretty hot and good at what she does," Blue Tie chuckled. "Hell, you never know, maybe she might throw one your way some time. Now that would be a great fringe benefit to being partners."

Jack didn't say anything. He stood up and tossed a twenty dollar bill on the bar before striding out of the room.

The two FBI agents just looked at each other and then started talking baseball.

PART TWO

53

THE FAT LADY SANG

Jack left the bar and walked out of the hotel. He started walking, slowly at first, and then built up to a power walk. What he had just heard kept echoing in his head. He had seen the kiss, he had seen the ass grab, and he had seen her arm go up around his neck. That was all that happened, she told him. That was all that happened. Now he knew what really happened. She had lied to him. She had lied straight to his face and even cried. The echoes slowly died away and were replaced by a stone-cold anger.

He turned and traced his steps back to the hotel. He opened the door to the room. It was dark. Suddenly he heard Yolanda's voice.

"Jack? Is that you? I'm sorry, Babe, I'm just exhausted, so I went right to bed. We'll have breakfast in the morning, OK?"

"Yeah, yeah," he muttered, "sure, go to sleep."

He didn't even get an answer. He walked to the bathroom and looked at his reflection in the mirror. His eyes looked tired and haggard. Then the anger came over him again. He started cramming his toiletries into his shaving kit. After he zipped it closed, he opened the door and left it open. The light from the bathroom brightened the room enough for him to see Yolanda in her trademark sleep pose with her head under her pillow.

He stepped over to the closet and retrieved his suitcase. Quietly he opened the dresser drawers and placed his clothing into the suitcase. He looked around the room to see if there was anything he had overlooked. Then he went to the desk and sat down. He took the cheap hotel ballpoint pen and began writing Yolanda a note. After he finished, he placed it under the base of the desk lamp. He picked up the suitcase and walked to the door. Then he stopped and put it down. He turned and walked back to the foot of the bed. He simply stood there for a long moment, looking at her sleeping form. Finally he turned and went to the door. He didn't stop this time.

■ ■ ■

Sunlight was streaming through the window the next morning. Yolanda hadn't bothered closing the curtains the night before. It always took her a little while to wake up. She wasn't like Jack who could hop out of bed the moment the alarm went off. She finally got both eyes open and discovered that Jack had already gotten up. *I wonder how late I slept,* she wondered. *Whoa, nine-thirty, no wonder he's up and gone. Probably down at breakfast.* She yawned and stumbled into the bathroom to shower. The bathroom mirror was all steamy after her shower. It didn't make any difference anyway, because she wouldn't put on her make-up until her hair dried. She decided to put it in a ponytail and go have some breakfast. She slipped into her bra and panties and put on a t-shirt and a pair of running shorts. It was just breakfast after all.

She looked around the dining room. There were just a few people eating and no Jack was in sight. *We must have passed each other or he's out doing something else.* She grabbed a bowl for some oatmeal and a second one for some fruit. She still felt a little tired and decided to try a cup of coffee for a change.

After breakfast she went back upstairs. Still no Jack. No big deal. This time, however, when she went into the bathroom to do her eyes, she noticed that all his stuff was gone, no razor, no toothbrush, no nothing. She put down her make-up and walked to the dresser and pulled the drawers open. Empty. Then she checked the closet and saw that the only suitcases left were hers. Puzzled, she looked around the room and then saw the piece of paper on the desk. She lifted it up from under the desk lamp and began to read it.

Yolanda,

I've been doing a lot of thinking the last few days and watching Roger and Grace made me realize just how old I am. I kind of liked our Confederate gold case for a while, but I've decided that it's really not for me. I think I'm just going to call it quits with that. So, I'm retiring from our so-called LLC. You can keep working cases without me, I'm just tired of it. As far as you and me go, you need to find someone closer to your age, you don't need me in your life. When we first met you called me a fossil. I still am, nothing's changed about that. Look, I'm going to hang out around here and maybe do some Civil War sight-seeing for a few weeks. You should go back to Indianapolis and take care of stuff there. Find yourself someplace to live and move your things out of the house. Maybe I'll check in at the office sometime to see how things are going, but it won't be for several months. I'm sorry, but I think it's best to make a clean break of this, so I blocked your number. I had to ask someone to show me how to do that. On the bright side, you get to fly back to Indianapolis instead of the long car drive. Bye, Yolanda, have a happy rest of your life.

Jack

"Jack?" she said out loud. "It doesn't make any sense, Jack. Why?" Her eyes started tearing up, and she curled up in a ball on the bed and started sobbing. The crying lasted for a long time, then she finally fell asleep again.

■ ■ ■

She woke up an hour later and then remembered the note. It was wadded up in her hand. She spread it open again and read it for the second time. She didn't cry. She got up and went into the bathroom. Her eyes were bright red and swollen. She blew her nose on a tissue, and then automatically went through her make-up routine. Her mind, thankfully, decided not to work, and she finished and put on some nicer clothes before going down to the front desk.

Grace was there.

"Good morning, Yolanda," she said. "My, sweetie, are you feeling all right? You don't look like your normal, happy self."

"No, you're right, I'm kind of out of it this morning. Say, have you seen Jack today? I haven't run across him yet."

"No, and I've been here since six this morning."

"And you haven't seen him?" Yolanda asked again. With dread in her voice, she asked the next question. "Can you look and see if anyone checked out last night?"

"Well, sure, sweetheart, just a second." Grace pulled the mouse closer to the computer and clicked it a couple of times. "Well, now, that's odd," she observed. "It appears that Mr. Clayton checked out of the hotel around nine o'clock last night!"

Yolanda couldn't help it, she started crying again.

"Land's sake, Yolanda, what's wrong?"

"He left me," she sobbed. "He just up and went and only left me a note. He didn't even say good-bye to me. I was already half-asleep when he came into the room last night. Now I know he just packed up and left when I was asleep."

Grace came around the counter and walked her over to one of the loveseats in the lobby. She pulled Yolanda down next to her and put her arms around her. Yolanda cried like a baby.

"There, there," Grace comforted her, "I don't know why he would have done that, Sweetheart, but it's going to be OK. You're going to get through this. Nobody knows what men think sometimes."

Yolanda sat up straight and wiped her eyes with her hands.

"Just sit here a minute and compose yourself, Yolanda, I'll get you a tissue."

In a moment Grace came back with a handful of tissues and Yolanda started repairing the damage to her make-up that the crying bout had done.

"Is Mr. Douglas still here?" Yolanda sniffed, then blew her nose again.

"I believe so, the only person who has checked out was your partner."

"I guess I'll have to get him back to Charlottesville, then I'm flying back to Indiana," Yolanda said.

"Uh, actually Roger, uh, Mr. Douglas has decided to stay here for a bit. He's going to give me a tour of local Civil War sites."

That did make Yolanda smile for a moment. "I'm glad that you and Mr. Douglas have hit it off, Grace. I think he's a very nice man. Oh, I need to tell you something; sometimes he forgets to take his medications. You have to be very aware of that."

"Gracious, I had no idea, thank you for letting me know." Grace leaned forward a little conspiratorially. "Maybe I needn't tell you this, but Mr. Douglas and I, well, we were actually intimate the other night. I swear, Yolanda, sometimes I don't know who I've become."

"That's OK, Grace," Yolanda said, patting her arm. "I suspected as much, but you know, times have changed, you are still a perfect lady."

Grace simpered at that remark.

"OK," Yolanda stood up. "Thanks for letting me have my cry, Grace. I think I'll stay here tonight and fly back tomorrow. You and Mr. Douglas enjoy your time together, you've been so kind to me."

That brought a tear to Grace's eye also and they hugged each other before Yolanda went back upstairs to book a flight back to Indiana. A single ticket.

54

JACK FINDS A MYSTERY, YOLANDA HAS A REVELATION

Jack really didn't know where to go or what to do. He had put his suitcase in the back of the Buick and climbed behind the wheel. He looked at his GPS, it wasn't going to tell where to go. He didn't even feel so angry anymore, just a little empty and a whole lot lonely. He drove to the west side of Richmond and found a Best Western motel. He didn't get much sleep. The image of Yolanda and Foster kept going through his head. He finally gave up and got up around five in the morning and checked out. There wasn't any point to hanging around Richmond, so he began driving west on I-64 back toward Charlottesville. He did stop on the eastern edge of the city, there was an exit off the interstate that promised a home-style breakfast and he needed to stop for a restroom break anyway.

The restaurant was crowded with the before-work diners. Jack ended up sitting at the counter and ordering. After the waitress put his eggs in front of him, he realized that he didn't really feel like eating. He put some jelly from one of those tiny, hard-to-open packets on one piece of toast and ate it while finishing his second cup of coffee. After paying the bill and using the restroom, he wandered back into the parking lot. He noticed that there were two identical vans parked on the right side of his Buick. Both of them had Greene County Schools emblazoned on their sides. Jack paused for a moment and then walked over and examined them more closely. The design was painted on.

Jack went back to his car and started it.

Greene County Schools? I wonder why that school district would have vehicles with painted logos and some with magnets. The day I picked up the car magnets, that guy's order had Green and Schools on it, I wonder if there was an "e" on the end of Green.

Jack started his car and began to pull out of the parking lot, then he braked and found another open spot. He went back into the restaurant and looked around for customers wearing coveralls or uniforms with the Greene County Schools logo. He located them at two tables near the kitchen entrance and walked over to them.

"Morning," he said, "My name's Jack Clayton, I just have a question about your vans outside. Is that OK?"

"Sure," answered a lanky, red-haired man. "What do you want to know?"

"Well, your school vehicles, are they all painted with the same logo?"

The red-haired man laughed, "Yeah, as far as I know. How else would they be painted?"

"I was just wondering if the district ever used magnetic signs instead of having them painted. It seems like it would be cheaper."

An older, heavier man at the table answered this time. "Probably would be, don't know about that. I ain't never seen any vans like that, but it wouldn't surprise me none."

I hate double negatives. "Thanks," Jack said, "I was just wondering." He walked back out to his car. *It's probably nothing, it makes sense to save money when you can.*

Jack got back into the Buick and started it. Just as he started to head to the I-64 entrance ramp, he changed his mind and turned back toward Route 29.

It's too early for the sign store to be open. He glanced at the clock on the dashboard. *Seven-thirty. I have to kill an hour and a half, I don't need any more coffee, so what do I do?*

Jack decided to go all the way up to the Sam's Club by the Doubletree. He spent over an hour looking at random tools, books, and gaudy Hawaiian shirts. They reminded him of Yolanda and her negative attitude toward his sizeable collection of similar shirts. *I guess I can wear anything I damn well please now.*

He finally gave up and drove to the sign store parking lot with about fifteen minutes to wait. He got out of the car, did some impatient window-shopping, and ended up waiting right in front of the entrance at nine o'clock.

As soon as an employee unlocked the door, Jack pushed through it and went to the counter. He pulled out his private investigator badge and quickly flashed it, hoping it would pass him off as an official law enforcement officer. It seemed to work, because the clerk, who appeared to be in his late teens or early twenties at the best, swallowed noticeably and adapted an ill-at-ease posture.

"I have a couple of questions regarding a recent order," Jack explained. "There seems to be a possible issue of fraudulent usage of magnetic car signs that may have been manufactured at your store."

The clerk swallowed again and nervously scratched at a recently erupted bit of acne.

"Uh, yeah, I guess I can help you with that," he said. "What kind of signs were they?"

"They were for the Albemarle County Engineering Department." Jack said.

"Got any idea about when?" he asked.

Jack smiled. "Yes, it would have been either the 9th or 10th of this month."

The clerk turned to the computer and typed in the 9th along with the name of the department. "Nope, not on the 9th," he retyped the date to the 10th. "Yeah, here it is. Uh, some guy purchased two signs, guess it must have been for a car or truck, because they were over-sized."

"Ah, I see," Jack noted. "Any name?"

"It says Roger Douglas, paid in cash, so there isn't an address."

"Can you print me out the list of the rest of the transactions on that date? It could provide an excellent lead," Jack requested.

"Sure thing," the clerk agreed. "Uh, don't you need a warrant or something though? I don't want to get in trouble with my boss."

Jack leaned forward. "Yes, I can get a warrant, but...," he leaned even closer. "That would also include personnel files of all the employees. You know, sometimes there are connections to things that just pop up when we start looking in-depth. As a matter of fact, just last month we uncovered a marijuana pipeline, just by a random employee file check."

That information caused the clerk to pale considerably, making his acne almost a glow-in-the-dark item.

"Oh, in that case, I guess I can just keep it to myself, no point in you having to get into all that paperwork," this statement was accompanied by a sickly grin.

"Great," Jack answered. "Look, I'll just look around for a few minutes while you get that printout done for me."

The clerk quickly went back to his computer, then hurried into a small office where the printer was obviously located. It only took five minutes before he returned with a manila folder.

"Here, officer," he said as he handed Jack the folder.

Jack peeked inside; there were six pages of copy paper listing the total transactions for that day's business.

"Thanks, so much, you've been very helpful," Jack praised.

"Uh, and that sort of takes care of everything, I mean like warrants and stuff?" the clerk nervously inquired.

"Yes, I think I'm done here, like I said, thanks a lot. I'll even try to keep your name out of the investigation. Unless," Jack added, "it becomes necessary."

One last hard swallow was the clerk's final contribution to the conversation.

Jack took the folder back out to his car and settled himself in before opening the folder.

OK, the guy with the Greene County Schools magnets checked out right in front of me.

Jack ran his finger down the list of names and found Roger Douglas halfway down the third sheet. Albemarle County Engineering Department was the job description. He moved up one to the Greene County Schools. Jack gave a low whistle, the customer name was Ahmoud Assan.

■ ■ ■

Yolanda didn't end up buying a ticket; every time she called she seemed to be on terminal hold. She wandered back downstairs and found Mr. Douglas firmly ensconced by the front desk chatting up Grace.

"Hi, Mr. Douglas, do you want to go and get some lunch? I'm kind of bored."

It took Mr. Douglas a moment or two to tear himself away from the endearing looks that Grace was giving him.

Good grief, Yolanda thought, *this is like a high school romance.*

"Oh, sure," he answered, "Grace, any chance you can join us?"

"I'm so sorry, Roger, but I'm on duty until two. I would love to go to lunch with you, but I can't."

"What if I come by at two and we can, uh, maybe go back to your house and talk about our, uh, trip?" he asked. Waggle, waggle, waggle.

Holy crap, it's like Jack thought. Once he got started with the sex thing, no woman, in this case Grace, would be safe from him.

"Oh, I would love that," Grace tittered.

Oh, God, no mental images, please! Stop!

"OK," Yolanda interjected, "let's go grab something to eat. Then I need to go by the museum and let them know I'm going back to Indiana."

"Where's Mr. Clayton?" Mr. Douglas inquired.

Yolanda sighed. "I don't know, Mr. Douglas, he decided to leave and didn't tell me where he was going. I guess our partnership has ended."

"Funny," he observed, "didn't see that coming."

"Me neither," Yolanda sadly said, "me neither."

By the time lunch was over and the required farewell trip to the museum was done, it was way past two o'clock. Yolanda ended up dropping an extremely impatient Roger Douglas off in front of Grace's house. She marveled at two things: first of all the speed he mustered in heading up the sidewalk and the speed that Grace displayed in yanking him inside. She could only imagine what was happening next, in spite of her best hopes to avoid it.

She drove back to the hotel, went up to her room, and stretched out on the bed.

I just don't understand what happened. Did Jack really mean what he said in that note? Why? He never let on that he was unhappy and then he basically sneaked out, that's so unlike him.

Eventually she fell asleep. When she woke up, she looked over at the clock. It said 7:20. She wasn't hungry, but thought she might as well go downstairs and maybe order a salad. For some reason, maybe a convention or tour group, the restaurant was full. The hostess directed her to the bar for a twenty minute wait.

She really wasn't interested in having a drink, but she didn't feel like standing at the hostess stand for that long either.

What happens when attractive young ladies sit down at a bar? Men are drawn as if by magic with offers of cocktails in hopes of later rewards. Surprisingly enough it was Blue Tie who landed on the stool next to her, although he was wearing a polo shirt and khakis.

"Hey, I know you," he started. "Can I buy you a drink?"

"No, I don't think so, just not interested in company this evening," she replied.

"But I wanted to ask you about that gold thing. You've been all over the news."

"Yeah, but seriously, I just don't care to talk. I'm just waiting for a table."

At this time Green Tie showed up, also not wearing his tie. He settled in on the other side of Yolanda.

"Let me apologize on behalf of my partner," he said. "Obviously he has been amazingly non-cavalier, since I see no beverage in front of a beautiful young lady."

"Stop," Yolanda said. "Look, I've had a bad day; I just want to get something to eat. I'm not in the mood to be hit on or engage in idle conversation. Buying me a drink will not get either of you any desired result."

"Bet you wouldn't feel that way if Galen Foster showed up," Blue Tie noted.

"You know Galen?" she asked.

"Sure, maybe not as well as you, but yeah, he's a fellow agent," Blue Tie continued.

"You're both FBI?"

"Yeah, we're working on the same task force as Galen." Green Tie said.

"He told me it had something to do with terrorist activities, something to do with Yemeni nationals," Yolanda said.

"That's it," Blue Tie said, "we were looking on the I-95 corridor, but it seems that there's more interest in activity connected to I-65 between Staunton and Richmond."

"You know," Green Tie smiled, "if you loosen up a bit and have a drink or two with us, we can give you some insight into the operation and you can tell us about the treasure thing."

"And maybe you'll see that we're just as friendly as Foster and maybe we might make this an evening to remember," Blue Tie added.

"Friendly? Yeah, I guess, I mean Galen and I were friends at the academy, it was just by coincidence that I ran into him."

The Ties both exchanged grins. "I guess you certainly did 'run' into him, so to speak," Blue Tie observed. Green Tie laughed.

Yolanda looked puzzled.

"Anyway," Blue Tie continued, "he told us all about you."

"All about you," Green Tie laughed.

"I don't get what's so funny," Yolanda said. "We were classmates at the academy, it's not like we ever went out or anything."

"Oh," Green Tie said, "I thought you and he had a dinner date not too long ago."

"Yeah, we went out for dinner, but it wasn't a date. We just wanted to catch up on things."

"Well, we would like to take you out for dinner too, maybe we could sort of catch up on things too," Blue Tie offered.

"What are you talking about? I don't even know you, what would we catch up on?"

"Look, you're right, you don't even know us. My name is Todd," Blue Tie said, "and this is Greg. OK, like I said, we're working on this Yemeni thing, we're friends with Foster and we thought maybe we could have some drinks, some dinner, and some fun later."

"Look, you're FBI, pay attention. I've already told you that I'm not in the mood for drinks and conversations."

"Well, maybe not tonight," Blue Tie said, "but there's always tomorrow night."

"Come on," Green Tie urged, "you solved a big case and you deserve a celebration of some kind. Besides, it doesn't have to be both of us, if that freaks you out. You can go out with Todd tonight and then you and I can go out tomorrow."

"What makes you think that I would want to go out with either of you?" she asked with a puzzled expression. "I don't get it."

"OK," Green Tie said, "we're here; you're here, I mean what's it going to hurt if you give us a little action like you gave Foster?"

"Action? What are you talking about?"

"Well, it's not like he was supposed to keep it a secret," Blue Tie laughed. "He said you were the best fuck he ever had. Hell, we're bored, let's get something to eat and head upstairs for the same wild ride you gave him. You don't want a threesome, sure, we get that, but like Greg said, one of us tonight and then the other tomorrow, unless you do want something a little kinkier."

"What?" Yolanda exclaimed. "I never had sex with Galen! He kissed me and pawed at me a little, but I told him I was with Jack."

"Your partner?" Green Tie asked. "We met him the other night. What do you mean you're 'with' him? Isn't he kind of old for you?"

"It's none of your business how old he might be," she angrily answered.

"You don't have to play innocent with us, we're all adults," Blue Tie observed. "It's no big deal that you fucked Foster. He said you were amazing. Hell, your partner didn't have any idea what a good lay you are. He couldn't believe it. One moment he was sitting next to us, then he just up and disappeared," Green Tie explained.

"Wait, you told Jack that I had sex with Galen?"

Blue Tie laughed, "Sure did, just about as graphically as Foster told us. I especially liked the part where you gave him road head on the outer belt."

"You told Jack all that?" Yolanda stood up.

"Where are you going? Seriously, why not hang around and have some fun?" Green Tie asked.

Yolanda turned without acknowledging him. Then she stopped and went back. "Where's Foster now? I need to talk to him."

"Talk?" Blue Tie asked with a chuckle.

"Fuck you, asshole; where is the lying son-of-a-bitch?"

"Whoa!" Blue Tie answered, spreading his hands in mock self-defense. "Foster's up in Greene County, north of Charlottesville."

"How can I get in touch with him? Do you know where he's staying?"

"I can give you his cell number. And I think he's staying at some Best Western off of 29. But you don't need to drive all the way there for some action, we remain dedicated to serving your every need, just like Federal Agent Foster did," Blue Tie winked at her.

"Just write down the fucking number," she snapped. As soon as Blue Tie finished writing on a bar napkin, she snatched it off the bar without saying another word. She didn't bother with the restaurant. She went upstairs and packed her suitcases and then called a rental car agency and arranged for them to drop the car off at the hotel. Then she lugged her bags down to the lobby and checked out.

Within fifteen minutes the rental car arrived. She had asked for a GPS and had looked on Google for the address of the only Best Western north on Route 29. It was called the Airport Inn. She quickly punched in the address and set it as the destination; it quickly guided her out of the city and put her westbound on I-64.

It wasn't until she got up to speed and put the car on cruise control that she allowed herself to digest what the two FBI agents had told her.

Oh, Jack, God damn it. Why did you believe them? Why didn't you come and yell at me? I could have told you it was all a lie. Tears came to her eyes. *You love me, you told me that. You mean I'm not even worth talking to? You take the word of two strangers about something that never happened and then you just leave? I'm going to find that lying asshole and fucking punch him in the face. Then you, Jack Clayton, are going to catch holy hell for running out like you did. Boy, will you ever!*

She forced herself to stop thinking about it and studied the GPS and the diminishing time until she reached the motel. The GPS directed her to exit before Route 29. She thought she would miss out on the traffic, but the road just shunted her to a different intersection. Traffic was still fairly heavy, even though it was after nine o'clock. She left Charlottesville behind her and drove on several miles until she was informed that her destination was just ahead on the right. It was a fairly new, three-story building with several shops in a semi-strip mall type setting. She parked in front and went inside.

"Can I help you?" the night clerk inquired.

"Yes, do you have a room available?" she asked.

"As a matter of fact, we have several. Queen? King? Double?" he inquired.

"I guess a queen will be fine," she answered.

"Just for you?"

"Yes, here's my credit card," she offered it to him.

He ran the credit card and then handed Yolanda a registration paper for her to sign. "How many nights do you plan to stay, ma'am?"

"I'm not sure, can I just let you know?"

"Sure, that's not a problem until this weekend, if you plan on staying that long. You'll have to reserve a room. We get booked quickly."

"OK, let's have me check out on Monday morning then, that will be five days. If I get my business done before then, I'll just check out early."

"Fine," he agreed, "Room 314, the elevators are down that hallway, breakfast is from 6:30 to 9:00."

"Can you tell me which room Galen Foster is in?" she asked.

"I'm sorry, we're not allowed to give out information about other guests, but if you go out the front door, there's a restaurant to your right. There are a couple of gentlemen in his party and they often go there in the evening."

"Thank you very much," Yolanda said. She went outside and considered taking her bags up to her room, but then decided that the most important thing for her to do was confront Foster and see if she was really angry enough to punch him. She moved her car to an empty spot, locked it, and then walked over to the restaurant.

Lord Hardwicke's? Seriously?

She pushed the door open and entered the restaurant. A sign on the hostess stand said "seat yourself." She looked around at the customers, hoping to spot Galen, but she didn't see him. She did see three men seated at the bar. They all had short hair and similar polo shirts on.

They are either FBI or Mormons, and since they're drinking beer, I'll guess FBI.

She approached them, setting off the type of expressions that one would expect from three men having a good-looking babe come up to them for a change.

"Hi, gorgeous!" said one, "C'mon, have a beer with us."

"Uh, no thank you," she said, "but can I ask you a question?"

"Sure thing, Babe, what do you want to know. I'm single if that's the question," he laughed.

"No, not that; you guys are FBI, right?"

They exchanged quick glances at one another.

"Uh, yeah. How did you know?" the one on the right asked.

"I could just tell, I graduated from the academy, but I'm doing private work now," she replied.

"Really?" the one on the right observed.

"Yes, here's my question. Where's Galen Foster? Isn't he supposed to be with you?"

"Wait a minute," the middle one put his beer down. "You're the Confederate Gold person, aren't you?"

"Ah," said the one on the left, "Foster kind of told us about you."

They all shared a hearty chuckle after that remark.

"Listen and listen good," Yolanda ordered. "Whatever that worthless son-of-a-bitch told you about something happening between him and me, it was a lie. That asshole made it all up and it was a lie that may have cost me the person that I love. I've already heard the story from your friends, Greg and Todd, back in Richmond. I'm here to tell that low-life bastard what I think of him, so where is he?"

"Well," said the one in the middle, "it's funny, because he's kind of gone missing. He was supposed to be back here last night, but he didn't show up." He pointed at the guy on the left. "He's partnered up with Jon, but they were following separate leads yesterday. I mean it's not unusual for one of us to be gone for a day or so, but we're supposed to remain in contact. If we don't hear from him by tomorrow morning, we'll notify the Bureau and they'll send some more agents to help find his whereabouts."

"But what is the FBI doing way up here? I thought you were concerned about the I-95 and the I-64 corridors, this is kind of off the beaten path, isn't it?" she asked.

"Yeah, well, this is none of your business really, but we got a tip from a couple of sources around here about some suspicious activity. They telephoned the DC office, just a couple of farmers, I guess, but we were told to come up and take a look around. Foster seems to have found something anyway," the left hand guy explained.

Yolanda thought for a second, then reached for her cell phone. She punched in the number that either Todd or Greg had given her. It rang six times, then went to voicemail. "Galen, this is Yolanda Tilden. I'm leaving my callback number. You need to call me immediately. We have something important to discuss."

"We've all tried that number several times," said the one on the right, "all we get is his voicemail too. Hey, my name is Tompkins, Charles Tompkins, I'm the head agent here."

"Any idea about this so-called lead?" she asked, ignoring the introduction.

"It was out west of Ruckersville, around some town named Stanardsville," Tompkins replied. "I don't know what got him interested out that way. I guess we'll find out when he shows up. Here," he said. He handed her a business card. "Just in case you do find him, tell him to check in with me or at least you give me a call."

"But since that might not happen until tomorrow, how about having that beer with us?" asked the one on the left.

"No thanks," Yolanda answered. "I've had enough dealings with FBI types today, I'm calling it a day."

That remark was met with definite shared disappointment among the three agents.

55

JACK CALLS A FRIEND

Jack needed some information and he knew where he could find it. He called his former lady friend in Indianapolis, the same one who worked for the Indiana Department of Education. She had given him the information about Lynn Salyer's attendance at the middle school. This time he needed her to contact Greene County Schools via email and inquire about an employee named Ahmoud Assan. She promised to take care of it and get back to him within the hour.

He drove downtown and parked near the walking mall. He stopped at a restaurant with outdoor seating and ordered a coffee. And then he began to think about Yolanda.

I miss her, he admitted to himself. *I knew there was something between her and Foster, but I desperately wanted to believe her. Maybe she did love me, but, if she did, why would she have done that? Sure, he was her age, he was nice-looking, but…just fucking get over it, Jack.*

His cell phone buzzed, he looked at the number. It was his Indianapolis friend.

"Hello," Jack answered.

"Morning, Jack, but it's almost afternoon, isn't it?"

"Yeah, it's getting there. Were you able to find out anything?"

"Yes, I sent an email that said he was looking for employment and I requested work records and employment history," she explained.

"And?"

"They have no record of anyone named Ahmoud Assan ever being employed by Greene County Schools."

Jack nodded slowly as he digested that information.

"Jack? Are you still there?" she asked.

"What? Oh, yeah, I was just thinking. Hey, thanks so much for that, it gives me something to go on."

"Why are you in Virginia, Jack? Did you move? I haven't seen you in ages."

"No, just on a job. I'll look you up when I get back to Indiana," Jack promised.

"That would be nice, Jack, I'll look forward to it."

"OK, I have to get on this, thanks again."

"Fine, Jack. Bye."

What do you want to bet that I won't be able to find the address of Mr. Assan either. OK, I have someone who purchased car magnets for a school that he doesn't work for. I'd better find out where Greene County Schools are located and take a look.

Jack solved that issue in the simplest way possible. When the waitress stopped to refill his coffee cup he asked her. It turned out that the schools were north of Charlottesville in the towns of Ruckersville and Stanardsville. Jack decided to go ahead and order lunch before driving up there. He had a BLT with fries. Not too long ago he would have caught grief about the fries. To be honest, he did feel a little guilty.

Shortly afterwards he was driving north on 29. He got stopped by the traffic light at the intelligence center and glanced up at the building.

If I were a terrorist, maybe I'd be taking a closer look at that place.

Jack continued on until he reached Ruckersville. It basically looked like what anyplace would look like without zoning restrictions. It was a haphazard strip of fast food places, implement stores, antique stores, and other shops offering odds and ends of goods. He saw a sign that pointed west to Stanardsville and he made the left hand turn. It didn't take long to reach there. He drove around and located the schools on the same street. There were three of them: an elementary, a middle school, and a high school. He also saw a couple of the district's vans, but they were all similar to the ones he had seen earlier that morning.

Schools, OK, why does this bother me? I'm not getting a feel for anything around here. I need to check out that Army building. I wonder how tight the security is.

Jack drove back to 29 and headed south. He turned in at the stop light and headed up the hill to the Army complex. He was surprised at how large it was. In addition to something called NGIC, he didn't know exactly what that stood for, there was another large building housing the Defense Intelligence Agency. He did know about that outfit. He pulled up to a guard shack and rolled down the window. A civilian security guard came out.

"ID, sir?" he asked.

Jack offered him his driver's license.

"No, sir, I need a military ID or a security badge," the guard said.

"You mean I can't get in and just look around?" Jack innocently asked.

"No, sir. This is a restricted area, if you have a military ID or retired ID, you can get into the open area of either NGIC or DIA, but a driver's license doesn't allow you access."

"Uh, what does NGIC exactly stand for?" Jack asked.

"The National Ground Intelligence Center. Excuse me, are you a tourist or something, because you don't really have any business being here. Like I said, it's restricted access."

"OK, OK," Jack responded, "I didn't know, I was just curious."

"That's fine, sir, but if you would just follow this circle drive, it will take you back to Route 29. Have a good day."

Jack nodded and followed the instructions, but instead of getting back on 29, he parked the Buick alongside the road and got out to take a closer look at the NGIC building. It was surrounded by a high, black, wrought-iron fence. It was a modern looking building with lots of glass and chrome.

OK, if I were a terrorist, what would I do about this? The point of entry is also the weakest; security guards don't expect someone to pull a pistol on them, so once they are taken out, I would have temporary access to either of the two buildings. I could pack a van or a truck with explosives and do extensive damage to either of the two. But would this NGIC place or DIA be a target to terrorists? Maybe, but I just don't know.

Jack got back in the Buick and turned north on 29. He pulled into the strip mall complex that contained a Best Western motel.

56

YOLANDA FINDS A CLUE

Yolanda woke up early. She went downstairs and found the breakfast dining room and contented herself with cold cereal and a peach yogurt. She went back to her room, showered, and put on make-up before leaving. She checked at the front desk to get directions to Stanardsville. In twenty minutes she turned off the main road and found a parking place near the center of the town.

That rat bastard is somewhere around here, she thought. *I cannot wait to smack him across his lying face. Trouble is, where in the hell is he?*

Stanardsville was not a large place and she really didn't have any idea where to start looking for Galen. She spent several minutes canvassing the small downtown area before giving up.

She got back into the rental car and spent a few moments thinking. *OK, supposedly he found a clue here, but a clue about what? This isn't near the I-65 corridor, this is up in what? Hillbilly country?* She started the car and began to drive back to the highway. She almost missed it, because it was way off on the side of the road, hidden by some scrub bushes. It was the back end of a black sedan.

Yolanda pulled off on the berm and got out of her car. The sedan had government plates.

This has to be Galen's car, she thought.

She peered into the interior, but didn't see anything noteworthy. Then she checked the doors. They were locked. She looked around on the ground and found a baseball-sized rock. *I can't believe I'm going to do this.* She went back to her car and retrieved her jacket. She wrapped her hand up in the sleeve and then smacked the driver's side window near the door lock. After two tries, she managed to knock a hole in it that allowed her to pull the door lock up. She opened the door, brushed the broken glass from the seat, and quickly slid in.

There were three manila folders on the floor of the passenger side. She leaned over and scooped them up. Then she looked in the back seat. There was a suit coat tossed haphazardly behind the driver's seat. She reached back and pulled it to the front. She checked all the pockets, but they were empty. She let it drop back to the floor before turning her attention to the file folders. The first one contained receipts for lodging and meals, the second one was empty, but the third one had several pages of lined notebook paper covered with untidy scrawls of handwriting.

Yolanda started on the first page; it was a rough draft of Galen Foster's notes about the operation. She quickly leafed to the last few pages.

Got to Charlottesville at rush hour, god what a traffic mess.

Jon and I are splitting up, a couple of yokels reported some foreign-looking types hanging around. Really? This place is just farms and cows and we get sent up here for a couple of days? He's looking at Ruckersville and up north towards Culpeper. I'm stuck going either east or west.

Stanardsville – one horse-town.

Talked to farmer; said there were "furriners" looking "shifty."

What the hell does that mean? I'm thinking anyone who doesn't look like a redneck farmer fits that description. He said there were enough Americans out of work, why was the school hiring "furriners?" So I guess he and the other guy that Jon is checking on don't like minority hires.

It can't hurt to check out the school or schools to see what the hell he's talking about.

Went online and found most of the schools are in Stanardsville, one is in Ruckersville, the ones in S-ville are all on the same street, that's easy.

Drove by schools, kids were in class. A couple of school vans were out in front of the middle school. Saw another school van parked downtown. It was different than the ones I saw at the school. Something different about it. Curious about it. Gonna see where it goes when it leaves, if it leaves. Probably a private contractor, but worth checking out. Flash the badge a bit, that always gets people talking. Parking close to it. Hopefully this won't take long.

That was the last entry.

Yolanda looked in the glove box, but there was nothing but an owner's manual. She got out of the car and looked under the driver's seat and then the passenger side, still nothing. She found the lever that opened the trunk. There was a small suitcase in it, she unzipped it and found a couple of changes of clothing and a small shaving kit.

She slammed the trunk lid back down and then saw something shiny on the ground by the front driver's tire. She reached down and retrieved it. It was a set of keys. She pushed the lock button on the fob and the sedan doors immediately locked. She unlocked them with another push of a button.

What the hell? Why are his keys just lying here? And he left his suit coat? Maybe I should call those agents and let them know I found his car. And what was so curious about a school van? What did he mean about a private contractor? God damn it, why didn't he put that in his notes?

She got back in the car and gripped the steering wheel. Then, before giving up, she reached up and pulled the sun visor down. There was a small notebook clipped to it. She opened it. *It's Galen's personal notes*! She flipped through from the back until she found the last entries.

Need to check with the school district. Why are some vans different than others? Drove downtown; there was an older school van with magnetic signs. All the other vans were newer and had painted logos. Could be the school was phasing out the older ones?

Here's another weird thing: The old van doesn't have school or commercial plates.

Kind of simple, I'll just stop and get the plate numbers and run them. That should take care of it, won't have to deal with the school admin. On the other hand, I'll just tail them and see where they go.

On a whim, she looked back until she found a mention of her.

Met up with Yolanda Tilden at the hotel bar. Gonna go out with her. Pretty hot, I'm hoping to get lucky.

Well, that didn't pan out. Seems she doing some old guy she works with. What a fucking waste of a dinner.

"Galen, you are such an asshole," she muttered. She went back to the last entries and reread them.

"That's what he thought was wrong, it was the license plates," Yolanda said to herself. She found the folder with the case notes and pulled out the last page, folded it, and tucked it in Galen's notebook before putting it in her purse. Then she pulled out her cell phone and quickly dialed the number that the agent had given her.

"Tompkins."

"Hey, this is Yolanda Tilden, I'm over in Stanardsville and I found Galen's car."

"But no Galen?"

"No, uh, just his car. It's funny, but the driver's window is broken and I found the keys on the ground." Yolanda figured she didn't have to tell that she was the one who broke the window; she would just report the incident.

"Anything about where he is or what happened?" Tompkins asked.

"Uh, no," Yolanda glanced down at the small notebook on the front seat. She picked it up and walked over and tossed it in her car. "No, it's clean except for three folders. One's empty, one has receipts, and the third one has his case notes." *Except for the last page about the school van thing. No sense in having the FBI muddy up the water where I'm going to be next.* "Oh, and his suit coat is in the backseat."

She did give him the location of the car.

"Look," he said, "are you going to hang around there until we arrive? I have to track down the other two guys and then we'll head over. We could use another pair of eyes."

"No," Yolanda answered, "I don't think so. It looks like the car was just abandoned. I suppose someone broke out the window to see if there was anything worth stealing. I don't have a clue why the keys were lying on the ground. They might have just fallen out of his pocket. Maybe you'll have better luck."

"Maybe," Tompkins replied. "Let's at least meet later tonight over at the bar to compare notes."

"Sure," Yolanda agreed, "That's definitely something we should do. OK, I'm going downtown to check around."

"Fine, we'll be over soon, maybe we'll run into each other."

"Maybe," Yolanda said and she hit the disconnect button on her phone. She got in the car and put Galen's notebook in her purse.

OK, so let me drive around and see if I can find a van like Galen described. Hopefully I'll be lucky, but first of all I need to go change into some jeans. I can't go investigating in a dress.

57

IT'S A SMALL WORLD AFTER ALL

Jack entered the hotel and asked for a room, the only one available had two double beds, but he didn't care, he just wanted some more time to check out that intelligence center. After he took his suitcase upstairs, he went back down and found the room that had computers for guest usage. He searched for the Google Earth app and downloaded it. As soon as it was ready, he zoomed in on the area of NGIC.

Looks like only one road in, but there is a service road right after the turn off 29. So, if I wanted to blow up either of those two buildings or maybe even both, I could bring two vans in, shoot the guards at the gate, pull right up to the front entrances, and detonate the truck bombs, just like in Oklahoma City.

Then Jack remembered what Mr. Douglas had said about the Army installation, something like being in the backwater of intelligence services.

I just don't know. Would this be a viable terrorist target?

Jack leaned back in the chair and studied the aerial view one more time. Then he closed out the program and left the computer area. He paused by the front desk.

There's something bothering me about this. I don't think it has anything to do with the Army place. After all, how many people even know it exists, let alone where it's located? The school thing is what has me puzzled. I have to figure out who or where Ahmoud Assan is.

Jack stepped outside and noticed a restaurant across the parking lot. Just as soon as he decided he might stop by and get a sandwich or something, a black sedan zoomed down the parking lot heading for the exit. He noticed it had government plates.

Huh, wonder where the fire is.

Jack went in, sat down at the bar, and looked at the menu. They had a soft-shell crab sandwich as the special. He wasn't interested, especially when he saw one being carried by. It was literally an entire crab stuck in a bun. He decided to go with a turkey-bacon sub instead. While he was waiting, he began going over possibilities.

Number one, I'm wondering why Mr. Assan needed Greene County Schools vehicle magnets. I know why I bought some signs and I suspect that he's up to something that will get him access to places he doesn't belong. Wait a minute! I think I know how to find him!

Jack told the waitress to make the sandwich to go, he paid the bill, and then hurried out to his car. Just as he got behind the wheel, a green sedan pulled into the parking lot two rows ahead of him. He was just getting ready to put it in drive when he suddenly stopped. Yolanda was getting out of the green car.

What in the hell is she doing here? Jack quickly turned the motor off and dropped down low in the seat, just in case she glanced his way. She double-checked the door lock and walked into the motel lobby.

Seriously, how did Yolanda end up north of Charlottesville? She was supposed to fly back to Indianapolis.

As soon as he was certain that she wasn't coming back out, he restarted the car and turned north on 29 back towards Ruckersville.

58

YOLANDA FINDS MORE THAN A CLUE

It only took Yolanda twenty minutes to change and start driving back to Stanardsville. Once she got close to the town, she saw a second black sedan pulled off on the berm where she had found Galen's car. Two of the agents were actually crawling around on the ground searching in the weeds as she passed by. They didn't notice her; she didn't see the third agent at all.

It didn't take her long to find the three schools; she drove by the elementary school and headed straight to the middle school. She pulled into the parking lot and stopped next to a row of school vans.

OK, so Galen saw two different types of vans. There were four vans parked there. Each of them looked fairly new and they had official license plates. These weren't the one that made Galen suspicious. There were some kids outside; it looked like a physical education class or something. A few of them waved to her and she waved back. She walked back to her car and drove to the elementary school and then the high school. No vans were in sight, just a couple of school buses. *Strike one; two; and three. What now?*

She was getting set to drive back to the hotel when she passed a gas station. There was a van at the pumps. *It's an older school van!* She slammed on her brakes, extremely irritating the driver of the car behind her, and darted into the gas station. She stopped near the air pump and waited. A moment later a man came out of the station carrying a Dr. Pepper bottle. He climbed into the van and drove off. Yolanda eased onto the street and followed him. He drove to a small supermarket and pulled into a spot in the back row. Yolanda drove by and parked out of the driver's line of sight on the passenger's side. She rolled the windows down and waited to see what he was going to do. Five minutes went by and she was growing impatient.

C'mon, damn it! Why are you just sitting there?

A few more minutes passed and then she saw him put a cell phone to his ear. It was a short conversation, because seconds later he had gotten out of the van and was standing by the back door.

Is he waiting for someone?

He was, because a similar van pulled up. There was a driver and a passenger in this one. The first guy opened one of the side doors and climbed in. The second van pulled to the intersection, stopped for a couple of cars, and then left the parking lot.

OK, here's my chance. Yolanda left her purse in the car and walked over to the van and peered through the windshield. There was nothing out of the ordinary, just the typical trash that accumulated in commercial vehicles: old coffee cups, crumpled fast-food wrappers, and carry-out sacks. There was a clipboard lying on the passenger seat. She walked around the car to see if she could make out any of the writing. It turned out that she could definitely make it out, but she couldn't tell what it said. It appeared to be in Arabic or something.

Arabic? Maybe. Galen's report mentioned "furriners," is this what those farmers meant?

She tried the doors. They were locked. She moved to the back of the van, the windows were so dirt-covered that she couldn't see inside, even after she brushed some of the dirt away. Then she tried the handle. To her surprise, it opened.

Holy shit, they didn't lock the back door!

The back cargo area of the van was lined with shelving. She looked around to see if anyone was around or leaving the store before climbing up inside. *OK, I guess this is a maintenance van, all this stuff looks legit.* There were several plumber and carpenter tools along with assorted spools of wires and an ample supply of duct tape. Right behind the front seats were six bags of something. They were heavily covered in dust. She looked around and found a rag on one of the shelves. She brushed off the top bag and read what it contained: ammonium nitrate fertilizer. *That's the same stuff McVeigh used in Oklahoma. Is this for real? Is this just for landscaping?*

Just then she heard a vehicle stop. She peeked out the side window. *Jesus Christ, it's the other van! What in the hell are they doing back here already?* She quickly considered ducking out the back door, but the van had stopped right in front of it. As she watched, the side door of that van opened and two men climbed out, joined by the two from the front. All four were dressed in the same coveralls with some logo on the front left, but it was too small for Yolanda to make out. One thing she did notice. They looked Middle Eastern.

Shit, what am I supposed to do now? I guess I can just step out of the van, flash my PI badge and bluff my way past them. Figuring that was about the only viable option, she fumbled in her pocket for her badge and crept to the back door. Just as she was getting ready to push it open, she looked down and saw something half-covered by a rag. *Is that blood?* She gingerly nudged the rag aside and uncovered a black, tasseled loafer. *A shoe? One shoe? Definitely not a work boot.* She examined the floor more carefully and saw what had to be bloodstains. *Is this what happened to Galen?* In that moment she changed her plan. If Galen was right and there was something going on with this van, maybe he came back here and managed to confront them. *Maybe they knocked him unconscious and took him somewhere in this van.* She heard the door of the second van slide shut and knew that she only had seconds to spare. She grabbed the corner of a blue tarp and hid herself as best she could under it. *Maybe they won't look back here,* she hoped.

She heard both front doors open and felt the van sag a bit as two men got in. She was in luck, because they didn't look in the cargo area. The van started. She felt it back up and then leave the parking lot. The conversation that was going on in the front was no help either, because, just like on the clipboard, the men were conversing in Arabic.

I guess it's too late to bluff my way out of this one. Hopefully I can sneak out of here when they get wherever they're going. If Jack were here, he would have told me to wait for back-up. God, I wish Jack was here.

Yolanda checked her watch. After fifteen minutes of driving, the van turned sharply to the right and bumped hard over something. Yolanda almost gasped out loud. One of the doors opened and she heard something like a garage door being raised. After a brief moment the van moved forward and then stopped again. Another van door opened and closed followed by the garage door noise again. It got very dark inside the van. She heard the voices fade.

OK, it's time to see what I've gotten myself into.

She carefully squeezed out from under the tarp and felt her way to the back of the van. She pushed one of the doors open. There was just enough light coming in from the cracks around the garage door to let her see that she was in a large area. There were three garage doors in a row. Another school van was parked in the furthest spot; the one next to her van was empty. She climbed out of it and softly pushed the door closed. As her eyes adjusted she could see a door at the far end of the parking area.

This must be a warehouse or something. She looked around. Besides the two vans, there were only stacks of something on pallets enclosed in plastic. One of the pallets was uncovered. It was too dark to see what was on them, but they were standard sized bags. *Is this more fertilizer?* She tugged the top bag from the stack and dragged it over to the garage door. It was identical to the six bags in the truck. *Jesus! Is this what Galen and that task force were looking for? Are these guys planning on building an Oklahoma car bomb out of this stuff? It's controlled now; they must have been buying small amounts from different suppliers.*

Then Yolanda remembered Galen. *Was that his shoe? Is this where they brought him? They must have taken his car and abandoned it. I have to see if I can find him. There was blood in the van, I wonder if he's hurt.*

Suddenly she heard the middle garage door begin to move. She ran to the far side of the van she had been hiding in, dropped to the dusty floor, and slid under it. She saw the wheels of a third van pull in and a single person got out of it. He grunted as he pulled the door chain down. She heard his footsteps recede and then heard the door open and close again, leaving her in the darkness.

OK, there's nothing for me to do in here. Maybe I should just try to open one of the garage doors and see where in the hell I am. She thought about that for a moment. *No, I need to see what's on the other side of that door. If it's clear, maybe I can find out what happened to Galen.*

She got up from under the van and placed her right hand on the wall. It helped guide her until her eyes adjusted and she found the door. She placed her ear on it and listened intently. There was nothing to hear. She gently turned the doorknob and eased it open just a little way. A bright sliver of light appeared around the edge. She listened again, still no sound. She opened the door a few more inches and was able to look inside. It appeared to be a normal hallway with six doors on the far wall from the garage, midway stood a tall, metal cabinet. Yolanda took a deep breath and slipped through the doorway, closing the door behind her. She quickly glanced to her left and right. She was alone.

Maybe I can hear voices. If someone comes out, maybe I can hide by that cabinet.

She scurried to the furthest door on the left and listened. Then she listened at each one in turn. It wasn't until she reached the last door on the right of the cabinet that she could hear muffled voices, punctuated by faint laughter.

OK, let me check the doors on the left and see if they're unlocked.

Perhaps it was luck or perhaps it was because the first door was the farthest from the voices, but it was unlocked. After she eased inside the room, she saw him.

The handsome FBI agent who took her out to dinner, made a strong pass at her, and ended up lying about her was now a bloody mess. He was tied to a metal desk chair. He appeared to be unconscious or asleep, his head sagged down onto his chest.

Oh, Jesus! "Galen! Galen!" she frantically whispered, glancing back to the closed door. She pushed his head straight up. His eyes flickered open.

"Yolanda!" he cried out.

"Shhh!" she whispered. "Don't let them hear us."

"Where's everybody else? Is Jon here too?"

"No, nobody else is here. Can you walk? Maybe we can get you out of here."

"I don't know. They worked me over pretty good. I was looking at a van when I guess I got hit from behind. I woke up here. Since then they've been beating me every so often."

Just then Yolanda heard a door slam. "Pretend to be asleep," she ordered. She desperately looked around the room for a hiding place. There was a wooden kneehole desk turned up on its back. She ran over and lowered herself into the opening. She tried to make herself as small as possible. She heard the door open.

"So, FBI man, you asleep?" She heard the sound of a slap. "Come on, you not tired, you need to talk some. How many FBI mans are around here?"

"Fuck you, Ahab," was Foster's reply. That earned him another sharp slap.

The door opened again. It sounded like more than three men had entered. Yolanda did a quick headcount. She had only seen three people. She didn't know how many people were in the third van, but she didn't dare risk looking.

"What he say?" someone asked in broken English.

"Nothing, he no say nothing. Maybe Amjad want to talk to him again."

After that something was said in Arabic, followed by loud laughter. Then she heard hard punches not slaps. She could hear Galen making pained sounds after every blow landed. Finally the sounds stopped. More Arabic, then the door opened. From the sound of it, everyone had left the room. Yolanda counted to ten, then she risked a quick glance over the edge of the desk opening. She and Galen were alone again. She climbed up and over the desk and checked on him. This time there was no doubt he was unconscious, blood was still running from cuts on his face.

Oh, fuck, how am I going to get you out of here? I guess it's up to me to get out and find help.

"Galen, maybe you can hear me. Look, I'm going to try and get out of here. I'll find your friend Jon and be back here as quickly as I can. Don't piss them off, Galen, tell them something, make something up. Don't give them an excuse to beat you."

Yolanda reached into her pocket and brought out her cell phone. She started punching in Tompkins' number when "no service" popped up on the screen. *God damn it, where in the fuck am I?*

She shoved the phone back in her pocket and whispered to Galen one more time. "I'm leaving now; I'll try and get out the garage door. Don't you worry, I'll be back to get you, I promise."

She didn't get any answering nod or grunt from him. She went to the door and peered into the hallway. It was deserted. She went through the door back into the garage area. She had to stop until her eyes adjusted to the darkness. She found the pull chain to the garage door and gave it a sharp pull. She tugged the chain until there was enough space to slide out under the door.

She stood up, dusted her hands, and turned to see which way she should go. There were three Arabs in Greene County Schools coveralls putting bags of fertilizer on a forklift.

Here goes nothing. She pulled her detective badge out of her pocket. "You're all under arrest for suspicion of domestic terrorism."

She didn't see the fourth man come out from under the garage door. All she knew was that everything went dark.

59

JACK VISITS RUCKERSVILLE

Jack was in a quandary. He couldn't stay at the same hotel that Yolanda was staying at; there was no way that he could avoid bumping into her. The hotel just wasn't that big. Ruckersville didn't look big enough to have a decent hotel and he didn't want to end up driving to Culpeper or all the way west to Harrison.

Damn, I guess I'll have to go back to the Double Tree; I really didn't want to have to make that drive. I'll wait until late tonight when I see her green rental car there, then I'll check out and relocate early tomorrow morning. It beats me how in the hell she ended up here. I didn't tell anyone where I was going.

Jack found the school in Ruckersville and there were some of the vans like he had seen in Charlottesville.

OK, if some guy named Ahmoud Assan bought magnetic signs, where in the hell are they? I only saw the Green... part, since they were wrapped in paper, but the printout from the store clearly said Greene County. I wish Yolanda were around, she could look up stuff like that on her phone. I don't have a clue. I can't go over to the hotel just yet, it's still too early. Let me take another shot at my buddy Ahmoud.

Jack turned his car south again and drove back to the sign store in Charlottesville. By coincidence the same young clerk was behind the counter. He noticeably paled when he saw Jack approach the counter.

"Uh, hello, Detective," he greeted Jack.

"Hi, there," Jack replied. "Say, you'll want to know that I told the Chief about how cooperative and helpful you were last week."

That started a huge smile accompanied by rapid up and down head bobbing.

"But there's one other thing," Jack continued.

The head bobbing abruptly ceased.

"When I was reviewing the printout you got me, I noticed the name of a wanted fugitive."

The clerk started his trademark gulping again.

"It was the infamous Roger Douglas," Jack explained.

"Infamous? Like as a little famous?" the clerk asked.

"Well, no, not exactly, it has a bit of a negative connotation. Here's the thing, right before that dastardly Douglas made a purchase, it seems a Middle Eastern gentleman made a purchase. Now it turns out that our department here in Charlottesville, and the FBI operating out of Richmond, think that Douglas may have stolen the identity of that man and is currently using his credit card."

The clerk just stared at Jack.

"So," Jack went on, "the feds and the Charlottesville police simply need the entire credit card number that was used in the Greene County Schools transaction."

"Uh, Detective, Sir, I'm pretty sure that we can't give out credit card numbers."

"Now, now," Jack reassured him. "Once again, I understand completely, but if the FBI has to request that information," Jack's voice dropped, "they have access to lots and lots of local criminal activities that my department doesn't. It would be a shame if someone here might, I don't know, uh, become a person of interest to the FBI, wouldn't it?" Jack smiled.

This time the clerk stammered out a positive response. "Yes, it would, it would be a shame. Uh, is this, I mean do you think you're going to come back here for more stuff like that?"

"Oh, no," Jack reassured him, "this will indeed be it." *I don't know what this kid is up to, but he'd better hope he never has to take a lie detector test.*

"Just a minute, sir, I'll be right back."

It took less than five minutes for him to hand Jack a business card with a 16-digit credit card number written on it.

"Is this a Visa, a MasterCard, or what?" Jack asked.

"Visa!" the clerk almost shouted, then repeated a bit more softly, "a Visa Card."

"Well, thank you very much, uh, Clinton," Jack said, peering at the clerk's name tag. "You can be assured that the Chief will again know what a good citizen of our city you are."

Smiling and head-bobbing followed Jack as he exited the store.

Jack drove until he found a small park. He got out of the Buick and took a seat on an isolated park bench. He pulled his wallet out of his pants and fished out his Visa Card. He flipped it over and called the 1-800 number listed on the back for lost cards. Within moments he had received the customary message about the call being monitored for quality assurance. *Yeah, yeah, just answer the phone.*

"Visa Lost or Stolen Credit Card Assistance Desk, how might I be of service?"

Jack wasn't really very good with Arabic accents, but he had watched the Simpsons TV show for several years and had developed a fairly decent imitation of Apu, the Springfield storekeeper. That was the voice he chose to begin the conversation.

"Well, I am unfortunate to say that my card of credit may have been taken," Jack explained.

"Ah," came the answer, "can you give me the number of the credit card, please?"

"Do I say 'dash' when the numbers separate, please?"

"No, sir, just read the numbers, no dashes."

Jack rattled off the numbers, in an accent that would make Arabic 7-Eleven clerks all across America quite proud.

"Fine, just a moment, sir." Jack heard some computer keys being punched. "So, am I speaking to Mr. Assan at the moment?"

"Yes, that is me, most definitely."

"I need to verify your identity; can you give me your mother's maiden name?"

"Oh, women in my country do not have such a thing; they take the husband's name when they wed."

"I see, what about her current residence?"

"No residence. She got blowed up."

"Pardon me? Blowed up?"

"Yes, back in Beirut, she got blowed up in Beirut. At the marketplace. Most distressing."

"Beirut? So your mother was Lebanese?"

"Yes, very much so, but she did favor men too, thus you have me as a result, you see."

"Uh, let me put you on hold for a moment, sir," the customer service person said. Before he hit the hold button, Jack heard him whisper something, "John, come here and listen in on this guy. It's hilarious."

Jack waited a few moments until he came back on the line.

"Mr. Assan, could you at least give me the billing address on the account?"

"Why most certainly; very gracious to be of assistance. It is 104 Ashton Street in Charlottesville, Virginia, that is my home," Jack intoned.

"Uh, Mr. Assan, that is not the address listed as the billing address. Let me see..., my computer says that is the address of a Mr. Roger Douglas."

"Oh, I am so angry!" Jack exclaimed. "That is the friend of my terrible brother-in-law Mahmoud! He is the one who has purloined my card of credit!"

"I don't know about that, sir. I just know that the address isn't in Charlottesville, it's 2420 Barnstable Road in Dyke, Virginia. Sir, do you simply wish to cancel this card? I can do that for you right now."

"Oh, yes, that would be so splendid. I must confront Mahmoud about this. It is not a family good thing!"

"Very well, Mr. Assan, would you like me to issue another card to replace this one?"

"No, I am not thinking so," Jack explained, "I must first deal with that scoundrel, Mahmoud. He is a rascally scamp to be sure, but I am thanking you so very much."

"Not a problem, Mr. Assan, I was happy to help."

You helped in a big way, Jack thought as he ended the call. *Now I just have to figure out where Dyke, Virginia is.*

Jack got back in his car and quickly entered the address on his GPS. It looked to be somewhere on the northwest side of Charlottesville. *If it takes me through Stanardsville, I'll stop and look at the schools again.*

Jack was getting to be quite a veteran of Route 29 traffic. Almost no one paid attention to the speed limit, but there were unexpected dips and hills along with an occasional traffic light that slowed everyone down. He drove up to Ruckersville and made a left hand turn as directed by his GPS.

It turned out that he did go by Stanardsville before reaching Dyke Road. He turned into the town and drove slowly past the three schools. As he was heading back to the highway, he drove by a parking lot. There was an isolated green sedan sitting in the back.

Hmm…I wonder if that's the car Yolanda was driving. Better check it out, but I don't want to run into her, but there are lots of green cars in the world.

He parked his car and walked over to the sedan. He looked carefully all around to see if Yolanda was anywhere to be seen, but the lot was deserted. He peeked in the window and saw a handbag on the floor of the passenger side. He went over and got a better look at it. *I'm no expert, but that looks like the purse that Yolanda carries. Why would she have left it in the car? Hell, I don't know for sure if that's her car or not. One way to find out.*

Jack looked at the back of the car and saw a small "e" sticker. He knew that stood for Enterprise. He got out his phone and studied it for a moment. *OK, there's a way to get on the Internet, it's got to be on here someplace.* He punched a few icons without much result, but on his fourth try, he pushed the one labeled Safari. He was rewarded with a Google search button. He typed in "Enterprise" and got a 1-800 number. He pushed the green phone icon and entered the number. Within moments a female customer service representative answered.

"Good afternoon, Enterprise, we pick you up," she greeted.

"Good afternoon," Jack replied. "This is Detective Jack Clayton in Charlottesville, Virginia. We have a car here that may be abandoned and it has one of your stickers on the back. Let me give you the license number. Can you check that for me?"

"Of course, does the car have Virginia plates?"

"Yes, it's A47 ML2, it's a green Chevrolet Impala," Jack explained.

"Just give me a moment Detective," she replied.

Jack checked to see if the doors were locked. They were.

"Detective?"

"Yes," Jack answered.

"It is one of our vehicles, it was rented to a Yolanda Tilden in Richmond. What leads you to suspect that it's abandoned?"

"Well, I might have been hasty in stating that. It's just that the car is sitting in the back of a store parking lot and there doesn't seem to be any reason for it being here."

"How long has it been there?"

"Oh, just for several hours," Jack replied.

"Well, due to the nature of our business, we don't make any quick decisions about abandoned cars. My computer indicates that it's an active rental and having it sit anywhere for a few hours wouldn't be any cause for Enterprise to make steps to retrieve it."

"Yes, I understand," Jack said, "I just wanted to check and see if it was indeed one of your rental vehicles."

"That's fine," she answered, "if the car remains there for a considerable amount of time, you might want to contact our Charlottesville branch. If it turns out that the car does need to be reclaimed, the Richmond office can overnight a set of keys there."

"Yes, we'll certainly keep an eye on it and let you know."

"Thank you for your call, Detective."

"You're welcome."

This car is the one Yolanda was driving. She was coming into the hotel parking lot around noon, so she must have had some reason to come over here. But where is she? And do women leave their purses behind? I'll check back when I get finished in Dyke.

60

OUT OF WHAT FRYING PAN?

Yolanda felt uncomfortable. Her back hurt, her shoulders hurt, and an acute foot cramp brought her completely awake. She was propped up in the corner of a dimly-lit room with her arms and legs securely bound with duct tape.

What the hell happened? I saw those three guys and then that was it.

She moved her head back against the wall and learned what had probably happened. There was a sizeable, tender, aching place on the back of her head. *Somebody hit me from behind. Damn, it hurts and I can't move my feet. Oww…stupid cramp!*

She squirmed a bit and managed to get her feet stretched out in front of her. That took care of the cramping. With that done, she took the time to survey her surroundings. There wasn't much in the room, just a couple of broken desk chairs and various boxes. Everything was covered with a thick layer of dust. No one had used the room in apparently a long time. She saw two sets of footprints flanking two long lines of disturbed dust on the floor. Apparently she was the source of the two lines; someone had dragged her in here and put her on the floor.

"OK," she muttered, somewhat comforted by the soft sound of her voice, "I hid in the van and then I found Galen in one of the rooms. He was in no shape to walk, so I thought I'd be able to get away and find help. Damn. Instead I bump into those three guys outside the building and then somebody hit me from behind. That sums it up."

She struggled to push her wristwatch up from under the duct tape. Finally she was able to make out the time, 4:42 p.m. *Shit, I got into that van around 2:30. I've been out for a long time.* She looked at the footprints again. *And no one has been curious enough to come back and check on me. I don't know if I should be happy or feel neglected.*

She listened carefully for a few moments. Other than a distant hum of some kind of machine or appliance, she couldn't make out any other sounds. It was deathly still.

The drive here only took around fifteen or twenty minutes. That wouldn't have got them back to Charlottesville, so I'm someplace else. And what is this place? A warehouse? An abandoned factory of some kind? There were three garage doors and this was obviously some kind of commercial building. How many of those guys are there? I saw four at the school and then the third truck showed up with just a driver, but were the three I saw outside the same ones? Shit, I don't know what I'm up against.

Then she heard the sound of a chain and the motor of a vehicle.

Somebody must be arriving. She tried to reach her wrists to try and bite through the duct tape, but whoever had taped her wrists had looped the tape around her waist several times. As hard as she tried, she couldn't reach them. Then she tried see-sawing her feet, that only served to roll the tape down, it didn't loosen it. Then she heard another door open and the sound of voices coming closer.

The door opened and let the bright lighting of the hallway into the room. She blinked her eyes several times to try and adjust them. Someone stepped into the room and flipped a light switch. Two naked bulbs suspended from an open junction box lit the room.

Two men, both Arabs, stood at the doorway staring at her.

"Who are you?" Yolanda asked. "Why do you have me tied up here?"

The men glanced at one another and exchanged a few words. One of them, a short, heavyset man, took one more look at Yolanda and then left the room.

"Do you speak English?" she continued. "Why am I tied up?" she asked again.

The man just stared.

Yolanda kicked out of frustration, managing to shove a carton a few feet with an explosion of dust.

A voice came from the door. "No, neither of them speaks English. And as for why you are tied up? You show up here for no particularly good reason and show my colleagues some kind of badge. You will remain tied up until I am satisfied about who you are and how you came to be in this building."

Yolanda studied the man closely. His English was good and non-accented. He was wearing a light brown suit with a shirt and a tie. She glanced down at his shoes, they were the two-tone brown and white shoes that she never thought were remotely fashionable.

The man gave what sounded like an order and the remaining Arab left the room.

"So, who are you?" Yolanda asked the man. "What kind of place is this? I didn't do anything. You just can't tie people up like this."

The man laughed. "In this place, I can do just about anything I want." The other man showed up at the door with a folding chair. It looked brand-new, in contrast to the broken and dusty furniture in the room. Nonetheless, the man took a handkerchief from his suit coat pocket and lightly dusted the seat of the chair before sitting down and crossing his legs at the knee. He replaced the handkerchief and produced a package of cigarettes. He pulled one out of the package. It was slightly longer and had darker paper than a usual cigarette. He paused for a moment and then offered the package to Yolanda.

"Here," he said, "perhaps you would like one also?"

"No thank you," she replied. "I don't smoke."

"Ah, yes, you Americans and your health habits. You don't smoke, but you eat like pigs and drink alcohol until you are all mostly fat."

"Do I look fat to you?" she said sarcastically.

"No," the man looked her up and down for a moment. "You seem to be an exception. But let's get on to other matters."

The other man quickly pulled a cigarette lighter from his pants pocket and lit the suited man's cigarette. He took a couple of long pulls on it before continuing.

"Here is what I find most fascinating. Three of my friends were in the back of this building. Oh, and to answer one of your questions, at one time this building served as a very small trucking and shipping firm. Suddenly you appear. You roll out from one of the garage doors and then show them some kind of badge. I must tell you, I have examined your badge and I don't find any connection with either the local or federal employees. I thought private detectives only existed on American television or sensational literature."

"No, I'm for real," Yolanda replied. "Now, why don't you tell about who you are?"

"It's really none of your business who I am. However it is my business to learn what you are doing here. By the way, only one of my friends speaks English. According to him you were placing them under arrest. That is quite humorous, you know. I'm curious, for what crime were you arresting them?"

Yolanda almost blurted out, "Because you've abducted and beaten an FBI agent." She immediately realized that the less known about her and what she knew could only be for the better. Instead she brought up a more immediate matter.

"I don't know how long I've been tied up here," she said, "but I do need to use the bathroom. Can you cut this tape so I can go?"

"Ah, yes, I understand," the man replied. "That does present a small problem. Yes, I will release you for a short time, but the door to the bathroom must remain open. Don't worry. I won't be observing you, just making sure that you don't attempt another of your 'detective' tricks. Also I must inform you that many of my colleagues are uncomfortable with you being here so inappropriately dressed."

"What do you mean inappropriately?" Yolanda asked.

"You're wearing trousers and your hair is not covered. Also the women in our country cover their faces for the purpose of modesty."

"So why don't you just let me go? I haven't done anything."

"No, not until I find out more about how and what brought you here. Now, let's take care of the restroom issue." The man stood and walked to her. He pulled out a pocket knife and used it to cut through the tape binding her feet and hands. She took the opportunity to rub her wrists and then bobbed up and down on her toes to stretch her leg muscles.

The man led her out the door and down the hallway. It was a different hallway than the one where she had found Galen. He stopped at a door clearly marked "Restroom."

"Go and take care of yourself," he directed. "I will stand here. Do not worry, I am not interested in watching you." He pulled out the package of cigarettes and lit another. Yolanda walked into the restroom, there were two urinals on the far wall and two stalls. She went into the first stall and started to latch the door.

"No, the door remains open. Take care of yourself, but be quick about it."

Yolanda could see his reflection in a mirror. It was true, he didn't appear to be watching her. He was leaning against the door frame still smoking his cigarette. She pushed her jeans and panties down and sat down. She didn't really have to go, but she forced herself. She didn't know when she might get another chance. The toilet paper roll was almost empty; she used the last of it and then stood and pulled up her jeans. She flushed and went out to wash her hands. The soap dispensers were empty and there weren't any paper towels, just one of the hot air blowers. She just rinsed her hands and pushed the button on the hand dryer. It really didn't work well and she finally wiped them on her jeans.

"Fine," the man said, "now let's go back and finish our chat." He pulled a cell phone out of his suit pocket and briefly spoke to someone in Arabic. When they got back to the original room, there were two more men waiting, one of them had a roll of duct tape. They had brought another folding chair and one of them pushed Yolanda down on it while the other duct taped her ankles to the front legs and pulled her hands around behind the chair before taping them.

At least I get to sit and the tape isn't as tight as before.

"So, you may begin to talk now," the suit man said.

"My car broke down and I was walking to find a gas station or something. I saw this building and I thought someone might be able to help me..."

Suitman walked over and slapped her hard.

Fuck! OK, Mr. Suitman, you are just a shithead.

Suitman smiled. "I am a nice man, but I don't like being lied to. Tell the truth. I or one of my friends can do things much more persuasive than a gentle slap across the face."

"You're brave too; it takes a lot of courage to hit someone who's tied up and helpless."

Suitman didn't catch the sarcasm and merely shrugged, "Bravery has nothing to do with it. You are an unexpected interruption and I need to be done with you as quickly as possible. Please, start over again and tell me what brought you here."

Lots of thoughts raced through Yolanda's mind. Obviously there was a flaw with the broken-down car ploy and she didn't want to get slapped again or the more persuasive things Suitman had mentioned.

"OK, I am a private detective. I was hired by a consulting firm to investigate a possible fraudulent use of public funds by Greene County Schools. It is believed that there are non-certified staff members, especially in maintenance who are falsifying time sheets and selling district property and supplies on the black market," she concluded.

"Seriously?" Suitman asked. "There is enough fraud and profit in school supplies that hiring someone like you would be warranted? That doesn't seem likely."

"But that's how I got here. I saw your van," Yolanda quickly interrupted.

"What about the van?" Suitman asked.

"It doesn't have commercial plates, it has regular Virginia plates. It made me suspicious."

Suitman stood, walked over and slapped her twice.

"God damn it!" she cried. "What was that for?"

He laughed, "Just keeping you honest. So, what you said; that's believable. But how did you get here?"

You smartass son-of-a-bitch.

"I checked the doors. The front ones were locked, but the back doors weren't. I thought I'd look inside and see if there were unusual items or supplies that shouldn't be there. Then I heard voices and there was a second van outside. Four men got out and I thought if I hid, they might take me to where they had stuff stored. The van pulled into this building and they got out. I left the van and looked around a bit, but it was nothing but an empty garage."

"Did you explore anywhere else?" Suitman inquired.

"Yes, I found the door that led from the garage and looked through it. There was a hallway with a bunch of doors."

"And did you look in any of the rooms?"

"No, I was going to, but then I heard voices, voices speaking Arabic. I got scared and went back to the garage. No one came in there, so I opened up one of the garage doors partway and went outside. That's when I saw those three men and then someone must have hit me from behind. The next thing I knew I was propped up on the wall over there," she gestured with her head.

Suitman stood up again. Yolanda flinched when he approached her. This time he simply put his fist under her chin and pushed it up until she was looking straight up at him.

"All right," he nodded, "that story seems much better than your first attempt and I think the gentle slaps you received helped you decide to tell the truth. I must admit, you are clever for a female. You noticed the license plates. There's nothing I can really do about that now, there's not enough time left."

"So, you're going to let me go?" she asked hopefully.

"In time. In time," he replied. "You don't know much, but you do know enough to be a problem. I'm afraid that I'll have to keep you here for a few more days. Don't worry, I have a room to put you in and you won't have to be restrained. You will get the same food and drink that my men receive."

"But I'm going to be missed," she protested. "People are going to come looking for me."

"Perhaps, but they won't be looking for you here. Wait a moment; I have to take care of something."

Suitman left Yolanda alone in the room. She struggled for a moment, but the man had been very generous with the amount of duct tape he had used.

That turned out sort of better than I expected. At least I didn't get beaten like Galen was. I wonder if he's OK. A few more days? I wonder what they have planned, it looks like it's going to happen soon.

Suitman reappeared. "I talked to the two men who were driving the van that brought you here. What kind of car were you driving?"

"What do you need to know that for?"

This time the slap was hard enough to actually knock the chair and Yolanda over on the side.

Fuck! That hurt!

"Don't question me, you American bitch. Just answer the question. What kind of car?"

"Set me back up, you bastard."

Suitman went to the back of the chair and yanked it violently upright, and then he got right in Yolanda's face.

"You will answer me. My colleagues will be more than happy to entertain themselves by beating you. You represent all that disgusts them in American females. They are getting tired of playing with another visitor whom we are holding and they would like nothing more than to move on to the next guest," he threatened.

"I get it. I get it," she murmured. "It's a green Chevy Impala. I don't know what year it is, I think it's new. It's a rental."

This time Suitman's hand went to her cheek and gently caressed it. "That's more like it. I would hate to see such an attractive face bruised and bloody." He slapped her gently three times, then he leaned forward. "But I promise you; if you try anything or do anything, I will turn them loose on you and you will regret it for the rest of your worthless life."

He turned away and spoke into his cell phone again. In less than two minutes someone came into the room. He handed Suitman a small leather case. Suitman opened the case and pulled out a hypodermic needle.

"This is for you," Suitman pointed at the needle. "I need to be sure that you will sleep for a while. When you wake up, you will be in your new quarters. I will have a book or two for you to read. I'm sending someone to retrieve your vehicle. I took the opportunity of removing your car keys when you were unconscious. Then, in a few days, if all goes well and you cooperate, you will be released. I promise you this."

"But I don't need a shot," Yolanda protested.

Suitman just grinned as the man pressed the needle into Yolanda's upper arm. His grin was the last thing she saw.

61

JACK VISITS A FARM

Jack followed his GPS on the short drive to Dyke. It turned out to be a small village with a nearby vineyard and winery.

It's obvious that this 2420 number must be a county route; this place isn't big enough to have houses or buildings in the 24 hundred block, more like a 200 block.

Jack turned on Barnstable Road and checked house numbers of the fairly isolated mailboxes. He started on the 2400's a mile or so out of Dyke and kept a close eye on each one, listening carefully to his GPS tell him how close he was getting to his destination.

Finally the voice said, "Your destination is ahead on the right."

Jack slowed down, but he didn't see any sign of a 2420 mailbox or driveway. He saw another mailbox a bit further ahead, but it said 2422.

What the hell?

He turned around in that driveway and slowly went back again. Still no mailbox, but this time he noticed a thin strip of gravel on the side of the roadway. It was a fairly narrow road, but there hadn't been any traffic so far. He pulled the Buick as far to the right as he could and got out of the car. He quickly discovered why there was no visible mailbox and no clear driveway. The mailbox was lying in some weeds, still attached to the post. The entrance to the driveway was covered with fairly expensive camouflage netting.

Wow, somebody doesn't want anyone popping in for a social call.

Jack wasn't certain what he should do next. He knew he couldn't leave the car out on the road. After a moment's hesitation, he pulled the edge of the camouflage net up and simply followed it to its end. It was tied to a large sapling. Jack ducked under it and found the driveway. It curved to the right in 30 feet or so. He couldn't see any house or outbuildings from where he was standing. He went back to the sapling and untwisted the four sets of wires that he found to be holding that end in place. Then he tugged the netting loose and dragged it across to the other side of the driveway. He went back to his car and turned into the drive. He didn't bother replacing the netting.

It doesn't look like anyone's been here, so I don't think it's going to be an issue. Besides I can pretend to be a county official if need be, I still have the fake tags from Ivy. Plus leaving the netting on one side will help make a getaway if I need to. Now, let's go see what's up ahead.

He reached the turn, the gravel crunching under his tires. It turned back to the left and went up a small hill. As the car crested the hill, Jack could finally see the house. It was a small, white-painted frame house. There was a small barn to the left, badly in need of a paint job and two smaller sheds, one was similar to the barn and the second was constructed in now rusty aluminum.

Time for the frontal approach.

He drove the remaining 50 yards, scanning the property for any sign of life, but either no one heard his car or there was no one there. He stopped and got out of the car. There was a gated opening and a mostly grass-covered walk to the front porch, but the gate was missing the top hinge and leaned wobbly to the side. Jack walked up to the porch and pounded on the door. There was no answer. He tried peeking in the front windows, but it was too dark. He made his way to the side of the house and tried another window. This let him see a small table and chairs with a dilapidated cabinet along a wall. *Dining room maybe?*

He turned the corner to the back of the house. There was a narrow cement back porch. At one end stood an old hand pump that looked like it hadn't been used in ages. He looked through the window of the back door. It was a kitchen, but there were dishes stacked everywhere. He tried pounding on the door again. Still no answer. It didn't take long for him to take his next course of action. He found a good-sized rock and simply broke out the glass above the door lock.

Being careful not to cut himself on the glass, he reached in and flipped the deadbolt and the door lock.

As soon as he stepped in, a nasty wave of odor hit him. It came from the random piles of dirty dishes that he had seen through the window. The plates were covered in mold, the refrigerator door had been left open and the contents were covered in black and green. Jack reached over and flipped the light switch. It was dead.

This place is abandoned. What were they doing here? What was Mr. Assan up to?

Jack happily left the kitchen and went to the right where he had seen the dining room. It appeared that the food remnants had been moved to the kitchen, because other than dust, it was fairly clean. The next room was the living room and it stretched across the front of the house. Jack saw the reason that he couldn't see inside. Each window had been covered with sheets of black plastic. There were three sets of sawhorses, each supporting a four by eight sheet of plywood. Jack examined each makeshift table. Besides the dust, there was a considerable amount of white powder on each one. Jack wet his finger and touched some of the powder and then took a tentative smell. *Wow, that's not drugs, it's ammonia based.*

He looked around the room and saw a narrow staircase. The stairs creaked loudly as he made his way upstairs.

If anyone is up there, I'm making enough noise to let them know I'm on my way.

Just like the kitchen, the odor emanating from the bedrooms and the bathroom was awful. Jack peeked inside each room, just to be sure no one was there. One bedroom was fairly neat. It had a double bed and was actually made up. Each of the two other bedrooms had three cots placed haphazardly in various places. There were papers scattered on the floor of one of the rooms. Jack stepped inside to take a closer look. They appeared to be printouts of an Arabic newspaper or news magazine. Jack picked up one, folded it, and put it in his pocket. The stench from the bathroom was so strong that Jack decided there was nothing in there he wanted to see, not even if an entire terrorist organization was hiding behind the shower curtain.

He went back downstairs. He looked in each room one more time, but there didn't seem to be any clues about what had happened there. He went through the kitchen as fast as he could, holding his breath the entire way. Once outside he decided to check out the sheds first.

Neither the aluminum one nor the ramshackle wooden one held anything of interest. Jack heard a car coming down the road. He listened carefully, but it zoomed right by the entrance to the farm.

He approached the barn. It appeared that the only entrance was through a large sliding door. Jack pushed as hard as he could, but the door barely budged. He took a deep breath and lowered his shoulder to the door and pushed off again. He was rewarded by a gain of a foot and a half. He looked inside, but he needed more light to make anything out. He looked up to see if there was something obstructing the door, but it just appeared to be extremely rusted. This time he braced his foot against the door frame and shoved. He heard a grinding sound and the door rumbled another three feet before a metal screech signaled the end of the move. Jack looked inside again; there was enough sunlight to brighten the interior enough to look around.

Just like in the house, there were four sets of sawhorses, but only one was still supporting a sheet of plywood, the others sheets were either leaning against a sawhorse or were on the barn floor. Jack saw two plastic 55-gallon drums in the back corner. He walked back to examine them. They were both empty. As he walked by one of the plywood sheets, he noticed a corner of plastic sticking out from under it. He got his fingers under the plywood and lifted it up slightly, so he could pull on the piece of plastic. It was a discarded plastic bag of some kind.

Jack took the bag over to the door to read it.

Holy shit, it's ammonium nitrate!

Jack ran back to the barrels and rolled one outside into the daylight. There was no label on the outside. Jack found the cap and struggled to loosen it. After a concerted effort, the cap turned. Jack put his nose to the opening and cautiously inhaled.

It's some kind of fuel oil!

Jack got an uneasy feeling in his stomach. He looked around the rest of the barn area and didn't find any other clues. He went back outside, not bothering to push the door closed again.

OK, here's what we've got. If this is a terrorist plot and they have enough ammonium nitrate mixed with fuel oil...oh, fuck, they are making a car bomb.

Jack ran back to his car and backed it around. He got to the road and checked for oncoming cars before turning back toward Dyke. Suddenly he slammed on his brakes and shifted into reverse, backing into the drive. He jumped out of the car and found the broken mailbox. He dragged it and the post to the driveway and opened the flap. There were five items in it. He placed them on the trunk of the Buick and quickly looked through them. Three were advertising flyers, one was a generic insurance letter, but the other item was a letter addressed to Mr. Ahmoud Assan.

Jack ripped the envelope open. It was a bill from a petroleum delivery company for fuel oil. Jack drove back to the house and found the fuel oil tank at the side of the house. He thumped the side of it. It was empty.

OK, I've got to get back and get the state police or the FBI in on this.

He tore along the country road as fast as he could safely go. He remembered Yolanda's car at the last minute and turned into Stanardsville. He was relieved to see that the green Chevrolet was no longer in the parking lot.

Good, at least she's OK. I still don't know what brought her here.

He got back on the highway and headed to the hotel. He needed to talk with the FBI agents and let them know what he had found. He didn't see the deer until the last moment. Everything went dark.

62

YOLANDA IS TRAPPED LIKE A RAT

Yolanda slowly struggled awake. She had a nasty taste in her mouth.

Oh, man, I feel like crap. What hit me?

Then she remembered the shot. "What the hell time is it," she muttered. She looked down at her watch. It read 8:30 a.m.

God damn it. I've been asleep for about twelve hours.

Then she noticed that something was drastically different. Instead of her jeans and top, she was wearing some kind of loose and shapeless kind of dress thing. She swung her feet to the floor and stood up and then promptly sat back down.

Whoa, dizzy! I don't know what they gave me, but I've got to be careful.

She looked more closely at what she was wearing. She peeked down the top of the dress. All she had on underneath were her bra and panties. She was wearing socks, but she didn't see her shoes anywhere.

This is not good.

She struggled to her feet and steadied herself by holding the back of a straight chair. She could make out a wall switch next to the door. She took a deep breath and stumbled towards it. She put up her hands and caught herself at the wall. She reached out and flipped the light switch. A dangling overhead bulb provided a dim light. She turned and braced her back against the wall while she got her bearings.

There was a single, metal, Army-style bed, a small night stand, a card table, and two chairs; the straight chair she had already used to steady herself, and a metal folding chair. The floor was cement, no carpet, although the floor had at least been swept and was sort of clean. There was a covered dish and two thick mugs on the table.

Yolanda shook her head a couple of times to clear it and then unsteadily made her way back to the table. She plopped down heavily on the folding chair and lifted the cover of the dish. There were three pieces of some kind of coarse bread, a paste that had to be hummus, and some dates. She realized how hungry she was, it had been almost twenty hours since she had eaten. She dipped the bread in the hummus and took a bite. The bread tasted kind of stale, but she didn't care. She looked at one of the mugs, it was milk. She took a big drink and almost gagged. It had been sweetened with sugar. She quickly took another bite of bread, just to get the taste of the milk out of her mouth. She took the other mug and examined it. It was tea. She took a tentative sip. It was also sweetened, but drinkable. It might have been hot at one time, but now it was just room temperature, even so, she emptied half of it in one gulp.

It didn't take her long to finish the light meal and it certainly made her feel better. She noticed three books lying on the nightstand. She went over and brought them back to the table. One was a science fiction novel, another was a romance novel. The third book was a biography of Yasser Arafat. *OK, he said I would have something to read. How bored am I going to be before I decide to start reading one of these?*

She did another search under the bed for her shoes and regular clothes, but they were not to be found.

I can't believe one of those bastards took my clothes off of me. God damn it, look at this fucking tent dress. Is this what they think is modest? I look like a walking trash bag.

She felt better. She stood up and walked around the room.

OK, is there any way out of here?

It didn't take long to discover that the only way out was the door. No windows, no skylight, not even a ventilation shaft offered a way to escape. She examined the door. Although there was only a doorknob on the inside, she could see that there was some kind of deadbolt lock above it. She tried it and the doorknob wasn't even locked, but she couldn't get the door to budge a fraction of an inch.

She pounded on the door in frustration and she even began to cry a little.

It's hopeless and I'm helpless. What in the hell am I going to do?

She wiped her eyes with one of the voluminous sleeves of her dress and sat back down at the table. She sighed and picked up the science fiction novel. *Well, now I know how long it took.* She opened it to page one.

Suddenly she put the book down.

Galen! I completely forgot about Galen! I hope he's all right. I hope they quit beating him.

She didn't pick the book back up. She went over to the bed and curled up in a ball. Within minutes she was sound asleep.

63

JACK IS WEARING SOMETHING LIKE A DRESS TOO

Jack woke up with a start. He looked around, completely bewildered. He was lying in a bed.

What the hell? Is this a hospital or something?

He looked down at his hands, there were clips and tubes attached to them. He lifted up the sheets and saw that he was only wearing one of those hospital gowns that tie in the back.

What the fuck? Where in the hell am I? Jesus Christ, my head hurts.

He felt the top of his head. There was a heavy bandage or something wrapped around it.

He looked around and found a call button. He pushed it several times.

"Slow down there, Parnelli," a sturdy sized nurse came into the room. "You only have to push that button once. It sounded like a bell choir down at the desk."

"Where am I? What happened? What do you mean Parnelli?"

"Well, here's what happened, Speedy. You were flying down Highway 33 towards Ruckersville and you and a large deer decided to have a rendezvous. Your airbag went off and smacked you in the face, it also threw your forearms into your head. Your wristwatch gave you a nasty cut. You're at the Culpeper Regional Hospital in Madison. As I understand from what the state trooper said, you're going to be able to buy yourself a new car. Your old one has already been hauled to a junkyard."

"Holy crap. OK, where are my clothes, I have to get out of here."

"You're not going anywhere until the doctor says so."

"So, where in the hell is the doctor? I have to get out of here."

"Sir, you may have a concussion, your face is cut and bruised, and, even if I gave you your clothes back, you don't have a car to go anywhere. Just relax and I'll get you a sedative."

"Look, I was speeding because I have some information to give to the FBI. I have to talk to them."

"So, you're sort of a James Bond type too. Good thing your car didn't have an ejection seat or you might be in worse shape," she laughed.

"God damn it, it's not funny!" Jack yelled. That was a mistake. It made his head hurt.

"Look, I'm sorry, but this is serious. I need to talk to a state trooper or somebody."

"All right, just stay calm. Let me go call and see if I can get a trooper here. I don't know how I would contact the FBI. Just give me a minute." The nurse disappeared.

Jack was impatient. He looked over on the night stand. His phone wasn't there, neither were his wallet or car keys.

Shit! I hit a fucking deer! God damn it to hell! He noticed the blood pressure monitor increasing dramatically. *OK, she's right, if I don't calm down they may keep me here for a day or so.* Jack looked for something green. He had read somewhere that the color green lowered blood pressure. The seat of the side chair was upholstered in green. He became intensely observant of that chair.

A few moments later, the nurse returned. "OK," she said, "I called the state patrol and a trooper will be here in a few minutes. Turns out that they need to fill out an accident report on you and your car anyway. I guess there's something about speeding too. They measured your tire marks after you hit that deer. Seems like you were indeed in a hurry."

"It's because I have to talk to the authorities!" Jack started out loudly then managed to soften it up by the middle of the sentence.

"Well, Napoleon Solo, you'll be talking to one shortly. Would you like some jello or something to eat?"

"How do you know who Napoleon Solo is?" Jack asked.

"My husband. He's a nut about spy shows from the 1960's. I have more worthless crap in my house that you can imagine. I married a ten-year old."

"Could I maybe get something like a sandwich?"

"Sure, I'll call down and get something sent up. I'll be right back." She left the room again. Jack looked around. All of his tubes were connected to a couple of large plastic bags hanging from a wheeled contraption, but the finger monitor was connected to a computer.

Shit, I have to get disconnected by an engineering genius.

This time when the nurse came back, she was accompanied by a Virginia State Trooper.

"Mr. Jack Clayton?" he asked.

"Yes," Jack answered. "Listen, there are three FBI agents staying at the Airport Inn off of 29. Can you get them here or get me out of here?"

"Not so fast, Mr. Clayton. You've been in a serious accident that appears to have been in part due to a high rate of speed. We need to take care of that first."

Jack sighed. "Yes, the high rate of speed was due to the need to talk to the FBI. Trooper, uh…," Jack looked at his nametag. "Roberts, the FBI is investigating a terrorist cell. I believe I found their hideout and I'm pretty sure that they built or are building car bombs. That's what I have to pass on to them. Can you please help? Look in my wallet, it may not mean much to you, but I'm a private investigator. I'm one of the people who found the Confederate Gold in Ivy, you've heard about that. Well, this is on the level too and it's urgent. Can you either get them here or get me out?"

Trooper Roberts looked thoughtful. "Yes, we've been briefed that the Bureau was conducting investigations along the interstates, but I wasn't aware that they were all the way up here. What are they looking for exactly?"

Jack's patience was ebbing. "We can get all that done at the same time, there's no point in me telling you, then telling them. We're wasting time. Can you please contact them?"

Trooper Roberts didn't answer. He simply pulled out a cell phone and punched in a number. "HQ, this is Roberts. Contact whoever is patrolling 29 by the Airport Inn. They need to check and see if there are some FBI agents there. If that checks out, have them brought up here to the Culpeper hospital. Some private eye here says that he has some information about their investigation. Sure, got it." He hit the disconnect button. "So, we just have to wait and see. Now, let's get to that accident report."

Jack let quite a few swear words loose inside his head. The blood pressure monitor got busy again.

64

YOLANDA'S BURKA IS SO BECOMING

Someone was knocking on the door. It woke Yolanda up, just as she heard the lock turn. Suitman and one other man came into the room. She sat up, still slightly groggy, partially from sleep, partially from the aftereffect of the drug. Suitman walked over and sat down. The other man was carrying a plastic bag. Yolanda wondered what was in it.

"I see you enjoyed your breakfast," Suitman said.

"You didn't have to drug me," she answered.

"What I have to do or I don't have to do is none of your concern."

"I need to use the bathroom," she demanded. "And I also need a shower. And what did you do with my clothes? This dress thing is ridiculous."

"The bathroom? Yes, I understand you need to visit it. A shower? Out of the question, we do not have bathing facilities here. As far as the clothing, my colleagues were unhappy with your immodest apparel. One of them had a dress he purchased for his wife. You don't have to worry about your modesty regarding your clothing being changed while you were sleeping. The men have no interest in an American female. When you leave here your clothes will be returned to you." He turned and spoke to the other man before turning back to face Yolanda. "Ahmed will have to accompany you; I have other matters to attend to."

Yolanda stood up and went towards the door. She really did have to use the bathroom; it had been hours since Suitman had taken her the last time.

The man named Ahmed motioned for her to follow him. She stepped out into the hallway. It was much like the one where she had found Galen, but there wasn't any cabinet. He led her to the end of the hallway and turned left. It was the same restroom that she had used before.

"You don't have to keep the door open," she said.

Ahmed just looked at her and shrugged. Then he rattled off something in Arabic.

So, no English. I really have to go; maybe he won't keep the door open.

She pushed through the door and turned to close it, but, to her surprise, Ahmed actually followed her inside.

I guess Ahmed is a bit more curious that Suitman. I hope he's not planning on watching me go.

She checked the second stall to see if there was toilet paper. There was. She stepped inside and started to push the door closed, but Ahmed came up and put his hand on it, shoving it back open. He pointed at the toilet and then went and stood over by the sink, giving her just a token of privacy.

Oh well, I guess there's not much I can do about it, I have to go. Badly.

She could see Ahmed's reflection in the mirror. Unlike Suitman, he was taking a healthy interest in what she might be doing.

Ahmed doesn't seem to be so taken with feminine modesty.

Yolanda had an idea. She finished up and flushed the toilet. She walked to the sink and unscrewed the soap dispenser. There was enough dried soap residue to wash her hands. Ahmed continued his close inspection of her actions. She glanced at him and smiled. She slipped both of her socks off and then she lifted her left foot up into the sink and pulled the hem of her dress up to midthigh. Ahmed's eyes bulged. She rinsed her foot and then did the same with her right foot.

OK, let's see what happens if I put on a little more of a show.

She reached up under the dress and pulled her panties down and stepped out of them. Ahmed was breathing through his mouth. Yolanda got a little more soap from the dispenser and briefly washed and rinsed her panties. Then she went to the hand dryer and pushed the button, holding the panties under the hot air until they were fairly dry. She smiled at Ahmed, then turned her back to him as she slipped them back on. She fluffed out the dress and turned to face him.

"Sorry, but I don't have any others to change into," she said with a big smile.

Ahmed's face was red. He motioned for her to follow him. She did notice that the process had caused an obvious physical response.

OK, Ahmed, you liked what you saw. I don't know if you call a tent a yurt where you come from, but you just made a swell yurt in your pants! What are the chances that you might pay me a private visit a bit later after Suitman leaves?

She purposefully brushed close to him as she went out the door, keeping the big smile on her face.

The door to her room was standing open. Suitman was gone. Ahmed pushed her through it, then he glanced down the hallway in both directions. He came into the room and closed the door behind him. He stood there staring at Yolanda.

OK, this might happen sooner than later, let's see how much I'm going to have to do.

She walked over to the bed and sat down on it. Ahmed didn't move. She did a fake yawn and stretch. Then she reached down and pulled her dress up above her knees. She leaned back onto the pillow, and slowly brought her left leg onto the bed, allowing Ahmed to get a very long moment to examine her black panties before she brought her right leg up. She took the pillow and placed it behind her back as she sat up. She looked at him and smiled. He was breathing through his mouth again. She tugged the dress up a bit higher and opened her legs slightly wider, keeping her eyes on him the entire time.

Ahmed finally reacted. He slipped his shoes off and unbuckled his pants. In a swift motion he pushed them down to his knees. He wasn't wearing any underwear.

Oh, boy, here we go.

He came over to the bed and stood next to it. He reached down and pulled her dress up until her panties were exposed. He took his index finger and ran it up and down the crotch. Then he took his right hand and stroked his erection a couple of times. He pointed at Yolanda's mouth and then at the tip of his penis.

Oh, Ahmed wants some oral sex. Maybe that's all that he wants, but he's going to get surprised at what he's really going to get.

Yolanda got up and stood next to him. He licked his lips in anticipation. She reached behind her and undid the back buttons of the dress and then slipped it down off her shoulders and past her hips. It dropped to the floor. Ahmed's eyes grew huge as he stared at her. Whatever fantasies he had entertained about American women appeared to be coming true. She smiled and slipped both of her bra straps off her shoulders. His erection was reaching epic proportions.

She smiled at him and then turned him around to face the bed. She came up behind him and reached around to take his dick in her left hand. She began to stroke it. He let out a soft moan and reached behind him, trying to slip his fingers inside her panties.

OK, Ahmed, I think that's just about as much of Yolanda as you're going to get.

She leaned back and was just able to snag the handle of the tea mug from the card table. She hefted it in her hand and then hammered it on the back of Ahmed's head with all her strength. The mug didn't even break, but Ahmed crumpled into a heap, half on the bed and half off.

Lights out, Romeo. OK, let's see if I can go find Galen and get out of here.

She reached down to pick up the dress from the floor. Then she glanced at Ahmed and got an idea. *He's about the same size as me.*

She lifted him up onto the bed and then tugged his pants down and off. She slipped them on. They were loose on her waist, but they weren't going to fall off, she buckled the belt securely. Then she unbuttoned his shirt and put it on. Ahmed was naked except for his socks.

I need to buy some time.

She looked around the room for something to use, but there wasn't much there. Then she saw the plastic bag. She went over to the table and looked inside. There was a leather case, similar to the one that had contained the hypodermic needle and drug they had given her yesterday. More importantly there was also a roll of duct tape. She opened the case.

No, too risky, I don't know how much to dose him, but duct tape? Yay!

She went over to Ahmed and pulled one of his socks off. It didn't smell good. Now he was naked except for one sock. His penis had turned turtle and had gone way back into its shell. She rolled the sock into a ball and forced it into his mouth. Then she found the end of the duct tape and covered his mouth with one end and wrapped it around his head twice before tearing it off. Then she used it to tie his hands and feet. She ran the tape around the metal headboard and footboard to further immobilize him.

So long, Buddy, it's been fun.

She went to the door and peeked out both ways. No one. She closed the door behind her.

65

THE GAME IS AFOOT

It took less than an hour. Trooper Roberts came into the room accompanied by three FBI agents. "This man here is supposedly a private investigator, Jack Clayton. He says that you're investigating something to do with a terrorist cell and that he's found a clue."

The man looked at Jack. "My name is Tompkins, I'm the lead agent on this task force. I don't know about a terrorist cell, but one of the agents assigned to me is missing. We got a lead from another detective already. She found his car abandoned over in Stanardsville."

"She?" Jack asked. "Was it Yolanda Tilden?"

"Yeah. How did you know that?" the agent asked.

"I saw her around the hotel," Jack replied, "we used to be partners."

"Uh, were you ever more than partners?" the agent inquired.

"More than partners? What do you mean?" Jack was confused.

"Well, she showed up here the other night, sorely pissed off at Galen Foster. She was going to read him the riot act or something more extreme about some story he made up about him and her. Turns out her partner left her because of it. Man, she was pissed."

"Yeah," a second agent added, "at the time we thought he was pretty lucky to be out on a case, now it doesn't look like that. He's been gone way over 24 hours and it looks like he must have run into something worse than an irate female," he laughed.

It was a lie? She didn't do anything with Foster? That's why she's up here? Oh, holy fuck! What have I done?

"Never mind that," the trooper interjected. "Let this guy tell you what he saw or did, otherwise he's getting a hellacious speeding ticket."

Jack had to put Yolanda out of his mind for the moment. "OK," he started, "let me take this from the beginning. Several weeks ago, I was purchasing some magnetic car signs. There was a man in front of me picking up some signs also. From what I could tell they were car magnets too and they were for Greene County Schools. So, yeah, I did leave my partner and headed back alone to Indianapolis. I exited on the east side of Charlottesville to get breakfast. There were Greene County School vans in the parking lot, but they were all custom painted. I found the workers inside and asked them if the district ever purchased magnetic signs. They didn't think so, but they weren't sure…"

"Sir, is this blathering going anywhere?" the trooper interrupted.

"Yes, damn it, just wait. So when the store opened, I went back to the sign store and kind of bluffed my way into getting the sales records for that date. The guy in front of me, I forgot to mention one important detail: he looked Middle Eastern, his name was Ahmoud Assan." Jack paused to catch his breath.

"Were you able to find him?" the first agent asked.

"No, not at all, but I did find out that Greene County Schools never have had an employee by that name. So, I went back to the store and got away with another bluff, this time I got Assan's credit card number and I managed to get the mailing address for the card."

"Well, you're not going to bluff your way out of a 100 mile per hour speeding ticket," the trooper tossed out.

"I don't give a shit about a speeding ticket! Listen, I went to the address. It's an old farm outside of Dyke. The place is deserted. It looks like they cleared out permanently. I would guess that there were about seven of them."

"Seven of what?" the second agent asked.

"Jesus Christ! Can't you people follow along?" Jack yelled. "Seven Yemeni nationals! When I went out to the barn, I found traces of ammonium nitrate and fuel oil. I found a bill in the mailbox for a delivery of fuel oil, but the tank was empty. Let me spell it out for you. That terrorist activity you've been looking for, it's car bombs. And if I don't miss my guess, there are probably three vans with fake Greene County School magnets that are going to be the bombs."

That tirade caused all three agents and the trooper to quickly begin punching numbers into their phones. The resulting babble was impossible for Jack to follow, so he took a moment to think.

Yolanda came here to find Galen Foster. Why? Because he lied about having sex with her. Jesus Christ, Jack, you are such a dumbass! Why didn't you confront her? God damn, I am such a fucking idiot. OK, she's probably coming back to the hotel tonight. I'll just fucking knock on her door and say I'm sorry, that's about all I can do. She can't be any angrier than she was about that snake thing back in Greenfield. Well, maybe she can be, I just don't know. Fuck.

The initial flurry of phone calls ended.

The lead FBI agent got Jack up to speed.

"OK, field teams and hazmat teams are going to show up in Charlottesville and Stanardsville tonight. The trooper put an APB out for Greene County Schools vans, if they're out driving around, we'll get them. By the way, why do you think there are three vans?"

"Assan order six oversized truck magnets. Maybe he ordered some extras, but it points at there being three vans."

The third agent finally spoke up. "So, any take on what the target is going to be?"

Jack thought for a moment. "Yes," he slowly said. "I don't think the school signs are simply a cover. I went out to Stanardsville. There are three schools in a row: a high school; a middle school; and an elementary school. I don't think they are after a high-profile type of target like that Army installation. I think they're going to try and blow up one or more of the schools. Look what damage McVeigh did in Oklahoma. Can you imagine the casualties a van loaded up with those chemicals will cause?"

That premise started another flurry of cell phone calls among the agents.

"OK," the lead agent said, after concluding the call. "First things first, we have to find the van or vans. Closing the schools would cause widespread panic. We just have to set up a perimeter that will intercept the terrorists before they get close."

"And don't forget," Trooper Roberts added, "it's not a lock that the schools are the target. School vans don't present much suspicion about illegal activities."

"You're right," Jack interjected, "but I like that scenario. This is going to be a terrorist attack. They could take out someplace like that Army base on Route 29, but it's still a government building. If they decide to take out schools and school children, that will put the entire country into a panic. Schools are soft targets. I think one or more of the schools was their plan all along."

"All right," the lead agent said, looking at Jack. "Let's get you out of here."

66

AND INTO THE FIRE

Yolanda paused for a moment in the hallway.

OK, the restroom is to the right. This building can't be too big, let's take a look to the left.

She peeked around the corner. It was a short hallway with a closed door at the end. She tiptoed to it and put her ear to it. No sounds at all, just the persistent hum of a ventilation fan. She eased the door open to another short hallway with two doors on either side. It looked like another hallway opened to the right at the end. Three of the doors were open. She warily looked into each of them. Two were empty and the other contained a haphazard pile of office furniture. She bypassed the closed door and approached the open end.

There's the metal cabinet! This is the hallway where Galen is!

She took a second to orient herself. The door to the garage area was to her left. That meant that the last door on the right side was where she had found Galen. She still couldn't hear anyone or anything coming from behind the closed doors. She scurried down to the last door and slipped inside. It was dark. She felt on the side of the doorway for a light switch and flipped it on.

Galen was still tied to the chair, his head slumped down, just like the last time she had found him. She walked over to him and shook him.

"Galen," she urgently whispered. "Wake up, it's me. I'm getting you out of here."

She pushed his head back and then she saw it. A bullet hole in the middle of his forehead. Horrified, she took a step backwards and banged into a broken chair.

Then she heard a voice from behind her.

"Everyone here has a certain duty to perform. When Ahmed failed to appear, we went looking for him."

Yolanda whirled around. It was Suitman.

"You killed Galen! You killed an FBI agent!" she cried.

"One less American doesn't really matter, does it? Americans have killed thousands of my countrymen, it doesn't bother me," Suitman said.

"He was tied to a chair, you coward!"

Suitman took out his cell phone. He spoke to someone for a few seconds and then disconnected. "I just told my friends to stop looking and come here. They were very amused when they discovered what you had done to Ahmed."

In a moment, four men crowded into the room. One of them was Ahmed. Somewhere he had found a pair of athletic shorts. He walked up to Yolanda and slapped her hard across the face. Then he pointed at his shirt and pants.

"Ah, my friend Ahmed wishes to reclaim his property," Suitman said. "Please be so kind as to remove them."

Yolanda didn't have a choice. She unbuckled the belt and undid the button. She pushed the pants down and stepped out of them, then she took off the shirt and threw it at Ahmed.

Two of the men came and each grabbed an arm.

"We are taking you back to your room. Unfortunately you have forfeited the limited freedom I afforded you. I'm afraid that you will have to be seated like your former friend." Suitman pointed at Galen.

"Fuck you," Yolanda replied.

"Ah, such vulgarity from such a pretty face," Suitman laughed.

He turned and led the way back to her original room. Once there, Yolanda was firmly seated on the metal folding chair. Suitman pulled a chair close to her and sat down.

"No dress?" she asked.

"No, you will have to be content with your undergarments. You won't be leaving this room, so you have no need of outerwear. Now, I have something important to discuss with you."

"You can just go fuck yourself," she said.

Suitman leaned forward and slapped her twice. "You will need to show a little more respect." He held up his hand in front of her face. "Slapping stings a little, but watch closely." He closed his hand into a fist. "Such a simple effort, the closing of one's hand, it can cause the instrument of a slightly hurtful slap into a much worse infliction of pain. Ahmed has a brother, Amjad, a similar name, but much different in personalities. Amjad greatly enjoyed his chats with your FBI friend and, believe me, there was no slapping involved. You humiliated his brother and he is very anxious to avenge his shame."

"Yes, another one of your brave countrymen who beats on helpless victims."

That earned her another slap.

"Your sharp tongue is little defense, but enough of that. I took the liberty of examining the contents of your purse that was in your rental car."

"So?"

"I discovered a small notebook that belonged to your friend and a large piece of paper. It seems that he was onto our activity. It also appears that the notebook provided the clue that led you to our van."

"So what?" she asked.

"Oh, it is trivial, I'm just in a sharing mood. It is almost amusing that you both ended up here in a similar fashion. Your friend made the same mistake that you made. He approached one of the vans and pulled out his shiny badge, expecting that it would intimidate the men. It simply led to him being rendered unconscious and thrown in the back, just like you, who decided to voluntarily take a ride."

"And now? What's going to happen now?"

Suitman studied her for a moment. "Well, I'm sorry to tell you this. First of all, we are executing our plan this morning. You will be left here. You will be taken to the restroom one more time, then placed back in your chair. We may return to this building or we may not. It depends on the outcome of our endeavor. It is an act of kindness that I allow you to use the facilities before we leave. If we do not come back, it may be a while before someone finds you."

"You're sorry to tell me that?" she asked.

Suitman sighed. "No, this is what I am sorry about. Amjad has been quite insistent about regaining the family's honor. I promised him that he could spend some time with you before we leave. If it's any relief, I told him not to kill you."

"Fuck you and your worthless goons."

Suitman smiled. "I will not slap you for your insolence again. I'm afraid that it will not prepare you for your chat with Amjad."

He stood up and spoke to two of the men.

"Farid and Yasif will take you to the restroom. When you are finished they will secure you to this chair. The rest of us will be making final preparations while Amjad comes to see you. I would not be surprised if Ahmed wants to watch."

The two men grabbed Yolanda and hoisted her up from the chair. This time there was no privacy afforded in the restroom. When they returned, they taped her feet to the two front legs of the chair and pulled her arms straight down and taped them to the back legs before leaving without a backwards glance.

Moments later, Ahmed and the short, heavier man she had seen earlier came into the room. She noticed that Ahmed had traded his pants and shirt for just the athletic shorts he was wearing earlier. He walked over and slapped her. Then he pulled her bra straps to the side and pushed it down to her waist. He stepped behind the chair and cupped both of her breasts with his hands and squeezed them hard. Yolanda clenched her teeth to keep from making a sound. He went back to the front of the chair and knelt before her. Looking intently into her eyes, he took his thumbs and forefingers and pinched both of her nipples until the pain finally brought tears to her eyes. That was what he had been waiting for. He stood up and pulled his shorts down. He was hard.

If he tries to stick that smelly thing in my mouth I'm going to bite it off.

Ahmed must have realized that fact and didn't act on it. Instead he thrust his hips forward and began twisting back and forth, lightly slapping her face several times with his erection. Then he stepped back and smiled at her. He took his right hand and started stroking himself. Yolanda studied his face intently. After a few moments she saw him tense up. When she heard him start to groan, she yanked her head to the side just as he began spurting on her face. She felt it run down the side of her cheek. Ahmed reached down and grabbed her chin and roughly pulled her face to him. He held it tightly as he smeared his semen all over her face with his other hand. He smugly smiled and slapped her one more time. He pulled his shorts back up and wiped his hands on them before sitting down on Suitman's chair. A grinning Amjad took his place in front of her.

67

JACK IS BACK

The doctor approved Jack's release the night before. He caught a little sleep in spite of the fact that he was worried. He had stopped at the Airport Inn on his way to Charlottesville. His detective badge got him Yolanda's room number, but she didn't answer the door. He looked in the parking lot and the green Chevrolet wasn't there. He even double-checked with the desk clerk to make sure she still had a room. She did.

It was now seven in the morning. Jack was standing outside an FBI van on the outskirts of Stanardsville. It was basically a council of war. The first question was quite logical.

"What makes you think it's today?" Agent Tompkins asked.

"I can't answer that," Jack replied. "All I know is this. The farm operation, their hideout, is deserted. If they were making car bombs, it's done. Those things are too volatile to keep in storage. If it's not today, we have to do this tomorrow and the next day until we find the vans."

State Trooper Roberts chipped in, "We have cars scouring every country road and highway in the area. We even have two choppers overhead. There hasn't been a single sighting of a van with the signs you described."

"They must be in a garage or warehouse," Jack observed. "Heck, if they aren't on the road, they could be behind a house or a tree."

Another FBI agent got out of an operations van with a detailed map of Stanardsville.

"Look," he said. "We don't have to deploy a large number of agents or troopers. Access to the town and to the schools is kind of limited." He traced the routes with the eraser end of a pencil. "Here's the 33 Bypass where we are with the intersection of Route 622, Celt Road. The original 33 comes up from the east, it turns into Spotswood Trail and then back to 33 west of town. There's the road from Madison and Ford Road. That's five lines of approach."

"Hopefully we'll spot the van or vans before they get this close," Roberts said.

"I have a question," Jack said. "What exactly are we going to do when they get here?"

Tompkins sighed. "Yes, we've been discussing that. We set up a roadblock. How do they react? If they don't get suspicious that it's for them, maybe they will try to bluff their way through. On the other hand, they might turn around and try to get away. One thing we do have to keep in mind is this. If they panic or get spooked, what if they detonate the car bomb? We could lose a lot of personnel."

"I have an idea," Jack said. "You guys have temporary vehicle inspection signs. Why not put some a mile or so out on all routes into town? That would allay any suspicions that they might have about seeing state police cars in their path."

"Good point," Tompkins said. "And that really wouldn't cause any traffic back-up, because we wouldn't actually be stopping anyone. We would just wave them through."

"Yes," Roberts added, "the last thing we want are several civilian vehicles involved in this."

"So now we wait," Tompkins said.

68

THE WAIT IS ALMOST OVER

All three garage doors were open when Ahmed and Amjad came into the garage.

"Is the family honor restored?" Suitman asked.

Amjad showed him the blood on his hands. "Yes, Ahmoud, I am grateful for your permission."

"Is she alive?"

"Yes, I was careful, but she will wish she was dead when she wakes up."

"Yes," Ahmed added gleefully, "Amjad was masterful."

"Fine," Assan nodded. "Now, both of you take the third van. Yasif is driving the first van and Farid the second. I will follow in my van. Once we have them in place, I will collect you and then I will detonate the bombs with the remote switch. We will be well on our way to D.C. before the authorities can react."

"This will be our greatest honor, to avenge our countrymen and show the Americans that they are not safe in their homes anymore," Amjad proudly said.

"Let's start that lesson now," Assan said. He waved to the two other vans and the drivers started the engines. Ahmed got into the driver's seat of the third van and waited for Amjad to climb in. The four vehicle caravan drove down the deteriorated concrete drive to the main highway. It turned left on 33 and headed east to Stanardsville.

It was dead quiet in the truck depot. Yolanda was mercifully unconscious in her darkened room. Amjad had indeed been masterful.

■ ■ ■

A state trooper jumped out of his cruiser. "They spotted them," he yelled. "They're on 33 heading here from around Elkton! A chopper spotted them!"

"Them?" Roberts yelled back. "How many vehicles are there?"

"Four!" came the shouted response. "They're about ten minutes out."

"OK," Tompkins said, "let's set up the roadblock where the Bypass goes back to 33."

"And we'll wait and see what our friends do," Jack added.

"We'll put cruisers out there, FBI vans don't do road inspections," Roberts noted.

"Good idea," Tompkins agreed, "we'll pull the FBI vans back to the next cross intersection in case something goes crazy."

"Seriously," another trooper added. "If one of those vans goes off, the fewer people we have around the better."

That observation caused quite a few throats to uncomfortably swallow.

■ ■ ■

Each occupant of the vans was deeply engaged in thought. That's why Yasif almost missed the sign on the side of the road. He pulled the van over and stopped, causing all the following vans to do the same.

Ahmoud Assan got out of his van and hurried up to the front where the others had gathered.

"What is it? What's wrong, Yasif?"

Yasif pointed at the sign. "Look, it says there's a vehicle inspection up ahead."

"Damnation," Assan exclaimed. "That could be trouble."

"What do you want us to do? Should we go on ahead?" Farid asked.

"No, one van might not be suspicious, but a policeman might think three vans are too much of a curiosity. Keep driving now, but turn left on the first road that you find. We will drive north a bit, then turn back eastward. We can approach the schools from the north."

The next road that intersected 33 wasn't far down the road. The caravan turned northward.

■ ■ ■

"They left 33," was the next shouted report.

"Where?" Tompkins asked.

"The chopper doesn't know, it's a county road about a mile and a half from here."

"God damn it! The inspection sign must have spooked them. Now what?" Tompkins asked.

They all studied the map.

"If they turn back east, they'll eventually intersect Ford Road," Roberts observed.

"Fine," Tompkins said. "Look, leave two cruisers here, just in case they do turn back. Let's haul ass up to wherever Ford Road is and set up there."

■ ■ ■

The caravan did reach Ford Road, but the inspection sign had been placed further out, so they didn't see it. Yasif's van came over a slight hill and he saw four cruisers about a half a mile up the road. He slammed on the brakes so hard that the following van almost hit him.

Once again Assan had to run up to see what had happened. He motioned for the others to remain in the vans.

"There are state troopers up ahead," Yasif explained.

Assan thought for a moment. "This is not a coincidence. They would not have inspection stations set up on different roads. Somehow they suspect something. I don't know how, the agent and the woman could not have shared the information about us."

"Should we turn around?" Yasif asked.

"No, we have come to avenge our country. Gather the others here, quickly."

Within moments the seven men were once again gathered by Yasif's van.

■ ■ ■

"Something's up," a trooper reported to Tompkins by radio. "I can see one van, it's stopped a little ways up the road. It looks like there are several men standing around it. What do you want us to do?"

"Just sit tight," Tompkins directed. "We'll wait and see what they do next."

"Affirmative."

■ ■ ■

The six men looked at Assan expectedly. He stepped in front of each of them in turn and placed his hand on their foreheads. After that he spread out his arms and began to speak to them.

"My brothers, it seems that our plan will not work out as we originally planned. We do know what task lies before us. We agreed before we accepted this responsibility that we would accept martyrdom in order to complete our mission. That time has come upon us. You will continue into the city and bring vengeance and glory to our cause. I will take the responsibility to announce your courage and sacrifice to our brethren. You will be honored for an eternity and your actions will inspire the hearts of others. They will be moved by your sacrifice to perform similar acts of courage."

A couple of the men shifted uncomfortably on their feet at that announcement.

"The policemen are there to stop us, but we will try something different. Yasif, you drive up slowly as if you intend to stop, then accelerate through and head to the elementary school. Farid, they will focus on Yasif, you take the road to the right. There is a small shopping center a short distance from there. If they are indeed aware of our plan, they won't consider it a target. It is not our planned objective, but it will send a message. Ahmed, you and Amjad must follow Yasif. If it appears you will not be able to get through, you can manually detonate the bomb. It should take a number of policemen to hell and your souls will pass them in upward flight."

They all nodded assent.

"My brothers, you will meet later today in heaven and I will someday join you there. An eternity of bliss awaits the martyrs of our cause. An eternity of bliss awaits you," Assan concluded.

■ ■ ■

"Agent Tompkins!" the trooper reported. "They're moving this way. At least the first three of them are. I don't see the fourth van."

"Hold tight," the agent replied. "Be ready to use force."

"Roger."

69

THE BALLOON GOES UP

Yasif slowed the van down as he approached the cruisers. A state trooper stepped out onto the road and waved him to a stop. Yasif rolled down the window.

"Hello, officer, may I be of service?" he asked politely.

"Good morning, sir, we are running a safety inspection this morning. Would you mind pulling your car over there and you and your partner step out of the vehicle?"

"Of course, officer," Yasif smiled and nodded his head up and down.

He put the two right tires on the grassy berm and then floored the accelerator. The state trooper fell down trying to get out of the way. Three other troopers opened fire as the van careened down the street. At that moment Farid roared up to the road block, then turned the wheel sharply to the right. The suspension of the old van groaned, but it didn't tip over. It bounced over a curb and then sped away toward the shopping center.

Yasif's van broke through the roadblock. Then he looked ahead and saw the FBI vans at the next intersection. The agents began firing at the van from the front. "Rashad!" he yelled. "We won't get through! It is time! Push the detonator!"

Just as Rashad brought the remote up to his face, a bullet crashed through the windshield and hit his hand, shattering the bones and the plastic detonator. At almost the same moment another bullet hit Yasif in the lower jaw. The pain caused him to swerve the van and it flipped over and rolled three times before it came to a smoking halt in a ditch. Rashad was thrown through the window and his body was lying in the middle of the road.

Ahmed was following in the third van when he saw the black FBI vehicles approach the first van from their back-up position. He saw Yasif's van flip up into the air and he slowed down momentarily.

"Don't slow down, Ahmed!" Amjad urged. "We have to get to the school!"

By this time Farid's van was bearing down on the shopping center just two blocks away from the shooting. Assan had been correct, there were no police or FBI blocking the road. He steered the van toward the main entrance and it struck the curb. Bashir was holding the detonator and the sudden jolt caused him to lose his grip on it. As he fought to keep hold of it, he accidentally connected the electrodes. In an instant the van and the two men disappeared in a huge explosion. All the facing windows of the store complex were shattered, along with most of the windows of the cars parked in the lot. Several vehicles caught on fire.

Ahmed's jaw dropped as both he and Amjad looked at the cloud of smoke. Then Ahmed glanced in the rearview mirror. He slammed on the brakes and threw the van into reverse.

"What are you doing?" Amjad screamed.

"Look!" Ahmed pointed back up the road. "It's Assan! He's already turned back! No, Amjad! I'm not ready to be a martyr!"

He slammed the gear shift into drive, floored the accelerator, and sent it hurtling after Assan's.

■ ■ ■

The trooper radioed in what he had witnessed.

"The last van has turned around and is fleeing the scene. We'll go after it."

"Yes, go right ahead," Tompkins okayed.

Jack heard the exchange. "Wait a minute, Tompkins."

"What?"

"The state troopers still have that helicopter up there. Ask them where the fourth van is going," Jack directed.

Tompkins connected with the helicopter through the trooper's radio.

"The last van turned around before the explosion," the pilot reported. "It's heading back down the way they came in. There's another van that just turned and is following it."

The trooper looked at Tompkins expectantly. "Sir, are we going after them?"

Jack butted in. "No, let's just tail them at a distance. Chances are they'll lead us back to their base of operations. Who knows what we might find there? And have them tell that copter pilot to maintain enough altitude that they don't realize he's up there. We've got them, there's no rush."

Tompkins nodded, "OK, that makes sense to me. Just a minute." Tompkins radioed the state trooper again and relayed the orders that Jack had given him. "Come on, Clayton, let's see where they take us."

Two other agents climbed in the back seat and they took Ford Road out of town, followed by four troopers in two cruisers. They made the turns that Assan and Ahmed had taken and soon found themselves heading toward the town of Elkton.

The radio crackled. "Agent Tompkins! The first van has entered what looks to be an abandoned shipping depot. There are no other vehicles in the area except a green sedan."

Jack leaned forward, "Did he say green sedan?"

Tompkins nodded.

"Ask him if he can tell what make it is?"

Tompkins relayed that request. In a moment the reply arrived.

"Negative, Jack," Tompkins shook his head. "The copter pilot says that if he got that close, they would know they were under observation. The second van is getting close to the depot."

"Tompkins!" Jack yelled. "That green car. My partner was driving a green car and she's disappeared! That could be her car!"

"Holy fuck!" Tompkins yelled back. "Do you suppose she's in that building someplace?"

"I don't know. I just know I haven't been able to find her since three days ago."

■■■

Assan was cursing to himself. *Damn Americans! How did they know? The only two people who could have known are still in the depot.*

He pulled up outside the building, the three garage doors still standing open. He started to go inside, but he heard a car on the highway. Much to his surprise it was one of the vans.

Why are they here? Why didn't they fulfill their mission?

The van turned onto the access road. He could see that it was Ahmed driving. He slowed as he approached Assan.

"What happened?" Assan asked. "Why have your returned here?"

"I am so sorry, my friend," Ahmed started. "My faith failed me and I could not go any further."

"But you swore an oath!" Assan angrily shouted.

"And perhaps I will be punished for my cowardice, but I could not continue after I saw what became of Farid and the others."

Assan decided on his next course of action.

"As you may well be," he agreed. "I am going to drive back and observe what is happening in the town so I might make my report. Drive the van into the depot and we'll disarm it when I return."

Assan quickly climbed into his van and reached the highway. He pulled off on the berm and watched as Ahmed drove the van into the garage. Then he reached over and picked up the remote detonator.

"Your duty was to die avenging our lost brothers, you coward. Now you can serve the purpose of destroying the evidence of our operation," he said out loud.

Then he toggled the switch marked Van 3.

The entire garage area went up in a massive explosion with flames and debris flying up in a billowing black and gray cloud of smoke. Assan smiled. *Now you can go be with your brothers.* He started back down the highway to Stanardsville.

70

YOLANDA

It was the pain. It was the pain that Yolanda began to feel as she slowly regained consciousness. She pulled her head up and tried to open her eyes, but they were swollen shut and caked with dried blood. She managed to open her left eye a tiny bit. She was alone. She began to cry, but the sobbing made her sides ache. It hurt to breathe. *I think he must have broken some of my ribs. Oh, God, I hurt so bad.* She looked down and, in spite of the dim light, she could see the bruises already apparent on her arms, stomach, and breasts. Amjad had concentrated on those body parts at the beginning, before eventually ending the ordeal by savagely beating her face. She was unconscious before he stopped. Yolanda tried breathing through her nose, but that only produced tiny, bloody bubbles, so she had to breathe through her mouth, in spite of the sharp pain that every breath demanded. She tried to control her crying, but she couldn't control the pain. *He said they might not come back. What if no one finds me? I'm so thirsty, I'm so damn thirsty.* She tried moving her feet to see if she could stretch the duct tape, but even that effort increased the pain in her chest. She slumped back down. *I don't know what to do. At least Galen got a bullet. I don't know how long I can last.* She had never felt so alone or so terrified.

She obviously wasn't aware of the drama that was happening outside, but suddenly a powerful force lifted her and the chair into the air. She came crashing down on the floor, striking her head on the metal footboard. For the second time that morning she was mercifully knocked unconscious, and was soon covered up by falling ceiling tiles and fragments of drywall.

■ ■ ■

"Holy shit!" came from the radio.

"What? What happened?" Tompkins asked.

"The building just blew up! One of the vans left the compound and then stopped on the highway. Just as soon as the other one went into the garage, the whole building went up in smoke!"

Jack looked ahead; he could already see the cloud of smoke.

"Can't you go a little faster," he urged.

"We're almost there," Tompkins replied.

As they crested a slight hill, a white passenger van flew by them.

"That was Assan! He's heading back to Stanardsville," Tompkins cried out. He grabbed the mike. "Assan is heading east on 33. Put some blowout strips on the downside of that hill on Ford Road. I don't want him to see them before he hits them. No shooting, take him alive and cuff him until we're done over here."

"Yes, sir, we'll get it done right away."

"That should take care of him anyway," Tompkins said.

Jack just nodded. He couldn't tear his eyes away from the billowing smoke. *Don't let her be in there. Don't let her be in there. She's on her way to Indianapolis.*

Tompkins turned on the access road and floored the sedan until it got close to the building. There were already several state troopers standing around watching it burn.

Jack jumped out of the car and ran over to the green sedan. It had been flipped onto it's roof, but hadn't caught on fire. He ran to the back and looked. It was an Enterprise rental car. It was Yolanda's.

Oh, please, God.

The front of the building was all on fire, the frame of the van was barely visible through the flames. Jack ran over to a chain link fence that went along the side of the building.

"What are you doing, sir?" a trooper inquired. "Where do you think you're going?"

"Someone may be trapped in there," Jack yelled back.

"You can't go in there. If there was anyone in there, it's too late for them."

"I'm going to find a way in. Get on your radio and get an emergency squad here!" Jack ordered.

"Suit yourself, but I'll call the squad. Most likely it will be for you," the trooper added.

Jack just looked at him for a moment and then clawed his way up and over the six-foot fence.

He ran along the length of the building. The initial heat from the fire kept him away from the garage area. He found a door. It had been blown off its hinges. Jack tried entering. There weren't any open flames, but the smoke and the heat pushed him back. He dropped to the ground and looked inside. Most of the wall separating the garage from the office area had been blown back, blocking access to the hall. There was one door left intact on the left side of the exit door. Jack pulled the bottom of his jacket up to shield his face. He took a deep breath and ran for the door. The heat was intense, but he managed to grab the doorknob and turn it. He stepped into the room. It was dark, but the heat was less intense. He could make out jumbled pieces of furniture strewn around the room, either by design or as a result of the explosion. Then he saw her. She was somehow strapped to a chair that had been blown against the far wall. Only her feet and her hands were visible. Jack ran to her.

"Yolanda! Yolanda!" he cried out. He pushed the debris aside until he could grab the chair legs and pull it free, then he turned it to him.

He was staring at Galen Foster's face.

"Foster," he breathed. Jack didn't need to check for any vital signs. He could make out the bullet hole in Foster's forehead.

Holy shit, Foster, what happened? God damn it.

It was growing hotter in the room. There wasn't any other exit and Jack didn't have time to try and untie the body. He set the chair upright and tilted it onto its back legs. He dragged it over to the door and braced himself for the ordeal. He took one large breath of the hot, smoky air and then flung the door open. The wave of heat struck him like a physical blow. He shut his eyes against the smoke and dragged the chair and Foster outside before he fell down to the ground. He looked back at the building. The fire had completely overtaken the hallway and was burning its way further.

He looked down at Foster. *Stay here, I'll be back for you. I promise.*

He ran down the rest of the length of the building. There were no more doors or windows. Jack turned to the back of the building. There weren't any regular doors or windows across the entire expanse of the back, but there was a small loading dock door in the middle. Jack climbed up on the dock. The force of the explosion had buckled the door about four feet up from the cement deck. Jack bent down, grabbed the handle, and lifted. It wouldn't budge.

"No!" he screamed in frustration.

He got down on his knees and grabbed the bottom handle. He gripped it with both of his hands and pulled as hard as he could. Sweat poured down his face, but he felt the door move a little. The bottom panels pushed up to where the door had buckled. There was just enough space to put his hands under the bottom of it. He took a few more deep breaths and then heaved with all his might. The door lurched up another ten inches then came to a metal-screeching stop. He had maybe twelve or fourteen inches of clearance.

Jack looked at the slight opening and, just for a moment, regretted the bacon and french fries he had been treating himself to. He struggled out of his jacket and threw it down on the dock. Then he got down on his back and stuck his head under the door. He brought his arms inside and pushed against the door, forcing himself further inside. The air was hot and smoky, but nowhere near as bad as where he found Foster. Once his hips made it under the door, he rolled onto his stomach and stood up. There was one door leading into the main building and it opened into a narrow hallway with another door at the end.

Jack reached the door and felt around it. It was warm, but not terribly hot. He knew what could happen if he opened it and the fire found fresh air. He threw the door open and jumped through it, slamming it shut immediately. No burst of flame came as a result. He let out a deep breath. He turned left and then made a right turn. He passed a restroom. The next hall turned to the right and there was a bank of six doors on the left hand side.

"OK, these are going to be hot," he breathed to himself.

He popped the first door open and only found scattered pieces of furniture like where Galen had been. He moved to the second door. There was a bed leaning crazily on its side next to a crumpled card table. He couldn't see anything else. He proceeded down and checked the other four rooms. It was getting terribly hot.

What if she was in that first hallway where Foster was? Oh, Christ, she wouldn't have survived.

Suddenly Jack had a thought.

A bed? Why would there be a bed here? They stayed at the farm!

He ran back to the second room. He went to the wall and yanked the bed away from it. Just like Foster, there was someone strapped into a chair under a pile of ceiling debris. Jack clawed his way through it until he uncovered the chair.

"Yolanda?" he whispered.

Her skin was covered with gray dust and her face was swollen and unrecognizable. He saw that she was bare from the waist up.

"Yolanda!" No response. He frantically put his fingers on her neck, feeling for a pulse. There was one. A feeble one, but she wasn't dead.

"Yolanda!" Still no response. Suddenly Jack heard a crashing noise from the hallway.

Shit! I have to get her out of here!

He examined the chair. They had used duct tape to bind her. He found the end of the tape at the front left leg of the chair and quickly unwrapped it and the right leg. Her hands had been secured to the back legs. Jack was able to tear the tape that was holding her wrists. Then he picked her up and put her over his right shoulder. She was a dead weight. He opened the door and saw what had caused the crash. The ceiling of the hallway that he had come down had fallen.

Looks like we go left.

He stumbled through the smoke and felt the hallway turn to the right.

This is going to take me back to the loading dock.

It did. Jack laid Yolanda on her back by the overhead door. He pushed her upper torso under the door before reversing the way he had earlier entered. Once he was on the dock, he pulled Yolanda the rest of the way from under the door. He climbed off the side of the loading dock and picked her up in his arms. He carried her a fair distance away from the burning building and found a patch of grass among the crumbled asphalt of the loading area. He looked at her in the daylight.

"Holy shit," he cried. "Yolanda, what happened?"

He brushed some of the dust from her face and could see the dried blood everywhere.

"Yolanda!" Jack burst out crying. "I'm so sorry, I'm so sorry. I shouldn't have left you! Please be OK! Please! I love you so much!"

He missed it the first time and almost missed it the second time, but he finally felt it. Her left index finger moved against the palm of his hand. Tap, tap, tap. For the second time in minutes he burst into tears as he buried his face in the palm of her left hand.

"I've got to get help," he said out loud. "I'll be back, Yolanda, I have to leave you for a minute or two, but I'll be back." Jack ran to the loading dock and grabbed his jacket. He raced back and knelt beside her. He brushed his hand softly against her face and then he gently draped his jacket over her bare chest. "I'll be back," he repeated.

He wiped at his eyes as he sprinted back toward the front of the building. The emergency squad was there, just like he had asked. He frantically waved them over to the fence.

"My partner is badly hurt! She's at the back of the building; bring your unit around the far side. I'll be waiting there! "

The ambulance made it around the building within minutes. The medics quickly placed Yolanda on a gurney and placed her in the back of the ambulance. Jack could see them putting IV's into her arm as the back door closed.

Jack stood by helplessly for a few minutes. Then the back door opened and an EMT stepped out. "How is she doing?" Jack anxiously asked.

"Looks like you got to her just in time," the EMT replied. "Her heart rate is improving and her respiration has too. She was covered in dried blood and her blood pressure was low, but it was within an OK range, so she didn't lose too much blood. She's stabilized and we've cleaned her up quite a bit. So now we'll get her to the hospital in Harrisonburg," the EMT explained. "Do you want to ride along with us? There's room."

"No." Jack was torn. "No, I need to settle some things here. You're sure she'll be OK?"

"About as sure as I can be, but I can't promise anything. You know that," the EMT replied.

"I am so grateful I found her. That explosion was huge and it banged her up so badly. She was buried under the debris," Jack said. "God, I am so grateful that she survived that. It was a close thing; I barely got her out of there ahead of the fire."

The EMT looked at Jack for a moment. "Uh, as far as I can tell, except for a slight head wound, she wasn't injured by that explosion."

"No? What do you mean?" Jack asked.

"Somebody gave her a severe beating. Those bruises and that blood were a result from someone pounding the hell out of her. It looks like her nose is broken and she may have lost some teeth. Nope, all that didn't come from the explosion, not at all," the EMT added.

Jack didn't say anything else. He just watched the ambulance maneuver around the corner and then speed down the highway to Harrisonburg. Another ambulance carrying Galen Foster soon followed. It didn't need to hurry.

71

LET'S PLAY A GAME

By the time Jack walked back to the front of the building and climbed over the fence, several more fire-fighting vehicles were there. A wrecker had already hooked a chain to the frame of the van and pulled it out of the garage. A county coroner was checking to see if there were any identifiable remains.

There was a makeshift picnic table under a tree. Tompkins and two other FBI agents were sitting with Ahmoud Assan. Jack walked over. Assan was sitting with his leg crossed over his knee, smoking one of the dark cigarettes he had once offered Yolanda.

"How did he get here?" Jack asked Agent Tompkins, pointing at Assan.

"They put out the strips like I ordered. He hit them so fast that it blew all four tires. I had them bring him over here so we could get some information out of him."

"So," Jack turned to face Assan, "things didn't work out so well today, did they? I expect you'll be spending a lot of time here in Virginia or in some federal prison somewhere."

Assan just smiled and took another draw on his cigarette.

"Uh, Jack," Tompkins said, "come over here a minute."

Jack followed him to the other side of the access road.

"What gives, Tompkins?"

"Jack, the son-of-a-bitch has a diplomatic passport. We can't arrest him. He's denying any involvement, only that he was there to check up on those men and to make sure they were adapting to American life. He says he was just as shocked as anyone with what happened today."

"You've got to be fucking kidding me," Jack spit on the ground.

"Nope, and the bastards killed an agent," Tompkins replied. "We can hold him 24 hours on a bench warrant, but then he's free to go."

"Is it OK if I ask him a question or two?"

"OK by me," Tompkins answered, "but he doesn't have to answer them."

They both walked back to the table.

"So, you're a diplomat?" Jack asked.

Assan merely smiled and nodded.

"Did you know what was going on in that building?" Jack continued.

"No, I thought they were school employees, just like everyone else. They kept everything very well concealed from me," Assan replied.

"There was a dead FBI agent in there," Jack said.

"That could only have been the work of the one called Amjad. You'll be pleased that he perished in the explosion here."

"And there was a woman," Jack added.

"Ah, yes, she stumbled into their base of operations three days ago," Assan noted.

"Is she dead too?" Jack asked.

Assan spread his hands, "I have no idea, perhaps she escaped, perhaps you will find her remains in the ashes."

"Was she beaten like the FBI agent was?" Jack continued.

"A most unfortunate situation arose," Assan stubbed his cigarette out and flipped the butt onto the access road. "Instead of cooperating like she was asked to, she took certain steps that humiliated one of the men, Amjad's brother as a matter of fact. You have to understand that in Yemen, women have quite a different social role than American women. This woman directly shamed Ahmed which brought a stain upon the family name. In order to expunge that shame, the woman had to be dealt with. As I understand it, Amjad punished her sufficiently to restore honor to the family."

"In other words, you had her almost beaten to death," Jack grimly noted.

"Oh, please, not me, I was merely a bystander in all these arrangements. Still, I don't think it can hurt the woman to learn a little humility."

Jack had to restrain himself from punching Assan in the face.

"So, am I free to go?" Assan asked Agent Tompkins.

"No, not just yet," Tompkins replied. "We still have some things to clear up. I wouldn't count on being free to go until tomorrow."

Assan simply sighed and reached for another cigarette.

A state trooper came up carrying a large, steel mechanic's tool box.

"Look what we found in the white van," he said.

The trooper opened the box. There were twelve neatly cut out half-circles in a piece of foam rubber that filled most of the box. Each one held a US Army-issue hand grenade.

Tompkins turned to Assan. "Do Yemeni diplomats carry cargo like this much?"

"My," Assan responded. "Heavens no, the others placed that box in my van. I assumed it was merely tools as is the purpose for such a storage device."

"Just put them in the trunk of Agent Tompkins' vehicle. Tompkins, give him the keys," Jack ordered. Tompkins tossed the trooper the keys to the car and the man walked over to the black sedan.

This time Jack motioned Tompkins to accompany him across the access road.

Once they got there, Jack turned to face him. "Here's the situation. You have a dead agent. This guy is clearly the one who ordered the torture and the shooting. My partner was beaten within an inch of her life, also by the orders of Assan."

"Yes, but we don't have a direct connection to any of that stuff and, besides, that passport trumps everything. The last thing the administration wants in the Middle East is a diplomatic issue."

"Here's an idea," Jack stated. "Have the troopers and your other agents go back and help with cleaning up the scene in Stanardsville. You and I can retain custody of Assan and we'll remain behind for a bit to see how things work out here."

Tompkins looked puzzled. "But why not just let the troopers take him and hold him overnight at the Greene County lockup?"

"I knew a warrant officer in the Army," Jack explained. "He was famous for getting things done quickly and correctly."

"So?" Tompkins asked.

"Sometimes he expedited things. Actually he almost always expedited things. That's how he got things done," Jack continued.

"I don't get your point," Tompkins said.

"God damn it, we're not going to let the son-of-a-bitch off. He's going to fucking pay for what he did to Foster and Yolanda."

"But how?"

"That trooper with the tool box gave me an idea. Let's get everyone out of here and I'll show you what I mean."

Within thirty minutes the entire area was clear. Even the fire response teams had departed, leaving a mostly wet, still smoky, mess.

Assan looked around. "Why haven't we left with the others? Is there something else to do here?"

"As a matter of fact there is, Mr. Assan. We're going to play a little game."

"A game?" he snorted. "Games are for children."

"Usually," Jack agreed, "but this one is more for adults. It's called Hot Potato."

"I have never heard of such a game," Assan said.

"Well, first of all we need to go find a small hill or ditch. Actually a ditch would be better for our game," Jack explained.

"I do not choose to participate in this so-called game," Assan insisted.

"I'm sorry," Jack replied. "Participation is mandatory."

With that said, Jack asked Tompkins for the car keys. He went to the car and rummaged around in the trunk. He was back in a little over a minute carrying a small plastic bag.

"Now, let's go find our playground," Jack said.

Assan reluctantly stood up and all three of them walked toward the far side of the compound. They found a small drainage ditch that led to Route 33, it was lined in concrete.

"Perfect!" Jack exclaimed.

"So what are the rules of this game?" Assan asked.

"It's simple," Jack said. "First of all, since you're our guest, you get to go first." Jack produced a bungee cord from the bag, dropped down, and wrapped it several times around Assan's ankles before hooking the two ends together. He did it so quickly that Assan didn't have time to react.

"Why did you do that? Remember I am an official of the Government of Yemen! Release me at once!"

"We haven't played the game yet, take it easy," Jack reassured him. "Now comes the fun part of the game." He reached into the bag again and brought out one of the grenades from the toolbox. "This," Jack pointed to the grenade, "is an Army-issue M67 hand grenade."

At this point Assan realized that something very unpleasant was going to happen and he tried to hop away. He made it a few feet before toppling over.

"Now look what you've done," Tompkins chided him. "You got grass stains on your nice suit pants."

"You must let me go! This is a direct violation of the diplomatic code!" Assan screamed.

"No, it's just a game," Jack calmly continued. "OK, here's where your part comes in. This grenade has a four second fuse. That means that after I pull the pin, four seconds will elapse before it goes off."

Assan turned paler than any Middle Eastern native had ever turned before.

Tompkins came up behind him and grabbed his arms.

Jack put his face close to Assan's. "Listen, you worthless fuck," he snarled. "I didn't like that FBI agent, but he didn't deserve to be executed while tied to a chair. And that woman? She's my woman, Assan. My woman. I love her and she is almost dead because of the beating that you allowed to happen. You know what else? You were hoping that you could kill hundreds of innocent little school kids. You think you're hopping on a jet and heading home tomorrow. No, I have better news; you're going to be joining your six dead buddies in hell."

"Please, no," Assan pleaded, "I have money. I can make you wealthy."

"No thanks." Jack laughed. "Look, you'll have a chance to win. I'm going to pull this pin and then I'm going to let go of the handle. Then I'm going to stick it right down your pants next to your pencil-dick and tiny balls. As soon as

I do that, Agent Tompkins and I are going to toss you in the ditch. You get four seconds to dig it out and throw it back at us. That's why they call it Hot Potato," Jack concluded.

"This is barbaric!" Assan screamed. "You are barbarians!"

"Nope," Jack replied, "just a couple of Americans who enjoy a good game of Hot Potato every now and then with a new friend."

He held up the grenade. Assan watched him pull the pin.

"Now, be quick and you can win the game, you asshole," Jack advised him.

He yanked Assan's shirt out of the front of his pants and pulled out the waistband of his underwear. Then he quickly let the handle fly as he jammed the grenade down his underwear.

"Hot Potato, Assan! Your turn!" Jack yelled.

Tompkins swung Assan around and pushed him into the ditch. As a precaution both he and Jack hit the ground and covered their ears. For two seconds they could hear some frantic shrieking and scrabbling on the concrete floor of the ditch, followed by a loud explosion. They stood up and looked down into the ditch. They saw the mangled body of Assan lying on the blood-covered concrete.

"Can you believe that?" Jack asked Tompkins. "He was going to use that grenade to be a suicide bomber and take all three of us out."

"And lucky for us, he stumbled and fell into that ditch!" Tompkins added.

"We'd better call for someone to come and clean this up," Jack said. "Can you handle it? I need to get to the hospital in Harrisonburg. Hey, could I use your car? Would that be OK?"

"Sure is, Jack. I'll catch a ride back. You know, that was a good idea you had. I thought that scum would get away with it."

"It's all about thinking like a good warrant officer, Tompkins, that's all."

Tompkins laughed. "OK, get going and see to your partner. Your woman, you said?"

"Yes," Jack replied, "I know it for sure now. She's my Yo."

72

YOLANDA FEELS BETTER

Jack rode the elevator up to the third floor, tightly clutching the scrap of paper with the room number that the receptionist had written for him. His usual dislike of hospitals didn't bother him; he was in too much of a hurry to find Yolanda. As he got off the elevator, a nurse at the desk stopped him.

"Sir, this is the Intensive Care Unit, visitors aren't allowed."

"I'm here to see how Yolanda Tilden is," Jack answered. "She's in Room 312."

"Are you family? Close relatives are the only people allowed on this floor."

"Not yet," Jack replied. "But she's my fiancée," he fibbed.

The nurse stood up. Her face showed immediate concern. "Follow me." She led Jack down the hall. "She's stable right now, but she is sedated," she continued. "She suffered severe bruising along with two broken ribs and a broken nose along with advanced dehydration. Don't be shocked when you see her and it's quite likely that she'll remain asleep. That's probably the best thing for her right now." She paused outside Yolanda's room. "There is one other thing, an oral surgeon has been by to examine her and she may lose her two front teeth. From the cuts on the inside of her lip, the doctor thinks she was struck squarely in the mouth." She looked at Jack quizzically. "Can you tell me or do you know what happened to that poor girl? I've seen lots of victims of domestic abuse and fights, but not to the extent that she's suffered."

"She was taken hostage and beaten by terrorists. That's it, plain and simple," Jack explained. "Please, can I go in now?"

The nurse nodded and pushed open the door. Jack went in and the door quietly closed behind him.

The room was dimly lit. The only sound was the soft beeping of the monitoring computer. He stepped close to the bed. If he hadn't known it was Yolanda, he wouldn't have recognized her. A blanket was pulled up to her chin and her head and forehead were covered by bandages. There was also a large bandage set across her broken nose. Her eyes were blackened and still extremely swollen. Jack could make out angrily-colored bruises on her face and neck. Bruises that continued down her arms, until the cluster of plastic tubes concealed them.

He took a side chair and turned it so the back rested on the side of her bed. He knelt on it and took her left hand and turned it upwards. He bent over and pressed his lips against her palm. Just like outside the building in Elkton, Jack began to cry. Between sobs he tried to whisper what he needed to say to her.

"Yo, please, get through this. I am so, so sorry. I left you, I was so fucking stupid. I let this happen to you. You would have been safe if I had been with you. Please, Yo. I love you, I do, I love you so much and I thought I did before, but when I found you, oh, God, it would have broken my heart if I had lost you. I know what you mean to me now." He sniffled some before continuing. "I promise I'll never leave you again, I promise, just please, please come out of this OK."

"Jack?"

"Yo!" Jack straightened up and looked at her.

"Jack?" she repeated in a soft, sleepy voice. "Don't look at me. I must look so awful."

"No, you're still beautiful, you're just sort of like a Christmas present; you're sort of gift-wrapped," he said.

"Not funny," she whispered.

"Yo, just rest. Let me tell you something. I don't know how much you learned about those men, but they were planning on exploding truck bombs outside of three schools in Stanardsville. We stopped them, Yo. That man that beat you? He's dead. The man in charge, he's the one who had you beaten, he's dead too. I won't tell you how until later. I just want you to get plenty of sleep. The doctor says it will take a while, but you'll recover from this. I just didn't want you to worry about them. They are all dead and in hell."

"Galen is dead, Jack." She began to cry.

"Try not to cry, Baby," Jack squeezed her hand. "I know about Galen. I found him. I got his body out of the building. They blew it up, Yo, those terrorists blew that building up."

"Jack?" she whispered again.

"What?"

"I like it when you call me Yo."

"If you want, I'll call you that from now on," he said. "I promise."

He didn't get an answer, she had fallen asleep, but Jack thought her face looked more peaceful.

THE DAILY PROGRESS

Charlottesville, Virginia

Agents of the Federal Bureau of Investigation and Virginia State Troopers foiled a terrorist attempt to explode three truck bombs. The terrorists allegedly targeted three school buildings in Stanardsville, VA. During the assault, one van was destroyed with both the driver and passenger killed by gunfire. A second van was prematurely detonated in the vicinity of a shopping mall, but only minor injuries, mainly to shattered storefront windows, came as a result of the explosion.

The third van attempted to escape and drove back to their believed base of operation, an abandoned truck depot on the outskirts of Elkton. Either by accident or by suicide, this van exploded inside the depot, starting a fire that eventually destroyed the entire structure.

Field Agent Roger Tompkins also reported that the remains of an FBI Agent, Mr. Galen Foster, were found inside the truck depot before the fire spread throughout the entire building. His death is being investigated as a result of the action of the terrorist cell. Another apparent hostage, whose name is being withheld for the moment, was discovered alive and is recuperating in a local hospital.

The FBI considers the attempted attack to be the work of a group of illegal aliens from Yemen. Both the Agency and the State Police are investigating the actual identity of the six men who were in the vehicles.

Hazmat crews and fire departments from Stanardsville and local volunteer fire departments have already finished cleaning up the debris. The bodies and the remains of the vehicles have been sent to Washington for analysis.

The FBI concludes that this terrorist cell was working independently and there is no longer a current threat of activity in the area.

Stanardsville schools were evacuated and remained closed for the remainder of the day, but classes resumed today.

THE WASHINGTON POST

Washington, D.C.

Mr. Ahmoud Assan, a high-ranking diplomat of the Yemeni government was killed yesterday in an apparent suicide bombing attack. Mr. Assan allegedly attempted to kill two men, FBI Field Agent Roger Tompkins and a private investigator, Mr. Jack Clayton, who was assisting the Agency in tracking the same terrorist cell that constructed three truck bombs that were intended to be used for an attack on Greene County Schools located in Stanardsville, VA.

Agent Tompkins reported that Mr. Assan was suspected of being aware of the planned attack, although was not considered to be directly involved. During a brief interrogation, Mr. Assan produced what appeared to be a US Army hand grenade. Citing a desire for martyrdom, Mr. Assan activated the device, but then lost his footing and fell. The grenade exploded before he was able to throw it at the agent and the detective. Both men expressed shock at his actions, because he was immune to prosecution and seemed to be cooperating fully with the questioning.

The FBI is planning a further investigation into the matter, but a government official reported that an examination of the site confirmed the testimony of the two men involved.

The government of Yemen has lodged a formal protest and has demanded custody of Agent Tompkins and Mr. Clayton for questioning and possible criminal proceedings. The US government has denied their claim.

EPILOGUE

Two months later

Jack and Yolanda were back in Indianapolis. She had stayed in the hospital for a week before being released. That release came with the stipulation that the bandages around her rib cage were to remain for another two weeks, so she wasn't allowed to shower or get into a bathtub for that period of time. She had to content herself with help from Jack. Jack was not opposed to helping with the bathing. In fact, he seemed to be overly helpful; extremely overly helpful in her opinion.

By the end of the two week period, the swelling and puffiness of her face had gone. The bruises on her chest and arms had faded, although there were faint reminders of the beating Amjad had given her.

One of the first things she did when she felt better was take Jack car shopping. He wanted another Buick, but she told him that he needed something nicer. She wanted him to buy a BMW. She overcame all of his early objections with one simple convincing argument. "Jack, it's a German car."

They had to get up early today. She had an important appointment.

Jack was already in the kitchen. Yolanda had purchased one of those new coffee makers, the one that could brew one cup of coffee at a time. She had also purchased a variety of flavors that Jack was testing. His only minor complaint about the purchase was the color of the coffee maker. It was purple. Yolanda's favorite color, not his.

As it began to brew his first cup of the morning, Jack happily started a little song.

"All I want for Christmas is my two front teeth, my two front teeth, my…"

Suddenly Yolanda stomped into the kitchen.

"So help me, Jack, if you sing that God-damned song one more time, I'm going to God-damned make sure that I'll be singing it about you next!"

Jack grinned. "Hey, Yo! How about whistling a tune for me?"

Yolanda picked up a small juice bottle and threw it at him.

"Hey!" he shouted. "No need to get violent."

"Listen, Jack Clayton, I've waited for this day for two months and I've heard you sing that stupid song so many times and, no, I can't frigging whistle, but today I finally get to go to the oral surgeon to get my implants, and I've finally had it! Enough is enough!"

Jack smiled and he walked over and took her in his arms.

"I'm sorry, Yo. You just look so damn cute without them, like you're a second-grader or something. It makes me smile."

"I do not look like a second-grader." She pulled up her T-shirt and flashed him. "See many second-graders with these?"

That got Jack's attention. He reached up under her shirt to double-check, but she caught his hand. "Not now, Jack, maybe later. Maybe later when I can whistle." This time she smiled.

"Promise?" he asked.

"Oh, Jack," she sighed. "You are such a baby. OK, I promise."

Jack retrieved his cup of coffee and Yolanda popped a hot chocolate one in the machine. After it was done, they sat down at the table.

"Yo, I've been looking at the case offers that have been coming in."

"And do you think there's one you like?"

"Yeah, do you remember after the Annie case? You told me that you didn't want our next case to deal with kids."

"I remember. I also remember what I told you that day at the hospital in Harrisonburg."

Jack nodded, "I know, that the next case could be about kids, dealing with the terrorists notched it up a bit too high."

"So," Yolanda nodded. "Does that mean our next case is a missing child or something?"

"Something," Jack replied, "actually it's more of a string of missing children over a period of several years."

"Interesting," Yolanda agreed. "Where is it?"

"Charleston," Jack answered.

"Oh, Jack, that's wonderful! I love Charleston. I love being close to the ocean. We'll have a great time."

"Uh, Yo," Jack started.

"What, Jack?"

"It's not Charleston, South Carolina. It's Charleston, West Virginia."

"That state we drove through with the house trailers falling into ravines? Oh, Jack, that's the one that got your interest?"

"I'll explain it to you on the way to the oral surgeon; you'll be OK with it. Trust me."

Later that morning, Yolanda could whistle again.

Later that afternoon, she kept her promise.

Later that evening, Jack was an even happier man.

The End

Made in the USA
Middletown, DE
27 February 2016